Catrin Morgan was born a...
she has drawn on her own...
THE VALLEYS, LILL...
COMFORT ME WITH...
several contemporary nov...
Jones. Her home is now in Anglesey, North Wales.

COMFORT ME
WITH APPLES

CATRIN MORGAN

Futura

A Futura Book

First published in Great Britain in 1991
by Macdonald & Co (Publishers) Ltd
London & Sydney

This edition published in 1991
by Futura Publications

Copyright © Merle Jones 1991

The right of Catrin Morgan to be identified as
author of this work has been asserted by
her in accordance with the Copyright, Designs
and Patents Act 1988.

*All characters in this publication are fictitious
and any resemblance to real persons, living or dead,
is purely coincidental.*

ISBN 0 7088 4999 7

Printed and bound in Great Britain by
BPCC Hazell Books
Aylesbury, Bucks, England
Member of BPCC Ltd.

Futura Publications
A Division of
Macdonald & Co (Publishers) Ltd
165 Great Dover Street
London SE1 4YA

A member of Maxwell Macmillan Publishing Corporation

Stay me with flagons. Comfort
me with apples; for I am sick of love.

Song of Songs, Ch. 2, v. 5

For Anwen Williams, who sets the
Gold standard for good neighbours.

PART ONE

To him that overcometh will I give to eat of
the tree of life, which is in the
midst of the Paradise of God.

Revelation, Ch. 2, v.7

PART ONE

>

CHAPTER ONE

South Wales, November 1926

Looka that sky, Arthur Gregg told himself. Bitta peace up there, all quiet, lovely black velvet quilt, embroidered with silver stars, and . . . quiet. Never seemed to get no quiet down here below any more.

He had been studying the night sky as much as possible lately. The past few weeks anything was better than looking around him as they walked down the street, seeing all them faces, hating him, waiting to get at him. And what if they did? This lot couldn't last much longer. And then what would they do to him? He shook his head angrily. No point thinking about that now. He was all right for the present. Time enough to get scared when these buggers was gone.

That reminded him. Over the past few months, he'd got so used to the regular tramp, tramp, tramp of their strong hobnails pounding along the road, they had effectively ceased to exist for him. They were there all right, though. The thought of them not being there abruptly brought his mind back to the creeping fears that had beset him moments before. He shivered and withdrew deeper into his old working overcoat.

There were twenty of them; strong, sturdy well-fed constables from the West Country – a good long way from the coalfield or any inconvenient sympathies for striking miners. They had been drafted in when the coal company discovered it had three men willing to cross the picket lines and go underground to work the South Celynen mine while their fellows were starving on the surface. In those days it had been forty coppers. In those

9

days! Arthur chuckled aloud at his own fanciful phrasing. That was just a couple of months back, although it felt like another century. Dolph Llewelyn and Harry Evans had felt like he did then and they'd all marched in together. What was it his godly wife had called them? That was it – terrible as an army with banners. And they had been. Showed all them buggers if you behaved like a bloody sheep you got cut out and slaughtered like one. He and his two good butties Dolph and Harry had thumbed their noses at the pickets, drawn the strength of the police force around them, and marched to work. Mind you, Dolph and Harry had been weaker vessels than him. Dolph had gone first. A gang of roughnecks from down the Ranks had grabbed his daughter and her kid on their way back from chapel guild one night. Hadn't laid a finger on them but it frightened Dolph's girl Beryl so much she hadn't gone out since. Her sister had to do the shopping and everything. Anyway, they'd told her to tell Dolph that next time it mightn't just be a friendly chat. Next time it might be a little walk down the canal with the baby to see if he'd like a swim. In six foot of stagnant water in early October. Dolph had been back out of that pit the day after, and he'd stayed solid with the Fed ever since.

Harry hadn't been much longer. There'd always been a bitta talk about Harry before the trouble blew up. Too keen on the ladies. Lorra people said it was him as got Jack Moseley's girl in trouble. Seemed like the boys from the Fed had thought so, too, because they'd stripped Harry off and painted his willy red and carried him through the village tied to a pole. Harry'd been back on picket duty the day after.

That had just left Arthur. Arthur had only the one daughter, unmarried, away in service down Cardiff. His wife, abetted by her God, was a bloody sight tougher than most of the men in the valley and if they threatened her she could stand up to them. Arthur himself had lived a boringly blameless life and had no secret sins for which they could publicly shame him. The police guard was scaled down to twenty and Arthur continued to do the long march, in solitary misery, to the pit every morning before dawn. There couldn't be many like him, in the whole of South Wales, because one afternoon on the way home, the local newspaper had sent a photographer to take pictures of him striding along with this column of police behind him. Looked like some crazy general, he had. Them all neat and clean in their uniforms, him in the middle of the front row, black from head to foot from eight hours underground.

Once he got to the pit, it was even lonelier than outside. No real point in being down. Nothing to do. You couldn't cut coal with one bloke at your disposal. But the company was very pleased with him. Hadn't Mr Gilchrist said, you keep it up, Arthur? You supply the backbone and we'll think out the strategy. It's important you're seen to be coming to work. That will break their will in the end. Just you wait and see if it don't.

Aye, he knew it would, in the end. But this last coupla weeks he'd been waking an hour or more before he was due to, cold and sweating at the same time, his head full of pictures of what would happen when they did break. It wasn't Gilchrist and his ilk who'd feel the push then. It was the likes of him, Arthur Gregg, front-line veteran, not praised and given a medal, but like as not taken down a dark side street and beaten senseless . . .

The pit winding gear loomed close in the pre-dawn gloaming. Here we go again, he thought. Wonder how many more days I got down there on my own?

As usual, the manager and under-manager were waiting for him. The sergeant at the front of the police ranks saluted smartly and said, as usual, 'Leave you to it, now, sir.' That was to Gilchrist. Neither the sergeant nor the constables ever talked to Arthur unless they had to. He shrugged, more comfortable now he was safe within the boundaries of the pit. Why should he care? He was doing what he thought was right. That was the important thing.

*   *   *

11

A couple of hours later, Tom Sloman and Haydn Walters waited in the upstairs committee room at the workmen's institute for Dai James to join them at the monthly union lodge strike committee meeting. The two men were close friends, never short of a topic of conversation, but this morning they were silent, morose in the knowledge of what was ahead of them.

Finally, Tom said: 'No use expecting a miracle from Dai, mun. You do know as well as I do what the books'll say.'

Haydn did not reply immediately. He seemed to find his worn-out boots a source of infinite contemplation. Now he sat, hands deep in his pockets, long legs extended in front of him, staring down the lean, almost starved, length of his torso at the ruined toecaps. Finally he said: 'Aye, my head do know, but my heart ent going to believe it, and neither is my voting arm, Tom.'

Sloman shook his head. 'No choice any more. Bloody miracle them funds have held out as long as they have. We ent going to take this lot through Christmas and New Year without some deaths, Haydn. You do know that as well as me. Women and kids and old sick people can't face a Valleys winter after starving for six months.'

Haydn's sigh was funereal. 'I think about my sister going to prison, and her kid getting rickets, and the whole bloody family half alive on the say-so of politicians and coal owners, and it do choke me. Christ, Tom, how *are* we gonna give in when the time do come?'

'Like we used to fight when we was winning, mun. With a band in the front and banners up the back, and singing. Never let the bastards know they've hurt you.'

Then Haydn cried, for the first time since he had seen the wreckage of his father's once-beautiful face and body, mangled in death by a colliery roof fall. He cried as if he had seen his whole family annihilated, because in a sense, he had. Tom came across the small room and rested an arm awkwardly about his shoulders. When he received no response, he cuffed his friend gently under

12

the chin. 'Come on, kidda – this ent the way class warriors do carry on!'

Haydn peered up at him through a haze of tears. 'You know something, Tommy *bach*? At this moment I'd swap every victory of the class war for a quiet warm house in green fields, with food and drink and new clothes for my family and no coal mines within a hundred miles, for the whole bloody workers' Utopia!'

Sloman turned away with a sigh. 'Aye, that's the trouble, ennit? Whatever the psalms and the politicians' promises do say, we've never had no chance to be led beside the still waters, or lie down in green pastures . . . if anybody ever had the sense to give 'em to us, there'd never be an industrial struggle in this country again.'

The shadow of a smile broke through on Haydn's lips. 'That do sound like something straight out of "All Things Bright and Beautiful". I think starvation must be softening your brain.'

Tom turned back and slapped his shoulder playfully. 'You had me worried there for a minute, you old bugger . . . '

When Dai James arrived, moments later, he found the two younger men engaged in a raucously mocking rendition of 'The rich man in his castle, the poor man at his gate, God made them high and lowly, and ordered their estate'.

He looked sombrely from face to face, then thumped his accounts book down on the table. 'Well, I'm glad somebody's happy,' he said. 'We got four pound in the lodge funds and there's a conference in Cardiff Saturday to see whether we give up or not.'

Two furiously militant faces turned on him. 'We'll starve first!' they chorused.

'And you'll probably get a chance to do that, an' all,' said Dai. 'From what I hear, though, we'll be doing it all by ourselves, that's the trouble.'

'What d'you mean? The lodge is a hundred per cent solid.' Haydn looked ready to punch him into agreement if he disputed it.

13

Dai waved his hand in denial. 'I wasn't saying nothing about our lot. Course they'm solid. But damn, Haydn, I been talking outside the village and it ent like that everywhere else.'

He dropped his voice as if afraid coal-owners' informers were outside the door. 'The Fed have lost seventy thousand members in this last coupla months, mun. We ent just talking about keeping blacklegs down any more. If we don't go back in good order soon, our own people will trample us in the rush.'

'I don' believe it. They'd rather starve – *I'd* rather starve.'

'Aye, Hayd, you said that before, but warrabout your wife and kids? You'm a bit luckier than many with your big family all pulling together. Some have felt the pinch a lot earlier, and they can't stand much more. They'm going back whether we do like it or not.'

'You gonna vote to go back then?'

Dai's chin jerked up and there were tears in his eyes. 'I didn't say that! Course I ent. But we'll be in a minority, Haydn. I'm just trying to get you used to the idea, that's all.'

Haydn looked across at Tom. 'D'you think he's right?'

'Aye, I'm afraid he is.' Tom stood up and stretched his big bony frame. 'Won't stop me voting to stay out, though – and it won't stop me carrying on with a little bitta private trouble after they've forced us back, neither.'

'Never say die, eh? You reckon they'll let us back down the pits, then?'

Tom shook his head, bewildered. 'Why not? They'll have us just where they want us, won't they?'

'I mean *us*, mun, the agitators, the union officers. You think they'll ever let us work again?'

'*Iesu mawr*! Never thoughta that.'

'Well I have, and I can't see no coal-owner ever letting either of us pick up a mandrel again. How the hell are we going to go on fighting the buggers if they won't even let us in the pits?'

14

Dai James uttered a heavy sigh. 'Look, boys, we gorra decide what to do. We can go on moaning like this all day, and it won't solve nothing. How do we vote at the delegates' meeting?'

'The men have mandated us to decide for the duration.' Haydn's tone was truculent. 'If we decide to stay out, there's no need to ask them again before we cast the vote.'

Tom Sloman intervened. 'Calm down, Haydn. You'm a better man than that. You know we got to ask them again on something as big as this. I propose a mass meeting tomorrow. We can get the word around by then and still have a decision in time for the conference.'

'Aye, all right. I s'pose we gorra give the poor sods their say. A lot do change in seven months.'

Two miles away, a similar thought was in the mind of Haydn's sister, Lily. She was kneeling on the kitchen floor of her house on the edge of Newbridge, packing pots and pans into a plywood tea chest. In her case, seven months had taken her first through a two-month prison sentence, then out of a neat villa with her husband's name on the freehold, to an uncertain future paying rent for one of the terraced coal company houses in which she had been born. She was not eager to renew the acquaintance.

'D'you really mean it, Mam? Right next door to Uncle Haydn an' everything, and can I play outside and go fishing down the canal and . . . '

'Hush, now. Of course you can. I said, didn't I?'

The enthusiasm of her son Tommy to live in the Ranks momentarily dispelled Lily's gloom, but soon it seeped back. She had felt low on other occasions in her life, but only once had she known sorrow as a physical lump pressing at the base of her throat and threatening to overwhelm her. On the previous occasion, it had been over the death of her favourite brother. Now it was the death of a dream.

The house was going – sold to settle the bills that her

husband had quietly been collecting throughout the lock-out, not only for their own needs, but for her mother, and her brothers' children, and medicine for her sister Rose when she was ill in the summer. David was a brave fighter, but he was a realist, too, and when he had told her the miners would be driven back to work within weeks, she knew better than to argue. He had sold the house, his pride and joy, back to the coal company for a fraction of its pre-strike value, and was using the cash to set the family straight.

'It's gonna be harder than ever for the next few years, Lil,' he had told her after they made the decision. 'Useless to saddle ourselves with all that debt on top of everything, just to say we got a bath and an indoor lav.'

Well, it had been nice while it lasted. And she was with him all the way – ahead of him at times. She thought of her husband with pride now – pride and deep love, neither of which she had felt when they married less than five years ago. If the strike had failed on all other points, it had taught her what a good man she had. Perhaps she had needed that lesson.

'Time to go, Mam – they'm outside with the horse an' cart. Can I ride up the front?' Tommy was bursting with enthusiasm. It was the greatest adventure of his young life.

'Yes, love, of course you can. Hurry up, now. There's a lot still to pack.'

Rising, she looked around her at the empty kitchen. Funny, it had once seemed so palatial. Now it appeared dreary and slightly out of date. Lily squared her shoulders and prepared to face her unknown future. There – it never paid to be satisfied with little dreams. A kitchen could never be more than a kitchen, here or in the Ranks. If you fought for something really big and important, it never tarnished. Perhaps she had set herself small aims for too long.

The mass meeting voted overwhelmingly to stay out. 'I won't fool you men,' Dai James told them. 'With funds

16

as they are, there's not even basic strike pay until we get some more relief money from the fund-raisers. Are you still game?'

'Aye!' It came as a single roar from a thousand throats.

'Right you are, then,' yelled Haydn. 'We'll know what to tell 'em down Cardiff on Saturday. 'Now, boys, have you gorra song to send us on our way?' And the miners launched into a spirited rendering of 'The Red Flag' as enthusiastically as if it were the first day of their dispute.

'I don't care whether I'm as much of a sinner not knowing as knowing. I prefer to trust in *your* innocence!' Margaret Ann Walters was on top form and determined as always that she would remain without sin if she could find a scapegoat. In this case a piece of scrag end of mutton was the point of contention.

Haydn made a face at Lily, who frowned and shook her head. Her look said, leave it: we've got enough trouble outside without quarrelling among ourselves. Haydn shrugged. He saw no reason why his mother should be protected from knowing that tonight's supper came directly from an elderly ewe who had strayed off the mountain just as a couple of hungry colliers approached, yesterday evening. There was a leg hanging in the pantry and this big pot of stew for tonight. Other families in the Ranks were cooking the rest of the beast at this very moment. That old ewe would have been happy to go in such a good cause if she'd known, Haydn reflected.

His mother had turned aside from the source of their meal to discuss what they were likely to do for Christmas. 'Starve, I should think,' he said cheerfully. 'I can't really see the coal company handing out the usual poultry and stuff to the officials, can you? And we certainly ent gonna have no money to buy the stuff.'

Lily slapped down the piece of mending she was doing on the table. 'When are we gonna start saying what we mean, instead of beating about the bush?' she demanded.

'In case you hadn't noticed, Haydn, we're still out solid – us and the Yorkshire miners, remember?'

Haydn's face was like an old man's now. 'Aye, and what about the rest? What about half our own membership? We can't hold it, Lil. The boys was great today at the meeting. Our lodge can hold its head up at that meeting on Saturday, but don't get the wrong idea. We'll be voted down on Saturday. Next week the owners'll have us on a plate; us, Yorkshire – the lot. There's no more to give.'

She snatched the half-darned sock again and shook it like a terrier with a rat. Her head was bowed so they would not see her crying, and her voice was harsh. 'We can't give in – we can't! They can't make us worse off than we are now.'

'Yes, they can – and they will, if they have to. This dispute have cost millions – far more than they'd have had to pay to settle with us. But once they've beaten us, they got us for a generation, haven't they? How many miners will strike in the Valleys as long as they remember this lot?'

Haydn had risen as he spoke, and now he stood behind Lily's chair, gripping her shoulders, holding her as though she would disintegrate if he let go. 'All we can do is try and persuade them to keep faith, Lil. But if we can't admit to ourselves that we've lost this time, how the bloody hell are we gonna learn how to win in the future?'

For once their mother did not criticise him for swearing. Instead, she busied herself at setting the table for supper. 'Come on, now,' she said fussily, when the silence had dragged on beyond decency. 'Get some food down you and it will look a bit better after.'

But nothing could paste an optimistic face on to this terrible end. At the Cardiff conference, delegates cast their votes. The final tally was more daunting in what it showed of non-voters than anything else. Fifty thousand opted to return to work. Twenty-seven thousand wanted to continue the dispute. It proved the worst fears of the South Wales Miners' Federation – that since the start of

18

the terrible dispute, they had lost around half their membership. At the beginning of 1926, there would have been 150,000 men voting. As the dispute lengthened, they had slipped away, the lucky ones to other industries, many simply to lie low and lick their wounds, reflecting that if this was all trade unionism got them, they might as well fight alone.

CHAPTER TWO

About time they showed some sense, Arthur Gregg thought as he laced on his big boots for the lonely march to the pit. Last time I'll be doing this journey with my escort, I expect. His fingers stopped their work with the laces. Aye, the last time . . . what would happen when they were gone? Nothing, his everyday self told him. The owners have won, haven't they? Beaten them silly sods so far into the ground it'll take 'em ten years to break surface again. Why should I worry? They ent gonna have no energy left to make trouble for me. Too busy trying to get their old jobs back.

He finished off the boots and straightened up. But under the bravado, a little, honest, frightened voice was saying: everyone needs vengeance. Even worms must want to turn round and bite the feet that trample them. They ent going to have a chance at the bosses now – I won't arf be handy for them if they want to knock somebody about.

This was crazy! Perhaps that last warning voice spoke the truth, but if it did, there was bugger all he could do about it. Hadn't he done the solitary walk all these months to prove he was right, that he wouldn't be intimidated? Well then, why act the coward now the war was won? Abruptly, his mind was filled with a memory of the soldiers who were killed on the Western Front as the clock struck on the eleventh hour of the eleventh day of the eleventh month of 1918 and Armistice was declared. The war had been over when they bought it, hadn't it? And weren't they just as dead all the same, over there in Flanders mud?

George shuddered. The worst part of it was that he had

no choice in the matter. He remembered saying, months ago, full of piss and wind, that everybody had a choice, always; that no man had to follow his leader blindly over the abyss. Well, now he was about to test the truth of his assertion. Did he any longer have a choice between life and death, let alone anything else?

In spite of his fears, it proved a totally uneventful day. Arthur realised he had been worried too soon. The decision had been made for the South Wales miners to go back, but it would not take effect until day shift tomorrow. Today's afternoon shift – his stint on the three-week rota the management had devised to make him as visible as possible – was unaffected. As usual, he marched in solitary splendour backed by his police escort.

But when he came up the pit that night, it was a different matter. The bobbies who waited for him even *felt* different – some breath of suppressed excitement they were giving off, perhaps, although he could not put his finger on it. They formed up behind him as usual and he led the way off into the winter darkness. All was normal until they passed the police station in Gwyddon Road. Two hundred yards beyond the squat granite building, his escort halted to a muffled order from their sergeant. Arthur had been walking drowsily, contemplating supper and a pipe and trying not to think of the events tomorrow might bring. The change of tempo snapped him back to reality.

He glanced around at the constables. 'What's up, lads? Where be we going now?'

The sergeant's smile was something from a nightmare. '*We'm* off back to the station, Arthur. Dunno about you, but I'd say you're on your way to Hell. We'll say goodnight to you.'

'B-but there's a good mile to go yet, up the darkest stretch of the lot . . . You can't leave me yer, mun!'

'Can't we? Just watch us, but. Strike's over, didn't you hear?'

Desperation was climbing towards panic inside

21

Arthur's skull. 'Aye – aye, I know, but not till after midnight, is it? Plenty of time to see me home before then.'

'Hmm – can't do it, sorry. This shift do go off at appast eleven, see, and there ent no provision for cover for you after our shift finishes. Time we get back down the station, we'll be all done for the day. Come on then, lads,' he added, turning to his constables. 'Back down the station, sharpish, and we may get a cuppa tea before we finish.'

Arthur watched in disbelief as the column turned, broke ranks and began to move down the hill towards the police station. For long moments he remained silent, his tongue dry against the roof of his mouth. Then, his voice no more than a croak, he yelled at their backs: 'But worrabout me? What will they do to me when they get me?'

A solitary, mocking voice called back: 'Same as people always does to scabs, I expect – knock you off!' Then a terrible silence enveloped him as the sound of their boots faded into the distance.

For some time he stood where they had left him, unable to make his legs carry him further up the dark hillside. He was sweating and his breath came in great gulps that were hard to distinguish from sobs. He stamped his feet, forcing strength back into them. 'Come on, you dull bugger,' he murmured, 'You can't stand yer all night!' He began to move towards home again.

By the time he reached the point where Gwyddon Road branched on to the hillside track which served Llanfach Farm, he felt better. Only a couple of hundred yards to go now, and no colliers lived up this far. He was getting childish in his old age, seeing hobgoblins where there were only shadows . . . Arthur started singing a hymn, faintly at first, but with gathering strength as the distance to his front door grew shorter.

'Happy in your work, are you, But?'

The soft, apparently friendly voice scared him so much he felt hot urine spurt down his leg. 'Who's that? What're you doing, lurking around up there?' he

22

demanded, imbuing his voice with every atom of aggression he could muster.

The figure emerged from the entrance to the farm track, but he was none the wiser. It was too dark to identify the man.

'What're you doing up yer this time a night, frightening honest people?' he demanded. As he spoke, he contrived to move a few steps further up the road towards home and safety.

'No need to hurry, Arthur, plenty of time, see.' The voice was smooth, beguiling. 'Gorra couple a the boys yer wants a little chat. You wouldn't want to be rude to them, now, would you?'

'Rude? Warra you talking about, mun? It's nearly midnight. No time for socialising. Talk to me tomorrow if you'm that keen.' He plunged off into the darkness, managing ten or fifteen yards before the silky voice stopped him again.

'No use hurrying away like that, Arthur. My butties won't be put off, and they'm all round you, just in case, you know, you didn't want to stop an' talk.'

'Leave me be – I never done nothing to you.'

'Didn't you, Arthur? Don't you think we'd have had a better chance if the likes of you hadn't ratted on us and gone back down? Don't you think we could have held our weak vessels if they hadn't had your rotten example to follow?' The false sweetness of the voice evaporated. 'Well, we couldn't get at you to tell you before, because of your big strong friends. Looks as if they'm otherwise engaged tonight, dunnit?'

Arthur screamed, as high as a woman, as the iron-hard hand gripped his shoulder. 'What's the matter, *bach*? Afraid our attentions ent of the best?' said another voice, sparkling with malice. 'Man your age should know who his friends are by now.'

'Keep away from me – I don't want no parta you!' Gregg turned, stumbling, from the man and ran a few shaky steps back down the road.

'Wrong way, Arthur,' said yet another voice. 'When

23

we do want you to go down that way, we'll tell you. Up there, now, there's a good boy. Sooner you come, sooner it'll be over, ennit?'

He tried again to break away. This time he was struck sharply in the back – at first, he thought, with a stone, but it was nothing more than a clenched fist. The knuckles of these men had grown sharp and bony over seven months of near-starvation. He stumbled and another arm shot out to stop him from falling. Teeth gleamed in the darkness and a soft voice said: 'Don't want you getting marked accidental like, do we?' Then they were bundling him up the farm road towards Llanfach.

The journey seemed interminable, but they took him no further than the little wood behind the Welsh Church – just beyond earshot of the houses in Upper Gwyddon Road, the only place he could have looked for help. Finally they stopped, deep in the dead bracken beneath the beech trees. Arthur remembered inconsequentially that in spring you couldn't see the ground up here for the thick carpet of sweet-scented bluebells. He wondered if he would ever see a bluebell spring again.

They were clustering close now, but it was still so dark he had trouble distinguishing more than half a dozen vague shapes. Arthur knew their intentions were anything but peaceful and desperation moved him to attempt escape again. He pushed forward at a narrow space between two of them but they were too quick for him. He reached out to fend off the attacker who moved to stop him, grabbing at the man's shoulder. Then, fleetingly, he realised why he could not make out their identities. He clutched at rough sacking. The man, like his companions, was wearing a hood. At least they must expect me to survive, if they'm bothering to disguise themselves, he thought. Then one of them shoved him, hard, and he fell against a tree trunk.

He waited for their big boots to start ripping into his prostrate body, but he was spared that. Then one of them said: 'Hold him still, an' I'll get his trousers rolled up.

Let the dog see the rabbit, eh?' His laugh was more of a nervous squeak, and Gregg realised with deepening dread that his assailants were themselves daunted by what they proposed to do to him.

Two of them held him down, and two rolled up his trousers. He was thrashing from side to side on the ground, trying to free himself, and therefore failed to notice two of the six moving away. The stillness of the others when they came back made him stop struggling to peer up through the darkness. What he saw made his blood run cold. They were silhouetted against the night sky, and he could see what they had gone for. Each carried a small sledge-hammer.

'Hold him tight, now,' one of them said. 'I don't want none of you getting hurt. Arthur, we don't like doing this: we ent men of violence. But next time we'm gonna win, so now we've gorra make sure nobody's ever tempted to try what you been doing this time. It's gonna be a hundred per cent when we do it again.'

And then he raised the sledge-hammer high above his head and brought it whistling down on Arthur's left shin. Gregg took four blows before he blacked out. As his consciousness faded he retained a grim picture of the two hammer-bearers striking turn and turn about. The fourth blow smashed his right leg like a matchstick.

When awareness returned, he immediately wished for oblivion again. A man was stooping over him, face contorted with mixed distaste and anxiety. 'Don't try to move, Mr Gregg. It's the doctor here. Keep still and I'll give you something . . . '

Arthur screamed, a long ululation like the cry of a wolf in the night. The two ambulance men who were bringing a stretcher down the steep slope shivered at the sound. When they reached him, Charles Henderson prevented them from putting Gregg on the stretcher until the morphine had taken effect. 'Otherwise I think the shock might kill him,' he whispered.

Arthur was still conscious, and knew he was in pain, but it was bearable now the drug was making it seem detached from him. Something was puzzling him. He must sort it out before he went off to sleep. 'D-doctor, who f-found me? I must be the luckiest bugger alive for anybody to come across me down yer on a winter night.'

Henderson's smile was without warmth. 'You weren't found, Mr Gregg. Someone directed us here. A note was pushed through my letterbox at two o'clock this morning and then someone hammered on my door until I went downstairs to answer it. It told me to bring an ambulance and come looking for you.'

Arthur was crying now. 'The bastards – the bloody bastards!' he sobbed. 'The whole village'll make them heroes for that.' And he turned his face to the dead bracken to hide his misery.

CHAPTER THREE

'If I thought one of our boys was mixed up in that business, I'd disown him!' Margaret Ann was working off her anger by banging about her immaculate kitchen, storming at Lily as she did so.

'Why are you so concerned about Gregg all of a sudden?' asked her daughter. 'He's not worth your sympathy.'

'Any man who have suffered like that is worth my sympathy. They do say his legs was pulp. Lucky to keep them . . . wouldn't have, if your Dr Henderson hadn't been operating.'

'Remind me to thank Charlie next time I see him.' Lily's voice was heavy with sarcasm.

'Lily! How can you be so callous? As it is, Arthur Gregg'll probably never walk again.'

'Good job, too, if he do use his legs to carry him past lawful pickets,' said Lily.

'You'd talk different if someone put you there beside the man and gave you the weapons to injure him. They say it was sledge-hammers,' Margaret Ann finished in a hushed tone.

'Maybe, maybe not. When I come out of prison and saw our Tommy's legs all distorted by rickets, I'd a been ready to pull the bugger's head off with my bare hands.'

'Arthur Gregg had nothing to do with Tommy getting rickets.'

'Didn't he, then? Who was sitting comfy, eating and drinking the best, when you was all starving for the cause? Arthur Gregg and that God-bothering wife of his – and thanks to the likes of him, we lost. The sick kids are his fault as much as the owners. Without rabble like

Arthur, the coal companies couldn't win.'

'And you do seriously think crippling him after the struggle have finished will help change the world? You'm tapped, girl.'

'In that case, so am I.'

Margaret Ann started violently at the interruption and almost dropped the saucepan she was holding. In her anger she had failed to notice Haydn's arrival. Her son came forward into the room, his bulk dwarfing its mean dimensions still further. Of all the male Walters children, he looked most like his dead father. 'Mam, surely you understand we ent finished for good? One day we'll try again, and we'll win. But we'll never have a chance if anyone do see the Arthur Greggs of this world getting off scot-free. There won't be anyone in the village willing to scab next time now they've seen what we do to them as have.'

Margaret Ann was staring at him accusingly. 'What d'you mean, "we"? What part did you have in it?'

He looked away from her. 'What happened up Llanfach Road was the whole lodge, not the few men that actually did him over . . . that's all I meant.'

'Did you? Well it never sounded like that to me. It seemed to me like you was all too familiar with it.'

Haydn was still unable to face her directly. He mumbled: 'Every man in Abercarn could describe it blow by blow for you, Mam. Now why don't you drop it? You can see me an' Lil will never agree with you.'

'Aye. And more shame to the two of you for that. But at least I know Lily didn't take no active part in it. I think you did.'

Guilt was rapidly maturing into anger in Haydn's tone as he said: 'Well, you better keep your bad thoughts to yourself. Thanks to Charlie Henderson attending to him, the police wasn't exactly dragged in at the double. Good bloke, that Henderson . . . but they'm interested enough now, and if they do hear a man's mother doing him down about it, he'll be inside before you can say Jack Robinson. That what you want?'

28

Margaret Ann pursed her lips and shook her head mutely. Lily uttered a heavy sigh and moved across to the hob to make tea. 'Come on, now, Mam,' she said. 'Best just keep quiet about it if you can't mend it. If you feel so bad about Gregg an' his legs, you can always go and pray for him in chapel. Add a bit on for his rotten cringing soul, too, if you got any sense.'

Her mother took a deep breath, ready to launch a counter-attack, but the back door opened again and her youngest daughter, Angharad, came in, effectively cutting off her line of attack. Instead she flashed a murderous glance at Lily, before greeting the younger girl with a flurry of questions about where she had been and what she had been doing.

Lily poured tea for Haydn and herself, and when they had drunk it she walked with him out into the back lane behind the house. 'Come on, Hayd, you can tell me,' she said. 'Was you one of them?'

'What would you say if I had been?'

'I wouldn't bawl you out like our Mam, if that's what you'm thinking. And I understand why Gregg had to be punished. But it gives me goose pimples all over to think one a my brothers could stand over a man in cold blood and smash his legs with a sledge-hammer.'

It was dark in the lane, but she saw the deep shudder that ran through Haydn's body. 'Gave me goose pimples, an' all, kidda. I couldn't a done it if I'd known before what it would feel like. They'm wrong when they say you get carried away by blood lust or summat at times like that – anyhow, I didn't. Oh, aye, I was mad with him, mad enough to bring that six-pound sledge down on his shins. But oh, Lil, the sound it made as it hit the bone . . . and the sound *he* made. When I come home I was sick all over the place.'

'D'you still think it was right?'

'Aye, but I must be a coward. I don't think I could ever be the executioner again. Do you forgive me for doing it?'

'Forgive you? Just 'cos I couldn't have done it myself,

doesn't mean I'm not with you all the way. I s'pose that's cowardly, an' all.' She stood on tiptoe and kissed his cheek. 'Go on home, now, there's a good boy. It's only Mam who'll cross-question you, and it'll be a nine days' wonder with her, wait and see.'

Haydn sniffed, rubbed the back of his hand across his eyes, and nodded. 'Aye, all right then. As long as you know I didn't just do it out of spite.'

'You haven't got a spiteful bone in your body, love. Goodnight.' She stood at the back door until Haydn was safely inside his own house, then turned back to her mother's kitchen.

A week before Christmas, half the family were gathered gloomily around Margaret Ann's fire again. The earlier antagonism was gone. Now the solidarity of poverty had welded them together.

'I shouldn't think there'll be more than stew or sausage on any Christmas dinner-table in the valley this year,' said Lily's brother Edmund. 'Even 1921 wasn't this bad.'

'We'll only be having mutton courtesy of our Elwyn, remember. Nobody else have got the money for it,' said Margaret Ann. She turned to Lily. 'It's your David I do feel for. That lovely house gone to keep our heads above water, and not enough left over for so much as a Christmas dinner. Cruel, I do call it.'

A wave of impatience washed over Lily. 'Aye, Mam, you've said that before. Remember it wasn't just *his* home, it was mine as well. And both of us would rather see our Rose get her medicine and the bills paid for your groceries and boots for Angharad than ten Christmas dinners, so let's drop it.' These days she often wanted to shake her mother, who always preferred to lament the absence of some unnecessary trimming like Christmas celebrations to thanking providence for important basics of everyday life. She concentrated on keeping her temper. None of them were at their best this month, after all. Why should Margaret Ann be any different?

Although she was reluctant to admit it, Lily knew the real cause of her own sudden irritation. Their brother Elwyn, generous to a fault, had slipped into the house just after the lock-out ended to tell them not to worry about Christmas: he had ordered and would pay for a nice leg of mutton for them, and put together enough dried fruit and extras for a plum pudding. Elwyn was the only brother who did not owe his livelihood to coal. He had a well-paid job at the local tinplate works and had sailed through the last seven months financially unscathed by the lock-out.

Normally Lily would have exulted in his good fortune, but now the very modesty of his Christmas contribution rammed home a distasteful reality she ignored as much as possible: the existence of Elwyn's wife Kitty. They had been married a year, and Kitty acted as if Elwyn were a combination of Rudolf Valentino and Richard the Lionheart. No one would have guessed from her demeanour that less than three years ago she had been engaged to another of the Walters boys, Lily's adored brother Emrys, who had died of emphysema before they could marry. Kitty, determined not to lose a source of financial support, had transferred her affections to Elwyn virtually at the deathbed, and had engineered the marriage as soon as it was decent – sooner, in the eyes of the female members of the family.

Lily detested her. She had found this quite easy merely on the basis of Kitty's relationship with Emrys. Even had he lived, Lily would have disliked her sister-in-law. But the subsequent seduction of Elwyn had added fuel to the flames, and the months of the strike had transformed her feelings into murderous hatred.

Kitty had been brought up a penniless ragamuffin, and had lived from hand to mouth until she married Elwyn. Then, abruptly, she became affluent – at least by her standards. She also openly enjoyed having more than other people, and the sufferings of the mining community had suited her admirably. Throughout the dispute she had continued to buy the best food, to wear silk stockings and smart frocks, and had even committed the unpardonable sin of snapping up a couple of precious pieces of furniture at bargain prices from families who had to sell them in order to eat. If the village found it hard to forgive her, Lily found it impossible.

No use blaming Elwyn. He was a pleasant, easy-going young man, unused to making his own decisions. Before Kitty came into his life, his mother had called the tune. He was accustomed to doing what he was told, and on balance he preferred to be dominated by a pretty, kittenish girl than a hard-faced matriarch. So when his much-needed contribution might have kept the family going a little longer, Kitty was spending it on clothes or furniture or luxury food. On consideration, Lily found it miraculous that Elwyn had stood up to her for long enough to hold back the money which would buy their modest Christmas dinner. Kitty had already extracted payment of a sort by arriving to gloat over the fact that they would enjoy the food only thanks to her own self-denial.

She had been expanding on the high price of mutton for some time when Lily's tolerance snapped and she said: 'Cost you the price of a coupla pair a stockings, did it? Poor bloody butterfly!' Then she had flung back her kitchen chair so violently it almost overturned, and stormed outside.

David had been with her, and had followed her out. They walked down the canal bank, Lily constantly slapping her left fist against the palm of her right hand in an effort to subdue her temper. 'It won't do you no good, love. Don't you see it makes her enjoy it more?' he had said after a while.

Lily had nodded, half blinded by the humiliated tears in her eyes. The incident had occurred scarcely a week after they moved back to the Ranks and she turned to him then, saying: 'If only we still had a bitta space, I could take it . . . It's easier to be civil to a cow like that when you can smile and bugger off upstairs to put your doilies on the airing cupboard or something just as daft.'

David had put his arms around her and drawn her head

32

down on to his shoulder. 'What are you doing, mun?' she said, almost scandalised. 'People will think we'm a pair of young lovers, not a respectable married couple.' But at least he had made her laugh a little.

He had turned her face towards his own and said: 'Far as I'm concerned, we are, always will be. Just thinka that when Kitty do get under your skin. P'raps it'll help.'

Remembering the scene now, a fortnight later, Lily shook her head sadly. If only it *had* helped! David loved her so much, and now she was far fonder of him than ever before, but it would never be a grand passion . . .

'Penny for 'em,' said Haydn. 'Where are you, Lil? You look miles away.'

She managed to smile at him. 'Best save the penny, love. My thoughts ent worth the price.' She turned to her mother, conciliatory now in recognition of her earlier surliness. 'I'll have a good look through the pantry when I go back, Mam, and see exactly what we got. We can always find stuff for a coupla roly poly puddings and a jam tart. None of our lot'll go hungry, you'll see.'

She rose and was reaching out for her thin coat when there was a business-like knock at the back door. Her mother looked up in surprise. No one knocked before entering a neighbour's house in the Ranks.

Haydn turned and opened the door. Charles Henderson stood just outside, another man a few paces behind him in the darkness. 'Ah, Haydn,' he said, 'How are you? I've been meaning to call and pay my Christmas respects to the family, and I thought I'd take the opportunity to introduce my new partner at the same time.'

'Oh, *Duw*, look at the state of the place!' hissed Margaret Ann, surveying the gleaming coal range as if it were covered in soot. 'And there ent even a fire in the parlour!'

'Bloody lucky there's a fire in yer, then, ennit?' said Eddy, grinning from his chimney corner. 'Don't be daft, Mam, they know the state everybody's in. Stop fussing and get 'em in outa the cold.'

Henderson had been hovering at the threshold, smiling

33

uncertainly, while this exchange took place. Now he stepped in, obviously wondering if he should have come. He and his companion were carrying a wicker laundry hamper between them. Now they put it down just inside the kitchen door and Henderson stood back to usher the other man forward. 'Permit me to introduce my new partner,' he said, 'Dr Peter Henderson.'

Haydn grinned and extended his hand to Peter Henderson. 'No need to ask if you're any relation, from the looka you,' he said.

He was right. It was as unmistakable as the resemblance between Haydn and Lily. Had it not been for the slash of silver that ran back from Charles Henderson's hairline, at first glance they might have been taken for the same man. Peter Henderson's hair was jet black, his features finely chiselled, his deep-set eyes the darkest brown, Spanish-looking. Looking at him, Lily felt as if someone was squeezing her heart. She turned away hurriedly, in case anyone noticed her confusion.

The younger Henderson was progressing around the room, shaking hands with everyone as his brother spoke their names. Too soon, Lily was dragged back into the limelight, as Charles Henderson said: 'And this is the best driver-receptionist in the Valleys – Lily.' The tenderness in his voice spoke volumes of his enduring love for her.

Lily blushed becomingly and shook hands with Peter Henderson. She remembered, long ago, Charles touching her hand for the first time. The tingling feeling she had experienced then exploded afresh on contact with Peter. Taken aback, she glanced up into his face, to find him looking equally surprised. Fortunately for them both, Charles Henderson had turned towards the door again, to get the hamper, and had the undivided attention of everyone else in the room.

'Mrs Walters,' he said, 'perhaps you'd care to come and see if any of this might be of use to the family. When I brought Peter back down with me from Northumberland, my mother loaded me up with ten times more than we shall ever eat. It will spoil if we keep it.'

Haydn stepped forward to help him, smiling broadly. 'Come on, doctor, let's give 'er plenty a room to see what you got. Bring it up yer.' He and Henderson took one handle each and swung the basket on to the kitchen table.

Lily never forgot her mother's face as she approached the prize. Her eyes were sparkling. If it was a full stocking on Christmas morning she couldn't be more thrilled, she thought.

Margaret Ann wiped her already-clean hands on her apron and reached out for the big hasp that held the basket closed. What she saw inside made her gasp in delight. 'Oh, Doctor – we couldn't . . . really we couldn't . . . ' she said.

Henderson gestured dismissively. 'Mrs Walters, you and your family have been friends of mine for years. This is a Christmas present – and I can assure you it cost us nothing. We're just redistributing our supplies more fairly. I shall be deeply offended if you refuse any of it.'

He's got her cold, thought Lily. She wants it more than she's wanted anything for years, and now he's made it clear he'll be insulted if she do say no – well played, Charlie!

As she watched, Henderson added: 'In fact, I shall help you start consuming it. I know you don't really approve of strong drink, Mrs Walters, but a little warming spirit never hurt anyone at Christmas. I suggest we all have a little of this.' And he took two bottles of single malt whisky out of the top of the hamper.

'Glasses – I dunno if we got enough glasses!' wailed Margaret Ann in anguish.

'Simple – you and your daughter will have cups, of course – I'm sure you prefer to take yours in tea, anyway.' At this he raised his eyebrows at Lily, silently daring her to dissent. 'And we men will be happy with whatever comes to hand.'

Oh, Charlie, you old devil, thought Lily. You'll have her drunk without her ever having to admit it's alcohol, coming out of a cup . . . It was worth wrecking her own first taste of the splendid whisky with tea just to mellow

35

her mother sufficiently for her to enter the spirit of things.

It did not take long. The contents of the hamper alone would have intoxicated Margaret Ann. As she unpacked pots of honey and pats of farm butter, Henderson slipped outside again and returned with a hessian sack. 'Mustn't forget the game,' he said, and whipped off the covering to reveal four brace of pheasant and a large hare.

'Hare! I haven't had that since I was a girl!' Margaret Ann was crowing with delight now. 'I'll jug it – I can get pig's blood from the butcher to thicken the gravy – and do dumplings with it. And pheasant . . . ' Her enthusiasm faltered momentarily. 'Don't think I've ever had that . . . '

'Then perhaps you'll permit me to come up and draw and dress the birds for you, Mrs Walters.' Peter Henderson was all smooth good manners. 'It's no job for a woman – far too messy.'

'Ooh, you are kind. Thanks ever so much. Maybe you'd like to come an' join us when we eat them.'

Henderson's face was comical as he looked around the little room. 'Where will we all sit?' he asked.

'Leave us to sort that one out,' said Lily. 'You'll both be ever so welcome.'

Eyes shining, Margaret Ann was back up to her elbows in her hamper – she had regarded it as her personal property from the moment she started unpacking it. Now she gazed across the sagging lid at Charles Henderson. 'God bless you,' she said, 'for being such a graceful giver.'

He smiled unsteadily, hardly knowing whether to feel pleased to give or guilty at having so much when they were without the most elementary comforts. 'You've given me much more than I could ever give you, Mrs Walters,' he said. As he spoke, his eyes shifted from her to her daughter, who, oblivious of his attention, was staring at his brother Peter.

CHAPTER FOUR

Incredibly, they managed to organise Christmas so that they could entertain the Henderson brothers as well as feeding the family. The furniture in Margaret Ann's little parlour was pressed back around the walls, and a trestle table installed down the centre of the room. The kitchen, already quite bare, was now dominated by its deal drop-leaf table, both the extensions in place as they never were when the family used the room as a living area. That left the parlour as the children's dining room and the kitchen for the grown-ups. On Christmas Day, Margaret Ann presided over a feast which would have been beyond her wildest dreams two weeks before.

Entering the kitchen, Peter Henderson suffered the momentary illusion that every child in the Ranks was in the room. In fact, as Charles pointed out, there were no more than seven of them – it was the adults who formed the crowd.

Margaret Ann turned aside from the kitchen range, beaming in a mixture of pleasure and embarrassment at the prospect of entertaining distinguished guests. '*Diawch*, you shouldn't have come in yer straight away,' she said. 'Angharad, didn't I tell you to take them straight into our Haydn's until dinner was ready?'

'She didn't have an opportunity, Mrs Walters. I'm afraid we followed the wonderful smell of cooking before the poor girl was able to stop us.'

'Well, you go in there now. Lily and Rose and some a the men is in there and you can have a nice talk till this is all ready.'

'Where on earth do they put them all at other times of the year?' Peter whispered to Charles as they moved next door. 'They look enough to populate the entire village.'

'A mere three or four houses full, dear boy. Evan Jones was a prolific man and a couple of his sons appear to be emulating him. Fortunately for her own well-being, luck or strategy have so far prevented Lily from following that road.'

Haydn's kitchen, next door, was more peaceful than Margaret Ann's, although here, too, the cooking range had been pressed into service. Only the hare and one of the pheasants – damaged by shot and more suitable for gravy than for the roasting pan – were being cooked at home. The tiny ovens of the Ranks houses were incapable of accommodating such plenty and, like most villages when they had big cuts of meat, the Walterses had sent the remainder to be cooked with the bread in the local baker's ovens. Dinner would be ready when the children brought back the finished roasts in large covered containers.

The intoxicating scents which already pervaded the two houses came from the hare and the stock pheasant. Maisie, Haydn's wife, beamed at them over a steaming pan and gestured towards the narrow passage. 'They'm in the parlour,' she said. 'Go and make yourselves comfortable for a bit, all right?'

In the cramped parlour, Lily, Tom and Haydn were chattering like a clutch of starlings, a mixture of banter and argument developed from a lifetime of familiarity. Rose, the quiet one, stood slightly apart as usual, clearly longing for the moment when she could take refuge once more behind her Albert. As the two doctors hovered at the door, reluctant to disturb their intimacy, Lily saw them and jumped up. 'Come on in, quick,' she said. 'We got the whisky in here so Mam won't see it – an' we got some peppermints, an' all, to suck while we're going in to dinner.'

Charles Henderson grinned. 'I thought you might be up to something like that. We brought a drop more, as there seemed to be so many people coming along.' Two bottles of whisky and two of port materialised from

38

beneath his bulky overcoat. 'I took it that wine with the meal would be considered inappropriate,' he added.

'You certainly know how to spoil a girl!' Lily twinkled at him.

They drank and chattered companionably until there was a loud hammering on the wall. 'Unless that's Santa coming a bit late, I imagine Mam's ready now,' said Haydn. 'Come on, in we all go.'

Lily's husband was unable to be with them. He had retained his deputy's job by a whisker after the return to work, and part of the price had been safety duty on Christmas Day. He would eat his Christmas meal that night after he came off shift, alone with Lily. Lucky blighter! Peter Henderson reflected, looking at her as she teased one of her brothers. She was all Charles had told him and much, much more. She was not the best-looking girl he had ever seen, although her strong features and startling colouring brought her within a hair's breadth of beauty. It was something in the way she looked at the world: clear-eyed, unafraid, ready to trust but equally ready to defend herself and those she loved. And quick, and funny, and, he was sure, passionate.

Charles nudged him sharply in the ribs. 'Over my dead body, little brother,' he murmured.

Peter smiled at him. 'It might come to that yet,' he said.

Margaret Ann had organised the event like a general planning a military campaign. 'Right,' she said, as they entered the kitchen, 'the children will eat first, with Maisie and Sal keeping an eye on them, and then go to play games in next door. The grown-ups will eat in yer and spread out between this room and the parlour once the little ones have gone in our Haydn's. All right?'

Peter Henderson fought an impulse to salute and snap 'Yes, sir!' and his face must have betrayed him, for he caught a mischievous grin and wink from Lily as he suppressed the thought..

Then the prospect of vast quantities of food diverted him. If Margaret Ann Walters knew anything about game chips and fried breadcrumbs as the traditional accompaniment to pheasant, there was no indication of it. But practically every other British winter vegetable was there. Buttered parsnips – 'Lovely, mind, now the frost have been on them,' said Margaret Ann – swedes, sprouts, a dish of leeks, mashed and roast potatoes and savoy cabbage jostled each other on the table. The hare was accompanied by herb dumplings and a great bowl of stewed red cabbage, in case anyone found the pheasant vegetables inappropriate to this heartier game. The leg of mutton was borne in on a separate plate, surrounded by yet more roast potatoes and baked onions studded with cloves. The gravy was served in the sort of jugs which the Hendersons were more accustomed to seeing carried to the fields full of cider to refresh the labourers at harvest time.

Charles Henderson stood at one end of the trestle-table, carving pheasants as though his life depended on it. Haydn was at the other, dismembering the mutton. Margaret Ann let the hare simmer gently on the hob, its dumplings bobbing like airy clouds atop the rich gravy, 'until we've all had a taste of this little lot'.

Abruptly, Lily said: 'Mam, why are we all cramped up yer when there's two seats still up your end? Everyone is here now, surely?'

Margaret Ann's cheeks reddened to an even deeper hue than had been induced by hours of cooking. She tried to meet Lily's eye and failed. 'Oh – didn't I tell you, love? Our Elwyn said they might come and have dinner with us instead of on their own.'

Peter Henderson watched the little drama with some perplexity. There was an ingredient here which he had missed. Why was Lily suddenly so angry simply because someone else was coming to dinner? There was certainly enough for everyone . . . he was not left ignorant for long.

'You missed a name, didn't you?' Lily's eyes were blazing. 'At least, I assume Lady Muck is coming with him.'

Margaret Ann's assent was virtually inaudible, but now she managed to look directly at her daughter, her eyes pleading for decent restraint in front of their guests. Lily was oblivious to such niceties.

'And to what do we owe the honour of a state visit?' she asked. 'I can't believe it was the prospect of eating their own dried-up old mutton.'

'I – er, that is, I did happen to mention Dr Henderson and his brother was having dinner with us, and Kitty said it would be nice to get better acquainted.'

'Christ Almighty – what it is to run a salon!' said Lily.

'Mind your language, my lady, or I won't be eating my dinner here!' Margaret Ann snapped back.

Lily subsided, but Peter could see her pleasure had been destroyed. He wondered what was so repulsive about this newly-mentioned sister-in-law. As if responding to a theatrical cue, Kitty Walters pushed open the kitchen door and simpered prettily at the party.

'Well, well, I never thought you'd get everyone in, Mother Walters!' she said. Lily's exaggerated eyes-to-the-ceiling exchange with Haydn said more than any words about what she thought of Kitty's way of addressing Margaret Ann.

Her mother came forward and kissed Kitty, took her coat and gave it to Elwyn to take upstairs. 'Come on, now, the two of you. Sit down before it do get cold,' she said.

The rest of the family closed ranks and began passing round vegetables, dishing out spoonfuls of this and that, while the newcomers settled in. They were all weary of conflict after seven months' industrial dispute and now instinctively looked for peace. Kitty seemed oblivious of her capacity to inflame Lily, and the moment she took her seat beside Margaret Ann, she was off at full gallop.

Turning to Charles Henderson, she said: 'I told our Elwyn, I know it's nice to be here cosy for only our second Christmas as man and wife, but family ties is family ties, and I don't want to come between anyone –

41

my own family is scattered, you know – so let's forget our little piece a pork and everything and go an have dinner with your mam. Nice to stick together this time of year.'

Charles Henderson nodded, preoccupied by Kitty's uncommonly sharp little teeth. Just like a small predatory woodland animal, he was thinking. I wonder who she has her eye on here.

Haydn had finished carving the meat and game birds and gave Lily a chance to calm herself by handing her a large platter of mutton slices for the children in the parlour. 'Yer you are, kidda, take this in to our Maisie. It's beginning to sound like a Berlin bread riot in there.' Lily flashed him a look of pure poison but took the meat and departed.

Returning, determined to be pleasant for her mother's sake, she was pitched straight back into fury by the first snatch of Kitty's chatter. Her sister-in-law was telling Charles Henderson: 'Of course, this time of year is never quite the same without the hunt, is it? My brother and sister and I used to be such enthusiasts! England wouldn't be England without all those pink coats and hounds in the inn yard on Boxing Day, would it?'

Haydn snorted with mirth and hastily covered his mouth to prevent food from showering his neighbours. Had Kitty taken leave of her senses? Everyone in the room, except the Hendersons, knew her origins. The closest she had ever come to a hunt was to gawp at it from over the gate of her father's wretched smallholding. Surely she didn't imagine they liked her enough to back her in such childish snobbery? Then he remembered – dear God, the leg of mutton! she really must think she had bought their loyalty with the paltry gift! Haydn turned unhurriedly to regard Lily, enjoying the anticipation of what she was about to do to his ludicrous sister-in-law.

But Charles Henderson had been Lily's fiancé for months, long ago, and knew something of her temperament. He also knew that an acrimonious Christmas Day might wipe out the benefits of the one carefree period the family had enjoyed that year. Without apparent effort, he smoothly intercepted any retort Lily had been about to make by saying: 'Ah! You rode to hounds as a girl, I take it?'

Only now, it seemed, did Kitty sense she might be entering a minefield. Her answering smile was less certain than it had been before. 'N-not quite. Father would never let me . . . I was delicate . . . he said it was too dangerous. No, we followed the hunt.'

'Mmm, I always found that a pleasanter pastime than riding. Hard to beat a good healthy tramp through frosty fields on a crisp winter day, isn't it?'

Kitty nodded gratefully, then abruptly said: 'Oh, Rose, I knew there was something I'd been meaning to tell you – excuse me, Doctor. If I don't say this while it's on my mind, I'll forget it for good!' And she was off on some slender conversational ploy involving a length of curtain material which she had seen in a Newport draper's shop a week earlier. Henderson smothered a satisfied smile and turned to Eddy, sitting on his right, to ask about work prospects now the lock-out was over.

The meal progressed, the participants mellow, now, with the best food they had consumed for as long as they remembered. Lily's resentment was banked down. Charles Henderson hoped it would not erupt before everyone had gone home that afternoon.

After the mounds of meat, a whole procession of puddings materialised: the traditional plum pudding was smaller than usual because it required so much precious dried fruit. But there were a couple of hot apple tarts, an apple suet pudding they all referred to as apple dumpling, and a couple of suet roly poly concoctions. More giant jugs, this time brim-full with custard, accompanied the sweet dishes. There was white sauce for the plum pudding, but none of the brandy or rum butter the Hendersons were used to seeing.

'You better make sure you'm full with all this,' said Margaret Ann, gesturing expansively. 'There ent no mince pies nor Christmas cake this year. Couldn't manage them even with the doctors' help,' she added apologetically.

Peter Henderson stood up and made a little bow to his hostess. 'I think it's just as well, Mrs Walters,' he told her. 'I don't think either Charles or I will ever walk again. It's a magnificent meal. Enough ballast there to take us right through January. We're most grateful you included us.'

After that, any lingering cloud of unease left by Kitty's and Lily's mutual antagonism was dispelled. The children were duly dispatched to play in Haydn's house, and ten of the adults crowded into the parlour, at Margaret Ann's insistence, while the dishes were cleared and washed in the kitchen.

After a while, Lily slipped out and cornered Margaret Ann. 'Mam, this is silly. There ent really room for all of us in there, and you know you're embarrassed to have strangers about with all this stuff waiting to be cleared. Why don't I take the doctors and Haydn and Eddy and Tom and Maisie down our house and leave the rest here? You could come down an' all, seeing that Sal and Angharad are doing the dishes. Elwyn's talking boxing with our Lewis, and Kitty is up to her eyes with new curtains and three-piece suites with Rose, so they're all right where they are. How about it?'

Margaret Ann glanced shrewdly at her daughter. 'Keep you out of Kitty's way, won't it? I think that might be a good idea.'

Lily embraced her lightly. 'I know you had to ask her, Mam, but she do drive me crazy. Let's just say it will make a better end to my day if we don't see it out under the same roof.'

'All right then,' said Margaret Ann, smiling. 'I won't come, though; I had my moment sitting at that lovely dinner table. Nothing could better that. Perfect end to a terrible year. You take them down the road and I'll stop yer.' She dropped her voice: 'Anyhow, it might need me to keep that Kitty from trailing down after you. Wait a bit. I'll put up a pan o' that hare and some veg for you

44

and David to have for supper. Angharad can bring tart an' custard down for you after we've cleared this lot.'

'Bless you, Mam. You'm an angel.'

'Gerron with you. I'll believe you if you do say it the next time I'm trying to stop you talking politics!'

Lily's small reward for resisting the temptation to a full scale row with Kitty was the sight of her sister-in-law's face when she announced she was taking some of the family and the Hendersons down to her house. She cut off Kitty's retreat by impressing on her that she was leaving her here to have a long gossip with Rose and Margaret Ann. Rose, who was as domestically acquisitive as Kitty, welcomed the chance to compare notes on household goods and Kitty's fate was sealed.

Lily's little house was a quiet haven after the bustle of her mother's home. A well-banked fire kept the kitchen warm and she put the covered pan of food for David on the stone hob beside it. Haydn went and lit a fire in the front parlour. He came back looking conspiratorial. 'Right, doctors,' he said. 'Where's them bottles – still some left, wasn't there?'

'But not for long, the way we mistreated them before dinner,' said Charles Henderson. 'Peter, why not drive back down to the surgery and get some more from the cellar? It wouldn't take more than ten minutes.'

'I'll go with you,' said Lily, a little too quickly. 'I dunno when I was last in a car. Bring back memories of easier times, eh Charlie?'

Charles's look was ambiguous. 'Perhaps . . . or perhaps something quite new. Look after her, Peter.'

Haydn, a straightforward soul, missed the implicit competition between the brothers and assumed Charles Henderson merely still nursed a deep tenderness for his sister that made him worry about her well-being. He found it quite romantic. As Peter and Lily left together, he accepted a glass of whisky from what remained of the stock Henderson had brought earlier, and sat down to talk to him.

* * *

45

'This is turning into one of the jolliest Christmases I can remember,' Peter Henderson told Lily as they drove down to the surgery near the Old Swan public house south of the village. 'It's certainly the strangest.'

'A bit different from the Peel, I'll give you that.' The Peel was his parents' Northumberland mansion, from which Lily, then engaged to Charles Henderson, had fled in misery at Christmas seven years before, after falling foul of his aristocratic mother.

Peter glanced at her quizzically before turning back to the road. 'The way I heard it, you didn't stay long enough to find out what Christmas was like there.'

'Oh, someone have told you about it, have they?'

'My dear girl, no one has ever got the better of my mother, before or since. She never got over it.'

'*She* told you?'

'Not quite, but she was the first to refer to it. She said something cryptic about this singular young woman whom Charles had "become entangled with" as she put it, and said she wished she had got to know you better. After that, wild horses wouldn't have stopped me prising the story out of Charles.'

'What did he say?'

'Always remember that Charles is besotted by our mother . . . even so, you came out of it rather well. He said he had been unfair to both you and Mother – but particularly to you – in throwing you together like that, and that you had behaved outrageously but with complete justification as a result. That made me more intrigued than ever.'

'Well it wasn't as dramatic as it sounds. It was awful. If your mother hadn't been armour-plated with emeralds, I swear I'd have strangled her.'

He laughed. 'I know the feeling. I once slapped her face.'

Lily's eyes were round pools of astonishment. 'What did she do?'

'Beat me within an inch of my life. No one lays hands on Mama and gets off scot-free.'

'How old were you?'

'Hmm . . . about twelve, I think. I still remember it vividly.'

'Doesn't sound as if there's much love lost between the two of you.'

'We hate the sight of each other.' He seemed supremely unworried about it. 'She wasn't keen on our eldest brother, Teddy, either. Charles was the one and only . . . she'd have made quite a Phaedra, I suppose. Just as well he got away from her as soon as he did.'

'Phaedra? I don't understand.'

'You must read the story of King Oedipus some time. Killed his father and married his mother. Phaedra was his mother's name.' Abruptly he changed tack. 'Still, mustn't be too hard on the old girl. She appears to have mended her ways since that brush with you. Now she fills the house with vigorous young men at every opportunity and goes off for long, long walks with them in the afternoons.'

'What does your father do?'

'Same as he's always done; a little shooting and a lot of fishing. Not a man greatly given to passion, my father. Ah – we seem to have arrived at the wine store!' He stopped the car outside the house he shared with his brother.

Lily went inside with him and stood in the stone-flagged hall while he went down into the cellar for bottles. Within minutes he was back, with three more bottles of whisky, two of port and two of madeira.

'That's a bit generous, ennit, considering what we've already had?' said Lily.

'It hardly seems fair that your husband should have been slaving away all day and come home to nothing. I propose to leave a secret bottle with you as a little present for him.'

She beamed. 'Oh, bless you for such a nice thought!'

'I haven't finished yet. Wait . . . ' He put down the bottles on the hall-table and ducked back inside the low cellar door. Moments later he re-emerged with a bottle of champagne.

'*Iesu, mawr*! You can't give us that an' all!'

'Oh, yes I can. You and your husband will have it with your supper. My brother tells me his best memory of you is the way your eyes sparkle when you've had champagne. I think that would be a good present for your husband, don't you?'

Lily moved closer to him. 'Look at you,' she said gently. 'You got cobwebs all down the side of your face. Look as if you been hanging in a cupboard . . . '

She reached up to brush away the spiders' webs and he caught her wrist as she did so, turning her hand palm up and kissing it in one speedy gesture. Without releasing her, he gazed into her eyes over the raised palm. 'Forgive me,' he said. 'I just couldn't resist . . . ' Then she was in his arms and they were kissing properly.

After a long embrace, she drew away from him and said: 'I should be the one to apologise. I really led you on . . . not fair . . . I'm a married woman after all . . . ' His arms were around her again and they kissed at greater length. ' . . . But I just couldn't help myself,' she murmured, as she surfaced again.

Eventually Peter said: 'I know this is all wrong, and we shouldn't even be thinking about it, but I feel as if I've always been waiting for you.'

'And me.' Quite without guile, she added: 'It's as if Charlie had been a sort of . . . sort of glimpse of what you would be, with the pieces not quite in place. Oh, hell, what're we going to do?'

Henderson's laugh was unsteady. 'It's absurd for us to think of doing anything, Lily. We've barely met.'

Her direct look silenced him. 'You know as well as I do that haven't got nothing to do with it. Whatever this is, I dunno how to cope with it.'

'Nor I. So for the moment, let's not. Kiss me once more and then we shall try to pretend nothing has happened to us until – well, until it happens again. I'm sure it will.'

She kissed him again and clung to him for a while, then said softly, 'Oh, yes, you can be certain of that.'

* * *

When they got back to the Ranks, Charles Henderson tried to reassure himself that the flush in Lily's cheeks and the sparkle in her eyes had more to do with the chilly winter air than with any special emotion, but it was hard to believe.

CHAPTER FIVE

Cardiff, February 1927

Lexie Walters eyed herself in the full-length wardrobe mirror and snorted with dissatisfaction. 'Bloody hell, girl, you look like a hippo!' she said.

Lexie was almost nine months pregnant and she hated her appearance. She had always been lithe and whip-thin. Now she had developed a smooth layer of extra flesh – and a greatly enlarged belly. To anyone else, she looked magnificent – her silky coffee-coloured skin radiating an extra glow, her long legs as shapely as ever and her graceful dancer's walk removing any possibility of ungainliness. She had allowed her formerly fashionable Eton crop to grow out during recent months, and now her lustrous black hair hung smooth and straight to jawbone level.

Someone rapped on the bedroom door. 'Come on in, Dad – I'm as decent as I'll ever be!' she called.

Rhys Walters walked in and surveyed his only child. Hell's teeth, he thought, I've been a sinner but I must have done something right to father one like this. 'Just looking in to see how you do feel before I opens up, Lex,' he said.

She flounced down on the side of her bed and scowled at him. 'I'd feel a damn sight better if you'd let me go on working in that bar,' she said. 'Way things is at present, you can't afford to pay a full-time barmaid while I'm out.'

'I was paying one before and I can do it again,' he said. 'I ent having my first grandchild born on a pub floor.'

That made her smile. 'No chance a that. I was always faster than was good for me, remember? I'd be back up these stairs quicker than you could say pale ale, the minute he started.'

'He? You'm sure it's gonna be a boy, ent you?'

'D'you know, it never entered my head it'd be anything else? Christ, I hope it is a boy!'

Rhys moved across the room and sat down beside her. 'Why, flower? I rather fancy having another pretty female face around the place. Yours kept me happy for more than twenty years.'

Lexie's brief flash of merriment had gone. Now her face was grim. 'No. It ent a girl – mustn't be.'

'Why not? Just hope it'll be fine and healthy, never mind the sex – why, Lex, you'm crying. I can't remember when you last did that. What is it, love?' He wrapped his arms around her and rocked her against his bulky body. 'Come on, now, you can tell your father. I meant what I said when you left here to go to London. Just remember you can always tell me anything.'

She turned and buried her head against his chest in a storm of weeping. 'If I'd stopped to think it might be a girl, I'd have got rid of it! I don't want no girl going through her life getting called nigger and blackie every time she pokes her nose outa the Bay, that's why!'

Rhys let out a relieved laugh. 'Don't be bloody soft, Lex. You'm worried about nothing. Your Mam didn't look all that coloured – you even less. Even you used to think you looked Spanish, remember? Well, your kid will look even lighter. Nobody'll even think about it.'

The tears had stopped. She was stony-faced, now, and was staring straight ahead. 'Oh, yes they will. Its father was as black as the ace of spades.'

'Oh.'

'Different story, now, ennit? D'you want me to clear out?'

Rhys looked as if she had struck him. 'What on earth could make you think that?'

She was glaring down at her hands, twisting them in

51

her lap, fighting to stay calm. 'Well, you know, the things everyone do say about going with coloureds . . . all that filth . . . '

His huge hand covered both hers and stopped their frenetic motion. He said, very gently, 'Lexie, what do you think made me fancy your Mam?'

'Dunno.' It was barely audible.

'Well I'll tell you. Her gorgeous brown skin and her little tight backside that stuck out prettier than any white girl's I'd seen. And that great pile a thick black hair. Closest thing to perfection I ever saw. Why would I blame you for having the right sorta taste in men?' He gave an exaggerated start. 'Unless you'm telling me he wasn't good-looking. I don't know if I could live with that . . . '

'Oh, Dad, I do love you! Wish I'd told you months ago, when I come home. Didn't you ever wonder?'

'Wonder what?'

'What he was like.'

Rhys chuckled. 'Our kid, you ent gonna like this, but I'll tell you anyhow. May give you a better idea about the way I looks at things. I didn't ask what he was like because I thought p'raps it was "them", rather than "him". It have been known in our family before, you know, and you never stayed alive in London and bought the sorta clothes you got by serving in no shop.'

She stared at him, momentarily shocked to the core, then she too chuckled. As they sat on the bed, smiling at each other, their grins turned to giggles and the giggles to uproarious laughter. Eventually, struggling for breath, Rhys gasped out: 'Ent as if I was exactly a good example a chastity, is it?' and that set them off again.

Abruptly, Lexie sat bolt upright. 'Oh, shit,' she said. 'Shouldna laughed like that. I think my waters have broken.'

They rushed Lexie into Cardiff Royal Infirmary after she had been in labour for nine hours. A last-minute caesarean operation saved her and the baby, but the surgeon told Rhys afterwards that there would be no more children.

'Right now that's the last of my worries – or hers, I should think,' he said. 'Will she be all right now?'

'Eventually, but it will take a while. No visitors before tomorrow – not even you. It's a very big operation when we perform it at such a crucial stage. Your daughter is fortunate. We often lose either mother or child when we have to resort to this procedure.'

'And you're sure there's nothing wrong with the baby?'

The surgeon smiled for the first time. 'Positive, Mr Walters. She's a fine healthy little girl, none the worse for her somewhat protracted entry into this world.'

Pity about it being a daughter, the way Lexie feels about it, Rhys reflected as he went up to the ward to see her the next day. Nevertheless, it was impossible to keep the broad grin off his face. Another girl! A girl to spoil, and tease, and take out . . . It made him feel thirty years younger just to think about it. Rhys Walters adored women of all ages, and preferred watching them, talking to them and having fun with them to any contact with his own sex. Lexie might have mixed views about this latest addition to the family, but her father approved whole-heartedly.

Lexie was in a small room on her own. Rhys had come down in the world since his days of prosperity after the War, but he still had enough emergency money to finance privacy for his only child. Now, as he entered, she levered herself up in the bed, grimacing as the movement tugged the row of stitches down her abdomen.

'Never believe 'em when they say you forget the pain straight after,' she said, scowling. 'That lot's tattooed inside my head for good. Not something I'll try again in a hurry.'

Rhys was so taken aback at her ignorance of her condition that he blurted out: 'But you can't have no more even if you want them. Didn't they tell you?'

Her eyes widened momentarily, and she shook her

head. Then relief replaced the look of surprise, followed by a big smile. 'No, they didn't, blabbermouth, but at present that's the best news I've had since they told me she was all right.' She nodded towards the neat crib which stood within reach of the bed.

Hesitantly, Rhys began to move over to the cot. 'How d'you feel about her being a girl?'

Lexie shrugged. 'The minute I set eyes on her I loved her so much that I decided to cross that bridge when we come to it. Maybe the world will be a bit better by then. If it ent . . . well, we Walterses was always fairly tough. No reason why she shouldn't be, an' all.'

'Good girl. Right then, let's have a look at her.' He pulled back a corner of the cot blanket and confronted the most perfect child he had ever seen. She was all smooth curves, and her skin was the colour of the darkest melted chocolate. The tiny rosebud mouth seemed to be blowing an unending kiss and, as he watched her, her eyelids parted to reveal a pair of midnight-black eyes big enough to swamp the rest of her face. Rhys's finger trembled as he extended it to brush the curve of the baby's cheek. He found it hard not to cry.

Lexie was watching him with an indulgent expression. 'It's all right,' she said. 'You're not going to pieces and turning into a soft old grand-dad. Half the nurses on the ward come in and coo over her every time they get a chance. Seems like me and Larry produced the world champion in the beautiful babies stakes.'

'You have as far as I'm concerned. Decided yet what you're going to call her?'

'Oh, yes, the minute I woke up. Georgia.'

Rhys was confused. 'I know your Mam took a fancy to royal names when she picked Alexandra for you, but don't you think that's taking patriotism a bit far?'

'I don't understand.'

'Well, Georgia. I s'pose it must be after the King, 'cos there ent nobody of that name in the Walters' tribe.'

Lexie laughed. 'You daft old devil. Stuff the king – her father was born in Atlanta in the state of Georgia. If she ent having his surname, at least she can have a first name to remember him by.'

Rhys nodded and sighed. 'Could be worse, I suppose. At least you don't want to call her Atlanta.'

'I thought about it, don't worry. But I think Georgia gorra nice sound to it.'

'Me too, Lex. The minute you come home, we'll wet her head with the last o' that champagne I got in the cellar.'

'Believe me, that can't come soon enough for me. I don't want anything to do with hospitals from now on.'

Back at the Anglesey Hotel, Rhys looked around him in deepening dissatisfaction. He had always kept a tidy pub – well-stocked and mahogany-panelled inside, freshly painted outside. He had driven expensive cars and gambled heavily, and had supported his extravagant ways by drug dealing and fencing stolen or smuggled goods. His villainy was no greater than that of many other dock-land publicans, and more modest than many. Anyway, in recent years the profits had tailed off, and with them the raffish high style of his pub.

Now the outside paintwork was blistered and peeling, ingrained with dust from Bute Street. Even the brewers' coloured tin advertising plates announcing their various beers had rusted and gone askew, and it had been a long time since any brewery had found it worthwhile to spend money on such promotion in this part of the city. Inside was better. Rhys was incapable of running an uncomfortable pub; nevertheless, the leather banquettes were cracked and some of the chairs had wobbly legs. The elaborate Victorian engraved-glass panels which divided parts of the main bar into booths were still in perfect condition, and the marble-topped cast iron tables were solid enough to last until the millennium, but everything else was distinctly down-at-heel.

Not that the Anglesey was exceptional. The port of Cardiff was dying on its knees – already dead, some said. After the War the coal industry had declined at breakneck speed, and, thanks to the indifference of the marquesses of Bute, original developers of the docks, no substantial alternative trade had ever been built up. As the coalfield languished, so did the seaports of the South Wales coast.

None of this had worried Rhys until now. Lexie had vanished from his life more than six years before and had not contacted him with more than the odd picture post-card saying that she was doing well. Lily had returned permanently to Abercarn shortly after Lexie's departure. Rhys had retained his expensive tastes, but he was slowing down. He was less interested in women, now, and the slump in trade caused him to spend more time behind the bar to compensate for the staff cuts made necessary by falling profits. That, in turn, diminished his interest in large flashy cars and prevented him from attending many race meetings. He had preferred the old high-spending days, but on balance he was quite content to rub along comfortably in reduced circumstances.

Now it was different. There was a future again, a future which revolved around Lexie and that beautiful little girl to whom he would have to be father as well as grandfather. That took money – pots of it, from what he remembered of bringing up Lexie. He walked past the bar entrance and trudged up the staircase to the first floor living quarters, which he eyed with new distaste. 'Say what you like about floozies, they don' arf keep the place looking tidy,' he muttered. 'Bloody place is a shambles, now. Gorra do summat about it before Lexie brings that kid home.'

Over the following days, he paid a local woman to spring-clean the living quarters, and had one of the old spare rooms freshly painted. In his first enthusiasm, Rhys had planned to refurnish the entire apartment, but common sense soon took hold and he decided what little he had in reserve was best kept for other, more pressing needs. Instead he bought new linoleum, a bright rug, a cot, a chest and a cupboard. A small table was painted the same colour as the nursery walls, and the daughter of

56

the cleaning woman ran up a pair of pretty curtains for him. When it was done, and looking better than anything else in the building, he uttered a sigh of satisfaction. It wasn't the Ritz, but at least Georgia would have somewhere pretty to come home to. He marvelled that he had grown so lackadaisical in his old age that Lexie had managed to dissuade him from such preparations earlier.

Every time he had raised the matter during her pregnancy, she had said: 'Plenty of time later on'. It was true she had borne her baby a couple of weeks earlier than expected, but even so, they must both have been crazy to let matters slide for so long.

Well, now it was different. That kid was having the best, even if he had to steal for it. Rhys laughed aloud at that. Steal, down here? He'd always been willing to do that from the right mark, but these days there was nothing worth pinching; no expensive, illegal powder coming in through the moribund docks for onward sale by a shrewd middleman; no Cathedral Road socialite's burgled jewellery to be fenced. Like commerce, even crime in Cardiff seemed to have come to a dead stop.

'Ah, stop maundering to yourself and go an' open the bloody pub!' he exclaimed. 'Something's bound to turn up in the end.'

When it did, it had the extra advantage of banishing some of Lexie's bitterness about never getting a fair deal in the city. A few weeks after she brought Georgia home from hospital, she ventured up to the smart shopping streets for the first time since coming back to Cardiff. The most decorative feature of the city centre was its network of Victorian and Edwardian arcades, which acted as shortcuts between the open thoroughfares and provided a unique covered area for women to shop when the weather was bad. Many of them were built on two levels, with wrought-iron galleries running above the ground floor, offering further commercial space. The upstairs levels included some shops, but also ran to small restaurants, business offices and places of entertainment. In one there were two dance studios.

Lexie had quite forgotten their existence in her years away. Now, emerging from an upstairs teashop, she glanced at the opposite gallery and remembered. Within minutes, she was inside the studio, talking herself into a job as a dance demonstrator and teacher.

Like the local cinemas, dancing schools and ballrooms were doing reasonably well in spite of the recession. People with little money and too much time on their hands could entertain themselves much more cheaply watching films or whirling around a dance floor than consuming expensive drinks at pubs. Ivor Daniels and his mother, who styled herself Madam Maude Danielova, watched Lexie dance and engaged her on the spot. It was a lower-paid but similar version of the arrangement she had, when she worked in London – a small basic wage and commission on the number of pupils she brought in. Lexie had no doubt that within a couple of months she would be earning a reasonable living.

Inevitably, Rhys grumbled. 'You ent fit enough for them sorta physical jerks, and anyhow, I've always been able to keep my daughter comfortably, haven't I?' he said.

'Aye, Dad, but times have changed and both of us knows that our little Madam over there is gonna be hard on both our pockets. You don't need me to remind you there ent a living for three in the Anglesey at present.'

When he made a serious assessment of recent takings, Rhys was forced to admit she was right. So, as soon as Lexie was completely fit again, she went off to work at the dance studios and Rhys began to divide his time between pub-keeping and acting as surrogate mother to his grand-daughter. He relished every second.

CHAPTER SIX

Abercarn, September 1927

'And I say that if you go on assuming they're all cruel-hearted Victorian ironmasters intent on grinding the faces of the poor, you're finished before you get started!'

The accent wasn't typical of the mining valleys, the sentiments only a little less so. Neither fact was surprising, since Peter Henderson had never seen a Welsh mining valley until the winter of 1926. It said much for his commitment to radical politics that he was already accepted by every left-wing organisation in Western Monmouthshire.

'Come on, Pete. You ent seriously suggestin' they'll do something about it if they see us that they wouldn't do if they'd just read about it?' Haydn Walters was regarding him incredulously.

'Remind me some day to show you a few of the photographs the Salvation Army circulated to the well-washed classes,' said Henderson. 'They'd talked themselves dry explaining how children were exploited on the streets of London, and society couldn't have cared less. Then some genius took photographs – posed a lot of them, I'm sure – and it worked. The sight of dirty cherubic faces and the stench of the slums always work better than rhetoric.'

'And because a that we gorra make ourselves into a raree show for the bosses' wives and children to gawp at? Just 'cos they'm too stupid to understand what it do feel like to starve?'

'That's exactly what I'm saying, Haydn. Never assume any intelligence in your adversaries.'

Haydn sniffed. 'Look, But, I never thought they was

geniuses, but if they was that daft, we wouldna lost all them other fights, would we?'

'It's not a question of intellectual ability; it's emotional immaturity. They hear it; they see it; they consider it against the good commercial principles they were raised with. And by those principles they reject natural justice. But if you show them – physically show them – the results of that thinking, they begin to grow up emotionally. That's the principle behind the hunger march.'

'I still don't like it. I've seen what happens on them marches. Our Lil's a case in point. Show 'er a copper and she turns into a whirling dervish. Her Mam's every bit as bad, if you can believe it. If they hadn't gone on a protest march, neither of 'em would ever of found out what they had in 'em, but they did. It was marching as put Lily in jail for two months.'

But Peter Henderson had no intention of being discouraged now. 'That proves my point, don't you see?' he said. 'Give them a march, and the emotions are crystallised. Confrontation between capitalist and worker . . . reducing us all to our essential equality . . . '

Haydn cut him off with a snort of mirth. 'When you'm face to face you notice the difference between the capitalist's broadcloth and your own moleskin trousers twice as much, mun. Sorry, but I still don' think it'd work. You gorra convince me them bastards is human beings to start off with.'

Henderson had spent the last twenty minutes trying to convince a group of miners at the Abercarn Workmen's Institute that a hunger march on London would promote their cause with Parliament and the coal owners. He had arrived at the institute flourishing a poster which announced a mountainside demonstration in the Rhondda Valley the following Sunday, to call for a march on London. Organised by the Rhondda Miners' Action Council, it was to feature massed silver bands and Arthur Cook, the national miners' union leader. Henderson proposed to commandeer the car he shared with his brother, cram it full of local activists and take an

Abercarn contingent to demonstrate the solidarity of the Monmouthshire village.

All of them except Henderson were sceptical about the value of the grand gesture. They had seen the whole of British industry silenced for nine days in support of their cause, and still they had lost. They had seen an official commission come out with recommendations that ownership of the industry should be put into the hands of the men who cut the coal from the ground, only to have its report set aside. They had seen death-dealing explosions scythe through the male population of flourishing villages, and had stood by, helpless, as the mine owners refused to compensate widows and orphans with enough money to stay alive. They had little faith left over to believe that a mere flaunting of their poverty would help to remedy the sickness of their society.

But it is hard to believe that your fellow man has set his face entirely against you, and the autumn of 1927 had given the miners fresh cause for dissatisfaction. The Poor Law had been tightened until it seemed to benefit no one, and a new Unemployment Bill was likely to make matters even worse. All along the valleys of the Rhondda, Rhymney, Ebbw, Sirhowy and Afon Llywd, colliers were telling each other that, could they but put a personal case to the privileged dwellers of Reading and Maidenhead and Mayfair, they would achieve some escape from the poverty trap for themselves, their wives and their children. In mining villages throughout south-east Wales, men like Haydn and Peter were arguing the merits of taking a mass protest to the doorsteps of the privileged.

Eventually they believed their own wishful thinking, and the skeleton of a great procession began to form – a march of the dispossessed to show the more prosperous members of society that parts of the body politic were mortally sick. It was to be dignified, well-organised, peaceful – and an abject failure.

Speaking on the Welsh mountainside on a breezy September afternoon, Arthur Cook added the vital spark which roused the colliers to the first of their hunger marches. In the week that followed, posters flooded the Valleys, announcing detailed plans for the protest to begin on November 8th, the day Parliament opened, arriving in London on November 20th. Each village was to supply one representative on the march; each marcher was to carry a safety lamp to symbolise the protestors' hopes. A few of the delegates were women, and the Abercarn representative was one of them.

'Don't you think you've done your bit for the cause already?' Margaret Ann Walters was pummelling the cushions on her Windsor chair as if she wished they were a human adversary.

Lily sighed, but her response was mild. 'Come on, Mam, even you gorra give up some time. I've come too far for turning back now, haven't I?'

'You've got a husband and a son to look after, and you'm planning to be off gallivanting for two weeks. What sorta way is that for a respectable married woman to carry on?'

Lily laughed at that. 'David would be tickled to death if he heard you calling me a respectable married woman!'

'And what else would I describe you as, may I ask? Shame on you both if you think that's such a light thing.'

Lily stood up and went over to her mother, embracing her with such vigour that the tiny woman was swept off her feet. 'Wharra you doing, you mad thing? Put me down this minute!'

'Just trying to butter you up. Who'll look after Tommy an' David while I'm doing my gallivanting if you don't?'

'No good expecting me to do it. I'll have nothing to do with any of it!'

Lily assumed an exaggeratedly woeful expression. 'What a cruel woman, leaving her own flesh and blood to starve . . . Mam, I thought you were a Christian.'

'Just you leave that out of it. I don't want none of your mockery. All right. I suppose you'll go whatever I do say – and if I don't see to the two of them, you'll talk poor

Maisie into it, when she've already got too much on her hands.'

'That's better, Mam. You'll have your reward in heaven, just you wait.'

Margaret Ann aimed a death-dealing look at her daughter and went outside to brush the step.

'Think this will work, then, do you?' Lily was striding easily along beside Peter Henderson, who had volunteered for the march medical team within two days of Lily's selection as the Abercarn representative.

His face was shining with boyish enthusiasm. 'I hope so – it's the first time I've had so much faith in anything since I refused to fight in the War.'

Her smile held a trace of sadness. 'Your pacifism didn't stop them all fighting, did it?'

'What are you saying?'

'Well, it do stand to reason. If you had faith that you'd stop people fighting by refusing to do it yourself, and you failed, it's just as likely we'll fail to make people see how we'm suffering just by rubbing their noses in it.'

He shook his head, angry at this questioning of the cause. 'If you feel like that, why are you tiring youself out by marching all this way?'

'If there's one thing I've learned, it's that you mustn't give up just because you'm likely to lose. There's always a chance, and it's worth a try for that reason. All I'm saying is, you'll take the blows better if you hope for the best and prepare for the worst.'

Henderson gave a snort of derision. 'The trouble with the working class if that it can never resist a good cliché – always preferable to adventurous thinking, it seems.'

If he had hoped to provoke Lily's anger, he was disappointed. She merely laughed. 'Aye, that's right, But. Nothing wrong with a good cliché. It rams home the message in words people remember when they have trouble reading and writing. It's not everybody do get a chance to master dialectic materialism in their holidays from boarding school.'

Reluctantly, he smiled. 'Checkmate, I think. I really must get out of the habit of patronising you because you speak with a Valleys accent, mustn't I?'

She shrugged. 'All the same to me. Working for your brother taught me accents change as fast as anything else. I talk like this now because the people around me talk like this. When I was working with him all the time, and living over the garage, I spoke something like the King's English. But I've always been saying the same thing – and I've read an awful lot of books, and understood them, whatever I do sound like when I'm talking about them.'

'Don't you ever feel . . . ' his words tailed off as he realised they might offend her.

'Feel what? Come on, you may as well tell me.'

'Well, that you might . . . influence . . . influential people more if you adopted a more educated tone of voice? That perhaps they'd take you more seriously if you sounded more as they expect educated people to sound?'

'That's a right bloody weasel of an argument, ennit? Sounds like good strategy, but what you'm really saying is that there's only one standard English for the classes, and if you sound different, you'm definitely masses. I know where I'm from. I'm comfortable here. I know they're clever, but I know I am, too. So why can't they come up with the same conclusion?'

'Because that's just not the way the world is!'

'Well it bloody well should be! Now, let's drop it, shall we? We'll never agree, and I like you too much to quarrel – not that I wouldn't, mind, given half a chance!'

It was almost two hundred miles by road to London, giving them a target of about twenty miles a day; easy enough for fit, habitual walkers, a harder task for people who had been half-starved for more than a year. The trade unions, with the exception of the miners, disapproved of what they were doing and would not back the marchers. But the ordinary people of the towns and villages they passed through turned out to greet them and cheer them on. They were fed and given shelter everywhere from barns and village halls to schoolrooms and private houses. By the half-way point, they were beginning to think they might win their case.

Sitting under a bright moon in the Oxfordshire village where they were to spend their seventh night, Lily splashed her blistered feet in the stream which ran alongside the main village street and beamed her pleasure at Peter Henderson. 'Even if this don't get us anywhere, I'm glad I came,' she said. 'At least, now, I know the people everywhere else are as good and bad as we are in Wales. I was beginning to wonder, the way the papers made us out to be a bunch of revolutionary beasts.'

He nodded. 'Yes, I know what you mean. In fact, I keep having to remind myself that there's bad in everyone, too, because we haven't seen much except the good side this past few days.' As they sat on the little built-up stone embankment from which Lily was swinging her feet, he slipped an arm about her shoulders. He felt her body stiffen momentarily, then she relaxed against him and went on gazing up at the night sky.

'I wish this would just go on and on for ever,' she said, 'no problems, no fights, no poverty. Just a bitta food and a glass a beer every night, and an open road with a bunch a good people around you in the day.'

'Is this the Lily Walters I've heard talking about the strength her family gives her, about the roots everybody needs?' he asked, gently mocking her.

But she did not take up his flippant tone. 'You may not know what I had to do last week. You were down Newport testifying at that inquest, then there was something or other you went on to in Cardiff, I think. Anyhow, it was Charlie saw me through what happened. You know Dolph Llewelyn done himself in?' Henderson nodded. 'Well, I had to cut him down and move him in the house – and clean 'im up a bit before his wife and daughter had a good look at him.'

Henderson stared at her. 'Why you? You weren't

related, and from what I hear he was the last man to be a friend. Strike-breaker, wasn't he?'

She nodded, grim-faced. 'Reckon that was what did for him in the end. He couldn't live with it. And in a way he was a double coward. Scabbed on his neighbours in the first place, then let them threaten him into rejoining the strike. Nobody would give him the time a day after the dispute ended. He was nothing to me, you're right. But for some reason, lately, people have started coming to me when they'm in trouble. Seem to think I'll know what to do.' She brooded on that for a moment, then went on: 'I think it was summat to do with me going to prison. When I come out they treated me like a war hero. And they expected me to be able to do things they couldn't – like cutting down their menfolk when they'd hung themselves in the lav.'

'And you were willing to go and do it?'

'Who else would have? Mrs Llewelyn wasn't sure the poor sod was dead when she come screaming across. I could hardly leave him hung up there like a line full a washing while they sent for your brother, could I? Knew he'd already had his chips, but I couldn't tell her that.'

'How did you know he was gone?'

'The smell. When he strangled, his bowels relaxed and he filled his trousers. It was the same with our Emrys when he died a few years ago. That's why I insisted on laying Em out. Didn't want Mam going in there with him in that state . . . ' Abruptly she snapped back to the present. 'Christ, you ask me a simple question and I start rambling, don't I? What I was trying to say was, that was the low point. After I'd got him in and cleaned him up, and Charlie had come and confirmed the death, I started to think about where my life was taking me. It wasn't a very nice prospect, I can tell you.'

A tear slid down her cheek and along the curve of her upper lip, apparently unnoticed. 'Don't get me wrong. I know what I'm doing and I think it's worth it. I hope my Tommy and Haydn's and our Tom's kids will grow up to something better because of what we're doing for them now. But oh, hell, sometimes I remember the fun I had down Cardiff when I was sixteen and I wonder where it all went to. I don't wanna get old without having any more times like that!'

As she spoke, she turned her face towards him. A second tear had halted half-way down her cheek and hung there now, a small diamond in the clean moonlight. He raised a finger and brushed it away. Then they were kissing, with a depth and passion which could foresee no denial in the future.

After a seemingly endless time, he murmured: 'There's a wonderful old barn behind the church hall where the men are sleeping. One end is already stacked with bales of hay. If I took my groundsheet in there . . . '

She pressed her fingers over his mouth to prevent him completing the sentence. 'Good thing I'm a heathen, ennit? Our Mam would have me damned for all eternity for doing what we're going to do tonight.'

'And you? What do you think about it?'

She shrugged, her face sombre. 'I was damned six years ago when I mistook your brother for you and then ran from him to a kind man I didn't love when I realised I'd made a mess of things. I can't do no worse than that.' Her tone lightened again. 'Come on – let's see if I can get it right this time!' She skipped lightly to her feet, picked up her walking shoes and socks in one hand and extended the other to him. Together they walked off to their barn.

CHAPTER SEVEN

They learned the hard way that marching would not get them anything but blistered feet. Proudly, politely, the men and women marched into London to present their case to Parliament. No one seemed to notice. Press cameras clicked as the march leaders handed over their petition to a group of friendly South Wales MPs. They were well looked after, but with nothing like the warmth they had received in the small settlements across the breadth of southern England on their way to the capital. London had seen it all, had turned away from its own poor, for long enough to remain untouched by the Welsh miners. Their protest lodged, their presence skimpily acknowledged, they climbed aboard a special train and were whisked back to the Valleys in a few hours. Within days, the country had once again forgotten their existence. The Means Test bit harder than ever, and coalfield trade unionism declined as membership of the Communist Party grew.

Back in Abercarn, Lily handed back David's Davey lamp and turned again to hearth and home. That was when she began to realise there was something wrong which would affect her more deeply than the collective troubles of the miners.

'You'm getting ever so short of breath, ent you, love?' she asked, concerned, as David leaned back in his chair and gasped for air. 'How long have it been feeling that bad?'

He made a dismissive gesture, still unable to speak. She went to make tea, more to occupy her hands than with any idea that it could help him. Every woman in the Valleys knew the symptoms he was showing, and they all knew that neither tea nor sympathy were effective remedies.

Eventually, David was almost normal again. 'It have been happening quite a bit lately,' he said, 'but you was so busy I didn't like to mention it.'

Busy? *Iesu, mawr,* any proper wife would have noticed his condition however busy she was, said Lily's guilty conscience. Yes, she had been immersed in politics, but she had been far more absorbed by her new-found love for Peter Henderson. Ever since their snatched nights of lovemaking on the London march, she had thought of little else, had drawn out her secret in quiet moments like a special treasure, and purred over it, or indulged in fantasies about forsaking everything and running off with him. And through it all, her husband had been struggling to hide a deadly illness in case it distracted her from her political activities.

'Have you seen the doctor yet?' Her question was sharpened by her own guilt.

David smiled wearily. 'Now when would I have done that, love? I been in work all day, and I'm with you all the time you ent off at meetings.'

'Well you better go tomorrow. Evening surgery will fit in all right with your day shift. Now, until you see Charlie Henderson, d'you think I could make up some sort of inhalant for you?'

He was regarding her steadily, patiently, like a sick animal. 'I don't think either of us do know of anything that'll shift this, do we, Lil?'

Blinking back tears, she shook her head, unable to speak.

'Well, then,' he went on, 'let's hang on and see what the doctor do suggest, shall we?'

In the end it was Peter Henderson, not Charles, whom he saw the next evening. The younger doctor listened to his chest, asked him endless questions, then referred him to a specialist at the Royal Gwent Hospital in Newport. It was a couple of weeks before there were any answers available, and then they were all too predictable.

Emphysema, one of the classic coaldust-related diseases, and in David's case progressing at an alarming rate.

David insisted on going alone to receive Peter Henderson's report on the consultant's diagnosis. Henderson skated around the truth for a while, giving him a name for his condition, but hazarding little information about how the disease would progress. Finally David fixed him with an unavoidable look and said: 'How long?'

'What? I . . . er . . . isn't that a trifle pessimistic?'

David's laugh was entirely without humour. 'I don't think so. Come on, doctor. I ent one a those who'll have you struck off if you get it wrong by a year or so. Won't break down in your waiting room, neither. But I'd like to know roughly how long I got to work, and how long I might stay alive. Not so very much to ask, is it?'

Henderson shook his head. 'Far less than you deserve, David,' he said in a voice which barely rose above a whisper. Then he forced himself to be disciplined again, and shuffled the papers on his desk while he tried to marshal his thoughts. There was no soft way out. Finally he said: 'You should have stopped work weeks ago. The consultant is surprised you can still manage a shift, given the state of your lungs.'

David's chuckle rasped painfully. 'Wet pits do 'ave some advantages,' he said. 'Rheumatism may be painful, but it ent a killer like dust. They've had me up the new workings in Graig Fawr this last six weeks and it's like being under the Bristol Channel up there. Up to your thighs in water most days. Dust don't have chance to fly. What are my chances of keeping on up there in the wet?'

'Don't even consider it!' Henderson snapped. 'Wet conditions in a confined space are only slightly less lethal than getting covered in flying coal dust. You must have been in agony for months now.'

'Aye, well, it haven't been easy, I do admit. But somebody got to earn the money. I gorra family, remember . . . That's the other thing worries me. I said to you just now, how long have I got after I have to stop work?'

Henderson shrugged, about to take refuge in medical uncertainty, then decided he owed the man more than that. 'I've seen men in your condition last three or four years, but not many. Most of them are gone in one.' He tried to inject optimism into his voice. 'And two or three have had remarkable remissions the minute they gave up work. They're still alive. You could be one of them.'

David shook his head. 'Ent no good to me, mun. I gorra policy on my life. Not much, but a bit. It'd give Lily a bit over a pound a week if I went. Nothing if I was alive and couldn't work.'

'But if you recovered a little, you might manage to find a pithead job . . . '

'With my record? Do me a favour – I was one of two deputies who stood out with the men against the management. Can't see 'em doing me no good turns now, can you?'

'No, you're right. But – but something else, perhaps. Something outside mining.'

'Oh, good God, mun, doin' what, chamberlain to His Majesty? I only know coal. What good would I be to anybody else. And you of all people, with your big political ideas, must have noticed the length of the queues down the labour exchange? Face up to it, I'm on the scrap heap. From now on, I'm worth more to Lil and Tommy dead than I am alive.'

'Don't you have anything at all to fall back on? I thought deputies had some sort of privileged sickness payment scheme.'

'Oh, aye, we do. A percentage of our full wages for a set number of weeks. After that, nothing. All very well for three weeks pneumonia. Not a lorra good if you'm just gonna fade away and die without ever getting better.'

Henderson could find nothing more to say. Both men sat staring morosely at the papers on the doctor's desk, Richards's death sentence. Then, abruptly, the miner broke the tension. He stood up quite briskly, slapped his thighs with his big square hands, and said: 'Well, there it is. Ent no good brooding about it. It have happened before and it'll happen again, no doubt; nothing special about me. Now I gorra think a some way to tell our Lil without her going daft.'

He started towards the door, then turned back, saying, 'Oh, *Duw*, where's my manners? Thank you for all your trouble. Ent your fault the news was bad. You done everything you could for me.' And reaching across the desk, he shook Henderson's hand.

Peter recoiled, feeling as if he had been burned, then hastily turned his reaction into a clumsy clasping of David's arm with his free hand. At that moment all he felt was overwhelming guilt. He had been making love to this man's wife while the poor devil was coughing his lungs out, alone at home. He realised for the first time that the tyranny of capitalist against worker was far from the only, or perhaps even the greatest, injustice.

PART TWO

And when he had opened the fourth seal, I heard the voice of the fourth beast say, Come and see. And I looked; and behold; a pale horse: and his name that sat on him was Death; and Hell followed with them. And power was given unto them over the fourth part of the earth, to kill with the sword, and with hunger, and with death, and with the beasts of the earth.

Revelation, Ch. 6, v.7-8.

PART TWO

CHAPTER EIGHT

London, Spring 1934

Bethan always blamed *Vogue* for her renewed entanglement with an old flame. Running into Pearl Pickles need have been no more than a brief revival of the dead past. If she had not weakened afterwards and bought the magazine, she would not have seen the gown. Had she not seen the gown, she would never have sold her diamond earclips to buy it. Had she not bought it . . . this was nonsense! Strung together like this, all the actions and consequences of her life could be explained away. What it amounted to was that somehow she was embroiled again with James Norland, after six years of estrangement. And once the novelty had worn off, she was not at all sure she liked the experience.

Bethan had come a long way since she was the clever but embittered young nurse who had forsaken her profession in 1924 to become a wealthy widow's private minder and later her son's mistress. In those days she had seen no way forward for a girl like herself, with brains and training but no suitable family background. Later, having learned the hard way that she was not cut out to be a rich man's bauble, she had left him for a completely different world, a world where she had found she was useful and highly valued.

As a full time birth control adviser in an East End clinic for poor women, she had found professional satisfaction at last. She had also found a more satisfactory lover than James Norland had ever been, for all his wealth. Her life should have been complete; but Bethan Walters had always possessed a capacity to want what she could not quite reach, and in recent months she had begun to hanker after glamour again. The copy of *Vogue* had turned undefined dissatisfaction into rampant desire for pretty clothes and lightweight entertainment, and before she knew it she was half way back to a world she had once considered well lost.

The fashion magazine was really the second step back towards her old role as social butterfly. The first whiff of her former life had come when she bumped into an acquaintance from James Norland's social set.

Bethan had been over to the Holloway Road clinic to a policy committee meeting, and was on her way back to Hackney when a high-pitched, imitation refined voice squealed out: 'Well I'm blowed if it isn't Beth Walters! Beth, dear, wait a tick, do . . . ' and before she had time to absorb more than the sound of her old nickname, she was enveloped in a cloud of silk and Shalimar.

'It's been such an *age*, and we were all *dying* to know where you got to, you naughty girl! Fancy running off like that, without telling anyone where you were going.'

By now Bethan had disentangled herself and discovered she was confronting Pearl Pickles, a dizzy blonde ex-telephonist of scant education but shrewd intelligence, who had used her looks and figure to clamber out of a City office into the fringes of Mayfair. She was still blonde, still dazzlingly fashionable. Bethan smiled appreciatively. 'I should be the one who's surprised to see you in a neighbourhood like this,' she said. 'The Pearl Pickles I knew didn't admit there was life north of Oxford Street!'

'Pearl Fletcher, now, dear, since six years come June. Nev finally made an honest woman of me. We live just up the road – Highgate, that is,' she added, her tongue lingering over the name of the comfortable suburb, which she pronounced Haygate. 'Neville thought there'd be more space and fresh air there for the kiddies, you know . . . listen, we can't just stand out here in the street. If you've got time, let's go and have some tea.'

Overcome with curiosity about what had happened to

her old set, Bethan agreed, and they found a café across the road.

'You were sadly missed, I can tell you – *sadly* missed!' announced Pearl, spearing a vast coffee eclair with her pastry fork. 'Jimmy quite went to pieces.'

Bethan's laugh was sceptical. 'I find that hard to believe. You and Neville might have found a happy marriage at the end of the road. All James had in mind for me was a cosy love-nest for as long as my looks lasted – and he seemed to think I'd put up with him finding himself a wife and having a family while he kept me in cold storage!'

Pearl's eyes widened at this disclosure. 'The crafty old devil – he told us you'd run out on him just when he was ready to settle down, and proved it by getting hitched to some society girl within six months of you going.' Bethan's heart sank, she had no idea why. After all, their affair had been dead for years . . . Pearl was still bubbling with chatter: ' . . . And then they'd split up in next to no time. After that it was on and off for a couple of years, but you could tell his heart wasn't in it. For a start, he'd got used to our set by then, and of course the Honourable Leonora Anthony wouldn't be seen dead with us.

'We wouldn't see him for months, then back he'd come – bit like a drowning man coming up for air, Nev always used to say. Tell the truth, after the first parting, I think he only went back to her to try for a family, because they had two a bit sharpish over the next two years – both boys – and then he left her for good. Said he'd had enough of the aristocracy to last him a lifetime. Don't think he's missed a big race meeting with us ever since.'

'Are they still married?' Bethan wondered whether the tremor in her breast was showing in her voice, but if it was, Pearl seemed not to notice.

'No – they arranged a quiet divorce. By then she was as anxious to be free as he was. Not such a disgrace these days, is it? Sometimes I think it's getting quite fashionable.

77

He's been fancy free for more than a year now, and still swears he'll never try it again.' She adopted a motherly tone and added: 'He needs someone special, though. Seems all forlorn, somehow, although there's always a pretty girl about.'

There was a lot more of such gossip, ranging from Norland to other members of their old group, and back to Pearl's dream of domestic bliss with her daughters, her big house in Highgate and her rich bookmaker. Bethan let her ramble, occasionally interjecting a suitable comment, but really hardly listening.

Eventually it was time for them to part. Pearl embraced her again and said: 'It really is lovely seeing you again, Beth. I'm sure Jimmy'd be thrilled . . . why don't you come over to dinner and, you know, I'll, just . . . reintroduce you?'

Bethan smiled and shook her head, hoping the gesture conveyed more finality than she was feeling. 'No, thanks all the same, Pearl. I don't think it's ever wise to go back.'

'Silly girl! What would you be giving up to see him again?' Her eyes swept over Bethan's serviceable ready-made suit, making it clear she thought her friend must have come down a long way since their rackety Mayfair days. 'Look – tell you what. Nev had some little visiting cards made up for me. Why don't you have a couple and get in touch? Doesn't have to be dinner with Jimmy along if you don't want to . . . Just come up one evening and say hello to Nev again . . . meet the girls. All right?'

Bethan nodded. 'All right, Pearl. It would be good to renew old acquaintance, I must admit.' She took the ostentatiously-engraved cards and put them in her purse. 'Now, I really must go. Lovely to have seen you.'

It was the next day that she saw the copy of *Vogue* on a news stand at King's Cross station. Until then she had all but dismissed Pearl from her mind. If she had been tempted to take up where they had left off years before, she had only to remember the pitying way the other girls had looked at her workaday clothes to realise it could never be. Then, as if someone else were directing her movements, she found herself paying for the magazine, and looking forward to it all the way home like a fat girl with a secret box of chocolates. As she turned the glossy pages back in her Hackney sitting room, she forgot the modest gas fire and the cup of cocoa at her elbow. She was once again in a world of champagne cocktails, Noel Coward first nights and interludes at the Embassy Club.

The gown was of creamy-white satin, skin-tight at waist and hips, fanning into an elegantly flared bias cut long skirt. A host of tiny rouleau shoulder straps held it up. The cut was everything: it had no need of fancy embroidery or frills. The headline said:

THE LOOK THAT SAYS MOLYNEUX
AT A FRACTION OF THE PRICE

An extended caption said that it was typical of the work of Rowena, a talented new designer-dressmaker who had set up a small workshop in Chelsea and was available for commissions. The moment she saw the feature, Bethan knew she was going to have the dress whatever it cost her, and to see Pearl and Neville again. She refused to contemplate the possibility of a reunion with James Norland.

Before she went to bed that night, she took out her jewel case, smiling at how shabby it had become, tucked away in the bottom of her wardrobe. She still owned the diamonds James had given her, but where did she ever go to wear them? She had not even looked at them for a year or more.

Now she considered the diamond earclips he had taken such pleasure in choosing for her. One pair was particularly fine. She put them aside, along with the little velvet-lined box that went with them, and went to find the insurance certificates that she had carefully kept up to date on all her jewellery. Yes, there it was: last valuation eleven months ago. One hundred and ninety pounds. James had always believed in buying the best . . . Bethan

79

put the insurance papers and the clips on her dressing table, then went to bed, her head full of plans to visit Bond Street the next morning.

It was a profitable trip. There were almost two million unemployed in Britain that year, but the more prosperous classes were doing well, and there was plenty of demand for good jewellery. The clips were in a plain, classical platinum setting – nothing that dated them – and a top Bond Street shop offered her £150 for them without hesitation. She took her booty and went off to Chelsea to find Rowena's studio.

'Beth, darling! I'd quite given up on you! You really will come along to dinner?' Pearl was delighted. Nothing gave her greater pleasure than to act as a matchmaker. Now that Bethan had finally telephoned, she had no intention of letting her go without engineering a meeting with James Norland. 'Just a minute . . . don't you go away, now! I'm just getting the diary open.' She flipped over the pages. 'Ooh, how about the seventh? If you can make that, it'll be ideal, because I've already asked Jimmy and he's said he'll only come if I don't confront him with yet another dizzy blonde. How d'you think he'll fancy a dizzy redhead?'

Listening to her, Bethan suffered a twinge of apprehension. 'I – I'm not sure, Pearl . . . truly, I rang because I thought it would be nice if you and I stayed in touch, that's all . . . '

Pearl dismissed that ploy out of hand. 'Nonsense! No need to run round the houses with me, dear. I think Jimmy's dreamy too, remember. If I'd been his type you wouldn't have got a look-in. No, I won't accept any excuses now. You come along on the seventh . . . dress sort of semi-formal, I think . . . and I'll organise the rest. You trust your Auntie Pearl.'

Replacing the receiver, Bethan was thankful she had gone mad with the money she got for the earrings. Once she had splurged on the satin gown, she had treated herself to a killingly smart navy and white linen suit and two cocktail frocks, one in black lace, the other in sea green crêpe de chine. The black would be a perfect foil for her red hair and creamy skin. Remind James Norland of exactly what he'd been missing . . . That brought her up short. What was she doing? He had never needed reminding. He had not thrown her over. She had walked out on him, without leaving any clue to where she was going. Why was it suddenly important to see him again, and to impress him?

She was still brooding on that when the door bounced back on its hinges and a cheerful male voice boomed out, 'How's the Cleopatra of the mining valleys this afternoon?' Max Grant, her landlord and, for the past six years, her lover, came into the room, embraced her and planted a smacking, turpentine-tainted kiss on her mouth. He had spent the afternoon upstairs in his studio, painting, and had obviously been absent-mindedly chewing on a brush as he worked.

She felt herself blushing and looked away, shame-faced, as he grinned and said: 'What d'you feel guilty about today, stealing the family silver?'

She clutched at the first excuse she could think of. 'I – I spent too much on a new suit, that's all,' she muttered. Well, it was almost true. She had bought the clothes two weeks ago, but had not told him. It would not occur to him that they were made to measure and therefore more expensive than anything she had bought since knowing him – and she had only admitted to one outfit instead of the four which were hidden in the cupboard behind her ordinary clothes. Better he should think she was being extravagant and vain than suspect her of seeing another man.

But Grant thought no such thing. He trusted Bethan completely and now was turning away from her towards the kitchen muttering about making them a cup of coffee between teasing remarks about her holding off middle age with the odd expensive dress. Bethan shrugged, impatient at her own over-reaction. She had done nothing beyond accepting an invitation from an old

81

acquaintance without telling Max. There was no hint that James Norland had any further interest in her and no reason why she should feel guilty. But she did. She knew exactly what was lurking at the back of her mind, and it went far beyond the prospect of sharing bisque de homard and boeuf à la mode with Norland.

Over coffee, she studied Max minutely while he flipped through an old craft magazine. Why on earth was she considering betraying this man? He was the answer to any sensible girl's prayer. What was it that drove her to such stupid dissatisfaction? He was attractive, intelligent, cultivated, an accomplished lover. He had a tendency to tease her when she became too stuffy, but he never stopped her doing what she wanted to and he supported her every step of the way in a demanding and often unrewarding career.

'I really must be mad,' she murmured, unaware she was saying it aloud.

He looked up from his magazine, grinning broadly. 'Yes, my dearest. I know that, but I'm amazed to hear you finally admit it. What on earth brought this on?'

For the second time in ten minutes, she blushed furiously, and blurted: 'Not to realise more often how lucky I am to have you, Max. You are so very good for me – don't ever let me go, will you?'

His smile dissolved and he looked troubled. 'Now why would you think I'd ever do that? What's the matter, Bethan?'

She shook her head violently. 'Nothing. Goose walked over my grave, that's all. Max, please bear with me if I do silly things from time to time. It gets a bit . . . well . . . demoralising, up at the clinic.'

He took her hand. 'I realise that, sweetheart. I couldn't stand it for more than five minutes. I'm always dumb with admiration at your fortitude in sticking with all those poor downtrodden women. If I feel down, I only have to paint myself a cheerful-looking canvas and I'm all right. You can hardly wipe out all the misery and pain of the East End when you get the blues, can you?'

'No, but sometimes I get frightened I might do something stupid in a moment of desperation.'

He misunderstood. 'If ever you feel like that, put on your coat and come straight back here to me. We'll get drunk, go out to dinner or a theatre – even head for the country for a few days. Anything but have you facing that on your own.'

'You are so good. I wish I deserved you.'

'My God – no one has sinned sufficiently to have that wished on them! Now, go and put on this sensational new outfit and I'll take you out to supper to cheer us both up . . . on second thoughts, perhaps you'd better wear your green jersey. I can only afford Luigi's this week and if you got pasta on the front of the new thing you'd murder me!'

CHAPTER NINE

Bethan told herself repeatedly that she would not attend
Pearl's dinner party. She would plead sickness, an unexpected holiday – anything to stay remote from temptation. But fate seemed determined to push her back into
James Norland's arms. Max abruptly decided to spend a
couple of weeks in Cornwall, working with two painter
friends who had lived at St Ives for years. He planned to
leave two days before Bethan's dinner date. Now she
would not even have to think up a lie to explain her
absence.

Until he told her about the trip, she felt reasonably
safe. After all, it was easy to contemplate cancelling
the engagement when she knew that to keep it, she would
have to slip out of the house with her party clothes in a
bag, and change somewhere else. Even the 'somewhere
else' raised problems. The clinic was almost as difficult as
home. Two of the staff knew Max and might say
something about Bethan's glamorous evening out . . . no,
the difficulties were insurmountable. She could not
possibly go. Then they were all wiped away and there
were no more excuses.

At 7.45 on the evening of May 7th, Bethan was
standing, dry-mouthed with nerves, on the front door-
step of Pearl's and Neville's Highgate house. You could
escape even now, she was telling herself, when a maid
opened the door and, before she had time for any more
misgivings, she was whisked back into a world she had
thought well lost for the past six years.

He looked better than ever. As she walked into the
drawing room, he turned from some small talk with
Neville and glanced in her direction. Bethan felt as if

everything had stopped. Without speaking, he touched Neville's arm, then moved across to her.

Clasping both her hands in his, he gave her the sort of look she associated with love-struck matinee idols, and said: 'Bethan, it's been longer than I'd have thought possible. Welcome back – and promise you won't go away again.'

Thank God I wore the black lace, she thought.

After that, her surrender was inevitable.

Months later, she wondered how she had come through six years of demanding work in one of London's toughest areas, seeing people at their best and worst, and yet had remained sufficiently naive for Norland's brittle appeal to win her again. It seemed that however much she thought she had grown up, there was a wide-eyed Valleys girl just below the surface, aching to be impressed by a rich man.

That first evening, she saw none of the flaws. Norland had been in Switzerland for some late skiing at the end of the season, and sported a spectacular suntan which was highlighted by his perfectly-cut dinner jacket. He had kept in good shape over the years, and the only signs of ageing were a few lines around his mouth and eyes. His stomach was flat, his shoulders as broad and his step as springy as ever. Conversation in this circle had never risen far above speculation on what would win the two-thirty at Kempton Park tomorrow, or whether Boulestin's or the Savoy were serving the best after-theatre suppers these days. But Bethan had forgotten how swiftly such chatter could pall. It was so long since she had taken part in a whole evening of amusing small talk that she lapped it up.

Too soon, she realised she must return to Hackney. She had travelled to the party by taxi, and planned to return home the same way, but, as Pearl had intended, James Norland insisted on driving Bethan home. They left amid flurries of invitations from Pearl to keep in touch. Already Bethan was mentally halfway back to her workaday world, and she realised in dismay that she was promising to see Pearl again as often as possible. Pearl means James, her conscience told her, and you know James means betrayal . . . As he drove smoothly away from the comfortable suburb, it was easy to forget such uneasy thoughts and revel in the luxury of the powerful car and its alluring driver.

'So you decided to give me another chance,' he said, carefully looking at the road ahead rather than at her.

'Of what?' Confused by his directness, Bethan decided stupidity was her only defence.

'Of getting you back, of course. Don't think I haven't realised a thousand times over what an ass I was with you, Beth. I took you so much for granted that I never realised your worth until you were gone. You had every right to leave me in the lurch.'

'And now? What would you do if you had me now?'

He laughed. 'Chance would be a fine thing! I'd put you where you should have been from the start, the centre of my life – and my home. No more secret Mayfair love-nests. Foxhall is where you belong, as Mrs James Norland.'

For a few seconds she was speechless. Then she said: 'We've been apart for eight years. In the meantime, you've been married, fathered a couple of children, divorced and made a few more millions. You've spent an evening in my company and suddenly you've decided you can't live without me. Isn't that a little sudden?'

'Hmm, it must look like that. Don't blame you for being suspicious. But – but . . . ' he took one hand from the steering wheel and grasped her wrist. ' . . . you never know the value of what you had until you've lost it, and that's what happened to me. If I seem over-eager now, it's only because I'm determined not to miss a second chance.'

'But what makes you think you *have* a second chance? All you know about me is that I have some sort of do-gooding job in the East End. Don't you think I have commitments – attachments?'

'I'd be damned surprised if you didn't – beautiful

woman like you, but come on, Beth, admit it – you're as bowled over by this as I am.'

'Y-yes. I can't pretend otherwise,' she told him, but her inner voice said, liar! You love the romance of this moment, but this smoothie isn't in the same class as Max Grant, not by any standards except wealth. She grappled with her own capacity to be impressed by glamour, and lost. 'What are we going to do?'

He pulled the big car in at the kerb. 'For a start, we need a long, long talk. Then I think I must let you get to know me properly, see what I'm doing with my life these days. I know this must be very difficult for you. I shan't ask you to make any snap decisions.' Then he leaned over and kissed her, and her body responded to him as eagerly as though they had separated only last week.

After a while Norland drew back, and said, purring with satisfaction, 'That's all I needed to know. I owe Pearl Fletcher more than she'll ever realise.'

'Now wait a minute, James.' Reality briefly reared its head again. 'One evening together? One kiss? And you know? I wish I were as sure.'

He was all smiles now. 'You will be – I intend to court you as you've never been courted before. Unless you're prepared to flee your present existence as abruptly as you made your exit from my life, you'd better start sorting out a story to cover your departure.'

After that, he made no further attempt at persuasion. He followed her directions back to Hackney, refrained from any comment on the shabby street where she now lived, and escorted her to the front door without asking to be invited in. As he turned away, he said: 'Tomorrow evening. Shall I pick you up, or would you prefer to meet me somewhere?'

'Tomorrow? I had no plans . . . '

'Well, you do now. And the next night, and the one after that. I'm in the City at the end of the afternoon. I'll call round for you directly from there, if you can stand dining informally.'

If you saw the contents of my wardrobe these days,

you wouldn't have to ask that, she thought. 'A-all right. Seven-thirty early enough?'

'Wonderful. I shall keep my City men in the office long after they like to be out on the golf course, and they can blame you for it.' He blew a positively theatrical kiss, and started down the short flight of steps. 'Until tomorrow, then.'

He persisted in his determination that they should see each other every day, and three evenings later, on Friday, he drove them back to his Eaton Square apartment. She could not even claim he had seduced her. When they arrived at the flat, he switched on subdued lighting, chose romantic background music, and opened pink champagne, none of which could be construed as signs that he planned to drive her home soon. It all looked and felt so right that she managed to ignore the fact that he was almost a stranger to her now.

By the time he suggested, oh, so tactfully, that they would be more comfortable in the bedroom, she was as eager as Norland himself, as much thanks to the opulence of the surroundings as to her mounting desire for the man.

In the bedroom, he undressed her with almost predatory enthusiasm, his powerful hands tearing her flimsy silk panties in his hurry to see her naked. Bethan was accustomed to the gentle, relaxed lovemaking of Max Grant, when passion and humour were never far from each other and he thought at least as much of satisfying her as himself. After that, the renewed contact with James was a shock, and perhaps the violent contrast with Max was what made it work for her that night.

It was like being the victim of a fantasy rape – fantasy because the violence never really hurt her, and because Norland made sure he excited her sufficiently to drag her along with him as a willing participant. Eventually, exhausted, she drifted off to sleep, but her last conscious memory was the disquieting picture of his face above her as he thrust his full weight on to her, mouth grim, eyes wolfish. As if he hates the whole world and this is the only time he can't hide it, she thought.

The idea was all but forgotten when she awoke, and physically she felt more fulfilled than she had for a long time with Max. But there was a loose tangle of bad feelings buried not far from the surface: bewilderment at a lack of any real affection; humiliation at the suspicion that she had been little more than an inanimate object of his desire, not a partner; sadness that she did not waken wrapped in his arms like his most precious possession.

When James woke up, such regrets melted within moments, because he turned to her once more with renewed vigour and this time, for whatever reason, he was more gentle and considerate. She basked in his caresses and told herself last night had been all in her imagination.

Over breakfast in his ultra-modern kitchen, she said: 'What a good thing we got so carried away on a Friday! I don't think you would have been too enchanted to have me dashing from your arms to my job at the crack of dawn.'

He merely grinned. 'Never leave anything to chance, dearest. It didn't just *happen* to be Friday, you know. I planned it. Just as I planned the bath things, toothpaste and underwear you'll find through there.' He gestured towards the second bathroom which led off the hall.

'Oh! So it wasn't the great impulsive gesture, then?'

'Darling, you knew me long enough before we parted the first time. How often have I ever acted impulsively?'

You've forgotten how little you ever told me about yourself, she mused. He had never discussed such matters with her in the past, and in fact she had remained convinced that their first rendezvous in an idyllic Thames Valley inn had been completely impromptu. Clearly she had been wrong. How many other things were different from what she believed.

Bethan pushed back her chair and stood up hurriedly. 'James, I think I want to bathe and dress and then go back to Hackney. I have a lot of thinking to do, and I shall never manage it as long as we're alone together like this. Perhaps your life is all neat and tidy, but mine isn't – at least, it isn't any longer,' she added, realising that it had been until he re-appeared a few days before.

Norland shrugged but did not move to stop her. 'All right, sweetie. I did have it in mind for us to spend a thoroughly self-indulgent weekend together, but I know how important this is to you. You go off and sort things out. But look – take my number, and if you change your mind, we can still salvage some of the time.'

He's being too kind, too considerate, she thought as she put the finishing touches to her appearance. The old James would never have been so co-operative, particularly if he thought I might be going home to some other man. So much about him failed to make sense, and yet Bethan found it impossible to pull away, as she knew she should. 'Perhaps when I've had time to think . . . ' she said.

Norland had showered and dressed while she was in the guest bathroom, and now he was waiting for her in the drawing room, looking ridiculously vigorous and handsome. He kissed her enthusiastically and then held her at arm's length, studying her with obvious satisfaction. 'If you had any idea how much good you're doing me, you wouldn't wonder why I'm so eager to fulfil your every whim,' he told her.

I wouldn't call this my every whim, Bethan reflected. So far, about all he's done is refrain from objecting when I say I must go home and sort myself out . . . But he was still smiling at her, and the whole feeling of him and this place was a world away from the shabbiness of Hackney and the misery of the women at the clinic.

He clearly thought she was overdoing it when she said she preferred to make her own way home. 'Whatever for? On a Saturday morning, it will take twenty minutes in the car. You'll be three times that on the bus or tube.'

'You forget the neighbours.'

'Oh, Beth, how unforgivably surburban! Why the devil should you care what they think?'

'For God's sake stop being so patronising! Don't you think for a moment there may be someone else to consider apart from us? I want this out in the open, but I certainly don't want . . . someone . . . finding out from pub gossip that I was brought home first thing in the morning by a strange man.'

He was full of contrition. 'Please forgive me. I can be such a blockhead at times. Of course you must go alone. Don't forget my telephone number, though.'

Her guilt and resentment lasted for less than half the bus journey. As the buildings along the roadside grew drabber, her memories of the past few days with James glowed warmer by contrast. By the time she let herself into the empty house, she was already regretting that she had said she would spend Saturday and Sunday alone.

An hour later, she had started some desultory work in the garden, hoping the gardening jobs would clear her mind for the major rethink she had convinced herself she needed. The telephone rang and she rushed to answer it, fighting to stop the disappointment from coming through in her voice when she realised that it was Max, not James, at the other end of the line.

'Darling, where on earth were you last night? I was quite worried.'

'Oh – er – when did you call?' She made an educated guess at after dinner, and hazarded, 'Was it about ten-ish?'

'Yes, that's right. What happened?'

'I thought it must be you. I was in the bath, and by the time I got to the beastly phone it had stopped ringing. You forgot to give me Fergus's number down there,' she added, accusingly, 'or I'd have got back to you straight away.'

'Blast – so I did! Sorry, Bethan. That was silly of me. But I couldn't get you first thing this morning, either.'

She felt guilty at the speed and ease with which the lie presented itself. 'I couldn't sleep, so I got up early and went down to the market. Thought that as the master chef was away, I might practise a bit of amateur cookery.'

He chuckled. 'That should make you suitably appreciative of my talents when I come back. I've never met a woman with so little basic grasp of food preparation as you. Good thing you have so many other talents.'

'Yes, isn't it?' She tried to inject the right note of lazy loving humour into her voice. 'Max, don't you think it would be sensible if you gave me Fergus's number now? I intend popping out to see a couple of films, and doing some late stints at the clinic, during the rest of your stay. Might be easier if I rang you every couple of days, don't you think?'

'Yes, you're right. You know what a worrier I am when it comes to you. Got a pencil handy?'

He gave her the number and she managed to dredge up the right sort of questions about how he was enjoying Cornwall and whether he was getting any work done. By the time she hung up, she was sure he had no suspicion that she was deceiving him. Then, thinking it over, she said, 'Oh, Bethan, you damned fool! That will make it even worse if you *do* have to tell him!'

But there were still ten more days until Max's return, and James Norland was only a couple of miles across London. Her gaze strayed back to the telephone. How long would she be able to resist ringing him to offer her surrender?

She managed to hold out until early Sunday morning. Then, after a wretched night when she realised she was not dithering between Max and James but wallowing in guilt about how to tell Max she no longer wanted him, she telephoned Norland's flat.

'If you haven't given up on me altogether, I'd love to take you up on the rest of your plans for the weekend,' she said. 'How soon could you drive over?'

She felt a wave of satisfaction pulsing in his voice as he said: 'But what if the neighbours see me and gossip?'

'To hell with the neighbours – I only have one life.'

CHAPTER TEN

James Norland had worn better externally than within. His apparently charmed existence had petered out abruptly shortly after his affair with Bethan Walters ended in 1926. All his life, Norland had affected a mock-democratic air which masked the profound snob he really was. He enjoyed the company of girls like Bethan, and took even greater pleasure in making his mother and the more hidebound of his business acquaintances look stuffy and old-fashioned by flaunting egalitarian attitudes at them. At heart, though, he was as conventional as they, and had always regarded girls of Bethan's type as no more than pleasant diversions. From the early days of taking over his father's booming automotive empire, he had cherished ambitions to marry into the aristocracy, and shortly after the rupture with Bethan he had done so.

Briefly, all had gone well. Then, to his dismay, he discovered that he truly preferred the superficial conversations of the Pearl Pickleses and Neville Fletchers of this world, and found either country pursuits or society gossip tedious in the extreme when unleavened by racier topics.

This, at least, was what he had told himself. His waspish sister Jessica had other ideas. When he confided his misery to her, she stung him by demonstrating a deeper understanding of his motives than his own. 'You'll feel better if only you admit you're never happy unless you can order people about,' she told him.

'What are you talking about? All I want is something a little more diverting than hunt balls and court presentations at every turn.'

'Nonsense, brother dear. Your trouble is that until now, you've been at the top of the heap. That's why you like those common little cronies of yours so much – they give you a sense of effortless superiority. I can just imagine what your women are like . . . Now, suddenly, you're in a world where no one cares about your newly-acquired money or your brilliance as a captain of industry. It would be bad enough if that applied simply to the types you meet at your club – but you're married to one of them, and from what I've seen of the Honourable Leonora, she never lets you forget her superiority.'

He had made some biting remark and slammed out of the house. But hours later, after he had picked up a tart and spent a couple of hours humiliating her in a sleazy back room in Shepherd's Bush, he was forced to admit there was much in what Jessica had said. When he told Bethan after the Fletchers' dinner party that she had been constantly on his mind since their parting, he had been speaking the truth. She had come to represent his ideal woman – spirited, physically attractive, elegant and accomplished, but socially and intellectually his inferior, willing to argue with him sometimes but always prepared to defer to him in the end. What could be better? What could make a more pleasing contrast to the aristocratic bitch he had married?

Meeting Bethan again had seemed like the realisation of an impossible dream, and now he had no intention of letting her go. He had seen enough marriages in which the husband had dragged up a socially inferior wife to his own level to know Beth would not hold him back. Anyway, he had no further ambitions to invade the aristocracy and she was eminently acceptable in any other social circle. The years of separation had given her more polish and self-confidence than she had possessed in her mid-twenties. All it needed now was a sufficient injection of money to get her some expensive clothes, and he would have re-created his perfect woman. James Norland seldom failed to get his own way, and he had no intention of doing so on this occasion.

So for the next few days he concentrated on making her feel like the most important woman in the world. He had caught her at just the right time, when she was feeling vulnerable about the passing years and depressed by her gloomy surroundings. It did not matter to James Norland that he might destroy other lives in sweeping Bethan out of her own world into his, and she herself lacked the strength of will to stop him.

She fought her desire to fall in with his wishes, trying to concentrate on the many facets of his character which disturbed her; trying to remember that he still had many of the habits of thought and behaviour that had alienated her so long ago. But within a week she admitted resistance was useless. She was in love with him once more, and drawn irresistibly by the glittering life which was miraculously being offered to her for a second time. She had no desire to hurt Max Grant, but if that was the price she must pay for her passport back to the world of parties and money, then she was prepared to do it.

There was the clinic to think of, too. They depended completely upon her. When she took on the job, the committee had been breathless with relief that they had found such a well-qualified and eminently respectable young woman. The dispensation of birth control appliances and information to working class women was almost universally regarded as a disreputable activity, and they always had difficulty in recruiting staff of the right calibre. Over the years Bethan had come to love the work, and to respect and sympathise with the women who attended the clinic. She was reluctant to leave the job, but all too aware that James would never tolerate her keeping it.

In the end, having agreed to leave Hackney and move in with Norland, who was proposing to marry her the following month, she went to see Joyce Gladstone, the doctor's wife who had originally recruited her to run the clinic. Joyce liked and respected Max Grant, so Bethan took care to skirt her reason for her departure from the area. Let Joyce think they had come to a natural parting of the ways – it was less embarrassing. Her main purpose was to ask for advice about the job at the clinic.

Joyce was horrified at her news. 'But Bethan, we'll never replace you! What on earth are we to do?' Her stricken look was enough to make the younger woman feel thoroughly ashamed of her proposed defection.

'Well – er – that's what I came to see you about. If there was a remote chance of my hanging on . . . perhaps resuming the post part-time in a voluntary capacity . . . do you think we could arrange something between us?'

They talked around it for an hour or so without reaching any useful conclusion. Then Joyce said: 'Would it help if you took, say, a month off, without actually leaving, to think it over? Not to think over whether you'll leave or not,' she added hastily. 'I can see your mind is made up about the full-time job. But enough to think over the possibility of some sort of voluntary commitment. Oh, my dear, it will be a tragedy if we lose you!'

Finally Bethan agreed to the plan. It would give her time to make the break with Max, and to see how things would work out with James. The unease she had felt that first time they had made love at his flat; the hastily-stifled misgivings about his behaviour; his apparent satisfaction with the friendship of his old racing and nightclub acquaintances – all fluttered at the corner of her mind as she thought over what she was giving up.

This is why you left him in the first place, remember? thundered her inner voice. What makes you think it will be different now? Because now he wants to marry me, she told it, almost as if she were arguing with a real person. No one had wanted to marry her before – well, not counting Max, of course – let alone anyone rich, and powerful, and handsome . . . and brutal, and shallow, and domineering, echoed the inner voice.

She had intended the parting to be painless – painless for her, that was. She preferred not to think what it would be like for Max. 'A scene wouldn't achieve anything,' Bethan told herself firmly, sitting down to compose her farewell letter. Everything else was done. Her suitcases were in the hall, beside a crate of books and the few mementoes she wished to keep. Much of what was in the flat was part of her life with Max, and she told herself she did not want to remove it from where it belonged. The truth was rather different. Contemplation of the small objects they had chosen together, or given each other on birthdays and minor anniversaries, would be painful. She preferred to cut her losses.

As she put the sealed letter on the hall table, a key turned in the front door lock. No – it couldn't be! Max wasn't due back until Monday and it was only Friday afternoon! Bethan glanced round in panic, as if there were hope of concealment behind her own luggage or in the under-stairs cupboard. Then the door burst open and Max stood there, beaming and already shouting some sort of absurd greeting-cum-explanation for his early return.

As he came in, he absorbed the meaning of the scene in front of him and his jovial boom faded to little above a whisper: ' . . . so I thought I'd take you by surprise. And I have, it seems.' There was no trace of a smile now. 'What's all this about?' he finished.

'I – this is – I didn't want . . . ' speech deserted her completely.

He saw the envelope, still in her shaking hand. 'No, so I see. The coup de grâce was to be delivered by proxy, I take it. When you've finished stammering, have you any intention of trying to explain?'

Bethan burst into tears. He made no attempt to comfort her; he merely went on standing where he had stopped, just inside the front door, staring at her. Eventually he said: 'Tears don't tell me anything. Perhaps you'd better give me the letter.' He reached out and took it, carefully avoiding contact with her fingers, then walked past her into the drawing room. He had left the front door wide open, his key still in the lock. Mechanically, Bethan removed it, then closed the door. She found it impossible to go back into the drawing room while he was reading her letter, and mooned about in the hall, pretending to check the security of the strap on her biggest suitcase, and to see that the cardboard carton was properly sealed.

After an age, he called out: 'You'd better come in now. Some things have to be said face to face.'

She inched round the door and raised her eyes to look at him. Max appeared to have aged ten years in the past few minutes. His expression held a mixture of incredulity and pain. Eventually he said: 'I won't ask you how you could do this. Clearly you *were* able to, or it wouldn't have happened. Maybe it was my fault for never probing into your past after you and I got together. Well, it seems I know about it now, chapter and verse. No point in raking it over. The only reason I'm even talking to you now is to say I think you're going to need me before this is all over. And, God help me, if you do, I shall be here.'

'Even after – after this?'

His sigh held considerable exasperation. 'Especially after this. Dammit, Bethan, five minutes ago I thought I was coming home from a painting trip to the arms of the woman I loved – and who loved me. I can't change that like a dirty shirt. I may get over you, but somehow I doubt it. And I don't think you'll get over me as easily as you imagine, whatever you believe now. I'll take my chances against Mr Wonderful. Just remember, if it turns out all wrong, there'll be no recriminations if you come back.'

'Why? I'd understand this better if you called me a lot of names and threw me out.'

'Believe me, I'm tempted. I just happen to think that there's another you under the little gold-digger who wrote me this letter – the woman I've been living with for the past six years or so. She's clever and funny and dedicated to a very important job, even if she can also be a contrary little bitch at times. I just have to pray that she'll surface again after a while, and push this other Bethan Walters back where she belongs.'

'Where's that?'

'If you really want to know, the gutter. The girl who wrote the letter couldn't belong anywhere else. And now, if you'll excuse me, I want to take a bath and then get drunk. I suggest you find a taxi and make your exit.'

Although she was still standing beside the door, Max contrived to pass her without touching her. Bethan ached to reach out and caress his cheek, but he passed her without a look and walked up the long staircase. Feeling empty and soiled, she left the house.

CHAPTER ELEVEN

The engagement ring was a half-hoop of emeralds big enough to blind Bethan to her own bad behaviour. Norland gave it to her over dinner at the Ritz. Much later, after dancing and drinking too much champagne, they strolled back along Piccadilly in the general direction of Eaton Square and Bethan smiled at a memory which drifted into her mind.

'This is like being given a chance to rewrite history to tell a happier story,' she told James. 'Years ago, you walked me along here on the way back to Mayfair, the night you surprised me with the keys to the flat.'

'Yes, I remember.'

'Hmm, but what you don't remember, because you never knew, was that little Miss Innocent here expected you to propose that night. I was so disappointed! The way I felt afterwards, no one would ever have known you'd given me the biggest present I ever got.'

To her surprise he looked sad. 'Poor Beth! I understood so little about you, didn't I? Of course you felt disappointed. I have a confession to make, too – I knew then that was what you expected. You were far too respectable a girl in those days to want to settle for less. Not really to be compared with the Pearls and Ethels of this world.'

She was surprised at the degree of bitterness in her own tone. 'That soon changed, didn't it? Every girl can learn to be a gold-digger if she tries hard enough.' Max Grant's insult still corroded her memory.

'Never mind, Beth. I hope I've learned now to treat you properly. Once we're married, you'll never have to think about any of that again.'

She wondered how that made her materialistic streak any less reprehensible, but decided that was something Norland would never begin to understand. It was a lovely May night. She was walking home with her fiancé from the sort of glamorous evening that featured in the best musical comedies. Why waste time brooding on her own weaknesses?

They were to be married at Caxton Hall, Westminster, at the end of the first week in June. The week before that, James was planning to launch Bethan into the main-stream of his social life by escorting her to a formal dinner at the Savoy. 'Time you broke out of the Pearl-and-Neville rut,' he said.

'Rut? The way Pearl tells it, I thought they were your nearest and dearest these days!'

'Well, in a way, I suppose . . . I do spend a lot of time with them. But my God, darling, you must have a pretty feeble opinion of my faculties if you think that chit-chat keeps me going all the time.'

'I was a bit surprised, but I thought maybe your business interests were so high-powered . . . '

' . . . that I needed nothing more than light relief? Not quite that bad yet, old thing. I *do* have other friends. Just hasn't been much doing with them lately. Now, you'll get a chance to meet them.'

'Them? All at once, at a restaurant dinner? It sounds terribly formal – are they all members of a club or something?'

'In a manner of speaking, I suppose. It *is* a sort of club, and the people who are my friends all happen to belong to it. They have a bit of a party every few months, in full fig, with a clutch of important speakers. We call ourselves the January Club.' He was growing enthusi-astic about the evening now. 'Should be a good one this time – Tom Mosley is the main speaker.'

'Do you mean *Sir Oswald* Mosley?'

'Yes, but that's just for the public. All of us call him Tom.'

Bethan felt cold. 'I take it this is a political club.'

That made him laugh. 'Political? I should say! Next week's do is the Blackshirt Dinner!'

'B-but they're Fascists!'

'Bravo Beth! With such perception, you should go into politics yourself!' He was still amused, still a million miles from taking her seriously. In James's world, women were decorative accessories. They did not offer opinions, unasked, on serious matters.

Time had blurred Bethan's memory of some aspects of her parting from James, but one thing that remained as sharp as it had been on May 4th 1926 was Norland's response to the strikers. Now it was all surfacing again. She had been unable to live with it then, although it had taken a trip round the East End finally to convince her. Would a wedding ring make it any easier to tolerate his bigotry?

She tried to salvage something, at least to understand him. 'Why do you believe in them?'

'Surely that's obvious? This country is finished as a democracy. You can't expect ordinary people to understand the complexities of government. It needs strength. It needs order. The common people just need a little bit of pride knocked back into them – that and a strong government telling them which way to go!' He stood back triumphantly, as if he had completed a masterpiece of oratory.

Bethan fought the impulse to scratch his eyes out. 'Rubbish! What they want is decent jobs and enough money to feed their families. They're at least as intelligent as you are. Won't you ever learn that poverty and stupidity are not the same thing?'

He stopped smiling. 'Darling, you know how this will end if we go on. Why not drop it? No one expects you to be political.'

'Oh, no! You just expect me to go out to dinner with a bunch of Blackshirts!' She had not realised until now that she cared so much about the Fascists, but it went beyond merely reading the newspaper reports of their exploits.

She had listened to the women at the clinic, telling frightened stories of the bully-boys striding into the East End and knocking people about, spreading their ugly doctrine of force. It was too much to permit her to remain silent.

When she had spoken her piece, Norland said: 'If you've finished, perhaps you'd care to go off somewhere and consider your position. You are my fiancée. You live in my flat. You have no job; as far as I know, no friends of your own any more; and if I chose to throw you out, you'd have nowhere to go.' The steely note in his voice softened. 'Don't misunderstand me, darling. I'm not threatening you. But I *am* pointing out that this is no time to stand on a set of principles about which you clearly know nothing.

'All you have to do now is come along to this dinner with me. Meet the people and listen to Tom Mosley yourself. I think you may get quite a surprise. If you still find it all too ghastly, you need never involve yourself again. Plenty of chaps' wives don't.' The hardness returned, 'But if you do feel like that, I'll thank you to keep your views to yourself. Because I happen to think it adds up to this country's future.'

In the end she went to the January Club dinner. There seemed little else she could do. He was right. She was alone. She had burned her boats and had chosen his world. It was her own fault that she had done so before finding out precisely what that would mean. Now she was stuck with it.

The dinner was appalling. Bethan fortified herself for it by dressing up in her beautiful new satin gown, with emerald and diamond earrings James had given her to match her engagement ring. 'People who wear emeralds shouldn't bite the hand that buys them,' she whispered at her reflection in the bedroom mirror, in a vain attempt to cheer herself up.

At the Savoy, it was obvious James was well thought of by the group of wealthy right-wingers who comprised the January Club. Most of them were in full evening dress,

103

the women dripping more expensive jewels than Bethan had ever seen, the men elegant in white tie and tails. Here and there the true fanatics appeared in the black shirts which were the closest the Fascist movement came to a uniform. At a table nearby two of these zealots, an Irishman named William Joyce and one of Lord Beaverbrook's various nieces, made loud remarks about the force and vigour of the new movement.

Bethan swiftly decided that if she had not been so offended by it all, she would have fallen asleep with boredom. A couple of self-educated colliers with the backing of a workmen's institute library could run intellectual rings around this lot, she thought, and they're supposed to be the master class!

'Cheer up, pretty lady!' A man with a bright red face, obviously rather drunk, had just sat down in the empty chair on her left. Her neighbour during dinner had moved across the room to greet an old acquaintance. 'Can't be that bad, can it?' he added. 'You look as if you'd rather like to murder Tom.'

Oswald Mosley had finished his speech and sat down to a storm of applause a few minutes earlier. 'I would,' she said through clenched teeth, not loudly enough for anyone else to hear.

The man beamed at her. 'Oh, I say, let's drink to that! Man's a bloody ass, isn't he, but you can't get any of these chumps to believe it!'

Fighting a desire to giggle, Bethan glanced around to see if anyone else had heard, but they were all moving about, exchanging greetings and gossip with people they had not seen recently. 'I thought I was the only one here who felt like that,' she said.

'Don't believe it, m'dear. My wife is a dragon. A *veritable* dragon. She dotes on every word that charlatan says. Means I have to climb into tails at the drop of a black shirt and be dragged off to hear some half-wit tell me how much better he'd run this country than anyone else.'

'Then you don't believe them?'

'Dear me, no! Can't imagine any sane man or woman

doing so! No, between you and me, I think the whole damned country's ungovernable. May as well give the anarchists a go. Everyone else has tried and failed dismally. But these johnnies can't even make their half-soaked ideas stand up among the simplest folk.' He snorted with laughter. 'In fact, it strikes me that they're the very ones who refuse to give the bounders house-room. Turn these BUF thugs loose in the East End and you invariably get a battle royal. Someone down there understands their poison well enough to reject it out of hand.'

Bethan gave him a radiant smile. 'What's your name?' she asked.

'Oh, nobody you'd know. Humphrey. Johnny Humphrey. Just a bumbling chunk of old England. But I'm not so bumbling I don't know a rotter when I see one, and this room's full o' them.'

She glanced around. 'See the tall, blond man over there, talking to Sir Oswald?'

Humphrey nodded, frowning. 'Yes. That young idiot Norland, isn't it?'

Bethan bit her lip. 'Would you class him with the rotters?'

If possible, Humphrey's complexion turned an even deeper shade of red than it had been when he joined her. 'Oh, I say, yes! He's pumping in thousands of pounds backing to these thugs. Definitely more than a fair weather friend to them. Are you – er – involved with him in any way?'

'We intend to get married next week.'

'Oh, my. There I go, putting my foot in it again. Always do when I'm tight, and I always get tight at bashes like this. Well, my dear, if you want some advice, I'd say, leave him at the church. Otherwise you could find yourself repenting at leisure. Now, I'd better buzz off before you tell me to mind my own business, hadn't I?'

'I shan't do that, Johnny. Thank you for being so honest with me. I'll think about it.'

She spent the rest of the evening drinking far too

much, and passed out gracefully soon after Norland got her back to the flat. He assumed that meant she had enjoyed the evening, and she was too depressed by the entire interlude to discuss it again. June 6th, her wedding day, was beginning to loom ahead of her like Armageddon.

CHAPTER TWELVE

June 5th was a lovely day. Bethan was a mass of over-stretched nerves. She had not slept more than a few hours since the January Club dinner. She spent every waking moment contemplating the appalling mistake she was about to make, and failing to see any means of escape.

She knew she was a coward, knew that eight long years separated her from the determined young woman who had walked out on James Norland in 1926 to find a new, worthwhile life. Now, it seemed she had destroyed her second chance, eliminating the new world she had built so painstakingly over the intervening period. For the first time, she saw clearly that she would have been unable to endure had it not been for the companionship and love of Max Grant.

It was not a miracle that she had found James Norland again, and that this time he wanted to marry her. Now she understood that the real miracle had been meeting Max. In her early days at the clinic, he had been no more than landlord, friend and confidant, but even that had been enough to get her over the first, hard months. Then it had changed to something else, and almost without realising it, she had slipped into being his lover. He had asked her many times to marry him, and insisted she was the first woman he had ever wanted as his wife, but she had always hedged, always secretly hoped that Prince Charming awaited her just over the hill. Well, now she had been proved right. Unfortunately Prince Charming wore a black shirt and wanted to help rule the world.

She had seen Pearl on Sunday evening, and had tried to confide in her. Pearl had no idea what she meant. After listening for a long time, with a look of agonised concentration on her face, she said: 'But why are you so worried, Beth? What does it matter about his politics? Nev hasn't got round to telling me how he votes after all these years, and I don't care. Why should you?'

It had taken Bethan some hours to realise that Pearl was not stupid. She was trying to make her friend adapt to reality as she herself saw it. Men were there to earn the money. Women were there to spend it. If the men got funny ideas about matters that had nothing to do with the provision and dispersal of that money, then it was a minor matter. Not advanced political philosophy, perhaps; but a useful working blueprint for a life like Pearl's. Bethan grew more convinced by the moment that it was not for her, but she could see no means of escape.

As usual, James had made perfect arrangements for Friday's marriage celebrations. The guests were invited, the caterers laid on, the wedding dress delivered and tried on with satisfactory results. They were going to Italy for their honeymoon, with a stop in Paris on the way back to buy Bethan some new clothes. What more could any bride want? Max Grant, if she had the sense she was born with, Bethan thought grimly as she dressed the day before the marriage.

She had been left to her own devices for the day. James was down in Oxford at the car plant, as he would not be back there for a month. He had left in high good humour, having provided her with a sheaf of banknotes and instructed her to do something amusing for the day. He was driving up from Foxhall first thing in the morning and going to Caxton Hall from a suite in the Ritz. 'Might as well get ourselves launched respectably on the big day,' he said. Pearl had offered to come and spend the night with Bethan at the flat, or to drive over first thing on Friday morning and help her to dress. Bethan had told her she would ring by mid-afternoon if she wanted her to come and stay.

Now she was footloose, out on her own with no one to take responsibility for her. Bethan knew it was an illusory

108

situation, but it still made her stomach hollow and her legs shaky. If only she had not deserted her family so long ago.

She dressed casually in a light summer dress and jacket and went for a walk. Shortly before noon, she was strolling along the Strand opposite Charing Cross station, when she saw the inevitable black shirts and thuggish expressions which seemed so much a part of London street life these days. Unable to ignore them, she moved in for a closer look.

The Fascists were grouping for a march on East London – from what they were saying it sounded like a dress rehearsal for a bigger rally the following weekend. Simultaneously repelled and fascinated, she began moving along the crowded pavement, parallel with the marchers when they set off.

It was a long walk, but she was wearing low-heeled sandals and had no trouble in keeping up. Along the way, small groups of people joined in for a few hundred yards, then drifted away again. On they moved, along Fleet Street, up Ludgate Hill and into the heart of the City. Messengers and clerks looked on admiringly as the bully-boys marched through the financial district.

By now Bethan was tiring – she had walked about three miles – and eventually she found a cab. 'Do you mind following the march?' she asked. 'I know it's slow, but . . . '

To her dismay, the taxi-driver grinned approvingly. 'Going to support the lads, are yer?' he said. 'That's what I like ter see!' And for the next half-hour she was subjected to a stream of opinion at least as offensive as what she had heard at the January Club dinner, all delivered in a friendly, all-mates-together tone.

At the edge of Whitechapel, trouble was waiting for the marchers. The taxi sighed to a halt and the driver said: 'I'm not sure I wanter 'ang arahnd 'ere, if it's all the same to you, lady. This cab's me living, and if it gets knocked about . . . '

'Yes – yes of course. What's on the clock?'

He had the grace to look concerned. 'Sure you wanter stay dahn 'ere on yer own? If there's trouble you could get hurt.'

'No, I'll stay well back. It's what I came for, after all.' She paid him and stepped out into the sunny street, glad to see the back of him but immediately feeling exposed. Ahead of her a line of young and middle-aged men were strung across the road, facing the Fascists. They looked poorly dressed and underfed. The marchers seemed like giants against them. Bethan backed into a doorway to watch, as one of the older men stepped forward to confront the Blackshirts.

'That's as far as you go,' he shouted. 'We've had enough a you lot dahn 'ere. Now bugger off back to your sewers before we show you some real trouble!'

The speed of the incident upset Bethan as much as anything else. One moment they were trading insults, the next, the front rank of marchers had closed with the line of local men and all hell had broken loose. Abruptly, the side streets erupted with reinforcements. The underfed guardians of the streets had not been without resources after all.

A handful of mounted policemen had escorted the marchers from the Strand. They were not out in the sort of force seen at full scale rallies, because this had the look of a small demonstration. Now, as struggling knots of fighters surged back and forth along the street, police whistles shrilled out and truncheons were drawn. With mounting panic, Bethan realised she was not as far from trouble as she had thought. Running, fighting groups could cover a lot of ground in a few seconds.

Suddenly the action swept towards her doorway and she let out a squeal of terror. The half-glazed door behind her was flung open and a short, bearded man stuck his head out. 'In here, quick, silly girl!' he said, and dragged her into the shop, locking the door behind her. 'Not much use if they smash the glass,' he said over his shoulder, 'but it may slow them down, neh?'

The noise outside was unbelievable now, with passersby screaming as they were embroiled against their will, and the ugly thud of police truncheons against the rioters' limbs and heads.

The man smiled at Bethan. 'I don't think you'll want to go out there for a while,' he said, 'but it isn't all that much safer in here. You could go out the back way if you liked. Keep going straight ahead and eventually you'll come out on the main road, far enough away for this not to matter.'

'But what about you?'

He shrugged. 'It's my shop. I'm not leaving it to that lot. Come on, I'll show you the way.'

The shop was long and narrow and when she emerged into the back alley, the shouting already sounded remote. The man gestured towards the sunlit street at the end of the lane and said, 'Turn left there and keep going till you hit the main road.'

'Thank you – thank you so much . . . ' Smiling, he cut off her gratitude and pushed her gently towards the end of the lane. The door shut with finality and she heard the chilling sound of a bolt being thrown home.

It was less peaceful out in the street. She was far enough from trouble not to be too worried, but the occasional pair of combatants would pass her at a run, fighting as they went. At the very end of the street, just before it joined the main road, two of them were scuffling in the gutter. An elderly Jewish woman, her wig knocked askew by the haste in which she had fled from their path, was sobbing inconsolably in the doorway.

Bethan stopped in her own headlong flight and went back to her, embracing her and drawing her close in an effort to calm her. 'It's all right now,' she said, 'really all right. They're away back down there, don't worry.' But the old woman merely went on crying and rocking against her. She was beginning to wonder if the weeping would ever stop, when the woman uttered a final, convulsive sob and looked up at her.

'You don't understand,' she said in heavily-accented English. 'My grandmother, they push her out of Russia

. . . then the Poles drive us west, always west. And then the Germans . . . ' she began to cry again at this ' . . . the Germans kick my brother to death in the street. My son brings me here, says it's safe, but it's not safe. This is how it started in Germany . . . it will be the same here . . . just the same . . . '

Bethan was crying too, now, wondering what she could say to comfort the old woman, despairing at the thought that there might be a grain of truth in what she said. At that point the adjoining front door opened a crack and a middle-aged woman looked out. Seeing that little was going on, she slipped out and joined them, saying something in Yiddish to the old woman.

'It is all right now,' she told Bethan. 'This is my mother-in-law. I will look after her.' She led the black-clad figure away and Bethan turned towards the main road once more. Dear God! Was this the brave, strong England of the future that James Norland was fighting to achieve? Hardly aware of where she was going, she turned westward along Commercial Road.

Joyce Gladstone was about to lock the outer door of the Holloway Road Family Planning Clinic at noon on Friday before eating her lunch. She had already pulled down the brown paper blind when she heard a feeble tapping on the glass and peeped around it. Outside, leaning against the door jamb and looking dishevelled and exhausted, was Bethan Walters.

Joyce fumbled with the lock and let the other woman in, supporting Bethan as she sagged, doll-like, against her. 'What on earth has happened, Bethan? You look as if you'd been out all night!' she said, guiding her to a chair.

'I have . . . I walked, and walked, and wondered what to do, and got lost . . . and there was just nobody . . . ' Tears were streaming down her cheeks but she seemed not to notice. 'In the end, I – I just gave up, and sat down, and it got dark.'

'But where? You can't have spent the night out of

doors dressed like that! You must have felt frozen. Where did you go?'

'Don't know . . . a park, somewhere. There was one of those little boxed-in shelters with benches. I sat there. Th-then, when it got light, I walked around for a long time again . . . '

'But darling, why? Why didn't you go home?'

'Haven't got a home . . . haven't got anybody any more. Never did, really . . . ' She crumpled forward on to the desk and laid her head on her folded arms. 'Oh, please, Joyce, get Max for me! Tell him I'm sorry. Tell him I was the worst fool in the world . . . ' The remains of the sentence were lost in muffled sobs.

As Joyce dialled Grant's number, she heard Bethan mumbling. 'Bet he won't come . . . wouldn't blame him if he didn't . . . oh, what a mess . . . what a terrible mess I've made!'

She uttered silent thanks when Grant answered at the third ring. 'Bethan?' he said, a note of rising hope in his voice.

'No, Max, it's Joyce Gladstone, at the clinic. But I have her here. Something awful seems to have happened to her – a sort of breakdown, I think. She's asking for you. Can you come and get her?'

'Just try stopping me! I'll be round there in fifteen minutes.'

By the time he arrived, Joyce had managed to piece together a little more of Bethan's wretched day, but it still made little sense because she had no detailed idea about the breach with Max Grant beyond a vague understanding that they might have agreed to go their separate ways. Still thinking Bethan was affected by a combination of general stress and rough handling at a Fascist demonstration she appeared to have got mixed up in, Joyce tried to calm her, dispensing hot, sweet tea and a lot of comforting, if meaningless, chatter.

Bethan appeared at last to be calming down, her sobs tailing off into occasional hiccoughs, her demeanour less agitated, when abruptly she froze. 'Oh, my God!' she cried, 'what am I doing here? I'm supposed to be getting married this afternoon!' Then she broke into a storm of fresh tears.

This time Joyce could get no sense at all from her. Finally she went through Bethan's bag and came up with a diary. The Hackney address and telephone number at the front had been crossed out and replaced by fresh details. She took the little book and went to squat on the floor beside Bethan's chair.

'This phone number: shall I ring it and tell them you're ill? Please, Bethan, try to be calm for a moment, then I'll leave you in peace. We must let them know – they'll be frantic about you!'

Real fear leaped in Bethan's eyes. 'Not him – don't tell him about it!' She seemed to be casting about for escape. 'Pearl . . . yes, that's right, Pearl Fletcher will be there by now. Pearl will help. Ring up, Joyce, and ask for Mrs Pearl Fletcher. Don't speak to anyone else – *anyone*, you understand? And don't even tell Pearl where I am. Tell her I'm safe and I can't go through with it. Say I can't come back . . . '

'But Bethan, she'll think I'm unhinged, a stranger telephoning out of the blue like that. Please let me . . . ' But before she could make any plea for disclosing a little more information, Bethan began to grow agitated again.

'No, Joyce – I just can't face it, really I can't. I'll explain when I can get my thoughts in order.'

'Very well. Now please, calm down. You know I'm your friend. I won't do anything to harm you.' Joyce went back to the telephone, wondering how on earth she would handle the call.

In fact it was Pearl Fletcher who answered the telephone. 'Oh, thank God for that!' she exclaimed, when Joyce told her, not quite truthfully, that Bethan was safe and sound. 'Her fiancé is on his way round here now – they're getting married at three.'

'No, I'm afraid they aren't,' said Joyce. 'Bethan is very distressed and there's no question of her going anywhere today, least of all getting married.'

'But she must! I mean – all the guests, and the reception and all . . . Jimmy'll look such a *fool!*'

Maybe that last remark gave Joyce the strength she needed. 'I'm afraid Bethan's sanity is far more important to me than some man's self-esteem!' she snapped. 'Whatever the poor girl has gone through in the past twenty-four hours, it's left her in no fit state for anything but rest. I think, Mrs Fletcher, that you'd better tell her fiancé to expect her when he sees her, and certainly not in the foreseeable future!' Then she hung up. Seconds later, she wondered how she could have been so impossibly rude, then she realised it was because she found it hard to understand anything reducing Bethan to such a pathetic state, and detested whoever had done it to her.

She was saved further speculation by the arrival of Max Grant. Joyce had re-locked the front door so they could remain undisturbed, and now Max rattled the handle impatiently. As she let him in, Bethan stood up shakily and said, barely above a whisper, 'Oh, Max, can you ever forgive me?' Then he was across the room, holding her, kissing her hair, easing her back into the chair. Joyce slipped out into the back room to give them some privacy.

Half an hour later she returned, bringing more tea, this time liberally laced with whisky from her secret emergency supply. Max sipped his gratefully and gestured to her to sit down. Bethan was calm now, but looked terrible.

'Well,' Joyce asked, 'have you sorted anything out yet?'

He smiled wanly and nodded. 'If you want her – after a little more leave, I'm afraid – you have your full-time clinic worker back. But first she's going to have a rest, and then we're getting married by special licence.'

Joyce's face must have shown her doubts about the wisdom of such a step, but Grant shook his head. 'She won't change her mind about me,' he said, smiling more naturally now. 'I didn't give her an option of saying no.'

CHAPTER THIRTEEN

The Cardiff–London train was racing towards Paddington, its wheels making a rhythmic sound on the tracks which imprinted itself on Peter Henderson's mind as Lily-I-love-you, Lily-I-want-you, Lily-I-need-you. What juvenile nonsense, he reflected. He remembered all the times in his boyhood when the train had been on its way home for the school holidays and he had spun his dearest wishes into the music of the wheels, convinced that if he could make them form the right rhythms, he would win them. I-want-a-pony had worked, but lots of them hadn't. He had even let it overlap into his young adulthood. He clearly recalled trying to force 'I won't be a soldier' into the right pattern, more in desperation than in belief that it would work.

That set him off on another daydream, and he hurriedly manufactured a a cough a moment later to hide the fact that he had started singing the disreputable song 'I don't want to join the Army . . . ' He had reached the line which announced that he'd rather hang around Piccadilly Underground, living on the earnings of a high-born lady, when he realised the ex-military type opposite looked ready to suffer an apoplexy.

Henderson's thoughts turned back to Lily. No use conjuring her with train magic. They had revelled in that wonderful year of love, and then her husband became ill. After that, it was brother-and-sister. Peter knew she was strong enough to bear the deprivation, although her nature was every bit as passionate as his. He was less sure about himself. It was even worse now that she was working back at the surgery again, and he saw her every day. Still, without ever mentioning that he knew what

116

was going on, Charles had made it better. He had kept Lily out of Peter's way as much as possible, and somehow always managed to arrive at the right moment to prevent something irreversible happening. But what a life to endure! Peter wondered how he managed it, and Lily's fortitude left him breathless.

It had been six years – six interminable summers and winters, seeing her and being unable to touch her. He had told David Richards there was a chance of remission of his sickness, more in the hope of cheering the man's last days than anything else. In the event, though, he had lasted longer than Peter would have thought possible, given his state when the condition was diagnosed.

David had encountered the usual stone-faced response to any claim for industrial compensation. The coal owners insisted in all but a tiny proportion of cases that their industry could not be linked directly with the men's fatal diseases. After submitting to a management medical panel, David received a piece of paper from a supposedly independent physician, stating that given his poor health, he was advised not to work underground. The rest was up to him. After pondering his own hospital consultant's view that he would hasten his own end considerably if he attempted to continue with his job, he remembered the benefits of his life insurance policy, gritted his teeth against the pain and returned to the pit.

Against all likelihood, he lasted well into 1928, but after that there was no question of any sort of work, even if the management had come up with a pithead job for him. He moved slowly and painfully about the village, wheezing hard, his shoulders hunched as if to protect his wasting lungs, and waited for the end.

Peter often wondered, now, how much difference it would make when Richards eventually died. Lily had reacted hysterically when she learned he would not recover from his illness. She could have faced David's death – people from her background lived with the possibility like an extra member of the family – but she could not quite forgive herself for having been

Henderson's lover while her husband was suffering the serious onset of the disease. Peter had tried to reason with her – tried to point out that it would have made no difference to David's prospects if they had never set eyes on each other. It had made no difference. For weeks, she retreated into complete silence. When she emerged, it was as a sort of madonna, purged of all sensuality. Henderson often wondered whether it would ever return.

David Richards had been confined to bed for the past three months, a yellow-skinned, living skeleton, only his bright eyes giving an indication of his former vigour. Lily had moved him into the little front parlour in the Ranks house, so that she could help him to the outside privy on his good days. From time to time she delivered a few well-chosen phrases about the system which had deprived David of the house he had bought from his life savings.

'At least if we'd still been there, the poor sod would have had an inside lav to rest his bum on!' she had said. When Charles Henderson attempted to soothe her by remarking that at least there was mains drainage from the privy, Lily retorted, 'Aye, and the temperature out there fit for the Arctic! I don't care about the drains, Charlie. Surely I don't need to tell *you* that when that cold air do hit his lungs he ent right for three or four hours? I'd be glad to help him do it inside, but his bloody dignity won't stand for it!' Silenced by her vehemence, Charles had left her to her grief and guilt and helplessness.

It didn't help that she seemed driven by some demon to work at the surgery, nurse a dying man, raise a boisterous son and still take an active part in the miners' unending struggle to improve their lot. Sometimes Peter felt exhausted by the mere contemplation of what a day in the life of Lily Richards must involve.

She also had an unnerving habit of seeing that others were as active as herself. That was why he was aboard the train today. Lily had decreed that this time, when they marched on the seats of power, they would speak with a voice that had a chance of being heard. Last time, she had said, they were herded about and given orders, and because they were friendless and over-awed by the capital city, they had permitted themselves to be sidetracked. This time they would reconnoitre in advance, and Henderson's years as a medical student in London made him uniquely qualified for the task.

He chuckled ruefully as he thought of it. He didn't really mind . . . for one thing it was a break from the grimness of the valleys. For another, it gave him a chance to renew old political acquaintances who for years had been no more than signatures on irregular letters. And most important of all, it flung him back into the heart of left-wing politics.

Peter Henderson was a perfect example of the belief that there was no prude like a reformed whore. Born to a rich, aristocratic, conservative family, he had listened to the theories of the Left and had liked what he heard. But there was no room for moderation in his thinking. He had stormed across the political spectrum and had fetched up proudly on the far shore as a Marxist. Today he was on his way to see Ben Abramovitz, an old friend from his medical school days, second-generation Polish–Jewish immigrant and as red as Peter with far more justification. These days Ben was an East End general practitioner, healing the poor by day, attending political meetings and anti-Fascist rallies by night. If the South Wales miners were to get a good hearing in London the next time they marched on the capital, Ben had the contacts to set it up.

The thought of a good political argument, followed perhaps by a good political fight, temporarily drove Lily from Henderson's mind. Now the train wheels were saying death-to-all-Fascists, death-to-all-Fascists, and Benny-will-fix-it, Benny-will-fix-it. They were sentiments which warmed the blood almost as excitingly as the thought of Lily's smooth flesh and welcoming body.

James Norland had consumed almost a bottle of whisky. When he arrived at the Belgravia flat on Friday to find

Pearl there alone and distraught, he had taken it calmly. He would have died rather than permit a vulgar little creature like her to see how devastated he felt. He had concentrated on maintaining the façade until he could get her out, and he felt unable to eject her until he had used her to cancel the caterers and the ceremony, and to telephone every guest who had not yet departed for the reception. After that, he was able to get her out by begging her to go along to the private banqueting room he had booked at the Savoy, to dispense champagne and platitudes to the few guests who had slipped through the net and departed for the party before she reached them.

Unfortunately for James's temper, Neville arrived before Pearl started out, and insisted on staying with the bereft bridegroom. 'Least a best mate can do, after all,' he said. 'I admit I feel a bit responsible for letting Pearl introduce you to the little cow again.'

After that the afternoon had merged into evening while the two men systematically worked their way through the contents of the cocktail cabinet. Finally, close to midnight, Neville had murmured: 'I don't think crème de menthe is really my style, old boy.' He had managed to get as far as the bathroom before he was sick, and had then gone off in a taxi, assuring James he would be far better off without Bethan.

On Saturday Norland awoke with an appalling hang-over – a condition which he regarded as a challenge. A couple of hours later a Turkish bath and a large breakfast had disposed of the worst effects of alcohol. Now he was left with a murderous hatred for Bethan, so strong it frightened him a little. Only the intensity of his reaction prevented him from storming over to the shabby Georgian house in Hackney – for he was sure that was where he would find her. Where else could she have gone? He knew that if he saw her now, he might lose control and injure her – maybe even kill her – and James Norland had no intention of ever losing his liberty for the sake of some treacherous female. There was a ball of hatred in his stomach, knotted as hard as indigestion, and he had to find some way of loosening it. That was when he started on the whisky. It had worked the previous night, after all. Maybe it would help now.

But it did nothing of the kind. Instead, it brought the knot of rage bubbling to the surface, until he found himself pacing about the velvety carpet, cursing under his breath and asking himself rhetorical questions about the unfairness of life and what he had done to deserve such treatment.

Then he remembered the rally. Of course! What better way to let off steam? They had ribbed him at the club when he cried off attending. Said he was getting married on the sixth merely to avoid the risk of getting his name into the papers as one of Mosley's biff boys. How they'd all laughed at that one! They all knew the biff-boys were lower-class types, what used to be called cannon fodder. Salt of the earth when one needed something done in a hurry, but no good asking them to think. James was one of the elite. He would no more be expected to go down into the arena and kick the shit out of the Reds than fly to the moon on a white stallion – now there was a prospect! Kick shit out of a few Reds . . . merely contemplating the act made him feel better. A lot better. Half of them would probably be Yids, too. What a feeling of achievement, to show those stinking Christ-killers they couldn't walk in and take over this country as if it were nothing more than a source of financial speculation.

With considerable surprise he realised the whisky bottle was empty. He stood up to go and find another. He had re-stocked that afternoon, following his mighty clean-out last night with good old Neville. Norland stood up and started to cross to the drinks cupboard, then realised he was a little unsteady. Silly, that. Pointless to numb oneself to later events. Dinner was in order – that was it, an early dinner. Something good and filling, then on to Olympia. He even had a pass somewhere. That mindless Aitken girl had given it to him and asked him to pass it on to someone who'd appreciate it. Well, he'd appreciate it himself, wouldn't he?

He looked at his watch. It was just after five. Black coffee, early meal, back here to change, and he'd still make Olympia by seven-thirty. Probably wouldn't manage to see Tom, but any of them would know him . . . shouldn't take too much trouble to fit him in as a steward. They'd probably be tickled pink at someone of his type being willing to get his hands dirty . . . Norland went to make himself coffee, then shrugged on a jacket and teetered off into the balmy early evening to dine before taking his revenge on the world for Bethan Walters.

'It's so obviously an act of deliberate provocation,' Ben Abramovitz said. 'Take a leaf out of Hitler's book and titillate the masses with an orgy of public violence – you treble your membership overnight. The only thing getting in the way in England until now has been the law about keeping the peace. A public rally means police presence. Police presence means no really bloody scrapping. So they've hired Olympia and turned the whole thing into a private function.

'They know as well as you and I do that our sort of people will fight to get in there and make their protests heard. In fact they've been deliberately making it easy for us by seeing that a trickle of tickets comes through. But once we're in there they'll use us as punchbags to stir up all the nastier bits of the British character. No need for me to tell you we'll get hurt, but what other way do we have of showing the people who can still think and want to do something to stop all this?'

'When have you ever known me able to resist a good political quarrel?' said Peter with a grin. 'Officially, I may just be here to drum up support for the miners' next march. Unofficially I'm all yours. It won't harm the miners' cause, either. I'm quite surprised you can spare me a ticket, though. Thought your lot would be forming queues to get in among the biff boys.'

'Oh, they are! But you have one big advantage, Peter. In spite of that black hair, you look so English that no one could call you Yid and make it stick. We want to show the world it's not just a bunch of victimised Jews protesting, but any civilised man or woman.'

Henderson sighed. 'Sometimes I wonder whether this sort of ugliness would happen at all if there were any civilised men and women left.'

'Me too, but we have to assume they're out there, ready to listen. Come on, it's about time we went and found out.'

CHAPTER FOURTEEN

However hard the Fascists tried to dress it up, Olympia was not Nuremburg. This was no Cathedral of Light, and the Blackshirts were not storm-troopers. Nevertheless they were capable of inflicting more than enough damage for London's taste.

Perhaps their lack of presence was the fault of the audience. Where Hitler could expect to strut before ranks of uniformed men, women and children, and even those without uniforms waved flags and stood in militaristic poses as they extended their arms in the Nazi salute, the crowd at Olympia was altogether more lack-lustre.

Between the wedges of correctly-attired Blackshirts the rank and file seemed to comprise downtrodden clerks and shopkeepers, men with shabby, sagging suits, celluloid collars and carefully repaired shoes. Their faces were flabby and greyish from the flabby and greyish food they ate, their bodies stodgy and slouching from sedentary occupations and lack of outdoor exercise. The women had dandruff on their collars and a defeated look in their eyes. They were the casualties of the peace of 1918, not victors of the intervening years.

Few of them had known any sort of plenty in their adult lives and they wanted to blame someone or something. They knew from long subjugation that their sort never triumphed over governments; governments had troops and money to back their will. But if they blamed foreigners . . . Who would bother to defend the Jewish shopkeeper if they broke his windows to show their disapproval of his profiteering? Who would protect the immigrants of the East End if the Blackshirts marched on their streets and showed them they were not wanted in

England? The prospect of vengeance dispelled the gloom of these people for a little while at least. Goaded by Mosley's oratory, they took refuge behind a cloud of rage in the brain and relished the flavour of blood on their tongues. The rage served to stop them reflecting that a few frightened immigrants and ruined shopkeepers were unlikely to redistribute the balance of power so that they got a better deal. It made no difference. At least it offered an escape, however brief, from the drab inadequacy of their lives.

'Someone seems intent on maintaining public order, I'm glad to see,' Peter said to Ben as they passed the army of policemen ranged outside the front of Olympia.

'Hmm – I read in the paper that there are over seven hundred of them,' said Ben, 'but don't get your hopes up. They'll all be staying outside.'

'Oh well, if there's going to be blood in the arena, it might as well be mine, I suppose.'

'If we go in there, you know it will be. They're counting on it. This is the last chance to go back out.'

Peter laughed at him. 'And have the decent people go on believing that gang of thugs are only interested in strong government and British dignity? Not on your life! Now is the time for all good men, and so on . . . ' They produced their admission tickets and walked into the building, suddenly aware of a sense of isolation.

The hall had been set up to mimic the German rallies as closely as possible. Full facilities had been granted to the cinema newsreel services. The Fascists were not interested in performing in secret. They wanted the world to see their strength. Banks of spotlights had been carefully trained on the platform, to maximise the dramatic appeal of Sir Oswald Mosley's big speech.

Peter and Ben split up once they were inside. Peter knew there were a dozen or so others with similar intentions, scattered around the audience, and guessed there would be other people whose individual convictions had driven them here tonight, to make their own protests against what was being preached. The British Union of Fascists' symbol was everywhere. Already the lighting was being used to heighten the portentous atmosphere.

Peter shivered, and wondered if he were equal to what lay ahead of him. Come on, you fool, he told himself, they're no more than a bunch of thugs. You're almost forty years old and you've never done anything really courageous yet. Now's your chance. It can't be as bad as the Western Front. It said much for his modesty that he did not class his conscientious objector's war work as courageous.

James Norland swaggered along Kensington High Street, his new black shirt still stiff against his flesh, his immaculate grey trousers showing off his long, muscular legs. He caught sight of himself in a shop window. Yes, not a bad example of the Master Race, if one were needed. Talked a lot of sense, that Hitler. Sometimes he wasn't altogether sure that Tom Mosley went far enough.

He had walked from Belgravia, partly to sober himself up, partly because he could not resist the temptation to show off in his paramilitary fancy dress. By God, he was going to enjoy tonight! It had been ages since he'd really let his hair down. This would be just what he needed to shake off the past. About time he involved himself in politics a little more deeply, too. He was paying through the nose to support what he believed in. They could hardly refuse him more practical involvement – not if they knew the value of money, anyway. He wondered how late the rally would go on. Having planned to be out of the country by now, he had taken only cursory interest in the planning stage. Still, if it finished that early, he could go back to the West End, maybe pick up a floozie somewhere, play a few games . . . some girls didn't understand who was boss unless they were slapped around a bit, and those trollops – well, someone had to keep them in their place!

With such titillating thoughts in his mind, Norland shouldered his way into the Olympia centre. He did not need to show his pass and within moments one of his cronies caught sight of him. 'Jimmy! This is quite a surprise. I thought you'd be half-way to the Italian Riviera by now.'

Norland smirked and shrugged. 'Decided this was far too important to miss after all. Anything I can do to be of practical help?'

'Oh, I think Tom would like you up there with us . . . there's a small group detailed to sort out trouble-makers. Interested?'

Norland's mouth was dry and his pulse racing. 'Yes, very. Anything to keep the peace, you know me!'

The other man winked knowingly. 'Precious little peace-keeping, old chap – although it will be quite peaceful for the agitators after we've finished with them. They won't be in a hurry to stir things up after that.'

'Just what I thought. Lead on.'

It had the inevitability of a Greek tragedy. Mosley delivered his poisoned oratory; in the audience a dissenter arose. The spotlight picked him out and biff-boys hurried towards him from various parts of the hall. There was no attempt at secrecy. As they hauled each protestor out into the gangways, they began punching and kicking. The newsreel cameras captured it in sickening detail. A group of all-party MPs who had come along on a fact-finding visit winced and looked away as the violence was administered.

Peter sat in the middle of row 'P' and sweated. He wondered whether he would have the courage to stand up when his turn came, to raise his hand, then to shout his protest at the inanity or offensiveness of what was being said. He watched first a man – someone he was sure had come alone, not with any political group – then a young woman, rise and demand that the obscene talk on stage should be silenced. The man was dragged out by the usual big male thugs. To Peter's intense distaste, he saw that the BUF had trained women for their ugly task too. When the female protestor tried to speak, five women – in the usual black shirts and grey trousers – closed in from the shadows and pulled her from her row. There was a novel twist to their treatment of the victim. They tormented her with open-handed slaps instead of the clenched-fist punches administered by their male counterparts. Presumably the sight of a feminine nose spread all over a pretty face by female fists was too much even for the iron stomachs of the Fascists.

And then it was his turn. As it happened, it was far more natural and far simpler than he had anticipated. Mosley delivered a sickening barrage of chauvinist falsehood and Peter surged to his feet, perhaps powered by angels' wings. He heard his own voice yell in outrage, as though from a great distance, and then felt the strength of the spotlight, sensed the grasping hands, the steel-tipped boots . . .

Ben Abramovitz's group found both of them in the alley at the side of Olympia, close to the railway track. Ben had lost his front teeth. The flesh below Peter's right eye had been cut by the ferocity of the repeated blows he received, and the muscle tissue beneath was clearly exposed. One of Ben's friends uncovered the injury and turned away for a moment to retch in the gutter.

'Hurts, doesn't it?' For the first time in his life, Ben was lisping. 'Only when I laugh,' said Peter, 'and I don't plan on doing too much of that in the immediate future.'

'Stop trying to be clever and see if you can walk.' Dave Cohen was the junior partner in Ben's practice. His task tonight was to see that any casualties were treated as quickly and efficiently as possible.

'Bloody Yids!' said Ben. 'Give 'em that much authority and they try to take over the world!' He began to stand up with exaggerated difficulty, then abruptly folded with a groan and collapsed again.

Dave rushed to support him. 'You silly sod, I told you to be careful! What is it?'

Ben was ashen-faced, now. 'Leg – m-my leg . . . feels as if it's gone in about three places . . . ' then he fainted.

Peter did not feel much better. Finally he allowed Dave to have him taken by stretcher to the makeshift ambulance they had provided. 'I know you're being the strong man,' Dave told him, 'but I got that from Ben, and look at him now. Roll on that stretcher and no more heroics.'

As he closed the van door on them, Peter hazily tried to piece together the details of the attack he had endured once they got him out of the main hall in Olympia. It was that big fair bloke who had really laid in to him. Proper Herrenvolk type . . . wouldn't be surprised if he was German . . . the shock of the attack caught up with him and he began to doze. So sure of himself. Definitely boss material, not like those pathetic sycophants in the main hall . . . wonder how he came to be mixed up in such an infra dig do . . . then he was asleep, and none of it mattered any more.

The blood was singing in James Norland's ears as his taxi drove eastward away from Olympia. By God, he had needed something like that! He chuckled with satisfaction as he massaged the knuckles of his right hand, which throbbed painfully from the impact with his victim's face. Not that he'd needed to use his fists much. Once the bastard was down, it was strictly feet first . . . That sounded less heroic and his brain sheered away into self-justification. Well, what did they expect, little Red runts, conspiring to overthrow a country that had given them shelter and opportunity? Kicks were good enough for that sort. Not worth a gentleman soiling his hands . . . but that second one had been different . . . that *was* a fully paid-up English gentleman if ever he saw one, but a renegade, otherwise what was he doing on the other side? Asked for all he got, betraying his class and race like that. And he'd certainly got it.

Norland remembered with a wince the soggy thud as his shoe had made contact with the man's cheek, tearing the flesh like tissue paper. He uttered another, this time rather angry, laugh. Just as well it was I who took care of him and not one of the biff-boys, he thought. They all had boots on. He'd certainly have lost the eye in that case.

His review of the evening was becoming faintly uncomfortable. He dropped the blow-by-blow examination and returned to revelling in the general feeling of satisfaction. He stopped the cab half-way up Shaftesbury Avenue. It was still quite early, really. Too early for sleep, anyway, feeling as charged as he did. Time for a little more fun before the night was over.

He found her in a pub along Dean Street. Her name was Amy and she was gorgeous: very small – not much over five feet – but with a sensational figure, good breasts and pretty legs. Her skin was as fresh as a country girl's under the obligatory layer of showgirl-style makeup, and she had pert little features, set off to perfection by blue eyes. But it was the hair that really attracted him. Bright red-gold and curly. From a distance, she could have been Beth.

They had several drinks together and he asked her whether she had eaten yet. She looked him over and apparently decided there was some sense of urgency in him, because she told him she'd had supper and wouldn't he like to come back to her place round the corner, 'just for a nightcap, o' course'.

'How much will this *nightcap* cost me?' he asked. Not that he cared, but it would be tedious to find she had mistaken his intentions in some way.

Again the calculating look. 'Fifteen,' she said. 'Twenty if you want breakfast.'

He laughed. 'Breakfast at the Ritz costs a lot less.'

'They don't serve it there the way I do, duckie. I'm one a the best.'

'At that price, you'd better be. I might want you to do a few . . . special things.'

Her smile stiffened. 'Depends what they are. Nothing too outa the way. But for a bit extra, I dare say we can sort something out. Come on, then, darling.'

She lived in St Anne's Court, a tiny side alley further along Dean Street. It was a tall, Georgian house with a precipitous staircase. Her room was on the second floor. He followed her up the steep stairs, watching the tiny,

130

tight backside undulating under the silk skirt. He longed to reach up and grab it, hard, and she probably wouldn't have objected, with what he was about to pay for, but best to save it. He had a lot of things in mind for little Beth.

'Amy,' she said. Good God, what had he said? He must have been thinking aloud. Sooner they got down to business the better.

'Sorry – Amy,' he said, smiling. 'You just remind me of someone, that's all.'

She unlocked her front door and led him inside, turning almost immediately and giving him a warm smile as she pressed her body against him. 'Call me Beth if you like,' she said, 'you know, if it works you up faster or anything. It's Liberty Hall here. Can't ask for the wrong thing.' She turned away and began to move into the room.

'I don't intend to, darling. Come here, now.' He dragged her back to him and put his hands up to the wide sweetheart neckline of her blouse. With a savage, outward motion, he tore away the fabric, leaving her breasts and shoulders bare. Her eyes flared wide in momentary alarm, but she was a professional and promptly decided he must be one of those who liked it rough. She could always charge him extra.

His mouth crushed down on hers and then he started biting and squeezing her body, pressing her back against the wall and pulling up her tight skirt as he did so. His hands slid over the silky thighs above the stocking tops – so like Beth's – and made contact with flimsy panties. He thrust his hand inside the gusset and again pulled with all his strength. The fabric shredded and he thrust his fingers into her with such force that she gasped with pain. 'Hey, hang on,' she said, 'that's human flesh there, mate!'

He tried to smile at her but felt the wolfishness of the expression without needing to see a reflection. To quieten her, he buried her mouth with his own again, pressing his tongue between her lips as his fingers continued to force a path into her body. She was moving with him, attemp-

131

ting to accommodate him without suffering too much discomfort, and momentarily he put the brakes on. He didn't want it all to end in tears too early, after all. This was going to be a good night. All of it . . .

'Don't wanta do it out here, do you?' she asked, a tremulous note hovering in her voice. 'Got a nice big bed in there. Come on, get outa your things and let's calm down a bit.'

'Y-yes . . . yes . . . that's right. Calm down. Sorry about that. It's been quite a day.'

Her laugh was shaky, too, but she kept her nerve. 'I can see it must have been! Well, you seem to have got me nearly ready for bed, one way an' another, but you're still all togged up . . . ' As she spoke she moved around the room, switching on two rose-shaded lamps and turning down the bed.

It was less of a floozie's room than many he had been in. No sickening little stuffed animals, or photographs of the inevitable child, off being raised and educated somewhere respectable. It was plainly furnished and comfortable. The only thing it had in common with most whores' bedrooms, apart from the rosy lamp, was the vast double bed with its ornate brass frame. Do all brass bedsteads end up in tarts' rooms? he wondered inconsequentially.

She reclaimed his attention instantly when she came across and started to undress him. 'No,' he said thickly, the excitement mounting again. 'You first.'

'All right,' she shrugged, 'but like I said, you've nearly done it already. Not much to take off.'

She started to undo the remaining buttons of the ruined blouse and he pulled her forward so that she stood between his spread legs, squeezing her breasts as she worked on her clothes. She undid the waistband of her skirt and he eased the tight fabric down over the swell of her hips. The torn panties came off with it and she stood before him, wearing only suspender belt and stockings. He forced himself to unhook that, instead of tearing it as he wanted to, and rolled the stockings luxuriously down her smooth legs.

His sexual impulses were more or less normal now. She was a very attractive girl, still young enough not to have been spoiled by her corrosive profession, and she was stirring natural excitement in him. Then she began to undress him. It was warm, and pleasant, and incredibly erotic, and he enjoyed every second. But when they were both naked, and she was stretched out beside him, fondling him and pressing his hands all over her own body, abruptly he remembered that this should have been the second night of his honeymoon.

Norland went berserk. He took hold of Amy by the hair and yelled: 'Why did you go off like that, Beth? What had I ever done to you? You crazy little bitch – I'd have given you the world!' Then he started slapping her, rhythmically, side to side, cheek to cheek. One blow must have pressed her inner lip against her teeth, and a thread of blood trickled out of the side of her mouth. That inflamed him even more. He stopped slapping her and rose to his knees, forcing her down on her back and pressing her throat in a stranglehold.

Amy Porritt had been a prostitute since she was fifteen, and she had learned survival the hard way. Now, with consciousness slipping away, she retained the presence of mind to raise her right knee with a savage jerk that plunged directly into James Norland's testicles. He gave a scream of pain and let go of her throat, rolling away from her across the bed.

Amy jumped out on the other side and dashed to the window, flinging it open and picking up a small, glinting object just inside the sill. It was a police whistle. She blew it now, with all her strength, and the second she heard running footsteps she began yelling: 'Help, police! Murder! There's a woman being murdered in Number Seven!'

Norland left Vine Street police station at eight o'clock the following morning, his heart sick at the thought of what might have happened if the girl had decided to prefer charges. As it was, she had delivered the final humiliation as she gazed at him coldly through the bars of the holding cell. 'No, thanks, Sarge,' she had said to the police officer who accompanied her. 'It might damage my reputation, being associated with that scum in public!'

As he looked for a cab along Piccadilly, Norland thought about Bethan Walters and the exquisite torments he would visit upon her if he ever laid hands on her again.

CHAPTER FIFTEEN

Abercarn, 1936

'This isn't the East End of London, Peter. This is South Wales, remember? And we want to make the top people understand what the Means Test is doing to us. It ent about Blackshirts, or Mussolini, or German stormtroopers. And it ent about Spain, neither. I wanna change things yer first, all right?'

Lily was furious. She was chairing a meeting to discuss policy on the impending hunger march to London and Peter Henderson had started raising side issues about showing solidarity against Fascism. These days, Lily found the stick-legged children of the Valleys used up every atom of anger and compassion she could produce.

'It's the same fight, can't you see that?' he demanded hotly. 'Widen your horizons. It's no good us struggling with tyranny at home, only to find out when we win that it's taken over the rest of the world.'

'When we win . . . *when* we bloody win, the man says! Listen, I don't think we gorra prayer of winning here, but we gorra try. I *know* we can't win out there. Now stop wasting time and let's get down to business.'

Plenty of other men in the hall shared Henderson's keenness to fight Fascism, but they found Lily more intimidating then either Mosley or Hitler and decided to keep their views to themselves for the present. Peter contented himself with looking daggers at them, for failing to support him, but there was scant satisfaction in that.

Now Lily was getting into her stride, and few did it better these days. 'I know marching on London never worked before,' she said. 'It looks as if they got hearts of stone and it don't matter how many times we tell them. But we must go on trying – even if it's only for the morale of our own people. The day we stop doing that is the day they really fall apart, and it'll be our fault because we've set ourselves up to lead the poor buggers.'

There was a murmur of assent from the front rows. 'Any thoughts about some handle we could turn this time to get a bitta publicity for the cause?' she said. 'No? Well how about this?' She picked up a page torn from a glossy magazine. 'Hope Newport Central Library haven't noticed it's gone yet,' she muttered with an almost girlish grin. 'This is – let me see – dancing at the Savoy with the after-theatre crowd. Take a good look, everybody. I'd say one of them frocks would pay the meat bill for this village for a week.'

The picture showed a cluster of women in slinky, backless satin evening gowns – that season's favourite style – dancing with men in immaculate evening dress. To one side there was a tantalising glimpse of a loaded buffet table.

'Very pretty, Lil,' said one of the men, 'but what good's that gonna do us on the hunger march? You don' think they'll sponsor us, by any chance?' There was a ragged laugh.

'No, I don't,' she reported, 'but somehow I don't think it would be so easy to ignore the state we're in if the papers got shots of us close up to that lot, us in our marching togs, just off the road, them got up like four-penny rabbits for an evening out.'

Damn it all, she's probably right, thought Henderson. That would shame some of the toughest nuts . . . She was talking again. 'Now in case you haven't studied your London street maps, I'll refresh your memories. We're planning to march into Hyde Park on arrival. Piccadilly's just down the bottom there, and guess what's half-way along Piccadilly? The Ritz, that's what – even posher than the Savoy if anything. How about it, boys? How about storming the Ritz?'

They were with her now. Jim Prothero said: 'I get the picture – no shouting and stamping, eh, Lily? Just quiet dignity . . . silent vigil, like . . . '

'Got it in one! We don't want anyone calling us an unruly rabble or that'd destroy our case. Well? Are you all game?'

'Yes!' they boomed with one voice.

'Peter – if you'm willing to forget your Blackshirts for five minutes, you can be a real help. Can your political boys get photographers there? No point in playing to an empty house, is there?'

He grinned. 'All right, you win. I'm with you – this time. But next time it might be another matter. Yes, I think I can lay something on.'

After that it was the usual straight strategic planning. Which towns and villages along the route would offer them hospitality. Where the best overnight stops might be. How they should return from London. Was there any point in a petition to Parliament this time? The march was scheduled for October. Peter volunteered his usual advance trip, particularly important this time if he was to persuade a couple of press photographers to turn up at the Ritz. After that, the meeting ended. No one headed for the pub. They could not have scraped together enough for a half-pint of bitter between them that evening. They shuffled off to the institute reading room or the billiard tables. At least it was warm in the institute, and there was company, and light.

Lily walked down the steps with Peter. A fine September moon sailed high over the village against a velvet sky. She sighed. 'It always looks so rich,' she said. 'Hard to believe it's looking down on such a bankrupt world, ennit?'

He was gazing at her intently. 'How have you been?' he asked, all abrasiveness gone from his voice now. 'Charles told me about David. How is he today?'

She blinked two or three times and swallowed hard before she was able to answer. 'Too good for me by arf,' she said fiercely. 'How do he hang on, Peter? I'll never understand it. What was it the specialist give him? A coupla years at most? That was nearly nine years ago, and the poor sod is still yer – and Christ, I do know he wishes he wasn't!'

'Is it so bad for him?'

'You're a doctor, mun. D'you need to ask?'

He shook his head. 'I just . . . somehow, hoped . . . '

'No. Fight, fight, fight, every step o' the way. And the really terrible thing is, all he do care for is this life insurance policy that would help me a bit if he was gone! He really wants to die, Peter, and he can't. He ent fighting to stay alive . . . just fighting . . . '

'Do you have to get straight back, or would you like to come for a stroll – blow away the cobwebs?'

She gazed up at him, longingly. 'We both know what that means, don't we?' she said, very quietly.

'Do we? It's been such a long time now, I was beginning to wonder whether it had ever happened at all.'

'Oh, Peter! It could be a hundred years and I'd feel the same about you. I may a lost you as soon as I found you, but I've been as true as if you were always by my side. Isn't it the same for you?'

'I never see any other woman but you, Lily. I'll wait for you forever if I have to.'

'You might, too, love. I still lie awake and think of us together – like that – and him, back yer in the village, coughing and drowning in his own phlegm. Dunno if I could ever lie down with you again and not feel his poor worn-out corpse between us.'

Her sepulchral tone made Henderson shiver. 'Don't say such things! You know he's a fine man. He'd have killed me for stealing you away when he was your big strong husband, but he'd be the first to say you need a man to love you and look after you when he's gone.'

'I know, but it ent his conscience, is it? It's mine.'

They had been walking down the village street as they talked, and now he stopped, in a patch of dark shadow where the little path to the distillery pond left the metalled road, and put his hands on her shoulders. 'I think you'd find you could live with your conscience, Lily, if you gave it another try. You're not going to save your poor, doomed David now, and God knows you've been a good wife to him since that one slip. Come down to the Swan with me, now. Don't question the invitation, just come. Sit down in the peace and quiet. Have a drink. Talk to me. And then let's just take it from there. We're not going to hurt your David any more than life has hurt him already . . . ' and he bent and kissed her gently on the mouth.

Lily uttered a little groan and leaned against him momentarily, as if he could remove all the troubles of the world from her shoulders. 'Aye, all right. Why not?' she said tiredly. 'I've had a real basinful these past few weeks.' She managed a smile and the old Lily started to surface again. 'As if everything else wasn't enough, our Mam have decided Angharad is too good to marry a miner!'

'What with the present unemployment rate around here, I'm amazed she can still find one!' said Henderson.

'Oh, Mam can always drum up a bitta trouble given the ghost of a chance. Angharad's just as bad as her, that's what worries me. The kid is going to have a rotten time of it if she ent careful.' She pondered the eccentricities of her family and then chuckled. 'You never guess what brought it on! Angharad landed herself a part in some tin-pot drawing room comedy the chapel dramatic society was putting on, *The Abercarn Heiress*. Angharad plays our young heroine – only she says it hair-ess – and I think she's really started seeing herself as one a the leisured class. Anyway, she's now threatening to learn shorthand and typing and go off and find herself a rich businessman husband. Mam's delighted, o' course.'

'Really? I thought your mother preferred to keep her offspring in the nest.'

'Oh, yes, but there's no real danger of Angharad going. It's all just a pretty daydream. Where the devil would Mam get the money for a shorthand-typing course?'

They had begun walking again, towards Henderson's surgery and house near the old Swan Inn south of the village. They had moved apart as soon as they emerged into the dim glare of the street lamps, and could have been any pair of friends casually discussing the small events of their day. Only they could feel the steel band of desire which fastened them together, and they both knew they could no longer fight it.

Peter had been visiting his political friends in London more and more often since the 1934 rally at Olympia. At first he had told himself it was merely to build a web of contacts to support and comfort the miners when they brought their campaign to the capital. But eventually, with only two marches in the two years that involved representatives from the Monmouthshire Valleys, he was forced to admit he was hotter for the fight against international Fascism than home-grown poverty. He went on attending miners' support group meetings at Abercarn, but that was as much to see Lily as for his ideals. His political heart was pledged to a more violent fight than the war of attrition being waged by the miners.

Now it was time to go off again, this time with a high heart at the prospect of arranging secret meetings with Lily along the march route, if not in London itself. He had telephoned Ben Abramovitz a couple of days before to say he planned a visit.

'Good boy!' said Ben. 'Make it this week. We need all the help we can get.'

'Why? What's happening?'

'Need you ask? Blackshirts again. They're planning a damned great show of strength through the East End on Sunday. The excuse is that Mosley wants to review the faithful. Of course, the review will need them to march through the heart of the Jewish streets. We're not standing for it.'

Henderson laughed ruefully. 'I'm supposed to be

coming to drum up support for the miners, Ben, but I admit I'm tempted.'

'You'll get plenty of opportunity to do that. Should be able to chat with a few sympathetic press men, too, and that won't do your miners any harm. How about it?'

And that was how Peter Henderson finished up behind a makeshift brick barrier formed around an overturned lorry, hearing for the first time the slogan which was to change his life – 'They shall not pass!'

'I'd be a lot less worried if the bastard was just an old-fashioned anti-Semite,' said Ben. 'That sort tends to knock Jews about when they cross his path and insult them when they don't, but it doesn't amount to much more. Mosley's realised he can use the Jews to scare a lot of people into supporting him who wouldn't touch him otherwise. He spouts all this rubbish about Jews and Communists conspiring to make the inner cities ungovernable, then he deliberately marches his biff-boys into the main Jewish slum areas, knowing the Jews'll have to defend themselves against the attack. The minute there's a scuffle between a few Blackshirts and a couple of our boys, you can guarantee there'll be publicity in the right-wing press about the Commie agitators running out of control. He seriously thinks he can get the majority of ordinary people behind him with that claptrap!'

'I'm glad to hear you don't seem to share his faith. I sometimes wonder.'

'Not a chance! Two great things about this country, from my point of view, anyway: first, you slung out all your Jews in the Middle Ages and didn't let them back in again until it was really too late to make them bogeymen like they became in Eastern Europe. Second, the closest this place ever got to Red Revolution, the 1926 strike, the middle classes treated it like a game of cricket and saved England from the spectre of Marxism. In their hearts, they all know us Reds'll never win, and that the Jews simply aren't a threat to them. You can't persuade people to let you run a police state over their heads when they think like that.'

Peter's politics had always been considerably less good-humoured than Ben's. He enjoyed the firebrand element of Marxism. He liked to think of old-fashioned privilege being swept away in a dramatic struggle; and he had a weakness for seeing Mosley and his like as sinister monsters instead of aberrant laughing stock. Abramovitz often tried to persuade him that laughter was a far more effective weapon against the Blackshirts than untempered belligerence, but he was preaching a lost cause.

Now Peter sighed in exasperation. 'If they're so unimportant in the main scheme of things, why are you all so determined to get out on the streets and fight them? According to your view they'll be blown away by history tomorrow or next week.'

Ben grinned broadly. 'That, my friend, is history. When I aim a kick at a Blackshirt's head, it's good old-fashioned revenge. Hath not a Jew fists?'

October 4th had been set by Mosley back in July as the day when he would take his followers on a triumphal march through the East End, stopping four times on the way to make speeches. Every mounted policeman in London and six thousand foot constables were drafted into East London for the event. The residents had little faith that it would be sufficient to protect them, and anyway by now many were itching to avenge the insults these political thugs had been heaping on them throughout the last few years.

The parade was to start from Royal Mint Street, after Mosley's first speech. By mid-afternoon, with the speech in full swing, more than one hundred thousand opponents of the Blackshirts had crammed themselves into the city block south of Whitechapel Road, bounded by Commercial Road, Cable Street, Leman Street and Cannon Street Road. Mosley inspected his two thousand Blackshirts and they formed up to march off. Then the police discovered that their route along Cable Street had been blocked by an overturned lorry. The barrier was reinforced with the bricks which had comprised the lorry's load, and which were now being put to use as a defensive wall and stock-piled as impromptu weapons.

The resistance was by no means exclusively Jewish. Much of it came from enraged Wapping dockers, who combined a loathing of Fascism with an almost equal resentment of the Metropolitan Police Force.

The police moved in to clear the barricade, and all hell broke loose. Peter Henderson and Ben were with detachments of fit, youngish men with experience of physical fights against the Blackshirts, their orders to filter down the side streets and attack the Fascists' flanks. By the time they emerged from a deeply-shadowed lane into the October sunlight of the main street, the battle was in full swing. Stones were flying, women were shrieking, and defeated demonstrators and policemen were fleeing for their lives all over the place.

Earlier that summer, far away in Spain, another, bigger, struggle against Fascism had broken out when right-wing forces under Francisco Franco had mounted an attack on the legitimate left-wing republican government. Half those who now struggled so violently in Cable Street knew of the larger conflict, and that the usurping forces were currently besieging the republicans in Madrid. The slogan of the Madrid defenders was 'No pasaran!' – 'They shall not pass!' Now, for the first time, Peter heard it used on an English street, in his own language. Someone among the scuffling dockers and policemen, seeing a weak point in the barricade around the lorry, yelled at the top of his voice: 'Come on comrades – give it to 'em! Remember: They shall not Pass! No pasaran!'

A multitude of voices took it up, until it thundered on the afternoon air – 'They shall not pass! They shall not Pass! No pasaran!'

The phrase, in its two languages, hammered through Peter Henderson's skull and it was like a Road to Damascus conversion. He had been waiting his whole life for this. He had not been preparing just to clear this

143

minor scum from the streets of East London, or to try and win fleabite concessions for starving miners from an uncaring government. He was alive to smash dictatorship, of whatever party, and then to help the deprived rebuild a decent world from the ashes. *'No pasaran!'* he heard his own voice as if it were that of a stranger, *'No – pasaran – no – pasaran – no – pasaran!'*

'Hey, Pete, remember me? We're not in Spain now, so grab this piece a wood and start separating those sods before they kill Dave!' It was Ben, dragging him back to a reality which, God knew, was exciting enough. But Peter went through the rest of the battle in a hallowed daze. He had found his Grail and the minute he could escape, he intended to go and claim it.

CHAPTER SIXTEEN

The week the marchers set out from South Wales for yet another appeal to the nation's conscience, a procession which swamped all memory of their campaign started from the North-eastern town of Jarrow. On the road, Lily read the detailed accounts of the daily progress of the north-country men and knew they could hope for no similar coverage. Nonetheless she felt incapable of resentment of this other band of paupers. Jarrow was the town that had been murdered but had still refused to die. With its last breath it had put together a march to end all marches and had sent it snaking off to London, accompanied by 'The Minstrel Boy' played on dozens of tinny mouth organs. If any march could waken the South-East, and the Government, from its shameful indifference, it was this one. Had they themselves not already been on the road, Lily would have suggested calling off their own protest.

Catching her reading the front page report on the Jarrow marchers in the *Daily Herald* one morning, Peter Henderson laughed bitterly and said: 'I don't know how you stand it! Doesn't it make you overflow with futility, just to look at that lot and know they're consigning us to oblivion?'

Lily's expression was inscrutable as she stared back at him. Finally she said: 'I think they'll have got rid of all the breakfast things now, and they'll be having a last cuppa tea before we get going. We were both up on the early rounds, we've earned one, an' all. Come on.'

She led the way inside the modest Gloucestershire church hall which had been their canteen and, partly, their sleeping quarters the previous night, got two mugs of tea and went to sit in a corner far from the local women who were handing out more drinks to those who had already been working that morning. She had not spoken since she suggested they go inside. Now she turned and stared at him again, the intensity of her gaze making him uncomfortable. 'Don't you think you'd better spit out whatever's getting at you?' she asked. 'You've been a changed man since you came back from that last London trip. What have gone wrong, Peter?'

His dismissive laugh sounded nervous, even in his own ears. 'Wrong? Why, nothing particularly. We're all under quite a strain – you and me especially. I expect it's just that.'

'Rubbish! It's something big and you know it. You've even changed towards me. Whatever the politics was, before that London do you could never wait to get hold of me – touch me, brush your hand on my hair – anything. Now you go half-way round the houses to avoid it.'

He stared down at the rough, splintery floorboards and said nothing. There was no acceptable explanation to offer. After a while, Lily went on: 'I know it ent just you going off me. God knows, that worries me, with all these political shenanigans we push down each other's throats when we should be whispering sweet nothings, but you've cooled down towards what we're all working for even worse than you have towards me.'

'Why should you say that?' His tone was excessively sharp.

'Why shouldn't I? You been like a cat on hot bricks the last coupla weeks. You used to love the workers, Peter, remember, call them natural aristocrats? Now you've started treating them like slow children – and slow children who are going all out to stop you achieving anything, at that.'

His irritability dissolved. He could never stay angry with Lily for long, particularly when, as now, it was unjustified. 'Oh, Lily, I know it isn't them! It's me. I'm going stale on everything I believe in, doing small, insignificant things when there are so many bigger dragons to fight.'

Her face seemed to close against him. 'That do sound awfully like the beginning of a big farewell speech to me.'

'I-I don't mean to sound like that . . . don't even know myself yet what I can do. I only know I'm not getting anywhere at this.'

'Liar! You're a bloody liar. There *is* something, or somebody, maybe. You just ent willing to tell me, that's all. You've got impatient with things before, but never like this. I've seen men getting ready to flit, and that's what you're doing now, so at least have the decency to be honest about it.'

'I-it's just that I don't know how to start . . . I need to be somewhere I can fight big battles, Lily, not the little day-to-day struggles of downtrodden people who'll never win unless we can change the whole world.'

A look of resignation replaced the anger on Lily's face. 'Ah, you needn't say much more, except when. It's Spain, ennit?'

That really took him by surprise. 'How on earth did you guess?'

'How do a reindeer know when Christmas is coming? Because it do start bloody snowing, of course! Peter, you haven't talked about anything except Spain ever since that Cable Street business. I've had the "They shall not pass!" speech till I wake up muttering it in the middle of the night. Christ, don't men *ever* grow up?'

'Now you've lost me completely.'

'I know I have, love, in more ways than one. This bit is simple, though. It's a hard, thankless job, seeing people stay alive and keep their hopes up day after day; convincing Valleys mothers it's for the best when their boys go off and walk to Redditch or Slough looking for work; comforting a woman when her husband kills himself with a bottle a Lysol 'cos he can't face another week picking coal off the tips and queuing to see if the Means Test have cut his money again. Trouble is, it's the most important job in the world – and you'd prefer to get your arse blown off by a Fascist bullet in someone else's struggle because you feel bored with all the poverty and unemployment in South Wales. Not arf as bloody bored as those poor buggers, mun – and they got dependants so they *can't* escape.'

'That's plain nonsense! What happens in Spain now will affect everyone's lives – theirs as much as yours and mine – more than anything else that's happening now.'

'Believe that an' you believe anything.'

'I believe in it so much, Lily, that I'm throwing up everything to go and do it. I've been agonising over it, weighing up what I stand to lose . . . and however much home and home ties matter, that's where I have to go. I just have to hope I'll find something of it waiting for me when I come back – you in particular.'

She had turned her face away from him while he spoke but now her head snapped round as she faced him again. 'Well, yes, a course . . . I'll be waiting, good old Lily, another coupla years older, another few dreams crushed . . . but Lily can stand it. Oh, yes! Lily's so strong. Couldn't manage without her! Don't you ever think I get sick a that – sick to the stomach? Don't you ever think *I* wanna run off and build a castle in Spain?'

'Lily – that's not fair! You talk as if I'm ducking out, just to rush off on a Boys' Own adventure.'

'Well, ent you?'

Now he was the one who turned away, his emotions an impossible mixture of outrage, shame and other unnameable things. 'If you refuse to understand, I see no purpose in our going on talking about this,' he said, not looking at her.

There was a slight rustle of clothing as she stood up. 'And *I* don't see no purpose in us going on at all,' she said. Then she walked out of the church hall, carefully placing her empty mug on the trestle-table and thanking the tea-makers as she went.

They remained distant from each other for the remainder of the march. Until then, on the first two nights, they had slipped away and found dark corners where they could be together after everyone had gone to sleep. That first night, Henderson waited in vain outside the school-room where the dozen or so women marchers were billeted. It was the same in Reading, and in Maidenhead. In Hayes, it was like old home week, because so many exiled South Welshmen who worked there turned out to greet their compatriots. No one got much sleep that night, some anonymous benefactor having donated a couple of crates of pale ale for the pleasure of the marchers. Even in the steamy good fellowship of yet another church hall, Lily did not unbend towards Peter. She sat among a group of people who had migrated from Abercarn five years before, swapping gossip, jokes and reminiscences. At the end of the little party, she passed Henderson on her way to the sleeping quarters as if he did not exist.

Kate Le Mesurier and Daphne Francis were dawdling over their tea at the Ritz. They had lunched and shopped together that day, but both of them had got hold of some fascinating snippets of gossip and they were far too interested in the latest scandals among their friends to want to separate yet. As they dissected yet another mutual acquaintance, Daphne said: 'If this little session goes on much longer, darling, we shall be going on from tea to cocktails without noticing the join.'

'I know, but such a pity to stop when one is enjoying oneself so much . . . do try another of these little sandwiches. Particularly delicious as an accompaniment to the demolition of Diana!' She uttered the tinkling little laugh she had been assured was thoroughly alluring, then realised it was falling into the sort of silence which occurred only in cathedral services and on great state occasions. 'Really,' she said, 'was it something I said?'

Then she turned and looked up. There, in front of her, stood a phenomenon which was so common outside as to become invisible. There were three of them, clad in boots which were about to disintegrate, their skinny bodies wrapped in old overcoats which had grown grotesquely oversized for their shrinking frames as they stopped eating properly. Their trousers were threadbare and they wore mufflers instead of collars and ties. On their heads were cloth caps, which looked as over-large as the coats, for much the same reason. A mouth organ dangled aimlessly from one man's hand. South Wales had come to the Ritz and found it hard to believe what it was seeing.

Dick Edwards nudged Bill Pugh, the one with the mouth organ, and muttered: 'Stop gawpin', mun – we'm supposed to be dignified protestors, not village idiots, innit?'

'But looka them curtains, Dick! I never saw no curtains like that in the pictures, let alone in a pub!'

'T'ent a pub, iss an hotel, the smartest one in the world. That's why we'm yer, remember? Now bloody behave!'

The photographer had slightly mistimed his arrival and the three miners were forced to stand where they were, waiting for their moment of immortality. A couple of members of staff began moving towards them, as unobtrusively as possible, but clearly half-believing that against all appearances, these were dangerous savages who might start attacking the tea-drinkers at any moment. The gilded boiserie and delicate green paintwork of the Ritz, the opulent deep-pile carpet and the brilliant table linen, threw the terrible reality of these men's poverty into high relief in a way no pavement scene could ever have achieved.

Kate shakily put down her cup, and said, very quietly for once, 'Dear God – I don't think I ever realised anyone could be that poor and survive.'

For a long, magic moment, the pain and the dignity of the three men percolated to the gilded world into which they had stumbled so temporarily. Then the spell was broken. Flashbulbs popped and the moment was captured for the next day's papers. A furious head waiter drew level with the men and somehow managed to shoo them out without resorting to anything which would provide the photographers with sensational shots of the Ritz oppressing the poor. That ended the incident.

All over the vestibule, people were gathering in scandalised groups, wondering long and loud what those dreadful Red agitators would do next. Daphne bounded to her feet. 'I say, Katie, we can't just go home after that! We must go and tell about it! Come along – I expect Margaret Vickers is at home . . . '

But Kate remained seated. She could not expunge from her mind the memory of that limp, emaciated hand, swinging pointlessly from its worn-out coat sleeve and holding the cheapest mouth organ money could buy. Finally she managed a shaky smile. 'No thank you, darling. I really don't feel too bright all of a sudden. I think I shall just go home. You go round and see Margaret.'

CHAPTER SEVENTEEN

David Richards had been in a light coma for nearly three days. Occasionally he stirred for long enough to murmur a few disjointed words, more often only to cough weakly before drifting down again into unconsciousness. His mother-in-law fussed about in the kitchen next door to his makeshift bedroom, complaining bitterly to Charles Henderson about how little David's wife understood her duty.

'I never agreed with them marches, any way whatever,' she said, 'but for her to go off on one with him this bad . . . I feel ashamed of her, doctor, I really do!'

Henderson strove to maintain his calm. He had violent feelings about the march, too, and Lily was responsible. But his response and the nature of his emotions were quite different from Margaret Ann's. Now he said, with studied patience, 'She feels she's doing something to prevent David's fate overtaking the next generation, Mrs Walters. Perhaps she has a point.'

'Even if she have – and I'm not saying that, mind – she've got a higher duty to her dying husband. Anyhow, it's men's work, making protests like that. How many other women do go on these marches? How many other women have been to prison for their politics?'

'Oh, a surprising number. You shouldn't undervalue what she's doing. David never has. He was always the first to say she should go.'

Margaret Ann assumed her most pious expression. 'That man's a saint – a real saint! He do worship Lily, and he'd do anything to please her. That's all this ever was. He've never been one for politics.'

'Be that as it may, he might have slipped away before Lily gets back. I think that would do terrible things to her. If only there were some easy way to contact her.'

'Not now there ent. They'll be on their way home by now. No telling where they are. I know Haydn had some sort of London address for getting in touch, but it will be too late for that. How long, d'you suppose?' As she asked her question she indicated with a nod of her head the room where David lay dying.

'I should think he'll last another twenty-four hours, but no more. Having said that, though, I'm forced to remember he should have been dead before 1930, according to the best prognosis I or anyone else was able to make when this disease first showed up. He may yet surprise us all.'

'If only he could see her again, talk to her one last time.'

Henderson sighed, exasperated. 'Mrs Walters, there's no question of that, even if Lily walked through that door in the next ten minutes. He is in an irreversible coma. He will gradually weaken from now on, perhaps with a few spasms of coughing or retching, then simply stop breathing. When I mentioned trying to get Lily home quickly, it was the thought of comforting her by enabling her to be with him at the end, not of making his last moments easier. He's beyond all that now.'

'So in other words he have died alone.'

Henderson was finding it increasingly difficult to keep his temper. 'No, that is *not* what I'm saying. He was conscious when your daughter went off on the march. They had an hour together just before she left. I remember vividly, because I had to ask her to come out of the room to let me give him an injection. It was barely an hour after that when he started to deteriorate. If you want to conjure up romantic deathbed scenes, that will stand in.'

'If I'd known it was that close, I'd never have let her go gallivanting off!'

'Really? I'm fairly sure they both knew. In fact, I think

David felt it relieved his last hours of the worry of having Lily suffer on his behalf if he had a lingering end.' He glanced at his watch. 'There's little more I can do now, Mrs Walters, and I have two more calls to make. I'm sorry you feel so strongly about Lily, but for what it's worth, I think she's been doing what both she and David think is right. They are the only ones who truly count in this matter.'

Lily felt empty and almost light-headed as she walked up the road from Abercarn station. The rest of the Abercarn representatives from the Means Test march had stayed in Newport to attend a meeting where they would report their progress. She had backed out of this in order to go home and see David. She knew he must be very near the end now. And there was another reason why she needed to be away from other people for a while. Peter Henderson had not returned from London. He had gone to meet a group of Communist friends and together they had departed to volunteer as soldiers. By now her lover was well on his way to Spain.

There was to be a small welcoming committee to greet the main delegation, but she was alone when she got off the train at Abercarn. Nobody expected her yet.

As she headed for the Ranks, she thought over the events of their latest mass protest. It had achieved precisely what all the others had achieved: nothing. The Ritz photographs had turned out well and had been featured in the newspapers the day after they staged the incident, but now she wondered what she had expected to emerge from that. The scene in the Ritz had proved to be the high point of the march. Once it was over, they completed their mission with the usual activities – mainly lobbying members of Parliament and pleading for some action to improve the lot of the poor. But even the mighty Jarrow protest had failed to move anyone who mattered. It looked as if they were all doomed to scrape along in misery until their whole society was shaken up by outside forces.

Was I too hard on Peter after all? she wondered. Maybe he's thinking straight and I'm not . . . maybe bloody revolution is the only way. But she knew that was not her reason for breaking with Henderson. Every grain of fairness in her had rebelled against the idea that it was acceptable to abandon the miners as a lost cause and go off to a more glamorous fight. Lily knew she was right about the miners having no choice whether they stuck to the struggle. In her eyes, Henderson was cheating by using his privileged position to escape when the truth of their desperate situation became unpalatable to him.

She glanced up the road and for a moment her eyes deceived her. He hadn't gone after all! There he was, hurrying down to meet her . . . then her mind cleared. It was Charlie, not Peter at all! Charlie, looking distraught. Could he know already what his brother had in mind? Abruptly she quickened her pace, anxious to get close to him, to comfort him.

But it was not she who comforted Henderson. As he reached her, he put his arms about and embraced her. 'Lily, my darling girl. I had hoped to save you this. For once your timing is too good.'

'I don't understand, Charlie. What have happened?'

'David. He's slipping away. Oh, my dear, I am so sorry. I was hoping to spare you this last pain. There's really nothing . . . '

But she was no longer with him. She had dropped the small knapsack which contained her marching gear and was running, running like a young girl, up the back of the Ranks, beside the canal. Henderson picked up the little bag, sighed and turned to follow her. He knew precisely what lay ahead.

As he walked through the open door of the Richards' house he heard her cry out – one long, animal howl, ululating for agonising seconds on the still afternoon air. Then silence. He entered the parlour–bedroom. Richards lay dead, his head arched backwards, as if still fighting for a last gasp of air. Lily knelt on the floor beside the bed, grasping his yellow, parchment-skinned hand

155

between both of hers. Henderson moved across to her and put his own hands on her shoulders.

'Lily, you know as well as I do that you said your proper goodbyes before you went off to London. Both of you knew he was unlikely to last much longer. I practically spelled it out.'

'But you've said it so many times, and he've still rallied. I thought, this time . . . '

'No, Lily. You had only to look at him. There was nothing left. Come on, now, out to the kitchen. Your mother will look after you.'

She nodded and got painfully to her feet, following him outside like a lost child. In the kitchen, Margaret Ann's demeanour was transformed. Lily's arrival home had killed any chance that the neighbours would gossip and that was what had bothered her above all else. Now she was full of solicitude. Lily sat down and dutifully sipped hot, sweet tea. Then she delivered the hammer blow which was to set Henderson himself reeling.

'You don't know the rest, yet, Charlie. It's your Peter. He've gone to Spain. Went on the boat last night. I don't think he's ever gonna come back.'

Peter Henderson was killed by a revolver bullet in his left temple in a night-time skirmish outside the town of Teruel, four weeks after he arrived in Spain.

PART THREE

And when he had opened the seventh seal,
there was silence in heaven for
about the space of half an hour.

Revelation Ch. 8, v.1.

CHAPTER EIGHTEEN

Cardiff, 1936

'I dunno whose home you'm going to, flower, your own or someone else's, but you ent staying here, so hop it!'

Lexie Walters was standing over the three drinkers who lingered in the corner at the back of the bar, and talking to the man nearest her. He beamed tipsily: 'No need for that, no need at all . . . can't a chap take 'is time over the last pint?'

'I hate to carp,' said Lexie, 'but none of you 'as been within sniffin' distance of a pint all night – you been nursing halves – and I don't see how even you lot could take much more time over the eyefuls you got in them glasses.'

The man's cheerfulness vanished. 'All right, if that's how you feel, we'll go. I can remember a time when there was always a welcome in this pub, no matter what time a night or day you come in, and no shoving you out the minute time was called, neither.'

'Yeah, well we was all better off in them days, weren't we? And you weren't drinking halves then, either – more like large whiskies. It's less worrying to risk your licence after hours on spirits than a coupla after-hours glasses of shandy – so *drink up*!'

Grumbling, they swallowed the dregs from their glasses and filed out through the door. Lexie heaved a vast sigh of relief and threw the bolt home. A sudden noise from the corner startled her and she glanced around. He was sitting in the darkest part of the bar, half-concealed by a monstrous old coat rack Lexie had never got round to throwing out, obviously trying to occupy the smallest possible space in an effort to escape notice. She had only seen him now because he had coughed. 'Oi, darling,' she said, 'you heard what I told that lot. It goes for you an' all. Now sling your hook!'

'Yes . . . yes, I am sorry . . . I just . . . I was . . . ' his explanation tailed off and he shrugged philosophically. 'Very well. I am going. I am sorry you 'ave to open the door again.'

She never knew whether it was his politeness, the irresistible French accent, or the state he was in which was responsible for what happened next. Maybe it was all three. As he moved to pass her, he staggered and put his hand against the table to steady himself. Oh, gawd, she thought, tight as a tick. We really do get 'em. But he was not drunk, merely too weak to walk steadily. Now, attempting to continue his exit unsupported, he stumbled again and fell. Something in the disjointed shape of him as he collapsed prevented Lexie from haranguing him where he lay. Instead she squatted beside him and pressed a hand to his forehead.

'My God, chum, you're burning up!' she said. 'Look, if this is just booze, I'll kill you when you get sober . . . but somehow I don't think it is,' she murmured to herself as she went over to the bar for some water.

He gulped it down and smiled ruefully at her. Lexie helped him up and pushed him into a seat. 'Okay, what's up with you?' she said.

He looked sheepish. 'I am really very sorry,' he repeated. 'It is not your affair. Nothing you 'ave not seen before. I finish the water and go.'

'Well you certainly don't *smell* drunk.'

He shook his head, still smiling. 'I could not afford water tonight, let alone anything stronger. I lost my job. I am starving . . . please, I do not mean to be a beggar. I hoped to hide over there because it is so cold outside. I thought . . . '

'Oh, who the hell am I trying to kid?' said Lexie. 'I'm about as tough as a marshmallow. God help you if this is a con, but I don't think so.' She crossed to the inner door to the living quarters, opened it and bawled up the stairs: 'Dad! Have we got enough soup for an extra one?'

Rhys's tones sang back, 'Yeah, 'course! Nice to 'ave a bitta company!'

'Can you walk upstairs?' she asked the visitor.

'I think so.'

'Right. You go first, then. If you fall, I'm nice an' soft to land on!'

'You tempt me, Madame, but I always try to be a gentleman!' Even in extremis, he was able somehow to preserve a touch of Gallic gallantry and Lexie felt a flood of extra compassion for this man who could retain his dignity in wretched circumstances.

She had already killed most of the lights down in the bar when she discovered the Frenchman, and had not taken a good look at him. Now, as she got him into the brighter light upstairs, she uttered a gasp of alarm. The poor sod looked half dead! As the thought formed, her father emerged from the kitchen, smiling companionably, to meet whoever she had brought up. As he caught sight of the new arrival, his smile froze. 'Christ, kidda, where d'you find the poor devil? Get 'im in there before he do fall!' And he stood back as Lexie ushered their guest into the living room.

The Frenchman was shivering uncontrollably now, still with the apologetic smile pasted on his face. 'Sit down by there – go on, close as you can get to the fire,' ordered Lexie. 'I hope your heart's up to this, because without it I ent sure the rest of of you will come through the night!' And she flipped open the cupboard where Rhys kept his private stock of spirits, seized a bottle of brandy and sloshed a large measure into a tumbler. The Frenchman took it and gulped at the brown fluid, his teeth chattering against the side of the glass as he drank. Lexie stood back impassively throughout the lengthy spasm of coughing which inevitably followed, then watched him finish the brandy.

'There, that's better. Never expect nothing in this house except kill-or-cure remedies. Like my cousin Lil

161

always used to say, there's only two sorts down the Bay, the quick an' the dead. Let's assume you intend staying with the first lot, shall we?'

She knew he was starting to recover when the terrible, beaten smile faded. She had seen men with that expression, begging on street corners and sleeping rough around the old abandoned warehouses along the dock. It was a last-ditch effort to please, to prove themselves acceptable when everyone had rejected them. And it never worked. Now the man leaned back against the comfortable upholstery of the shabby old sofa, closed his eyes and sighed as if taking his last breath. Lexie said nothing, merely perching on the arm of the sofa, near enough to help if he got worse. Eventually he passed a hand across his forehead and looked up at her.

'Why are you helping me?' he asked.

'Because I'm either an undercover worker for the Sally Army or recruiting bouncers for a South American brothel. You gorra guess which.'

'No one has been good to me for so long . . . I had almost forgotten . . . '

'That's always the worst part, ennit, mate? P'raps that's why. I know the feeling too. Look, stop worrying about tonight and tomorrow, at least. We'll give you some food an' a bed and then sort you out. Think that'll help?'

'That you offer it helps more than anything.'

Don't cry, you stupid bitch, she thought, standing up hurriedly and turning back towards the landing. 'I'd better see what my old villain of a dad have done with that soup. Don't go away, now.'

In the kitchen, Rhys was ladling fragrant Welsh cawl into three big earthenware bowls. 'Is he gonna be able to take this, Lex? Looked as if gruel woulda been too much for him when I seen him out there.'

'Amazing what your cognac does for a chap on a cold night!' she said, chuckling.

He regarded her like a mournful bloodhound. 'Lex! You didn't . . . '

'Dad, I did. With your blood pressure it don't do you no good at all, and it didn't arf 'elp him.'

He put an arm around her and patted her shoulder. 'You'm a good girl, even if you're the bossiest kid as ever walked. Why don' you go an' see if Georgia have settled down while I'm doing this?'

Georgia was peering sleepily over her bedclothes when Lexie looked into the room. 'Who was it with that lovely voice?' she asked. 'I always wanted to learn to talk like that.'

Lexie moved across and pushed her back down into the bed, smoothing the child's hair and lightly caressing her cheek. 'The way you look, you'll soon be jail-bait enough without that sort of accent into the bargain! Come on, now, settle down. He's just a visitor who've come for supper and to spend the night. You can listen to 'im all you like tomorrow.'

Back in the living room, Rhys had put bowls, bread, glasses and bottles of stout on the table, and was holding a chair for the Frenchman, who was still moving very feebly. 'Ah, yer's Lex,' he said, looking up. 'Lexie, meet Jean-Baptiste Berard, master chef and knight of the road.'

Lexie's eyes widened. 'You're a master chef and you're in this state? Now that *must* be a story!'

A genuine smile now curved his well-shaped mouth. 'Oh, it is! I think I can sing for my supper, if I can do nothing else.'

'Well, let's have the supper first, mate, or you may not be fit for it,' responded Rhys. 'Oh, and by the way, take a tip from one who've been in your state more than once, and don't gulp your food. Some of it may come up anyway, after, but all of it will if you hog it on an empty belly.'

Jean-Baptiste nodded. Lexie broke in: 'One thing, flower, if you puke on the rug up yer, it won't be a great tragedy.' She looked down at the threadbare object. 'Might even add a bitta colour,' she observed darkly.

'Lex! Shurrup. You'll put the poor sod off his food

before he do even start. Come on, eat your supper. You must be bloody peckish, an' all.'

They all set to and ate the soup – the unthickened traditional broth which was cooked throughout Wales to stretch fragile budgets to feed big families. Neck of mutton, onion, leek, swede, carrots, potatoes and parsnips were diced and cooked in large quantities of water until the meat was tender and pulpy, and its richness had permeated the liquid. For the poorer families, the soup pot did double duty on the second day with a top-up of vegetables but no more meat. Harassed mothers everywhere swore the stock gave an illusion there was still meat somewhere in the stew. Their children knew better, but at least it was food.

The Walterses did better than that, but they still ate cawl at least twice a week to spin out an income from the pub which had shrunk alarmingly as the decade advanced. Rhys often thanked his lucky stars that he had taken up an offer from the brewery to sell him the freehold of the Anglesey which had coincided with a substantial win at the races. Had he been no more than a tenant, he was not at all sure he could have kept a roof over their heads.

Rhys had slowed down a lot, but that was hardly surprising, he often reflected. He was seventy-eight this year, and had never been renowned for taking care of himself. His idea of a good time had always involved too much alcohol, food, sex and tobacco. The sex was only a golden memory these days, and he had given up the tobacco and cut back on the drink, but he had assumed the damage was already done by the time he got round to such remedial treatment. Apparently not. He tired easily, but still ran the domestic side of their ménage while Lexie looked after the pub. After a series of dizzy spells a couple of years before, even Rhys had been forced to admit that was too much for him now.

On balance, he was a happy man. Life had treated him well, and when his time came he would go easily, he often thought. His one reservation was a nagging anxiety about what the future held for Lexie and Georgia – especially

Georgia. Lexie had proved she was as tough as tempered steel, but Georgia was small and soft and innocent and they had both protected her so far. How would she ever manage alone without a cushion of family support behind her?

Rhys shrugged mentally and returned to his supper. No point in worrying over what you couldn't remedy. P'raps something would come up before he bowed out. His good luck had always come from unexpected sources in the past. In the meantime, they had a guest – an interesting one, too, it appeared – and he was one hell of a lot worse off than they were. Rhys turned his attention back to Jean-Baptiste, who was mopping the last of the cawl from his bowl with a big chunk of bread.

'Bit more bread an' a chunk of cheese hurt him, d'you think, Dad?' said Lexie.

Rhys shook his head. 'Shouldn't think so, not if he do take it slow. That went down all right, didn't it, But?'

Jean-Baptiste's smile was radiant. 'The best food I ever ate! After that, yes – I think I even manage some of your terrible English cheese!'

Father and daughter glared at each other indignantly for a second and then burst out laughing at the Frenchman's effrontery. 'Bloody Frogs! Give 'em an inch an' they take a kilometre!' said Rhys.

Jean-Baptiste had the grace to laugh at himself. 'I am sorry – old habits and tastes die hard, you know.'

'Speaking of which, as you don't look ready to collapse yet, I think it's time you paid for your supper and told us what happened to bring you down to hiding behind the hatstand in a down-at-heel Tiger Bay pub on a cold winter night,' said Lexie, opening a second bottle of Guinness.

There was nothing dubious about Jean-Baptiste's claim to be a master cook. He had gone to work in his family's restaurant in the Dordogne valley at the age of fourteen, and, before the age of nineteen, had become a chef of supreme skill, specialising in the rich duck, goose and truffle dishes of his region. Eventually his parents had

165

retired and handed over the business to himself and his elder brother, Edouard. But he and Edouard had never seen eye to eye, and shortly after his father's death they quarrelled bitterly. Jean-Baptiste sold out his interest in the restaurant for a pittance and went to England to try his hand on the grand hotel circuit.

At first all went well. He worked at some of the best hotels in London, but quickly learned that the British system was different from that of France. In France, a top chef was valued whatever his seniority in a large kitchen. In England, it seemed, the head chef was idolised, particularly if he were an Escoffier, but the dozens of only slightly less exalted talents who helped make the reputations of the Escoffiers were anonymous to the upper-class English diners, and doomed to remain that way.

Jean-Baptiste had laboured on for a few years in growing misery, when he heard two people comparing notes about a recent visit to the lower Wye Valley on the South Wales borders, and saying how like the Dordogne it was. Beset by discontent and homesickness, he had taken a short holiday and travelled there, staying at a small country inn near Tintern. He fell in love with the countryside, and with a local girl, found a job in the area and settled there, at a fraction of his London wage but already a happier man.

He had saved his money while working in London, and added it to the nest-egg from selling out his share of the French business to his brother. Now he revived an earlier ambition to open his own restaurant. Alice, his wife, was a farmer's daughter, and eventually she inherited a little money from her grandmother. It was enough. They bought a small, pretty country pub on the main road that carried holidaymakers and racegoers between the Wye Valley and Chepstow, and worked themselves into the ground to establish a successful French restaurant with rooms for overnight guests.

By 1931, in spite of the gloomy economic conditions, they were beginning to see some return on all their effort.

They were still not sufficiently secure to start the family they both wanted, but were close to it. Then, towards the end of that summer, their busiest yet, Alice had taken their little van into Chepstow to pick up a delivery of fruit and vegetables from the wholesalers. On her way back, the van went out of control on one of the hairpin bends that twisted up the valley and plunged over the edge, overturning in the rich meadows that flanked the river. Alice was thrown through the windscreen and killed instantly by a skull fracture.

'All I could think of after the funeral was to escape from that cursed countryside,' said Jean-Baptiste. 'When she died there, it was as if it became my own Périgord country, which had thrown me out all those years before, and now it was doing so again. I wanted to get into a town, lose myself far from anything that reminded me of her, or the business . . . ' He stopped and gazed blankly ahead.

After a while, Rhys prompted gently: 'But that don't explain how you lost the business an' all. Why didn't you just sell up?'

Jean-Baptiste shrugged. 'If you think of an answer, my friend, please tell me. I did not. Even as I decided to leave, a terrible misery fell on me, blacker than my first grief after Alice died. For days I did nothing except sit in our small kitchen upstairs, holding a picture of her, talking to it. I expect I became a little crazy. Sometimes I remembered to eat, sometimes not. I had never been close to my wife's family and after they came a few times and I was rude, they did not come again. Nor did the customers. Sometimes they would not find me open at all. Other times, if I *had* managed to throw something together, it was all so far below my old standard, soon they did not come again either.

'And then the bank came. But *they* did not go away, of course. We had needed to borrow a lot of money to get started, and the property and my skill had been good security. But all that was gone, then. They took everything. That was when I realised my desire to leave the countryside was to be granted. In fact I no longer had a choice.'

After that his downhill path had been inevitable. He had moved on, first to a country inn a few miles outside Cardiff. But although the area was different from the Wye Valley, the rural atmosphere reminded him forcibly of his dead wife and their happiness together. Lacking the initiative to resign and find somewhere with less painful associations, he provoked his fellow workers, insulted his employer and clients, and soon contrived to get himself dismissed.

The next job had been as sous-chef in a high class hotel–restaurant in the centre of Cardiff. That was certainly different from what Jean-Baptiste had known over the previous few years, but it failed to pull him out of his misery. Compared with his former role as owner-chef-entrepreneur, this new job was nothing. He let his contempt show, and within weeks he had made enough enemies to ensure his enforced departure the next time there was a slump in profits.

There were to be no more prestigious jobs. After the hotel, he was a short-order cook in a series of increasingly dowdy roadhouses in and around the city. No one cared when he produced a perfect sauce bearnaise to accompany the tournedos; the chances were that they did not know it was a tournedos and rejected the sauce as what they called fancy foreign muck. Jean-Baptiste sank further into depression and went downhill from job to job.

Finally he was cook at a small, dirty chop-house in Bute Terrace. Even there, he could not entirely let his standards lapse. The proprietor had looked into the kitchen one evening to find him putting a half-pound pat of butter into a saucepan to cook mushrooms for that evening's steak dinners. There was a row – not even a major one, far less impressive than he had known at some other establishments – and Jean-Baptiste had taken to the road for the last time.

This time there was no meaner restaurant to which he

could resort and make a living. He had simultaneously run out of eating houses in the Cardiff area and the initiative to move elsewhere for a fresh start.

He still had a little money – even in the places where he had been working, a man who left the stove only when it was time to go to bed, and did not go out again until he went on duty next day, did not use up the most modest salary. He lived on his haphazard savings until they ran out. Then the boarding-house evicted him and he roamed the streets for a while, spinning out his last pennies on doughnuts and coffee to keep himself warm and give an illusion of being full. When the February cold spell struck dockland, he had been down to his last halfpenny and had not eaten for three days. The hide-out behind the coat rack in the Anglesey had been his last resort against freezing to death.

Lexie's face was blank. 'What're you gonna do now, then?'

He shrugged. 'That I cannot tell. All I know is that you and M'sieur Rhys have brought me back from whereever I was. I needed to know there were still people like you in the world. I wonder why no one ever showed me that before? Now, if I can just get a job, I will be all right.'

Rhys guffawed. 'That'll be the day! There's a bloke on every corner down yer, looking for just the same thing. I know you gorra skill, and a good one, but all those ex-bosses are hardly gonna give you glowing references, are they?'

Jean-Baptiste smiled at him. 'I do not mind. I will try anything until I get a proper chance. You two good people have given me the new hope I needed.'

Lexie was surveying him, a speculative look in her eye. 'He don' look like a bloke who do eat too much to me, do he to you, Dad?' she said eventually.

'Hardly notice 'im, really,' said Rhys.

'Well, Georgia was just saying when I tucked 'er in what a lovely voice Jean-Baptiste have got. What if he helped me down the bar and taught her a bitta French in between? No money, mind,' she added hastily, turning back to Jean-Baptiste. 'Just a roof and food. But it's better than nothing, while you're looking round, like.'

The Frenchman's eyes were shining. 'Very much better, Madame Lexie! I hardly like to accept. I think perhaps you are extending Christian charity.'

Rhys hooted at that. 'Listen, But. In this house, whatever charity it is, Christian en' in it. But it's worth 'aving, just the same. Are you on?'

'I'm on, M'sieur Rhys. When do I start?'

'Soon as you'm strong enough to pull a pint,' said Lexie, 'and looking at you now, I'd say that's at least six weeks away! Just one little thing, though. I dunno how Dad do feel about "M'sieur Rhys", but "Madame Lexie" makes me feel like Black Bet with one foot in the grave. Unless you wanna wake up without your front teeth one morning, I think just plain Lexie would be a bit better.'

He smiled. 'Very well. I will save "Madame Lexie" for when I have made all our fortunes.'

Lexie gave an exaggerated sigh of relief. 'In that case, I'm safe for ever on your present record!'

CHAPTER NINETEEN

Soon it felt as if Jean-Baptiste had always slept in the little back room over the pub and helped in the bar during opening hours. For a couple of years, Lexie and Rhys had been struggling to do the cellar work between them. They had managed, but invariably emerged with Rhys flushed and panting and Lexie furious that she lacked the strength to take this over-demanding task away from her ageing father. Now, within days, Jean-Baptiste learned the knack of tipping the barrels on edge and rolling them into place, to clean and condition the feeder lines from cellar to pump, and generally to get the cellar back into the prime condition it had enjoyed in Rhys's heyday. With painful slowness, the pub picked up a tiny fraction of its former trade.

But still it was not enough, and Rhys grew increasingly conscious that there was no provision for Lexie and Georgie after his death. He would not have minded if he could have looked forward to ten or fifteen more years, but at his age he knew he would be lucky to survive until Christmas.

The presence of Jean-Baptiste Berard made him feel a little better. He was well aware of the sparks that flew between the Frenchman and his daughter, even if Lexie herself seemed not to have noticed it yet, and he hoped that some day there would be another man to look after his little nest of womenfolk. But on its own, that was not enough. Berard had been through the mill. He could reach the heights again, given half a chance, but no man could be reasonably asked to do that from rock bottom, and that was what it would mean for Jean-Baptiste. Rhys decided he needed to pull off some sort of financial coup

171

to set them up. The trouble was that he could see nothing which might provide such a windfall.

Then, one spring day, he was looking after the bar at the quiet time of the afternoon when these days they had very little trade. Jean-Baptiste had gone off with Lexie to see the ridiculous mock lighthouse in the middle of Roath Park lake, set there as a memorial to the Antarctic explorer Captain Scott. Lex said it was longer than she could remember since she had an afternoon out, and had jumped at the invitation. Rhys was secretly delighted. Sooner those two got together the better. He didn't have too much time left to keep an eye on them.

Half-way through the afternoon, he was sitting behind the bar on a backless chair, glancing through the early edition of the *South Wales Echo*. The bar was empty save for two old ex-seamen playing dominoes at one of the back tables.

'Wassamarra, Rhys, takin' a rest cure?' The voice was rasping, familiar, though long half-forgotten. Rhys looked up to see Joe Mathewman eyeing him across the counter.

'God almighty, Joe, I thought the pox or the booze would have got you years ago! What brings you back to these parts?'

'Bloody bad luck, I s'pose,' said Mathewman. 'Thought I'd made my pile back in '28, but it went faster than it come in and I'm back on the old treadmill. Interested?'

'In what, exactly?'

'Well, you know, snow an' that . . . plenty of other stuff about now, an' all. Market's narrower, but them as still buys is spending tons more. We need a quiet depot – something just like the Anglesey, you know, outa the way, private, like. Shouldn't think you've 'ad a raid for ages.'

Rhys snorted in contempt. 'Come off it, Joe! You should know me better than that, even after all these years. I never 'ad a raid down yer all the time I was running my . . . er . . . business interests. A sweetened

172

copper is a non-nosey copper in my book. Always was like that, could be again if it was worth the trouble . . . What have you got in mind?'

What Mathewman had in mind was exactly what Rhys had been dreaming about: a few months, a year, if he lived that long, and there'd be enough to tide the family over until this terrible threadbare time was past. They said there was a war coming, and once that happened . . . Rhys had fond memories of the last international hostilities and the amount of unearned income he had raised from them. Given Jean-Baptiste's talents and Lexie's adaptability, they'd never look back. But he didn't *know* there was a war coming, and he had to provide for them just in case.

'Lexie, I do not like these new customers we are getting. There is something . . . something *gangsterish* about them. I do not understand it.' Jean-Baptiste was looking along the mahogany bar counter at a knot of men in loud suits who stood at the far end, drinking large whiskies.

'You're right, flower, and I *do* understand it. I've seen 'em all before, and I outgrew 'em years ago. I don't like people who profit from the misery of others, even if my Dad is tied up with it.'

'Rhys? Rhys is familiar with these men? I cannot believe it.'

'Well you better had. He ent the same bloke now as he was twenty years ago, and I'm bloody glad an' all. My Georgia softened 'im up a lot. Trouble is, I think it's Georgia who've got him into this.'

'Please? I do not follow you.'

'Course you don't. You don't know the whole story, that's why. In the old days, this pub would sell anything that was too hot for anybody else to handle.'

'You mean, stolen goods?'

Her laugh was bitter. 'Stolen goods, smuggled goods, and drugs. Mainly drugs. And I think it's the drugs that have come back now.'

'Oh. It is something I have only read about.'

173

'I'm glad to hear it, an' all. The Dordogne an' the Wye Valley are hardly hotbeds of that sorta thing, are they? Anyhow, I don't see there's much I can do about it now. Just wish it wasn't happening again, that's all.'

'Why has it anything to do with Georgia?'

'Oh, surely you understand that? He's terrified me an' her'll go to the wall when he snuffs it – an' he's an old man, now, although he looks as strong as a bull. So he's trying to put summat by for when he can't help no more, and he ent too particular about how he gets it.'

'Can't you tell him you do not want money that has come like that?'

'He'd never believe it! Never worried me when I was a kid. I used to take the pocket money and the fancy dresses and drive around in his big car with him – and I knew even then it all come from snow and fencing. I can't suddenly come over Miss Purity just because I'm thirty-eight instead of eighteen, can I?'

'I don't see why not. We are all supposed to learn from experience.'

'Yeah, but don't you see? That's the bloody trouble – Dad *haven't* learned. He'd hold it against me till his dying day if he thought I had.'

'Lexie, I do not understand any of it. Why not assume these men are just here for a drink, and there is nothing bad going on?'

'Because there *is* summat going on – you noticed it as soon as I did. You brought it up, remember? Dad do know I ent daft. He's doing this for me, but there's nothing straightforward about him. He'll only do it for me on the unspoken understanding that I know where it do come from, and then he catches me because I know if I show any disapproval, he won't forgive me.'

Jean-Baptiste gave an exasperated sigh. 'You damned British! Nothing is ever simple. I did not understand any of that. I only know Rhys is doing something dangerous and it is upsetting you. I do not like that, but you leave me helpless to change it.'

Lexie smiled and took his hand. 'It do help even that

174

you noticed, flower. Try not to think about it, eh? Dad do always do what he wants to anyway, and he usually comes out of it smelling sweet. Let's hope it's the same this time.'

But times had changed, and Rhys no longer had the sureness of touch he had enjoyed in the early 1920s. He was mixing with more dangerous men than before. They took more risks and they were less trustworthy than the old underworld fraternity. And when they encountered trouble they were sufficiently careless to let it spread among their associates.

Edmund Halliday lived at the expensive end of Cardiff. He had risen the hard way to a business empire of considerable prosperity, and had been determined to see his only son did not grow up as a pampered waster. As a result, the boy was thrust through the most expensive toughening-up processes available in the form of preparatory and public schools; and when he went home for the holidays he was greeted coldly and treated more like an employee than a son.

The minute he had finished his education and taken his place in the family business, Christopher Halliday started extracting his revenge for such a rejection. He worked hard enough, but once he had finished for the day he disappeared with a group of friends whom his mother feared as too fast for her only child, and his father regarded as only slightly removed from Lucifer. This made Christopher doubly enthusiastic about their company and, within a couple of years of his return to Cardiff, there were very few expensive vices he had not tried.

One in particular had become something of a preoccupation lately: at a very private party, someone had introduced him to heroin, and he had become well and truly hooked. His suppliers were the same men who had begun haunting the bar at the Anglesey, and their interest in Halliday did not end with selling him heroin at inflated prices. Soon one of them became greedy, and suggested to Christopher that if his father learned of his latest vice, he could say goodbye to any future in the family business. Abruptly, much of Halliday's social activity stopped. He was being so efficiently bled of funds that he could no longer afford his heroin habit and his visits to nightclubs, racetracks and expensive restaurants. In any case, as the drug took hold of him, he was less interested in such childish fancies and increasingly saw pleasure only in a hypodermic syringe.

Joe Mathewman had watched Christopher's deterioration with growing disquiet. Get someone of his background so thoroughly hooked, and you normally had a long-term customer. But this boy was screaming downhill so fast they'd be lucky still to have him around in a year or so. Joe considered Alf Patullo's little extortion racket with Halliday to be overdoing it a bit. No doubt the blackmail had thrown their mark into drugs faster, harder and deeper than he would have gone otherwise, and now it appeared Alf was about to kill the goose that laid the golden egg.

Halliday's end came faster than even Mathewman had anticipated. He had less ready cash than either of his persecutors had realised, and when Patullo made one demand too many from Christopher, the young man filled a syringe with uncut heroin and injected it, killing himself in the most sensational way without leaving any note of explanation.

His father was not a loving man, but he was vengeful. When the police reported the manner of his son's death, Halliday hired a private detective and tracked down the people who had supplied Christopher's drugs. Then he went looking for them.

Edmund Halliday had many faults but cowardice was not one of them. To a man of such overweening arrogance, such an attitude was unthinkable. When the detective told him his son's suppliers frequented a rough pub in Bute Street, Halliday set out alone to confront them with what they had done.

Lexie never found out exactly what happened that evening in the Anglesey. Jean-Baptiste was in the cellar and she was serving behind the bar. Suddenly a brawl broke out between the flashy men she disliked so much and a well-dressed stranger she had never seen before. Squabbles were common enough in this part of the world, and Lexie took no more notice at first than to keep a watchful eye on them. Then the incident heated up and she saw Joe Mathewman give the newcomer a violent shove. She put down the pint glass she had been filling and hurried to the cellar door.

'Jean-Baptiste – up here a minute. There's a bitta trouble blowing up.'

The Frenchman hurried into the bar and approached Mathewman, a friendly smile on his face. 'Come along, Joe, you know better than to do that in here . . . ' He broke off with a gasp as the lamplight gleamed on the silver-blue of the switch-blade knife. Mathewman had produced. Jean-Baptiste spun towards Lexie. 'Tell Rhys it's a job for the law!' he cried, lashing out in an attempt to strike the blade from Mathewman's hand.

But Mathewman was a veteran of countless knife fights. He had no desire to lose the useful haven of the Anglesey and Jean-Baptiste probably owed his survival to that. Instead of stabbing him, Joe aimed a smashing blow at the Frenchman's temple with his free hand, then stepped over his body as he fell and continued his interrupted advance on Edmund Halliday. He had backed the businessman against the panelled wall when a deep, deceptively gentle voice said: 'Not yer, Joe. Nobody gets cut up in yer, remember?'

'There's a first time for everything, Walters!' grated Alf Patullo, moving to form a barrier between Rhys and Mathewman.

'Not yer, I said,' repeated Rhys, brushing Patullo aside as if he were a frail child. 'Now, Joe, what the bloody 'ell is going on? This bloke ent no pusher, nor a user, neither, by the look of him.'

'My business,' said Mathewman. 'Out the way, Rhys, or you'll get hurt.'

'No bugger tells me what to do in my own pub.' And

Rhys reached out, twisting Mathewman's hand sideways and back until the younger man let out a sob of pain and the knife clattered harmlessly to the floor.

But Mathewman was not the only armed man in the bar. Patullo, furious at such contemptuous treatment by a man old enough to be his grandfather, jumped up and threw himself at Rhys's back, springing open a switchblade and jerking it in a short upward arc between the big man's ribs as he did so. Rhys uttered one great gulp, then muttered 'Lex! I . . . ' and slid forward to lie face down on the floor.

Lexie was beside him in moments. 'Dad? Dad, say summat . . . where do it hurt?'

Rhys was alive – just. Now, some echo of a well-loved voice penetrated down into his receding consciousness and he reached up from depths of oblivion to touch it briefly. 'Yer, Lex . . . I'm yer, love . . . always yer . . . ' His eyes fluttered closed again and a trickle of blackish blood began to run from the right corner of his mouth. His great frame shuddered as he made one last, supreme effort. 'Where's that Jean-Baptiste? Tell him . . . tell him to k-keep the place. Keep the place, times'll get better . . . ' His harsh breathing changed to a convulsive grunt and the trickle of blood became a fountain. Lexie held him in her arms and was covered from breast to knees in her father's life-blood. Rhys's back arched in a final effort to hold the spark of vitality inside him, then slumped against his daughter, his huge frame finally vacated by the spirit that had held it together.

Patullo and Mathewman had melted away like snow in springtime. Edmund Halliday, a stranger to physical violence, stood aghast, staring at the scene his action had engendered. Only Jean-Baptiste moved in this terrible tapestry of death. 'Lexie . . . dearest Lexie. Let me help. There is no more you can do . . . ' He squatted beside her on the floor, trying to ease Rhys's great bulk away from her.

She turned on him like a wildcat. 'No! He ent dead! Get the doctor, you! He ent dead, I tell you . . . A blood

178

transfusion . . . yeah, thassit . . . a blood transfusion. He'll be all right. Get the hospital, Jean-Baptiste, quick. And the bloody law. I want them murderers behind bars!'

Jean-Baptiste knew then that she had accepted her father's death. She called them murderers, not just thugs. But her heart would not let her see what her mind knew to be a fact. He studied the dreadful little tableau for a moment, then sighed and stood up. He could do Lexie no greater service than to comply with her orders.

As he dialled the hospital's emergency number in the cubicle where they kept the telephone, Edmund Halliday jogged his elbow. 'Police first, you fool!' he said. 'You can see as well as I can that the man is dead mutton!'

Jean-Baptiste replaced the receiver and turned on him. 'You call the police if you feel like that. Rhys Walters died for you. I want his daughter to feel everything has been done that could be. Now shut up and let me make the calls!' Then he contacted the hospital, said there had been a stabbing, probably fatal, and the emergency service was needed, and only after that did he ring the Bute Street police station to report the fight.

By now, Edmund Halliday was gibbering. 'Those swine were responsible for the death of my son and they've just killed another man. You gave them more time to get away . . . I hold you personally responsible – *personally*, d'you hear me?'

Jean-Baptiste advanced slowly on the businessman. 'You listen to me, Mr Bigshot. Rhys Walters just died to protect you. The very least you can do for his daughter is to let her think we did all we could to save him, even when she knows in her heart it is useless. Will an early arrest wipe out your own loss?'

Halliday flushed and turned away. 'Damned foreigners!' he muttered. 'No idea of how to conduct themselves . . . '

CHAPTER TWENTY

Rhys Walters's death was as flamboyant as much of his life had been. Half of old Tiger Bay turned out for his funeral, marching behind the hearse, scorning the cars which had been provided. The wreaths were shaped like pint-pots and dartboards and whisky bottles and the messages they carried bordered on bathos. Rhys would have loved it.

After the last sympathisers had departed from the pub, Lexie sat down to consider their assets. It did not merit lengthy contemplation. 'Give or take the odd half-bottle a whisky, I reckon we'm cleaned out,' she told Jean-Baptiste.

'Really, Lexie, don't you think you are being a little melodramatic?' he said. 'After all, Rhys owned the Anglesey. That is a considerable asset.'

'Would be if I had any way a raising the cash to stock it. But I 'aven't. How d'you run a pub with no beer?'

Jean-Baptiste was all optimism. 'The same as Rhys did, of course – use the brewery account. He always managed to repay what he owed within the twenty-eight-day limit.'

She uttered a mirthless laugh. 'Oh, aye, and so could I. There's just one little snag, ent there? They won't let a single female – a *black* single female – have the same credit. Simple as that. I own the building but unless I can get my paws on fifty quid or so, I can say goodbye to the stock.'

'Fifty pounds?'

'Guarantee against my falling down on the account. New customer, you see.'

'But the brewery know you are Rhys's daughter. They

180

must realise you have been running the Anglesey for a couple of years.'

''Course they know. They'd just rather I was a man, that's all. So they're using the easiest way out they know. T'ent as if they was closing down one a their own tied houses. This is a free house. All they do is cut the risk of a silly little woman failing to pay up on time. Like the man said, Jean-Baptiste, we ent just broke, we'm ruined.'

'That is plain nonsense! There have been countless times when I would have given almost anything to have a place like this in which I could get started.'

'I bet! And you've taught me enough about French thrift to make me sure you'd have a sock fulla money ready to stock it all up.'

He made a face and shrugged. 'We can find money somewhere.'

'Where? There's a bloody depression on out there, remember? Arf the Bay is outa work. Oh, sure, I could scrape up enough to keep me an' Georgie by going back to work in the dance studio. Madam would jump at it – she always said I made the men come running. But if I was up there earning our keep, I couldn't be down yer running the pub, could I? And we certainly couldn't pay any staff. In any case, all I could earn would go on our living expenses. We still wouldn't have the fifty pound for the brewery.'

Jean-Baptiste scowled and plucked his lower lip. 'Hmm, you are right – and it would be the same if I went to work as a chef again. I am sure I could get a job, but it would not let me save so much for at least a year. Too long, no?'

'Too long, yes. No question. The Anglesey shuts and I go back to the dance studio. You find a job chef-ing again. You know there's room for you to live yer as long as you pays your way – in fact I'd miss you summat rotten if you went, now. But the Anglesey's finished, Jean-Baptiste. Face it.'

'No – Rhys told me to keep it going. With his dying breath he told me . . . '

181

'Dead men's requests!' Lexie made an exaggerated gesture. 'If his ghost is out there watching us now, the poor old sod's probably cursing himself for saying summat so daft. Dad would never hold either of us to any nonsense like that.'

'I wasn't thinking anything so childish. He was right. He was trying to say that if we could only hold on, we would do well eventually. And it's true, Lexie. It is the best chance either of us will ever get.'

She nodded glumly. 'Maybe so. But I can't see any way of making it happen, Jean-Baptiste. End o' this week I put up them shutters for good, unless you come up with some alternative.'

'I will try.'

When it came, Jean-Baptiste's proposal was certainly novel. 'I will go to sea, Lexie. It is the one thing I can do that will save the money and pay my keep at the same time.'

Lexie stared at him solemnly for a long moment, then burst out laughing. 'Have you ever been on a ship except to go back and fore to France?' she asked.

'No, but some of those old tubs do not ask for certificates or anything.'

'Maybe. The way I hear it, times are so hard now they've got men with master's certificates working as deckhands on some a the ships outa the Bay.'

'Not the ones I was thinking of. Please, Lexie, listen to me. I mean it. If I find a berth for a long voyage, and save every penny, will you make me two promises?'

'Don't like promising when I don't know what it do involve.'

'First, will you be my partner to start a restaurant here in the pub – my savings, your premises. Second, will you do it as Mrs Berard?'

Lexie's eyes widened until they appeared to swamp her face. 'You wanna *marry* me?'

'Is that so very strange?'

'Dunno about strange. It's bloody unexpected.'

'Only to you, it seems. Your father knew. Why do you

think he tried to ask me to keep the Anglesey open? Not from any concern for my welfare, I assure you.'

Lexie was still gaping at him, but now she was thinking, too. He was certainly an attractive sort of chap . . . Georgie adored him, and already chattered away in French as if she had spoken it from birth. She liked him a lot herself . . . so why was she hesitating now? *Larry! Larry Hines!* It had a dying echo, now, even to her. Of course no one could ever take his place, but he was never coming back, either, and a woman could get very lonely with only a daughter to give her love.

Lexie gave Berard a ravishing smile. 'Thank you for asking me,' she said. 'Yes. If you manage to get a stake for us to restart this place, yes, Jean-Baptiste. You're a good man and I think I could be very happy with you.'

He twinkled at her. 'And you are a very *bad* woman. I love you, and I know I could be happy with you!'

She laughed, inexplicably pleased that he had not asked her for a declaration of love, but had still been content to make one to her. All of a sudden this looked like a man she could spend the rest of her life with.

Jean-Baptiste eventually carried out his plan to go to sea, but he did it the hard way. Lexie was right when she said berths were hard to come by in the port of Cardiff in the summer of 1936. For the couple of weeks during which Lexie managed to keep the Anglesey open, he picked the brains of any customers with the slightest connection with the sea. Finally, a decrepit old cider-drinker, hearing him cross-examine an ex-seaman, leaned across and tapped his arm.

'Only way you'll get a berth is to do a pierhead jump, mate . . . yeah, a pierhead jump . . . only way . . . ' he cackled into his cider and said no more. Jean-Baptiste looked enquiringly at the ex-sailor. 'I do not understand. What is this thing?'

The seaman's smile was humourless. 'Didn't know you was that desperate or I'd have told you. The way the docks is built down yer, every vessel leaving has to slow down on the way out. You usually gerra chance of a quick word with the skipper, and if they'm a hand short . . . well, they take almost anybody, long as he's strong enough to jump aboard. But d'you think you could stand that, mun? Three months without the option, aboard some old scow that was so lousy it couldn't get a full crew up even at times like these?'

'I need the money.'

'Well, in that case, get some kit together and take your chances down there. There's a few leaky old tubs in port at the moment. Any one a them may need somebody.'

He lost his nerve about telling Lexie. She had gone up to the Arcade Dance Studio to see Madam and ask for her old job back. Jean-Baptiste took his chance, left a note for her, snatched up the few belongings he thought he would need, and headed for the pierhead.

As he started along Bute Street, his heart lurched. Georgie was skipping along in the other direction. She ran to meet him. 'Hallo, Jean-Baptiste. Going somewhere nice? Can I come along?'

He tried to invent an excuse to get rid of her, but had no heart for it. He could not depart with no one to see him off. 'Walk along with me for a while,' he said. 'I'm off to make our fortunes.'

She gazed at him, hero-worship shining in her eyes. 'Really? Where are you off to?'

'I do not know . . . Rio, or Surabaja, or San Francisco, maybe all three. But I will come back by the end of the year and we will all be together for good.'

The bright eyes had filled with tears as he spoke. 'But I don't want you to go! Why can't you stay at home with us?'

'Because we are poor now your grandfather is gone, and we must have more money. I promise I will be back sooner than you expect. Will you take a message from me to your mother? She does not know yet that I am going today.'

Momentarily, Georgie looked ready to argue. Then she

184

changed her mind and said: 'Only if you let me see you off.'

'It might be a very abrupt departure, Georgia.'

'I don't care. If you must go, I want to be with you till you leave. Come on, then, or you'll be late.' And she strode off slightly ahead of him, on the lifelong port-dweller's assumption that if he was going to sea he was doing so from the pierhead.

A likely-looking vessel started nudging its way down the dock within minutes of their arrival. Jean-Baptiste crossed his fingers that it would take him. He did not think he could stand Georgie's overwhelming sadness for long.

She was called *Bute Princess* and was so rusty she seemed held together by corrosion. The master, a slovenly, unshaven man, was on the bridge. As she drew level, Jean-Baptiste cupped his hand to his mouth and shouted: 'Hey, Captain, do you need an extra hand?'

The master eyed him impassively. 'I might, an' I might not. What d'you do?'

'A bit of everything. At sea since I was a boy.' He felt rather than heard the sharp intake of breath from Georgie at this vast lie.

The captain grunted. 'Don't s'pose you can cook? My bloke got laid out in a pub fight three hours ago an' I didn't get a chance to replace him. The crew'll mutiny when they taste the slop his usual number two serves up.'

Jean-Baptiste beamed. This was almost too good to be true! 'I am a short-order cook sometimes when I am ashore.'

For the first time, the master's expression changed and a faint smile cracked his rugged features. 'Well, you're a bloody cheeky liar, I'll give you that. Okay, mate – jump for it and you got a job.'

Jean-Baptiste threw his kitbag aboard and prepared to leap, then, almost as an afterthought, he shouted: 'First, tell me – where are you bound and how long?'

'River Plate, four months. Take it or leave it!'

'I take it! Goodbye, Georgie, tell Lexie she must wait

and pray for four months. And tell her I love her!' He planted a smacking kiss on the child's forehead and then took a flying jump aboard the steamer. Soon, through her tears, all Georgia could see was a faint speck at the deck rail of the departing vessel. She had no idea whether it was Jean-Baptiste or not.

Black Bet O'Donnell came to see Lexie a month after they buried Rhys.

'Duw, love, I wish I'd been yer,' she said. 'Losing Rhys was worse than losing one a my gentlemen. First 'oliday I'd had in ten years, an' all. Month in Eastbourne – terrible, ennit, when even us rackety ones gets old enough to want somewhere quiet like that. Then I went an' made it worse by getting a bitta bronchitis and having to stay an extra fortnight. That's why I never come before.'

'Oh, I know you'd have been at the funeral if you'd known, Bet. No need to apologise. Our Dad would be just as happy if you'd bought a drink in his memory, you know that.'

'Course he would! No, I didn't mean that, love. I was thinking of you. He left me summat for you – summat he didn't want no thieving hands on.'

'How long ago did this happen?'

'Oh, lotsa times, since back in the spring. He come to see me just after Easter and said he wanted me to hang onto some cash for you. Said he didn't want it going through the pub and if he got in any trouble he didn't want nobody taking it away. Said he'd already taken too many chances to get his hands on it. He gimme two hundred quid, Lex. Six weeks later he was back – it was two hundred an' fifty this time, and then another two hundred later on.' She opened her big black leather handbag. 'I nearly had heart failure coming along Bute Street with it on me today. I never carry money from the business unless one or two a the boys is with me to keep the jackals away, like.'

Lexie was goggling at her, oblivious of her chatter about safeguarding the money. 'You got six hundred an' fifty quid in that bag that Dad give you for me?' she finally spluttered.

'Aye, that's right, love. Seems a bloody shame you've 'ad to keep the pub shut all these weeks when the money was just there waiting for you, dunnit? I'm awful sorry . . . ' she winked, the old dockland tart in her bubbling back to the surface. ' . . . never 'ave survived in my line a business this long if my timing was always this lousy, would I?'

'Bet, the last of Dad's single malt is in that cupboard. You an' me is going to finish it to see the lovely old bugger off. I know where that money come from and I don't care. In the end he paid for it with his life-blood.'

She re-opened the Anglesey two weeks later, her new account with the brewery in good order, the shelves behind the bar better stocked than they had been in years. Lexie knew there was no longer the prosperity in dockland to merit such outlay, but she wanted to do it for Rhys's memory and to ensure that Jean-Baptiste came back to a place that looked worth saving, after what he would have gone through by then in order to help her keep it. Rhys had managed to harvest so much from his illegal enterprise that even after stocking up and getting the outside of the pub re-painted, she was still able to deposit a good sum in the bank to earn interest until they needed it for their restaurant.

For the first time in her life, she had no thought of rushing out to buy herself pretty clothes with any of the money. As long as she used it only for the business, she managed to persuade herself that it qualified as legitimate spoils of war. Somewhere deep in her heart, though, she felt that if the clothes on her back were financed by drug profits, she would be degraded by it. She knew there was no logic in her viewpoint, but it made her feel better.

Jean-Baptiste arrived back from the River Plate two weeks before Christmas, his skin tanned a deep mahogany shade and his kitbag packed with small, exciting souvenirs for Lexie and Georgia. He also brought Georgia a glowing, smoky-gold topaz, and Lexie a cottonwool-lined box containing three medium-sized, flawless emeralds. 'Your engagement ring, when I get to a jeweller to have them set,' he said with a complacent grin.

'But how could you afford them? You can't have any of that pay left that you worked so hard to get!'

He laughed. 'Precious stones are crazy-cheap in some parts of South America. Don't think about British prices. Come to that, I don't want to talk about me at all for a while. I want to hear all about how you managed to keep going after all.'

She explained, and as she did so he relaxed visibly. Finally he said: 'I cannot tell you how relieved I am! I am afraid I'm no good at selling my unskilled labour – too used to what they pay master chefs, it seems.'

'Why, what happened?'

'Well, before I set out on my voyage of discovery, I asked the captain where the ship was bound. I neglected to find out what he was paying. Guess how much I have saved for our restaurant business!'

'I wouldn't know where to start.'

'However low you went, I think you would be wrong. By keeping every penny, I have made sixty pounds profit on four months away.'

They stared at each other, momentarily aghast at the enormity of his sacrifice for so little. Then, warmed by the posthumous windfall from Rhys, they began to laugh, clinging to each other as if tipsy at the irony of the situation. Jean-Baptiste said: 'At least it looks as if it might work out all right. I was almost afraid to come back and face you with so little. But, Lexie, it will mean you are the boss and I only work for you. Sixty pounds cannot make me your partner.'

'You silly sod – you're gonna marry me, ent you? How much more of a partner can you be? I wouldn't know how to get going on a restaurant if you weren't going to organise it and do the cooking.' She paused, then added,

'Anyhow, d'you reckon we'll have enough even with the rest of that money from Dad and your sixty quid? It seems like small change if we're talking about a business.'

'It is, it is – but what is our alternative? We risk everything on one shot and we might succeed. We will never earn enough from this pub to keep us. Remember you own the building, and that is the biggest expense of all. You have the brewery account, too. I'm sure they could be persuaded to switch the balance of the order to wine and spirit supply and make the beer less important. That will wipe out another big down-payment. As long as we can keep enough to buy food supplies and make the Anglesey look like an attractive place to eat, we have a good chance.'

Lexie's voice rose almost to a wail. 'I musta been mad even to think we could do it! A few hundred pound will never do all that. My God, all them tables an' chairs and cutlery and glasses . . . '

He silenced her with a gesture. 'Trivialities! We are not equipping the Caprice. I will buy old tables and cheap, plain kitchen chairs. There will be bright-red checked cloths to cover the old tables, cheap tumblers for the wine, and old-fashioned horn-handled cutlery. Alice and I found out that people liked that. Half the country restaurants in France look like this, and they love the hospitable atmosphere. It makes them think they are abroad.'

She was regarding him dubiously. 'I know the sorta place you mean. There was enough a them in Soho when I worked in London. They did all right there. But in Cardiff? Could we get enough customers to a place like that to live on it?'

'Trust me. I may be lousy at negotiating seaman's pay, but I am a genius in the kitchen!'

And, against all Lexie's fears, it worked. They were married just after Christmas, and went on running the Anglesey as a pub until a month before Easter. It was no roaring success, but at least they scraped a short-term

189

living without dipping into their meagre capital. Then, in March, they closed and transformed their seedy pub into a little piece of provincial France. The old panelled bar at the Anglesey was painted white, its flagstone floor covered with rush matting and the cheap furniture Jean-Baptiste had bought was installed. He got hold of a musician who had found no regular employment since the end of the 1920s when talkies swept away cinema orchestras, equipped him with an accordion, a beret and a striped jersey and installed him as the restaurant entertainer. As a final, vital promotional touch, he employed a sign-writer who had seen better days as an artist, and got him to paint an extravagant design on the board which had once simply said ANGLESEY HOTEL. Now the two-foot wide panel running above the restaurant entrance showed a picture of a well-rounded amphibian, table napkin tied around his neck, spoon between webbed fingers, about to pitch into a steaming plate of soup. Alongside him was the legend: THE CONTENTED FROG.

Bet O'Donnell, who had maintained an almost proprietary interest in the project since arriving with the money which was to finance it, took a look at the place on the eve of its opening and said: 'Tell you what, kid – I'll see that every one a the gentlemen visiting my girls gets a recommendation to come yer. No riff-raff among my clients, mind – best South Wales can offer, there.'

They advertised discreetly in the *South Wales Echo*, then stood back nervously to await their first evening's business. Five hours later, as Lexie helped the last couple into their coats and saw them out into the night, she turned to her husband tiredly and said: 'We're gonna make it, ent we?'

'If three-quarters of them decide to come back, yes. I think, Madame Berard, you have earned yourself a glass of champagne.'

Lexie burst into tears and flopped down on one of the kitchen chairs near the door. 'That's the first time anyone have said that since Dad opened his last bottle to celebrate Georgie's arrival!' she said.

Jean-Baptiste ignored her tears. 'Then I think we might let Georgia get up, just this once, and enjoy a glass with us,' he replied. 'I will bet the whole night's takings that she has not had a wink of sleep since we sent her to bed!'

CHAPTER TWENTY-ONE

Abercarn, 1938

At times Lily felt that the rigours and disappointments of the 1920s and early 1930s had prepared her to ride calmly over what came afterwards; whatever the reason, none of it seemed to hurt as much as some of the more dramatic events of her earlier life. For a while after David's death she had moved about as if in a dream, barely in touch with everyday matters.

It took her a long time to understand why his passing had come as such a blow; she had hardly been unprepared for it, after all. Then the news came of Peter's death, and she began to comprehend. Guilt had driven her, and now that guilt seemed to be expiated. Sometimes she wondered if that made her some sort of monster. What kind of woman found her own bad conscience over the betrayal of one man assuaged by the sacrifice of another man's life? Invariably, though, that was where her native good sense took over. She could spend a lifetime in such pretend heroics, when there was still work to be done.

Charles Henderson had broken the news about Peter on a sullen autumn day in 1936. Lily, still half-submerged in her mourning for David, was sitting by the kitchen fire, re-living all her small failures in a welter of bad conscience which was almost pleasurable, when she heard Henderson's familiar, brisk rap on the back door. She turned to greet him, summoning the beginnings of a false bright smile. Then she saw his expression.

His face was sheet-white, the eyes burning dark and

agonised against the chalky flesh. The hand he rested on the door handle trembled violently and his mouth twitched almost in synchronisation with its jerky movement. Lily's own smile froze. She got up and hurried over to draw him into the room. 'He've had it, haven't he?' Her own voice sounded harsh and vulgar to her ears.

Henderson slumped into the Windsor chair where David had been in the habit of sitting in happier times. He leaned forward, resting elbows on knees, covered his face and burst into great, racking sobs. 'Lily, oh Lily!' he eventually managed to gasp out. 'How can you ever forgive me? When he went to Spain, I actually caught myself praying for this!'

For once he caught her off-guard. The utter certainty that he had come to tell her of his brother's death had steeled her to whatever he might say; but this? 'Wharra you on about?' she asked, bewildered.

'I-it's like some dreadful judgment. I loved him far better than many brothers, and he was just as fond of me. And yet, I was so jealous . . . so jealous of you and him, that when he went off to that benighted country all I could think of was that he wouldn't be taking you away any more . . . that if he didn't come back . . . ' His next words were lost in a fresh rush of tears.

Lily came to him, took his head between her hands and pressed his face to her body, comforting him like a mother with a lost child. 'Hush now . . . hush, there's a good boy . . . cry it all out, it'll be better then . . . '

After a while the storm of weeping ended. He drew back and looked up at her. 'How can you comfort me like this? How can you find compassion for me when you must be dying of grief?'

She shrugged. 'I 'spect that will come later. This minute, I'm empty of anything, but pity for you. Oh, Charlie, love, what a lorra suffering I seem to load on every man who do ever look at me! I run from you and marry poor David, and you never get over it. David do follow me round all his life looking for crumbs of love because I never loved him enough in the first place; and then Peter takes every grain of passion I got, and there ent nothing left for the rest of you.' She uttered a small, bitter laugh. 'And if you wanna know the truth, I don't think that poor devil loved me at all, in his heart of hearts. I was just some sorta working class madonna he could idolise – not that he didn't fancy me like mad, mind, but I think love of anything but big causes was right outside your little brother's nature. And I had to fall hook, line and sinker! Proper punishment, really, for all my other sins.'

'Do you really have such a low opinion of yourself? He adored you – all the men in your life always have.'

'Rubbish – you just all saw what you wanted to see in me. You saw the free spirit. David thought he saw the perfect wife and mother. I just told you what Peter saw. None of them was real. I'm just a show-off with a big mouth and a nose that won't stay out of other people's business, that's all . . . Oh, Jesus, Charlie, why am I talking like this when what I really want to say is how did the poor sod die, and where, and when?'

Henderson took out a crumpled letter, creased where he had crushed it convulsively as he read the news. 'Nothing dramatic,' he said. 'This is from a comrade of his who was with him. They were besieging the town of Teruel in Aragon. Peter was on night watch and he caught a sniper's bullet in the temple. Wasn't even a rifle, just a revolver . . . talk about an unlucky shot.'

Lily could not look him in the eye. 'A-any sign of Famous Last Words for either of us?'

He reached for her hand and squeezed it. 'Nothing. Peter always did think he was immortal. Just as well. In my experience a last love letter or fond adieu to the family only extend grief instead of healing it. Better just to let him fade away in our memories, Lily. He was never meant to make old bones.'

She disengaged her hand from his and thumped one fist in the other palm in her characteristic gesture of anger. 'My fault!' she said. 'He was forty years old. He could have had a wife and a family to hold him here, keep him safe. And I went and strung him along all those years so he never took on any real ties at all. He'd never of gone if he'd had a few everyday responsibilities.'

Henderson stood up and gave her a little shake. 'Stop it, Lily! That's pure self-indulgence and you know it! Neither Peter nor I was meant to settle down in that way, and it was as much our dear mother's influence as anything you did to either of us. Any fool with a medical education and a little personal insight can see that. Let's have no more breast-beating. Grieve for him, by all means. We both loved him and he deserves that from each of us. But don't clothe his life in sorrows that were none of your doing – didn't really exist, come to that.'

'Your mother have been dead for four years.'

'Yes, and have you seen either of us hurrying to do anything about the inheritance? I was wrong all those years ago when I said that I might find it difficult to give up the Peel in the end. I let it go without any regrets. I only held on to it after Father died to give Mama the illusion that it wasn't all going to end in ruin. But she was the only one who knew me intimately who ever used the title in addressing me, and I made damned sure I renounced it as soon as she was dead and buried.'

Lily was gazing at him with a new understanding. 'I'm only just beginning to realise . . . what a bloody fool . . . you've turned into that man I once thought I had, haven't you, and I never noticed?'

His smile was ineffably sad. 'I think perhaps I have. And I'm terribly afraid that Peter's death has made it too late for any going back.'

Two huge tears released themselves from her eyes and trickled slowly down her cheeks. 'I wouldn't be too sure a that. Just give me time to think about this one. A lorra time. Whatever I did or didn't mean to him, there was a big bitta your brother that was my knight in shining armour. Gorra get him out of my mind. After that, who knows what'll happen? We might *all* be dead next week.'

Henderson thought of recent newspaper headlines and

gave an involuntary shudder. 'Don't tempt providence,' he said.

But the war clouds had held off for long enough to permit Lily her period of mourning and 1936 dragged into 1937. Small improvements began to take place as the worst of the Depression faded. Outside the Valleys there was a certain air of optimism abroad by the time 1938 came in. Nowadays there were plenty of new light industries along the Thames Valley, and enough South Wales families had relatives already working there to be hopeful about new jobs and new futures away from the dead hand of the coal mines.

Now, as her son Tommy raced towards manhood, Lily faced a dilemma. Had the boy been exceptional, she would have done anything to provide him with an expensive education. She worked full time for Charles Henderson now, and he insisted on over-paying her so that she earned as much as many skilled men in full-time employment. Tommy had an instinctive skill with his fingers, was fascinated by electrics and anything mechanical, but would never be a brilliant student. He had scraped into the local boys' technical school by passing an examination at the age of twelve, a few months before his father died, and Lily had haunted the headmaster's office during 1938, seeking advice about his next step. She might have been asking for the moon.

'I wish I could offer some truly constructive suggestion, Mrs Richards, but I cannot think of anything which would get your boy away from what his family has always done,' said Joseph Thomson.

Lily eyed the man sceptically. 'If you mean send our Tom down the pit, you can forget that straight away,' she said.

'I assure you that we're not talking of the bad old days,' he said, trying to inject some enthusiasm into his tone. 'Tommy will have no trouble in securing an apprenticeship underground. You hardly need me to tell you they're like gold in surface jobs. The only children

196

signing indentures as electricians or engineers in the Valleys these days are the sons of other electricians and engineers. I'm afraid it's mining or a move away.'

'Move away? The boy's only fifteen this year.'

'That's why I suggested you should consider the mines. There's no reason why he shouldn't be in senior management by the time he's in his mid-thirties, and I believe he's got too strong a family life here to be happy moving to the south-east of England.'

It was the phrase 'senior management' that had done it, Lily reflected later. Her son, one of the boss class? It would never work. He'd cut himself off from his roots in the worst possible way. Better send him away than that. Under her surface indignation, though, she realised that was only part of it. What she really could not stand was the thought of her only son confined down there in the dark. She remembered Billie's halting accounts of his early days as a collier. Coal hewer or apprentice, did it matter what you were doing if you had to do it lying down there in the black dust with millions of tons of mountain over your head? Not my Tommy, she promised herself.

The boy himself eventually provided the answer, although she did not like it. Two weeks later he arrived home from school waving a sheaf of recruitment literature from the Royal Air Force. Lily bit her tongue, realising she must sound the worst of killjoys, as she chorused along with her mother: 'The RAF? But Tom, they'd send you away!' Margaret Ann turned on her favourite daughter in open satisfaction, her look saying: I knew you'd agree with me one day, girl.

Lily took a deep, resentful breath and started again. 'Tell me right from the beginning, Tommy *bach*. What's so special about going off to the RAF?'

His look was level. 'I been talking to Uncle Billie, Mam. And I been watching you.'

'And what do that mean?'

'I dunno which of the two a you is more scared a that pit, him or you. It killed your dad. It killed our Dad. It killed arf your brothers. It frightened the living daylights out of Uncle Billie so he can't bear to think about it no more, all these years after. And you think that's better for me than going away?'

'N-no, love. I didn't mean that – don' know what I meant, to tell the truth. I been trying to work out what I want for you, but I do know it ent that bloody pit. That's all that's holding me back – that an' the fact that you'm only a little boy.'

To her consternation, he threw back his head and laughed. It sounded just like her father, in the days long ago when he had a carefree moment and matters were running well for him. Lily looked at her son with new eyes. *Duw*, but he was big! Why had she thought he was such a little boy?

She laughed, shakily, as if coming out of a bad dream, reassured by reality. 'I been blind, kidda. I do still think of you as a child, and you ent. Wharra my trying to protect you from? Nothing could be worse than that bloody old pit. Tell me about this idea of yours.'

Eagerly, now truly a child again, Tommy put the pamphlets on the table. 'Now this one yer is for the Boy Entrants' scheme. They do pay you a wage – and board – and you get a proper apprenticeship, same as in outside industry mind, while you'm in. You train as an aero engineer.'

'Hell, what's an aero engineer?'

'Same as car engines but building and servicing aircraft. Think of it, Mam. When I've finished, I can build planes. It's the future. Nobody'll still be using cars in another generation.'

'Hang on, now. Nobody in the Ranks 'ave even *gorra* car yet!'

He gestured dismissively. 'Good reason why I should join the RAF, then, ennit? Bad enough bein' one generation behind, lerralone two.'

That made her laugh. 'You'm a cheeky little bugger, I'll give you that. Taking after your grandfather again, I 'spect.'

Margaret Ann boiled over. 'Lily, I will not have you swearing and giving the boy wrong ideas about Evan. He was a fine upstanding man, you know that.'

Lily bit back a retort, looked chastened, said 'Yes Mam', and squeezed Tommy's hand conspiratorially under cover of the tablecloth.

Tommy – insisting they all called him Tom from now on – was inducted to the Air Force at RAF St Athan the following September. A couple of weeks after the boy completed his basic training, Charles Henderson marched decisively into Lily's office as she put away the last files from evening surgery and said: 'Unless you have life or death objections, we are getting into the car and driving out to Usk for dinner at the Three Salmon tonight, Mrs Richards. I may even permit you to drink me under the table.'

'What's all this in aid of? You got bad news for me?'

'It speaks volumes of the way our relationship has deteriorated that you no longer look forward to such occasions as magic moments. Go on, now – take the car, change into your best frock and get back here as soon as possible. While I'm waiting, I shall book a table and order something special.'

She grinned at him. 'You are a nice man, Charlie. I won't be more than half an hour.'

Champagne cocktails awaited them at the Three Salmon. They dined on Usk salmon, followed by wild duck with a delicious vintage Burgundy which he had ordered and asked them to open when he booked the table. The old-fashioned dining room was almost empty and Lily sighed with contentment, stretching out in her carver chair and kicking off her shoes to toast her toes before the log fire.

'You are *so* good at spoiling women,' she said, 'you make me feel nineteen again. It's bloody hard to believe I'm forty.'

'It may be hard for you, Lily. I find it impossible. To me you'll always be nineteen.'

199

'Keep talking like that and the answer is yes, whatever the question turns out to be.'

'You're on dangerous ground there, my girl. I don't want to trap you.'

She caught the underlying seriousness of his mood. 'What is it? Nothing awful have happened, have it? I didn't think there was much worse *could* happen . . .'

He smiled. 'No, nothing awful. But now your life has straightened itself out a little, and your commitment to Tommy has eased off, there was something I wanted to ask you.' He groped in his waistcoat pocket. 'I wondered if you'd care to consider accepting this again, and wearing it with all the implications it held before.' As he spoke, he put something down on the dinner table. It was the engagement ring she had returned to him almost twenty years before.

Lily gasped and stared at the ring, but made no move to touch it.

'What's wrong?' said Henderson. 'Have I made yet another blunder?'

She gazed at him, eyes suspiciously bright. 'Oh no – not this time. Fancy – you kept it all these years!'

'Somehow I could never bear to part with it. While I hung on to the damned thing, I never quite gave up hope that some day you'd take it back again. Will you?'

'I-I don't know what to say . . . I'd need time to think . . . it's been a long time. Oh, Charlie – this was the last thing on my mind!'

His face had darkened as Lily dithered. 'Then you couldn't love me again?'

She laughed in his face. 'You dull bugger! I've never stopped loving you! Nothing there that need worry you. I'm just wondering whether I'm fit to live with any man now.'

He beamed. 'I hereby volunteer to be your guinea pig.'

She picked up the ring. 'I'll wear it again,' she told him, 'but don't push me for a while. Let me have a bitta time to think. I'm too old to change now, Charlie, too old to give up my good causes, or stop work, or talk posh again. Are you ready for me warts an' all, instead of a green little girl ready to be changed?'

'Warts and all. You were quite something then, Lily, but now you're worth a hundred times the value of that green little girl.'

She stood up, leaned across the table and kissed him lightly on the forehead. 'Just staking my claim,' she said. 'I'll spell it out in full when we're nice an' private, all right?'

'I can hardly wait.'

Lily glanced around, mischief sparkling in her fine eyes. 'P'raps it won't be as long as you think . . . d'you reckon this is the sorta place where they'd turn a blind eye to' – her voice dropped to a husky whisper – 'forbidden assignations?'

'Lily, what *are* you suggesting? This place has been a respectable next-to-last resting place for ex-Indian Army colonels and genteel maiden ladies since the turn of the century! I think that stuffed salmon would revolve in his glass case at the very idea of any naughtiness!'

'Just as well we're too old to be naughty, then, ennit? Go on, be a devil. Book us a coupla rooms for tonight and if you're very lucky I may come an' be your hot water bottle.'

'But what do we tell them back in Abercarn? What will your mother say?'

Lily crowed with mirth. 'Nothing, if she've got any sense left, which I sometimes doubt. Mam knows me well enough by now to recognise when to leave well enough alone – and if she don't, what on earth can she do about it? I only care about Tommy, and he's tucked up safe down St Athan. Come on then – you still going to turn a warm woman down?'

His own laugh was explosive. 'You really *are* outrageous! What if I were doing surgery tomorrow morning?'

'Don't be daft – I make up the rotas, remember? I got a morning off and your partner is doing the morning stint, so we'm free as birds.'

Henderson uttered an exaggerated sigh. 'Then I suppose I must simply let you have your way with me. The things I do to oblige a lady!'

'Only *this* lady, I hope!' said Lily. 'Now, to business. You get me a nice big whisky – calm my nerves, you know – and while I'm sipping it, you can see if they'll take us in.'

'Very well, you hussy, but if you won't let me make an honest woman of you after this, I shall tell everyone in Abercarn about your disgraceful behaviour!'

'That'd brighten things up in the Ranks for a bit!'

Her room was ridiculously romantic. When she saw it, Lily abandoned all thoughts of joining Henderson and told him he must come to her. It was in the oldest part of the inn, with a mullioned window left slightly open so that she could hear the river chuckling past below. A log fire crackled in the enormous stone fireplace, reflecting on the overstuffed furniture and transforming the shabby upholstery into the jewel shades of precious tapestry. The broad bed boasted a vast feather mattress which demanded they jump into it.

Lily shivered in anticipation as she began to undress. 'Daft ha'porth you are!' she told herself fondly, 'acting like a batty little girl with her first boy, when both of you are old enough to know better!'

In recent years, Lily had let her hair grow long again, as it had been when she was a girl, and usually she wore it caught up in a loose chignon. Now she undid it and it tumbled down her back, almost to waist level, as thick and vital as ever, although there were a few silver hairs now. She brushed it vigorously with a small brush she had in her bag, and it sparked with static electricity. So much for beauty treatments! She had no scent, no alluring nightgown, only her own still shapely body and a tender passion for Charles Henderson which, to her surprise, was surging through her now as strongly as it had when she was young.

When he came in, she was sitting in front of the fire,

quite naked, partly veiled by her hair, gazing into the flames. His sharp gasp of pleasure at her beauty brought her head up and round to face him and she smiled radiantly. 'Something unfair about this, really,' she said. 'All my life I've laughed at women who read those silly romantic stories about being swept off their feet by handsome princes in exotic places – and I end up in the middle of one!'

Henderson was self-deprecating, as always. 'Precious little of the Prince Charming about me, I fear. Gammy leg, hoary locks – more like Father Time than Young Lochinvar.'

'Never did fancy Young Lochinvar overmuch. Stop apologising and come over yer by me.'

He crossed the room, half-reluctant to step within the magic half-circle of firelight around the hearth in case it dissolved into a dream. She pressed him down into the squashy armchair, then sat on the floor, her long, strong, bare back pressed against his good leg. Almost of their own volition, Henderson's fingers twisted gently through her hair, relishing its springy smoothness as his mind played with the long-cherished memory of her body melting into his.

After a while, Lily took his hand in hers and stood up. 'We'll drop off here in front of the fire if you don't get your clothes off and in that bed!' she said. 'We can spend as long as we like sitting around like this back home.'

His eyes devoured her splendid unclothed shape and he said: 'We can hardly sit around in front of the fire like *that* – what would the housekeeper say?'

'Do it up my house and you wouldn't have to worry about the housekeeper – just the kids staring in through the kitchen window.' Then she stopped talking and drifted smoothly against him, covering his cheek and jaw with tiny, butterfly kisses. Suddenly he realised there were tears on his face.

Lily's fingers moved to them, wiped them away, then she said: 'Have it been so very bad for you, Charlie?'

'Worse than you could ever imagine, my darling. I

203

never stopped wanting you for a second, and being halfway decent about it all those years was probably the hardest thing I ever had to do.'

'Oh, hell, why have I always managed to make so many people suffer?'

He gave her a little shake. 'You shouldn't need me to answer that! Because you gave so many people pleasure, and hope, and joy as well, you idiot. We all have to suffer some pain for the good things.'

'You seem to have suffered an awful lot for a few scraps.'

'Oh, no, Lily. Look what I've got now.' His long hand slid down over her firm white breast, cupping and weighing it with delight. 'You *will* marry me, I don't care what you say now, and tonight will be the first night of our honeymoon.'

'Daft old bugger!' she said with a giggle, but the notion clearly pleased her. They sat side by side on the big bed and slowly, teasingly, she helped him to undress. When he finally slid beneath the puffy eiderdown beside her, he was as excited as a boy, and Lily pulled him down to her, caressing, whispering, encouraging. His last cogent thought before he slid off on a cloud of pure physical pleasure was of her saying: 'It's better now than it ever was, before, Charlie . . . p'raps it took me till now to find you.'

She married Charles Henderson in July 1939 and they went to France for a short holiday. When they returned, no one talked of anything but war, and Lily realised it was not only her private world which had changed for ever.

PART FOUR

One woe is past; and behold, there come
two woes more hereafter.

Revelation, Ch. 9, v.12

CHAPTER TWENTY-TWO

July 1941

Billie Walters had no desire to leave his fields that afternoon. It was a hot, sunny day, perfect for hay-making, and he had a good chance of finishing by nightfall. Then he remembered he had been promising Lily for months that he would go down and see her. Some things mattered more than hay-making, and a promise to Lily was one of them.

In the end he compromised and left it rather late before he harnessed up Daisy Belle and they set off down the valley at a relaxed amble. He noticed something unusual seemed to be happening about half-way down Gwyddon Road. At this time, most people were either having tea or, on a day like this, going off to enjoy a walk in the late afternoon sunshine. But today a remarkable number of them seemed to be heading for the village. He speeded up the pony, curious now about what was going on.

The market square was in a ferment by Abercarn standards. Billie guided Daisy Belle around the top of the Ranks front row and down the first back lane. He was tethering the rig to Haydn's coal-house door when Lily came out of the house.

'Billie – just the boy I wanted to see!' she exclaimed, her face alight with pleasure. 'I knew you'd get around to taking a coupla them poor kids eventually, with that great barn of a house of yours!'

Billie recoiled, wondering what his sister was getting him into. 'I – I only come down to see you, Lil,' he said lamely.

'Well we can soon change that. Come on, down you

get. I'm on my way over Central Hall. We'll go back down the Swan for some tea after.' And before Billie could object, she was dragging him in her wake down the side street that led to the canal bridge and the large Presbyterian church building on the other side – the biggest hall in the village.

She had reached the door of Central Hall, still chattering so volubly he had no chance to ask what on earth was going on. Now other people were converging from all directions. Finally Billie stood still, almost tripping up a couple who were hard on his heels. 'That's enough, Lily!' he said. 'I wanna know where we'm going and what for before I take another step.'

'To see the evacuees, of course. I wanted to take one, but Charlie said over his dead body. He reckons there's far too much work for me in the practice to take on a kid an' all.'

'He's right, too. So why are you going in spite of it?'

She smiled. 'Our Rose. Mam finally persuaded her to have someone – two children, I believe – but she's as timid as ever and Mam said I'd better go and see she don't change 'er mind at the last minute.'

'That does it. If our Mam is gonna be there, I ent. Now, out the way.'

'Oh, calm down, for God's sake! Why d'you think Mam wanted me there? She's gorra go up the Garn tonight for something. I think I'm supposed to be her proxy.'

'I'm only coming if you promise not to involve me. Strictly to keep you company, mind.'

'All right, I promise. But honest, kidda, it would do you the world a good – young faces around you, someone to help with the work.'

'For the last time, Lil, no. N-O. Got it?'

She giggled and made a lip-buttoning gesture across her clamped-shut mouth, then they went inside.

Albert and Rose were a few feet inside the chapel doors, looking shy and anxious. Oh, Lily, thank goodness you'm here!' breathed Rose, glancing around in case someone overheard her. 'I nearly lost my nerve an' went!'

'But why? I thought you was looking forward to it. God knows you got enough room for the kids.' For ten years, Rose and Albert had lived in a three-bedroomed house with a large garden on the new housing estate in Llanfach.

Albert sighed heavily. 'Aye, I thought she was, an' all. But the last coupla days she've been polishing everything that don't move of its own accord and saying none of it is up to having people coming to stay. Another day of it an' she'd of 'ad us both in the asylum!' Billie winced at the allusion and Albert compounded his gaffe by saying 'Oh, sorry, But – I forgot. No offence, innit?'

Groups of people were standing about chattering, speculating on where the evacuees would come from and how many there would be. Time started to drag. Then someone dashed in from outside and shouted: 'They'm yer – four bus loads – look tired out, an' all!'

Five minutes later a bedraggled procession of strangers began to wend its way into the hall. Rose uttered a gasp of dismay. 'There's women with them.' Nobody said nothing to me about no women!'

Lily glanced at her sister and realised this could well be where Rose backed out of her promise. Unobtrusively she threaded her way over to Henry Evans, the local registrar, who had been asked to deal with allocations of evacuees to individual families. 'Henry, if you don't give our Rose unaccompanied kids, I'm afraid you'll lose billets for a couple of the people you got down there,' she whispered.

Evans looked harassed. 'Oh, hell, not another!' he said. 'Lily, they're all saying the same. For heaven's sake, how were we to know they'd change our allocation at the last minute? Instead of unaccompanied children, we've been given an emergency evacuation of mothers with children as well as unaccompanied, because a lot got bombed out night before last. But how many women do you know in this village who'll be willing to share their kitchen with a stranger?'

Lily's smile was sphinx-like. 'Come on, Henry. You'm a good chapel type. Where's your faith in their Christian charity?'

He leaned closer and whispered in her ear: 'If there wasn't an audience, I'd smack your bum for vexing me like that. You know what this lot'll say to women like these.'

Sadly, she did. For a few seconds, it might be funny. But there was no humour in the situation for women who had lost their homes over the past couple of days, and whose husbands were away fighting heaven knew where. Now they were facing rejection by the very people they had hoped would take them in. Lily shuddered with distaste at the way the poor were willing to treat strangers of their own kind. 'I'll take a mother and child, Henry,' she said firmly. 'Mind the woman do know she'll have to do most of the housework, though. I can't have no fly-by-night who expects me to house-keep as well. I work full time, remember, and you know Mrs Jones retired six months ago.'

'Bless you for a saint, Lily!' said Evans, adding, again in a whisper, 'even if it's a Red saint!'

She patted his arm. 'You find me a nice one – I couldn't care less if she's respectable, as long as she's nice and not lazy – and I'll come back to collect my prize after. And mind what I said about our Rose. Now I better go and stiffen her backbone a bit, or you won't even get her to take unaccompanied kids!'

And that was about the position with Rose when she got back. Billie and Albert were both attempting to persuade her, but she was already saying that if there was any doubt about having a mother, too, she would prefer to have no one.

'Come on, Rose, behave yourself. Our Mam'll have your guts for garters if you go back an' tell her you're not doing your bit for the war effort,' said Lily. 'I told old Evans you wouldn't have no mams and kids. He's trying to sort you out a coupla singles now.'

'Oh, Lily, this has quite upset me! I don't really think I can manage anyone at all.'

'Don't be bloody daft! Mam'll kill you. Wait an' see what Henry do find for you.'

Evans was only partially successful. There was a multitude of mothers and children and only a scattering of unaccompanied boys and girls. But when he did get across to them, the registrar proved he could judge his targets well. He was leading a slender, nervous, good-looking boy aged eleven or twelve. The child was immaculately turned-out and obviously at least as shy as Rose. She took one look at him and it was as if she were seeing the son she had never been able to bear.

'Rose,' said Henry Evans nervously, 'this is Leonard – Leonard Crowthorn. He comes from Chatham and he's here to stay with us because they've blown up the houses near the dockyard. Do you think you can take care of him until his mother and father think it's safe for him to go home?'

Rose's eyes were shining. 'Oh, yes, I'd like that . . . would you like to come home with us, Leonard? We gorra big garden and a Sealyham called Tich, and a nice back bedroom you could have all to yourself.'

The boy smiled and it was as if the sun had risen on a beautiful landscape. 'Yes, I think I'd like that very much,' he said. 'But can you tell me, please, what's a Sealyham?'

Under cover of their talk, Lily turned to Henry Evans and said: 'If you can come up with another like that, I might even *let* you smack my bum, an' all!'

But Rose felt she had done her bit. 'I think we'll take Leonard home now, Mr Evans,' she said. 'He must be ever so tired after that long journey.'

'But what about the other child?' Evans's question was hardly more than a formality because he was virtually certain he had already placed all the unaccompanied children. It was irrelevant to Rose, anyway.

'I think we'll get on lovely with Leonard, and that's enough,' she said. Then, turning to the child, 'd'you like

gooseberry tart and custard? Our garden's full of goose-
berries.'

Henry Evans shrugged and turned away towards his
other charges. He still had too much work undone to
waste any more time on Rose.

Lily's evacuee was entirely to her liking, a woman of
around thirty with wickedly bright brown eyes and a cap
of blonde hair, the colour of which owed nothing to
nature. Her knee-length skirt showed off shapely legs
and, to the outrage of the local women sentenced by
shortages to lisle stockings, she appeared to be wearing a
pair of the latest super-fine nylons with arrow-straight
black seams up the back. The natural rebel in Lily took to
her on sight. To add the cherry to the cake, her name was
Sadie.

'It's Sarah really,' she confided, having decided the
attraction with Lily was mutual, 'but I thought that was a
bit ordinary.' She turned and introduced her companion.
'This is my Elaine.'

She drew forward an equally perky-looking little girl
whose hair really was blonde – a soft, glossy ash shade,
braided into two thick plaits. Sadie patted it – 'Marvellous, innit? Takes me arf me time to get my hair this
colour, and she gets it as part of the basic equipment!
Who says there's any justice?'

Lily was relieved that Rose and Albert had gone by the
time she rejoined Billie. She wanted to prepare Margaret
Ann for the sight of Sadie herself, without a doubtless
highly-coloured taster from Rose. Rose took pains
to dress smartly, but she regarded anything beyond
a touch of face powder and a hint of natural pink lip-
stick as the work of the devil. Seamed nylons and hair dye
would have outraged her.

Billie, who was better with children than with adults,
got to know Elaine while Lily was talking to Sadie. Lily
was secretly delighted to hear him invite the child to come
up to the farm with her mother some time, and enjoy a
country day out. That, at least, was a start.

Her interest in her own new family had distracted her

from the general movement in the hall. Now, looking up, she discovered only three people were left, standing forlornly in the centre of the vast space, looking frightened and lost. She could hear Henry Evans saying worriedly: 'I'm terribly sorry, Mrs Chandler, but if you'd been prepared to separate the children it would probably have been different.'

'They've been through enough this past six months without that an' all. They need each other and they need their mum. I'll go back to London rather than split up from them!' As she rose to the defence of her children, the woman's apparent apathy fell away and she visibly tensed to face the ordeal which was undoubtedly ahead of her.

Evans ploughed on, determined to help her in spite of herself. 'But just for a few weeks . . . We could place your boy here in Abercarn without trouble. If you and the girl went to the overspill centre in Risca overnight, I'm sure we could sort something out for you tomorrow, then in a month or two perhaps something could be done to get you all back together.'

Her eyes blazed at him: 'You don't really expect me to *leave* him here on his own? Do me a favour!'

'But, madam, that's what other mothers all over the country are doing. It's only a very few who actually go away with their children at all.'

'Yes, and once we do, you see to it that doesn't last long. No thanks. I'll find some way of getting back to London tomorrow, if we can all go to this centre tonight.'

Lily realised she was not the only eavesdropper on the scene. Her brother was staring, outraged, at the little group. Now he said, fiercely, as though to himself: 'I'm damned if I let them do that to anybody!' and almost before Lily grasped what was happening, he had joined Evans and the women.

'No need for anybody to go to no centre,' he said. 'If your little ones don't mind travelling in the back of a pony trap, missis, I'll give you all a home.'

Lily thanked the God she did not believe in that there

was no reserve on the woman's face, only a glow of gratitude. 'D'you really mean it?' she asked, 'not just tonight – a proper permanent place?'

Billie smiled and nodded. 'No point taking you five miles up the Gwyddon just for tonight, is there now?' He squatted to bring himself eye-to-eye with the children. 'I'm Billie. What're your names?'

There was a second's silence, then the girl's hand emerged from its hiding place inside her overlong cardigan sleeve, and slid into his like a shy but friendly animal. 'I'm Shirley,' she whispered, 'and he's Paul.'

'Well, Shirley an' Paul, I hope you do like animals, 'cos from now on you'll be lookin' after a pony and feeding the chickens. I'm very particular about who I ask to look after my animals.'

The children's mother had turned her head away momentarily and Lily realised, through a mist of her own tears, that she was trying not to show she was crying. She made much of going over to the corner of the room to pick up their meagre luggage and Billie came back to see Lily about them eating together at her house before they set off on the long journey up the valley.

'You're a one, ent you?' she teased him, her tone loving. 'What suddenly brought on that change of mind?'

He was unable to meet her eye. 'I don't remember much about the first three months back in the asylum after France,' he said, 'but I *do* recall overhearing the superintendent saying if our Mam would have me back home, I'd probably get better quicker. The almoner just said to him: "As far as Mrs Walters is concerned, he's no responsibility of hers; no responsibility of anybody's." It have always stayed with me, and when I saw those three, it was as if somebody was saying it about them. I can't let that happen to anybody if I can do something to stop it.'

'I love you, Billie,' she whispered, 'and whatever our Mam do think, I know you're one hell of a bloke.'

He responded with a rueful grin. 'You'd better hope I live up to your opinion, then. Don't forget I've been on my own up that valley for twenty years or more. What if I do fail?'

'You ent gonna fail, Bill. I'm surer of that than anything. Go on, now, get 'em over yer and we'll all have some tea up our house.'

CHAPTER TWENTY-THREE

Angela Chandler had endured a tough war. Her husband had volunteered in the first week of September 1939, soured by the decline of work in the docks and the growing hollowness of their marriage, and she had seen him only twice since then. To the children he was no more than a name, vaguely associated with a uniform.

Angela herself was twenty-eight years old and out of the usual run of young East London women. She was the daughter of small shopkeepers who had dreamed of a good education and an advantageous marriage for their quick, pretty only child. Angela had won a place at grammar school, did well in her school certificate and was working hard to go away to teacher training college. In the evenings and during school holidays, she served in the shop. And that was where she met the big, burly docker who deflected her from all thoughts of a career and estranged her from her parents.

Still under eighteen, and head over heels in love, she had gone to her parents and asked their permission to marry Steve Chandler. Her mother cried and her father threatened to beat her, although they both knew he would never nerve himself to do it. They refused to consider the marriage, forbade her to see Chandler again and stopped her from working in the shop in case she was led astray by some other young man. But she contrived to go on seeing him, with the help of a girl-friend who pretended to be at the cinema or youth club with Angela two evenings a week. Fumblingly, uncertainly, they became lovers, and it was inevitable that she learned she was pregnant only weeks before she was due to take up a place at teacher training college.

This time the family recriminations were even worse, but to a respectable couple like her parents there was no real doubt about what must be done now: Angela must marry her docker for the sake of her reputation, and spend the rest of her life repenting the opportunity she had missed. At first she had not felt deprived at all. Chandler really loved her, and she was still starry-eyed about him. She was healthy, and her pregnancy presented few problems.

Then their baby was born, and prospects were less bright. She worshipped her son, Paul, but Steve began to resent the baby. He also ran into work trouble, and was often only given two or three days in a week, instead of the steady six he had been doing when they married and he had been able to afford to set them up in a neat terraced house with its own back garden. Now it was hard to find enough money for rent, food and clothes. He complained constantly that she was spending more than she needed to on the baby, then started saying that if she persuaded her mother to have the child at the shop, she herself could get a factory job to boost their income.

Harassed by his nagging and worried about the worsening shortage of money, she tried to persuade her mother to co-operate. She refused indignantly, and was backed by Angela's father. 'Oh, no, my girl – your mother works herself into the ground already. You made your bed, now you must lie on it!'

He delivered the last line so smugly that Angela decided he must have been saving it ever since her marriage. A full scale quarrel developed and, almost before she realised it, Angela was storming out of the house, swearing she would never return. She had kept her resolution, too, even when the birth of their second child, Shirley, worsened her predicament and made it more important than ever for her to find a job.

Somehow, she managed. An old woman who lived in their street was glad of a warm room and her meals during the daytime, items she could not afford at home on her tiny income. Angela gratefully installed her as child minder and went off to work at the soap factory. She loathed every minute, but at least, now, she was not totally dependent on Steve for housekeeping money, and did not have to go through the week dreading the moment on Friday evening when he grudgingly handed over the small supply of cash, impressing upon her that their misfortunes were largely at her door.

His reason for blaming her changed from week to week. Sometimes it was her stupidity in alienating her parents, who would have been a soft touch according to Steve once they saw their grandchildren growing up. Alternatively, the line was that he had never wanted kids anyway, and she had trapped him into early fatherhood, or worse, marriage itself, by getting herself pregnant. At least, once she started supplying half the housekeeping money, he limited his complaints to the occasional bitter aside. Almost anything was better than the constant, whining abuse she had been enduring before. That was less easy to keep in mind in the noise and stink of the soap factory, or when her children begged her not to go off and leave them in the morning, but she often reflected it was amazing what you could put up with when there was no choice.

By the time the war started, she was glad to see the back of Steve. But what lay ahead was hardly an improvement.

It said much for the stress she was enduring now that she was willing to talk about her past. In normal circumstances a girl of her respectable background would have died rather than take strangers into her confidence. But she sensed that these were kind, understanding people who had suffered themselves. And she was almost at the end of her endurance.

Over strong tea, liberally sweetened with black-market sugar from Lily's store cupboard in the rambling doctor's house at the Swan, she told at least part of her story to her new friends. 'When that bombing started last September, I think I was more frightened than I'd ever been in my life,' she said. 'But it's amazing how quickly

218

you get used to things. After a bit we'd be going out to the Anderson shelter without really waking up, and me going off to work in the morning and the children to school as if it was just another day . . . s'pose it was, in a way.

'It wasn't doing Paul and Shirley any good – they're so jumpy now when they hear loud noises, and they hate fire – but we were still alive and fit and we had a roof over our heads. And Dad came home twice on leave, didn't he?' For form's sake she slipped in this last reference, but her audience were no more fooled by the forced cheer in her tone than her own children, who nodded gloomily. Then Paul smiled: 'But not for long, that second time, eh Mum?'

Angela laughed in spite of herself. 'Naughty boy! You weren't supposed to notice.'

'What happened?' Lily prompted her.

'Well, he came home, must have been last Christmas, all full of himself and how dangerous things were where he was posted. Wouldn't say where, or what he was doing, but he sort of suggested that he was a marine commando. All I knew was he was in the forces. Could have been the commandos, but I wouldn't care to bet on it . . . anyway, he came home a week before Christmas – seven day pass because after that he was off on this big hush-hush mission. First night home, the Luftwaffe came over an' chucked everything they had on Silvertown.'

Paul broke in now, quite animated at last. 'It wasn't all that bad compared with some of what we'd had the week before, but it saw Dad off. He nearly trampled me in the rush out to the shelter, and then he sat there curled up in a ball for a couple of hours. Wouldn't come back inside after. Said he knew where he was well off. He went back the next day. Recalled to his unit . . . ' Even to an eight-year-old boy this had clearly not been convincing. Paul delivered the line with a cynical half-smile.

'How did that happen?' asked Billie. 'In my experience, the military ent usually that obliging.'

Angela shrugged. 'That was the big mystery,' she said. 'Steve's story was that he'd left the phone number of the pub on the corner with his commanding officer in case there was an urgent recall and, surprise, surprise, first time he went down the boozer, that dinner time, there was a message for him to contact HQ. He was gone by teatime.'

'D'you miss him?'

Angela responded with a long, level look at Sadie, who had asked the question. 'Now what do you think? I miss a nice dad for the kids, but I think p'raps we'll be better off on our own in the long run. Don't you, children?'

They both nodded. 'We like it better with Mum,' murmured Shirley. Her voice dropped even lower. 'Tell the truth, I was a bit frightened of my Dad.'

The grown-ups exchanged significant looks and the conversation made an abrupt change of direction. The rest of Angela's story could wait.

When they eventually set off for Trywn Farm, the sky had turned a clear turquoise and the bright green of the summer trees had softened in the evening light. Daisy Belle gave a snort of disapproval at the sight of so many extra passengers, but Billie bribed her with a wrinkled apple Lily had found somewhere, and the pony promptly forgot her resentment in the fuss the children were making of her. Both of them insisted on clambering down and walking along sections of the route, exclaiming in delight over great swags of pink foxgloves that were bursting out along the verges, listening enchanted to the faraway gurgle of the Gwyddon brook in its hidden valley below the lane.

Angela Chandler sat on the front seat beside Billie and looked about her dazedly, as if locked inside some magician's spell. For a while that suited Billie, who was never prone to excessive talk. Eventually, though, he grew a little anxious. 'Is anything the matter, Mrs Chandler? You'm ever so quiet.'

She turned to him as though awaking from a dream, and gave him the sort of smile he had seldom imagined this side of heaven. 'Matter? Why, no – quite the opposite. I feel as if somebody's going to pinch me any minute and I'll wake up back in that rotten bombed-out street in Silvertown. I'll never be able to thank you properly for what you've done for me and those children – never.'

He looked at her pretty, slightly worn face and felt an absurd desire to protect her from harm. 'It wasn't that much, you know,' he said. 'I got plenty of room up the farm.'

She shook her head. 'You're a good man – one of the best. I don't need to know you better to understand that. I saw you in that hall, hanging back, arguing with your sister about taking people in. And then I saw the look on your face when that old fool tried to separate Paul from me and Shirley. You've been hurt, as well, haven't you?'

He nodded, and instead of reserve and embarrassment, felt a huge smile forming somewhere deep inside him, bubbling upwards and turning into a chuckle, then a full-throated laugh, as it erupted from his body. 'Welcome!' he shouted, 'welcome to the Trwyn! You'm just what it do need to lay the ghosts!'

The two children, who were walking a little ahead of the trap, glanced back in surprise at the sudden noise from this hitherto quiet man, saw the look of happiness on their mother's face and turned back to the foxglove clumps, knowing instinctively that all was well.

Back at the Swan, Lily looked admiringly at Sadie Ryder's legs and said: 'I thought I had a weakness for black market goods, flower, but I confess you got me beaten with those. How did you ever get your hands on 'em?'

Sadie was bewildered. 'What are you talking about?'

'Them nylons. I've only seen them that sheer in the movies. I certainly haven't met anyone wearing 'em around Abercarn.'

Sadie's giggle was delicious. 'Show you summat, if you promise to keep it to yourself,' she said, then stood up and turned away from Lily, spitting on her fingers as she did so. She rubbed her stocking seam just behind the knee and it smeared, then disappeared. 'Well-shaved legs, a steady hand and a good quality eyebrow pencil, love. That's all it takes,' she said. 'Mind you, it gets bloody draughty in winter!'

Lily was more impressed than she would have been by some major contribution to the war effort. 'But how d'you twist round and get them so straight? You must be a contortionist!'

'Nah – Our Elaine's just a quick learner, thassall. I showed her how to do it, made her practise until they were dead straight, and Bob's your uncle. I keep telling her no wonder she's so good at art in school when she can draw seams like that.' Her voice dropped to a whisper. 'Course, it's more fun when you gotta fella to do it for you, but those days seem to be just a beautiful memory at present.'

Lily's laugh held an element of nervousness. 'I think you and me'll get on terrific, Sade, but God knows what you'll do to our Mam's blood pressure!'

They finally arrived at Trwyn Farm with the last shreds of daylight. The lovely old house snoozed on its rocky platform, its well-tended walled garden holding at bay the wilderness of broad-leaved forest that plunged into the valley beyond. In spite of the warm weather, a hospitable trickle of smoke threaded its way from the squat chimney. Above them the sky was a translucent dome of clear deep blue, with tatters of faded pink and gold along its western edge.

'This is the most beautiful place I ever saw,' said Angela. 'I used to look at pictures of places like this in books and wonder if I'd ever see one.'

'Well, now you 'ave. Welcome, and I hope you and the children will be as happy here as I have been.'

'Oh, I haven't got any doubts about that,' said Angela, following him up the uneven garden path.

He lit a couple of lamps and said: 'I expect you'll be needing some supper after that long ride. Tea and bread-and-marge down Lil's is all very well, but these kids is growing.'

'You won't be able to find supper for us, Mr Walters. I haven't even had time to dig out our ration books yet.'

Billie grinned at her. 'Haven't spent much time around

farmers, have you love? If I had to live on what they gets from the shops down Abercarn, I'd never be strong enough to run this smallholding single-handed. If you keep livestock, you always got enough to get by, even with the men from the ministry buggering about the place from time to time. Now, how about some milky cocoa for the kids, and a bitta toasted cheese?'

It sounded, and eventually tasted, like a banquet. By the time Paul and Shirley had finished their huge mugs of cocoa, they were nodding off to sleep, emotionally and physically exhausted by the trials of their long day.

'Beds ent made up, I'm afraid,' said Billie. 'As you gathered, I had no plans to find three lodgers. But there's plenty of space and the front rooms is always kept aired. I'll just take some sheets up.'

She went to help him, and they made up a double bed and two singles in adjoining rooms over the huge old kitchen. Billie's own room was at the far end of the landing. 'Furniture's a bit funny, I'm afraid,' he said. 'I picked it up over the years, or made some for myself, see. Seemed like a pity to leave all these nice rooms bare, and I never really had no money to furnish them all. So I put scraps together bit by bit, mainly when people was throwing things out. Hardly anybody to stay in them, anyhow – Lily, or Haydn and his wife now and then, and o' course the kids have always come up for a coupla weeks in summer. But apart from that it was only me.'

'You must have been lonely, sometimes.'

'Suppose I have been. But it do always depend on what you'm coming away from, don't it?'

She sighed. 'You're right, there. There were plenty of times before this war started when I'd have given a lot to be lonely from my husband. Still, mustn't whine about that, must I?'

'If you want to, I'd like to hear, once you get those two little 'uns to bed. And by the way, don't call me Mr Walters. Nobody've called me anything but Billie for thirty years at least.'

'All right . . . Billie . . . I'm Angela.'

'Come on, then, let's get the children off to bed . . . Angela.' He spoke her name as though savouring its sound, then went off along the landing, his mind full of pleasure at the prospect of having children and a woman around to look after and cosset.

Once Paul and Shirley were in bed, he raked up the fire, banked it and re-heated the last of the milk for their cocoa. Sitting opposite her in the glow of the fire, he smiled wryly. 'Of course, in the films, they have scenes like this with deep snow outside and bottles of fine wine indoors, and the beautiful lady refugee is being comforted by someone really glamorous like Paul Henreid or Errol Flynn. All you got is a batty old recluse and a cuppa cocoa!'

'You *are* a funny bloke – you're not a bit like that.'

'Like what?'

'A batty old recluse. You're a really nice man with the warmest smile I ever saw. Not a trace of the hermit anywhere if you ask me! And where does the "old" come in?'

He laughed, then. 'What age are you? Twenty-five? Twenty-six, maybe?'

'Flatterer! Twenty-eight this spring. Remember, I've got a son who's nearly ten.'

He shrugged. 'Even so . . . I remember enough about my own twenties to know anyone over forty is ancient then . . . And I have been in my forties this long time.'

'How old *are* you?'

You're blushing, you silly sod, he thought, then said: 'Fifty-two. One foot in the grave.'

'And you look less than forty, you daft man! The solitary life must suit you.'

'Suppose it do, an' all.' He was silent for a moment, then added, 'O'course, there's them as would say you don't age if you don't live. P'raps I've never lived, really.'

'I don't believe that, either. You have this lovely little farm, you've got a great family – at least if your Lily's anything to go by – and my kids think you're about one step down from God after just a couple of hours in your company. I think that adds up to someone really special.'

'Go on – kids like anyone with a pony an' trap.'

'They don't like men – not mine, anyway.' Her face had taken on a pinched, shut-in look.

'Something happen to them, did it?'

Angela nodded. 'Their bloody father. They don't remember, really, now, thank God. It's a couple of years ago and Shirley was barely five. The boy was seven. More of it stuck with him, poor little devil.'

'Will it help if you tell me?'

'D'you know, I think it will? You look as if anybody's secret would be safe with you . . . ' She took a deep breath. 'Don't s'pose it's that awful, not to anyone but me, that is. 'Spect it happens every day, somewhere . . . He came back home on his first leave. The house isn't – wasn't – very big, and the walls were like flypaper, they were so thin. Shirley had flu. Really bad, not just sniffles, and she was in bed. I was dead on my feet, working full time, queuing at the shops for food, looking after her, seeing Paul wasn't left out – well you can imagine. And all of a sudden, there was Steve. None of us had seen him since September 1938. And he looked so big, and frightening, in that uniform.

'Anyway, he came in, all hail-fellow-well-met, didn't like it because the kids didn't behave as if the conquering hero had returned, and then went straight off to the pub. I'd used the whole week's meat coupons for a decent supper, and of course he got stinking drunk and staggered home hours later. By then it was dried up all over the place and I'd gone to sleep by the fire.

'He bawled at me for spoiling the food, then Paul came downstairs asking what was wrong, and I – I went for him when he belted Paul.' She was looking away from Billie now, into the depths of the fire. 'I-I'd undressed earlier on, got into my nightie and dressing gown. No Marlene Dietrich, mind you – men's winceyette to keep me warm – but it left me defenceless. He smacked Paul again and then he started mauling me. Shirley was down by then, too, crying that her throat hurt and what was the

225

noise about and was anything wrong. He went mad. Pulled off the dressing gown and had me, there and then, in front of them. I was fighting and crying and trying to stop him but he wouldn't listen.'

She was crying, now, as she relived the humiliation of that night. 'He – wouldn't – bloody – listen. Afterwards he just collapsed on me with a sort of groan and I think poor Paul thought he'd killed me – he'd never seen people doing that before, you see. He ran over and started hammering Steve's back. I tried to stop him but it was too late. Steve got up, picked his leather belt off the chair and strapped Paul senseless. When I tried to stop him he knocked me out. I came to, don't ask me how much later, and poor little Shirley was kneeling down on the hearth rug, rocking my head in her arms. Paul had got a cloth from somewhere and washed the blood off his face. It took me weeks to get rid of the bruises that swine had left on his back.'

She considered her story in silence for a while and then said: 'Who am I trying to kid? They'll never forget it, will they? And I used to wonder for a bit why they were nervous around men! Let me tell you something. You're the closest thing to a decent bloke they've had anything to do with yet.'

Billie had no idea what to say. He knew he wanted to reach out and take her in his arms, comfort her and tell her it was all right, he would see nobody could ever hurt her again. But he was powerless. She trusted him sufficiently to tell the awful story. It would take much longer before she trusted anyone enough to commit herself further. Finally he said: 'What happened the next day?'

'Oh, he was on a forty-eight hour pass. I think he was a bit ashamed – not about raping me, but about beating up the boy and letting both the children see what he did to me, that's all. He stayed out most of the day and when he came in he was very quiet. Brought them presents that he said had been in his kitbag all the time, but I don't think he'd even considered that before he came home. I think he'd got some mate of his down the pub to get the presents there and then so he could try to buy the children off. It didn't work, of course. He went back the following day, and we all breathed easier afterwards. Then I had to start trying to put the pieces back. I was just getting somewhere with it when they bombed us out of Silvertown.'

'Dear God, it don't rain except when it pours, do it?'

'Not for me. We weren't hurt, but half the area was flattened, and some good-hearted idiot sent us all the way to North London – Woodford, then Walthamstow, and finally Finchley.'

'Was that so terrible? I'd a thought you'd want to be out of your own streets if they'd blown up your house.'

'Yes, we would. Only one snag. We still worked at the soap factory in Silvertown – seven of us, all tucked away up there in Woodford, and Walthamstow, and Finchley, with those fractured transport lines back. Never stood a chance.'

'What happened?'

'We lost our jobs, of course! There was always someone down there looking for work, and the minute we didn't turn up on time they sacked us and got new people.'

'But your husband's pay – surely, that . . . ?'

'We never saw enough from him to keep a flea alive! Honestly, since last October I've been wondering what on earth will happen to us. That first night, when we were bombed out, the council was supposed to look after us. They put us on a bus to Woodford. You'll never guess where they put us when we got there – in the Majestic cinema! We had to spend the night on the cinema seats. You can imagine how much sleep any of us got. There were no toilets or bathrooms apart from the ordinary Ladies and Gents in the picture house. We spent three days there – three days with me worrying myself ragged about the job, and the kids getting more and more fretful at being cooped up on those *bloody* seats! Honest, if this war ever ends, I don't think any of us will regard going to the pictures as a treat again.

'They took pity on us eventually and put us back on the

buses. We were that pleased! Anything, I thought – anything as long as it isn't a cinema. Miss Innocent was thinking of a YMCA hostel or something. Now that *was* a joke! They'd found us a church in Walthamstow. Not even a church hall, mind you. For one awful moment when I saw it, I thought they'd make us sleep in the pews! It wasn't that bad. They put straw down on the floor and we lay there like a bunch of farm animals. Still nowhere to wash or anything, mind, just the straw and an outside toilet behind the vestry. For eighty of us. Lovely.

'That was when me and the other girls from the soap factory heard we'd lost our jobs. The manager very kindly sent someone up to tell us we'd been replaced. If ever I came close to doing myself in, it was then. But I looked at the kids, and I thought, you selfish little bitch! At least you've had a bit of life, even if it wasn't all you could have wished. They've had nothing. Nothing. You owe them. Put up with it, girl. Something will change.'

'And did it?'

'Well, in a way, I s'pose. We had another few days there and then they found us a place at Finchley Rest Centre. It wasn't paradise, but it was no worse than an Army barracks or something like that. At least you could keep clean and get a little bit of privacy. And the children could start going to school again.'

She smiled fondly at the memory. 'I was lucky there. Steve always said I was a bit of a snob, teaching them proper table manners, and seeing they spoke nicely. But what of it? It was the way I was brought up, and there's nothing wrong with having standards, is there? When some of the children from Silvertown went along to the school in West Hampstead, the local kids gave them a terrible time, called them cockney scum and things like that, because they had these awful accents and held their knives and forks in that funny way.' She blushed. 'To tell the truth, I don't think some of them even *used* knives and forks. I think they just picked up their dinner and guzzled it. Bit difficult when it's mutton stew.'

As she said this her sombre mood broke and she gave

Billie a brilliant smile. 'My God, I sound a right moaning Minnie, don't I? Don't take any notice of me. I wasn't worse off than anyone else there, and better than a lot. At least none of us was hurt or anything. And what I was going to say about the children at school was, mine fitted in all right because their manners were nice and they spoke properly. Made the world of difference to them.'

He shook his head in wonder. 'I think it's marvellous you coped with it at all,' he said.

'Well, what else is there? Once you've got children, there isn't a lot of choice.'

'How did it sort itself out in the end?'

Angela shrugged. 'It didn't – not altogether, anyway. We had to stay at that wretched centre. I had a bit of good luck – a local shopkeeper was short of help and when I told him about growing up in a corner shop, I had a job straight away. Not well paid, but they treated me all right and they used to give me little treats, under the counter, you know, for the kids. We managed like that right through the winter.'

Billie's sigh sounded almost like a sob. 'I think that woulda killed me.'

'Which bit of it?'

'Having to live with all them people . . . never alone . . . ' He laughed at his own eccentricity. 'Daft, ennit? I'm one of a rugby team a kids – always had a house popping at the seams. Slept about five to a bed when I was little. But when I got back from the Army I promised myself, never again. A man gorra be private when he wants to be. Only way I've lived this long.'

'Then you can imagine how I felt about it. I was an only child. Always had my own bedroom. Even my parents knocked before they came in. Then Steve went off so early in the War and there were only the three of us . . . oh, yes, that was the hardest bit all right. I never want to do it again.'

He gestured around him. 'Well you won't have to, now, will you? You gorra nice spacious roof until Mr Hitler promises to stop fighting us. How about that?'

Her eyes followed his hand around the firelit room. 'You know, I feel as if I've been here all my life. I can't tell you how much I hope nothing will happen to drag us away from here.'

'Now what could do that?'

'My husband. He won't go away that easily.'

That had never occurred to Billie, any more than he himself would ever have considered leaving a wife and children of his own voluntarily to go and fight a war. 'He'll be coming back, then?'

'I'm afraid he will. To tell the truth, I wish he'd run off with some exotic piece he meets on his travels, but I don't kid myself it will be that easy. There's no future for Steve and me after what he did to us – 'specially what he did to Paul. I'd never live with him again.'

'Well, there you are, then.'

'But who says he'd agree with me? He's a great big brawling bully, one of those men who always looks brave when he's facing down women and children.'

'I know the sort.' Billie's tone was grim.

'Hmm, well, don't discount the possibility of him coming to look for me . . . Still, that needn't be your worry. We'll have gone back to London long before that, I'll be bound.'

'Don't bank on it,' said Billie. 'Wars have a habit of going on a lot longer than you'd expect. Anyhow, we'll cross that one when we do come to it. Tonight, what about settling for a nice clean bed and the promise of eggs for breakfast?'

Her look told him she thought he stood only a little way below God. 'I can't think of anything I'd like better,' she said. 'Now, I really must stop keeping you up and go off to bed.'

Long after she had gone, Billie sat before the dying fire in his Windsor chair, gazing at the embers. Eventually, rising, he blew out the one lamp he had left alight, and went upstairs in the darkness, saying: 'There ent no fool like an old fool, is there, Billie?'

CHAPTER TWENTY-FOUR

To Lily's amazement, it was not Sadie Ryder who excited Margaret Ann's hostility, but Angela Chandler. Billie was not at all surprised.

'Why bear a girl a grudge just 'cos she *looks* a bit fast when you can hate one who really *is* fast?' he said, by way of explanation.

Lily was bewildered. 'I'm beginning to think the Great War did something to your brain after all,' she said. 'That Angela is about as fast as a minister's wife.'

'Well, I'm glad somebody thinks so. Don't you really understand the way our Mam's mind is working?'

She shook her head.

'Good-looking young married woman with two kids turns up in the village on the evacuees' bus. All the evacuees do get placed except her. Funny, don't you think? Then, hey presto, when Henry Evans gives her the choice of a home for her boy and a perfectly comfortable night at the reception centre for her and her girl, what does she do but turn him down. Miss hoity-toity, ready to go back to London rather than slum it in Abercarn, eh? And then, to cap it all, she do get her hooks into that half-witted Walters bloke, and before you can say Jack Robinson he's smarming all over her and she and the kids have got one a the best billets in the valley, one that more respectable families woulda given their eye teeth for.'

He stopped for breath and by now his sister was goggling at him. 'But Billie, that's the daftest thing I ever heard! I was there, remember? I know as well as you do it wasn't a bit like that. You saved the Chandlers from either being split up or going back to take pot luck in London, that's all. And she certainly didn't ask for any favours, from you or anyone else. What's so different from you having three evacuees and people all up and down the valley taking them?'

'None a them is Margaret Ann Walters's funny son, the one who never fitted in, are they? And how many of them are attractive women lodging with single men, miles away from where prying eyes can get at them?'

As he spoke the last words, Lily began to laugh. 'I'm glad it do amuse somebody, any rate,' said Billie grumpily.

'Oh, I am sorry, kidda, but when you said that, I suddenly realised. Of course, that's it – it's just that whatever you do, she won't know. You could bump the whole family off and bury them in the farmyard and nobody in Abercarn would be any the wiser – including our Mam!'

'Bloody good job an' all! Angela's a nice woman, who've been through a lotta trouble lately. Last thing she'll want is a scandal-monger like Mam stirring things up for her.'

'D'you think she and the children will settle down all right up there? It must be like the outback after London.'

'From what I can see, she's taking to it like a duck to water. Lil, this may seem a bit fanciful, but in a way it's like it was for me. She really have taken a mauling: parents who disowned her, awful husband, homeless since she was bombed out nine months back, barely enough money to keep going. They'm not the same things that drove me daft, but I don't think she was much further away from breaking point all the same.'

Lily was beaming at him. Billie stumbled to silence, then after a while said: '*Now* what's on your mind?'

'I think you've got a crush on your lodger, Billie-boy!' She leaned forward and hugged him. 'Now don't get all worked up. I'll keep it to myself. It's just that if you have, I'm glad. You been on your own too long.'

He knew he was red-faced again, and muttered:

'Wharra you on about, girl? I'm fifty-two this year – old enough to be her father.'

'Well, yes, if you'd started young, I suppose . . . but plenty of girls marry men with that sort of age difference and it don't do them no harm. Does the men a lorra good, an' all, so I've heard!'

'Lily Richards, if you breathe a word . . .'

'Cross my heart an' hope to die. I'm only teasing you, Billie, but I hope it do work out between you. That one's a really nice woman – and the kids, too, come to that. Anyhow – that's your business an' I'll drop it. I've had some really marvellous news – tell the truth I can hardly believe it.'

She dipped into the pocket of her wraparound pinafore and produced a letter. 'Listen to this,' she said, 'it's from Tommy.'

> Dear Mam – can't write much because they won't allow us to say a lot and someone will only put a blue pencil through it if I chatter on too much. I've been posted at last. You'll never guess where in a hundred years – Singapore! There you are. You always did say the further away from the front line I was stationed, the better. Can't get much further than that, can I?
>
> I did some training on the sort of planes they use there, so they're sending me as part of a small advance group before our main force. That's about all I'm allowed to say, except that we leave at the end of the month and I'll get a forty-eight-hour pass before I go. Have your shopping list ready when I get home. I intend to come back loaded with silk and jade for you!

'There – how about that? I've been dreading them sending him somewhere really dangerous, but if it's the Far East, the journey out will be about the worst he'll have to cope with. I'm so relieved!'

Billie smiled lamely, trying to think of a response

233

which did not betray his own feelings. He was far from sharing Lily's faith in the invulnerability of Malaya. He, too, had read the 'Fortress Singapore' newspaper headlines which were obviously the source of her relief, but he did not believe them. And with what they said about the inevitability of Japan joining in on the German side . . .

'What's the matter, Billie? Ent you pleased?'

'Aye, if it makes you happy, of course I am: I just wish there wasn't no war and boys of Tom's age were back here where they should be, just enjoying being young, that's all.'

'Well, we can't have everything. I suppose in a way the war saved him from the pit. There'd hardly have been a demand for apprentices in the RAF if they hadn't known we'd be going to war, would there?'

What a world, thought Billie, as he climbed back into the trap for the journey back to Trwyn Farm. How old was Tommy now? Seventeen? Couldn't be much more. And he'd been in the Air Force since just after his fifteenth birthday, and now he was being sent thousands of miles, possibly to die, before he'd had a chance to understand his own back yard. I'm glad I ent young any more, he thought, and glad that however long this one do go on, Angela's kids are too young to get caught up in it. He jerked the reins and Daisy Belle headed for the one place Billie always knew would be his safe, peaceful haven.

It was inevitably only a matter of time before Billie and Angela fell in love. At first they both resisted the growing attraction between them, mindful of the difficulties Angela's children had already endured as much as anything else. Eventually, Billie had Angela's husband to thank for the consummation of their affair, if only indirectly.

He was on his way to bed late one November evening, long after Angela had retired for the night. Passing her door, he heard her cry out and then, sobbing, apparently trying to fight off an attacker. Without a second thought, Billie dashed into the room, only to find Angela alone, terrified, still three-quarters asleep, and struggling with a tangle of bedclothes.

He put down his oil lamp and hurried to the bedside. 'What on earth's the matter?' he asked. 'I could yer you shouting out from half-way down the stairs. Thought you was being attacked.'

She burst into fresh sobs and clung to him. 'Oh, Billie, I can't tell you . . . the dreams, they're dreadful. I can put that bastard out of my head in the day-time – it gets easier all the time thanks to you – but at night, back it all comes. He's always chasing me, or beating me . . . or – or worse.' She buried her head in his shoulder. 'Please don't ever let him take me back.'

Her voice was muffled and he could hardly believe his ears. Hesitantly, he said: 'I could never do that, Angela. I do love you more than anything else in the world.'

That stopped her crying. She sat back staring at him, her cheeks still wet with tears. 'You're not just saying that to comfort me?'

He shook his head, unable to express his love in any greater detail. He waited in dumb misery for her to tell him she could never return it, that she must leave as soon as possible. Instead, she said: 'Oh, thank God for that! I was beginning to think you were just being kind to me.'

There was no need for either of them to say more. Silently, she moved further into the wide bed and patted the empty space to indicate he should join her. With trembling fingers, Billie undressed. He reached over to put out the lamp but she gestured to stop him. 'No,' she whispered, 'I want to look at your lovely face.'

He slid into the bed beside her and felt as if all the years of solitude slipped away with the first touch of her fingers on his skin. Some time later, he heard himself say: 'I wouldn't care if I died tonight, my love, after what you've given me. It'd be worth it.'

She pressed soft fingers against his lips. 'Hush! No need for that. We've got half a lifetime together. This is just the start.'

* * *

It should have been the best Christmas of Billie's life, but it was marred by the vast catastrophe which overtook Lily. On the night of December 6th, the Japanese invaded the Malay peninsula. Throughout the next two months, they pushed the European military and civilian population inexorably south towards Singapore, the fortress with brilliant sea defences and no landward protection worthy of the name.

Finally, in mid-February, Singapore fell, and with it Lily's last hopes of seeing her son again before the war ended. In due course he was posted missing, believed taken prisoner, and Lily returned to a semblance of normal life. But there was no longer any zest in her ceaseless round of activity, and apart from putting aside a large white five-pound note as the reward for whoever would one day bring her news of Tommy's freedom, she was helpless to do anything about her private pain.

CHAPTER TWENTY-FIVE

May, 1944

When their Silvertown home blew up under his wife and children, Steve Chandler was in the Western Desert with the Eighth Army. He had never been a great one for writing letters, and following his shameful departure after only one night of his last leave, he found it impossible to communicate with them at all. He kept promising himself that next day, or next week, he would produce a long, newsy, loving letter, somehow telling Ange just how much he thought of her and that he knew she and the kids had real guts to stand up to all that punishment, but somehow it never happened. As his silence lengthened, it became less and less possible for him to break it.

So he went on with his war and left them to theirs. Now the two seemed to be coming together again. Along with the rest of his company, he had been given seventy-two hours leave on returning from Italy to England. They all knew there was something big in store when they reported back in a few days, but could only guess wildly at what it might be. Now Steve was home, in search of love from his children and passion from his wife.

He found a derelict street, the houses gutted, boarded up, and clearly long-abandoned. He stood and gaped at the sight. Somehow it had never occurred to him . . . but it should have, shouldn't it? his conscience said. You knew there'd been a Blitz . . . tried a taste for yourself and didn't like it . . . she'd never have written to you again after that first leave when you forced her . . . you knew that . . . up to you to find out about the rest . . .

Raw with guilt, he wandered eastward along the terrace. Around the corner, a few signs of normality survived. The Queen's Head stood four-square amid the rubble and fireweed, its doors open and welcoming. Let's hope Harry Shaw is still the gaffer, thought Steve.

He was. He treated Steve to a pint on the strength of his uniform and the shock they both agreed he must have suffered at seeing his home was no more.

'You've never gone this long and not heard a thing, mate?' Harry was exaggeratedly sympathetic. He knew Steve's reputation with the fists and was unsurprised that pretty little wife of his had seen her chance and run for it. Not before time, either. Seemed a pity somehow to stick him on to her again. Still, mused Harry, I'm not the Lord God, am I? Let 'em sort it out for themselves.

'Town 'all,' he told Steve. 'That's what you wanna do, mate, try the town 'all. They was all shifted somewhere up North London way for a coupla weeks and your Angela did her level best to get back to the factory in the mornings in time for work. Couldn't keep it up though, and they sacked her, and the other women who was bombed out. Plenty of vultures ready to take their jobs, then, too. Last time my missus saw her, she said summat about them getting evacuated – you know, some a the mothers was allowed to go with the kids, even if the kids was a bit older than babies, providing the mums was still in emergency accommodation. And from what I heard, your Angela was in emergency accommodation all right.'

Steve left his kitbag with the landlord and trudged off to the town hall. Hours later, in a filthy temper, he had finally managed to unearth the information he sought. Angela and the kids were somewhere down in South Wales. Mining village called Abercarn. The only onward address they had was the area reception centre, but they were sure he would be put in touch with them from there.

He spent the night as Harry Shaw's guest at the Queen's Head. Next day, after interminable delays at Paddington, he eventually caught a train for Newport. By now, Steve's initial waves of sentimental anticipation

238

at seeing his family after so long had vanished beneath self-righteous anger at being dragged half-way across the country to find them. A Londoner born and bred, he had seen more than enough of abroad and had no desire to explore the rest of Britain on his return. Now he held Angela personally responsible for his mission, and already half-believed she had quit London to evade him rather than to escape the Blitz.

Finally an even slower train than the one that had brought him from London deposited him on the platform at Abercarn. The station was over half a mile from the village centre, and he stood outside the ticket hall in perplexity, looking around for anyone from whom he could seek directions.

The elderly man who doubled as guard and ticket-office manager came shuffling back from waving out his train. 'Hey, mate, can you help me?' said Steve. 'I'm looking for a young brunette woman with two kids – boy and girl – name of Chandler. Mrs Angela Chandler. Someone said they'd come 'ere to stay as evacuees. Don't suppose you've heard the name, have you?'

Steve was ignorant of the tightness of Valleys communities or it would have been unnecessary for him to ask. The old man's face cracked into a knowing grin. 'Oh, aye, I think I do know who you mean all right,' he said. 'Take a bitta doing for you to find them on your own, though – outa the way, see. Tell you what. I know just the lady who can help. Mrs Walters. Lives in a street up the village called the Ranks. Go along that road down there until you get to the village centre, then turn left up the main road and ask for Mrs Walters. Margaret Ann Walters. Everybody do know her. She'll put you right.'

The sinister grin still played around his lips and Steve wanted to shake him. The old bastard knew something about Angela, but he wasn't going to say what. And this Walters woman. If Ange wasn't staying there, why the hell should she know anything? Barely managing to mumble a civil word of thanks, he set off towards the village.

Eventually he found the small terraced house in the front row of the Ranks and rapped on the door. A tiny, neat woman opened it and looked him over, her face momentarily clouded with alarm. 'You ent from the Air Force, are you?' she asked.

Remembering he wanted a favour, Steve struggled not to bite her head off. He touched his cap with false humility and said, 'No, ma'am – Army. If you're Mrs Walters, someone said you might be able to help me find my wife and kids. They're evacuated down here.'

She continued to look apprehensive for a moment, then broke into a secret smile which had a disturbing similarity to that of the old railway guard. 'Oh, aye. Name of Chandler, by any chance?'

His heart bounded in a mixture of relief and anger. 'Yeah – that's right. You know where they are?'

'Well, yes. But it will be a bit of a trick for you to get there. Come in a minute and have a cuppa tea. You must be parched. I'll see what we can arrange.'

He drank strong tea and ate Welsh cakes in the cramped parlour while Margaret Ann looked outside in the back lane for a child to run an errand for her. Finally she persuaded one of the Webb boys to go, and scribbled a brief note to the doctor. Charles Henderson was the only local person she could think of who might have a vehicle and enough petrol to take Steve Chandler where he wanted to go. Secretly she hoped it would not be Charles and, automatically, Lily, who got the note, but Henderson's woman partner. Lily might try to keep the man away from his wife, and somehow it didn't seem fair after he'd come all that way, special, with so little time to spare.

It turned out that Lily was driving Henderson to an emergency call in the inaccessible mountainside row of houses known locally as the Spiteful. Twenty minutes later, Maureen Lawlor, his female partner, arrived in her little four-seater.

'Sorry about Dr Henderson, Mrs Walters,' she said. 'It sounded a bit desperate, if this poor chap has to rush back to London soon, so I thought I'd come to the aid of the party. I'm not doing anything at present.'

As Margaret Ann got into the back seat behind the doctor and Steve Chandler, she wondered if there really was a hint of sulphur in the air, but dismissed it as a by-product of her over-fertile imagination.

Margaret Ann had not been up to Trwyn Farm in all the years Billie had lived there. Now, bumping up the old dirt road, it was like being thrown back through time to another century – another life, where madness and jealousy and something deeply evil about this place had conspired to form one of the worst experiences of her life. The thick trees closed in overhead and far, far below she heard the brook chuckling as if it knew a terrible secret.

Something primeval and deadly stirred deep inside Margaret Ann. I told Billie this was a wicked place, but he wouldn't listen . . . did wicked things to me, did Billie . . . left his poor Mam and went to live with that fancy piece of his father's. Left her and then disgraced her by coming back years later, not quite right in the head. Well, she'd told him this place would find him out, and now it looked as if it had. No good would come of it.

Abruptly she realised that Dr Lawlor had asked her the same question three times. 'Oh – sorry doctor. Yes, I know it's remote. You don't realise till you get up yer, do you? Never think the valley'd go back this far, so steep and so narrow? I never understood how our Billie could bear it up yer.'

'Billie? That your son, missis?' said Steve, adding, with exaggerated detachment, 'Bet 'is wife has summat to say about being so far from the shops.'

Margaret Ann was all innocent surprise. 'Oh, he ent married! Wouldn't catch a girl from Abercarn living all the way up yer. I always wondered how Mrs Chandler put up with it.'

'You mean she's been tucked away up 'ere for two years with some strange single bloke an' my kids?' The rising note of rage in Chandler's voice dented even Margaret

Ann's complacency. 'There'd better be a bloody good explanation for this!'

Maureen Lawlor flashed Margaret Ann a warning look in the rear view mirror, but the other woman deliberately turned away and studied the scenery. The doctor adopted her most soothing tone: 'Really, Sergeant Chandler, from what I've heard of the matter, Mr Walters did your family a good turn. I have a fair bit to do with the evacuees in this area – sit on a couple of committees – and I remember the registrar telling me Mr Walters took them in at a time when they'd have been split up otherwise.'

'Yeah, I bet he did – and I can imagine why, an' all! Two innocent kids and a cracking bit o' skirt like my Ange! Bet he'd a paid for the privilege, given half the chance!'

'I think you're being grossly unfair. Your children have had a better life up on that farm with Mr Walters than they could have hoped for elsewhere in wartime. They're two of the healthiest youngsters on my books. You'll find them changed beyond recognition from the pale little waifs they were when they arrived.'

'I bloody bet I will! What'll they be doing, calling this geezer Uncle and forgetting they've got a real dad who's out trying to make the world safe for them?'

'I'm sure neither their mother nor Mr Walters will have let them forget that – and just as a point of interest, everyone I know calls Mr Walters "Billie". I assume that includes your children.'

'Bet it bloody well includes my Ange, an' all!' he snapped.

Maureen Lawlor stopped the car with a jerk. 'Sergeant Chandler,' she said, 'I agreed to drive you up here because I thought it was vital for you to see your wife and children before you went back on active service – I assume that's why you're home now. But I have no intention of taking you to the farm if you plan to wreck a perfectly decent, human arrangement which has worked well for a couple of years. Now, unless I have your word that you will conduct yourself in a civilised manner, I have no intention of driving you any further.'

Steve sat hunched in the passenger seat and chewed his thumbnail, too angry to reply. Then he realised he still had no idea which of the winding woodland tracks led to the farm, and that he would have to rely on the doctor for at least the rest of the outward journey.

'All right,' he said sulkily, 'but their story better be good.'

'If you simply let them tell it, I am confident that it will be,' said Maureen Lawlor, secretly praying that was true.

In the back seat, Margaret Ann said nothing, only hugging himself in secret anticipation of nemesis finally claiming Billie.

'This is the sort of day you wish would go on for ever,' said Angela, stretching her arms luxuriously above her head as she gazed out across the valley from the farm garden.

Billie emerged, grinning, through the farmhouse door, bearing a tray laden with tea, scones, butter and a huge honeypot: 'And is there honey still for tea?' he said, in what he called his posh voice.

'Where'd you get that from? I did it for my school certificate!'

'Didn't know farmers had poetic souls, did you? It just so happens the poor sod as wrote that died in the same war as I fought in, and when I read it was typhus as killed him, not a bullet, I read his stuff. Love that one, although the patriotic rubbish he wrote was another matter entirely,' he added.

'Well, I like *everything* he wrote, so there!'

'Oh, Miss lah-di-dah, showing us you're the big reader in the family, eh?' He put the tray down on the weathered wooden garden-table, and came over to embrace her. 'God, but you'm a gorgeous woman, and I can't think what I ever done to deserve you.'

She kissed him and said: 'You were just a lovely, honest, gentle man, that's all. Promise me you won't ever change.'

'I will if them idle kids don't hurry up with that watercress,' he boomed, having seen Paul and Shirley clambering up the steep path from the valley with their spoils. Hearing him, they squeaked like a pair of mice, and rushed forward with their booty. 'It was lovely down there today, Billie,' said Shirley, 'all thick and fresh and so much we coulda got enough to sell to people.'

'Hey, watch out, kidda – you'm getting quite a little Welsh accent there – what'll your London friends have to say to that?'

Shirley's smile vanished and an expression of deep anxiety replaced it. 'Oh, don't say that, Billie – I don't ever want to go to London again!' And she ran to him, butting him in the midriff as she threw herself against him in a fierce little rush.

He stroked her hair and held her off, gently, saying: 'Come on, now, no need for that. It's a free country, ennit? That's what we're fighting this war for. Of course you don't have to go back unless you want to.'

The gloom lifted. 'Promise?'

'Cross my heart and hope to die!'

'All right then, I believe you . . . '

Paul and Angela chorused: 'Thousands wouldn't!' and they all giggled as Angela herded the children towards the tea table.

Casting about for something to keep Shirley's mind well away from any gloomy prospects of London, Billie said, in mock-sepulchral tones: 'Watercress do always flourish there, you know why? Dead – men's – bones!'

Both children gasped sharply. 'What? Is it a ghost, or a norrible murder?' asked Paul.

'Oh, definitely a norrible murder,' said Billie, making suitably exaggerated faces.

'Long before I was born, there was a farmer living up yer had a wife who went funny. One day they found her drowned in the stream down there, with her foot trapped in the grid of the sheep dip. Some said suicide, some said murder . . . and then, a generation later, guess what? They found her son in the same place. Weighed himself down with a millstone from the farmyard, he had . . . and when they dug under the other arf a the stone, they found his poor wife, who he'd murdered while she was making the jam . . . '

'Oh, Billie, stop! It's not true – is it?' quavered Angela.

Billie grinned, somewhat shamefaced at having got so carried away with his murder story. 'Afraid it is, love – but I wouldn't worry about them – they'll enjoy the watercress all the better for knowing, won't you, you bloodthirsty little devils?'

They both nodded, agog at having learned this was a place with such a gory history.

After the children had finished their tea and run off to play again. Angela said: 'Was that really true about those people who used to farm the place, Billie?'

'Yes. Sorry if it upsets you – but I knew the children would love it. Kids always enjoy being scared about that sorta thing.'

She nodded. 'Oh, yes, I know that. As long as there's no *real* bogeymen in their lives, they won't worry. And you keep the real bogeymen away.'

'Do I? For you, too?'

'Especially for me. I don't know how you do it, but I'm really happy and safe for the first time in my life.'

He leaned across and kissed her lightly. 'Well you keep it that way, 'cos I'll make sure nothing do happen to you or them.'

Angela squeezed his arm. 'Come on, then, tell me about all these murders.'

'Well, that's about all there is, really. Only one murder for sure, although some said the son's mad father did the mother in, rather than her killing herself. I found out because my damned mother tried to make a big "this place is cursed" thing out of it to scare me off the farm.'

'And you had to lay the ghosts.'

'That's right. At first I told myself she was making it all up. But I know her better than that. Mam is the sort of woman who do only lie by telling some a the truth, if you know what I mean. Seems to feel it keeps her right with her 'orrible Old Testament God. Anyhow, after a bit it got to preying on my mind, and I actually started hearing funny noises about the place the winter after she tried to poison my mind with it. So I promised myself I'd make a special trip down the county library and the newspaper office and read up about it. And I did.'

'And was it as bad as she said?'

'Only in a way. It do just prove you make your own place. All I just said to Paul and Shirley really did happen, but I think the poor woman probably took her own life. Her husband was odd, too, and that, sort of, nudged her closer to the edge, I think. Then along came their poor boy, half-barmy from their misery, and married a girl who couldn't fill the place with kids of their own. And the same thing happened again. Only this time there was no question. The wife was murdered. She had her head bashed in. Afterwards, the poor fella staggered down the mountain and drowned himself where his Mam had done it all those years before.'

He uttered a humourless laugh. 'The really sad thing was, the wife was our Mam's friend, and Mam was the one who found the husband's body in the sheep dip. Don't show her up very well, do it, that after it have passed, all she can use the grief for is to try and scare off the son she don't like?'

Angela touched his cheek. 'Oh, Billie, I'm so glad I found you. Whatever she tried to do to you, whatever the Army tried to do to you, they all failed . . . you're the best.'

He kissed the palm of her extended hand. 'As long as you think so, I don't care about the rest.'

They sat quietly in the sun for a few minutes, then she said: 'What you said about that poor woman not being able to fill the place with children . . . d'you think that makes a difference?'

He nodded. 'Oh, aye. I'm a bit funny about kids. I think even just having them around, like your two, laughing and crying and growing up here, do make a place live a bit more. But when children are actually *born* in a place . . . it breathes new life in. Just as good for the land as it is for the people on it.'

'I'm glad about that, Billie, because we're going to have a baby.'

He sat back in his chair and let out his breath in a huge, astonished gust. Then he threw back his head and yelled, 'Way-hey-hey! You hear that, God? We've done it! We've brought new life back yer to break the old spells!' He jumped up and pulled her to her feet. 'I love you so much I wanna burst with it!' he said, 'and if you like this un when it comes, I want a houseful of kids – d'you hear me?'

'I hear you, you bloody mad Welshman – and we'll have as many as you want!'

CHAPTER TWENTY-SIX

'Who could be coming up here today? That engine isn't the forestry van, and Lily said she wouldn't have time to come up before the weekend,' said Angela, listening to the chuff of a labouring motor approaching, up the farm track.

Billie shrugged. 'We'll know soon enough, won't we? T'ent as if it's gonna be the last judgement.'

The figure which disembarked from Dr Lawlor's car might have been just that, with the doctor and Margaret Ann Walters as stand-ins for the horsemen of the Apocalypse.

Angela's hand flew to her mouth. 'Oh no!' It was almost a sob. 'Get inside, Billie. That's Steve.'

She was staring at her husband and away from Billie, but she could tell her lover had made no move to go. In mounting panic she hissed: 'Stop playing games – he's twice your size and fifteen years younger.' Then she glanced for the first time at Billie.

He was standing, loose-limbed and relaxed, the hint of a smile on his lips. 'I think maybe *you'd* better go in, love – and keep an eye open for the kids, an' all, in case they come back while this little lot is going on.'

The trio from the car began to advance on the garden, Steve in the lead by several paces. Angela was close to hysteria now. 'Billie – for God's sake – he'll kill you! Let me talk to him, then, maybe, after . . . ' She fell silent. They both knew there could be no 'after' in this confrontation.

'Just this once, woman, don't argue,' he said. 'Go in. Close the curtains, if you like. I don' give tuppence about

Mam's finer feelings, and Dr Lawlor will have seen a lot worse. But you'm different.'

There was a note in his voice that would stand no disobedience. She turned towards the door, brushing her hand down his arm as she did so. She noticed he was standing easy and relaxed, poised with his weight slightly forward, his arms hanging away from the body, almost in a wrestler's stance. Suddenly confidence leapt in her. He's going to beat him! she thought. He's going to show him you don't have to be a bruiser to come out on top! Nothing would stop me watching this!

She went indoors and stood behind the curtain by the nearest open kitchen window. Chandler had come in through the gate, now, and was storming up the path to confront Billie. Without any other introduction, he yelled out: 'I want my wife, you Welsh bastard!' His colour was high and so was his temper – so much so that he choked on his own words.

Maureen Lawlor, who until now had been moving slowly, in an effort to let the man exchange a quiet greeting with his wife, realised what was about to happen and surged forward like an athlete, intent on getting between the two men before they came to blows. She was a tall, powerful woman, but Chandler thrust her aside as if she were a dead leaf. 'Mind your own business,' he muttered. 'This is my fight, and if you stay out of it you won't get hurt – you and the old lady, all right?' Then he resumed his advance on Billie.

Billie made no move to meet him. He merely stood on the flagstone path, limbering his arms and swaying gently on the balls of his feet. His easy stance unsettled Chandler, who was big enough to be used to men moving out of the way if he approached them in anger. Eventually he stood only inches from Billie, gazing down into the Welshman's silver-grey eyes, without the man having stirred from the spot.

'Well,' said Steve, 'let's be havin' her. I got plans for you, mate. I'm gonna spread you all over this poxy little garden, and then I'm gonna take my wife an' kids back to

London where they belong, but first I want her out 'ere to see what an apology for a bloke she got hold of. Christ, you look as if you got one foot in the grave already!'

'She ent coming out yer, and she ent going anywhere she don't want to. Same goes for the children. Now, are you gonna behave, or do I 'ave to ask the doctor yer to drive you all the way back down the valley? Or p'raps you prefer to walk – cool off a bit, like?'

That pushed Chandler's temper over the edge. All thought of humiliating this Welsh gnome in front of Ange disappeared. A red fog suffused his brain and all he wanted to do was strike out against this vermin until it had dispersed. 'Right,' he said. 'You fucking asked for this!' and drew back a fist the size of a small ham, lining it up with Billie's jaw.

As he began to lunge forward, Billie pivoted slightly on one foot, almost like a ballet dancer. The other foot came up in a short, graceful arc and the curved hobnail-studded toecap caught Chandler squarely in the genitals. It hurt too much for him to scream. He merely uttered a breathless grunt and started to double forward. As he did so, Billie hunched slightly, then made a lightning-fast, rigid jab forward with his whole upper body. His forehead made contact with Chandler's as the bigger man collapsed towards him, with a crack that Angela heard clearly from inside the house. Then Billie stood aside, with the grace of a successful bullfighter completing a pass, and permitted his victim to complete his fall to the ground. Once Steve was prostrate, Billie delivered a couple of sharp kicks to the kidneys to ensure he remained there for a while.

He glanced up at Maureen Lawlor, who had just drawn level with them. 'Sorry about that last bit,' he said, grinning apologetically. 'That was a bit of revenge for what he done to the kids, see.'

Dr Lawlor stared up at Billie, awestruck. 'Where on earth did you learn to do that?' she asked.

He shrugged. 'If you'd ever known Evan Jones, you wouldn't need to ask that. He was my father.'

'Don't you *dare* associate your father's name with such carryings-on! I never saw such a disgusting exhibition in my life!'

Margaret Ann, who had remained beside the car until now, prepared to relish Billie's downfall, came storming up the path. 'That man was here to take his own wife and children – the woman you've been doing goodness knows what with up here for so long, thinking nobody'd ever know. Well, now you both got your come-uppance!'

Sensing he might need her beside him now, Angela had come back out of the house. Margaret Ann glared at her and turned back to Billie. 'Well, why don't you tell the trollop to pack her bags and get ready to go?'

Billie merely gave her a pitying smile. 'Angela ent going nowhere without me, Mam, ever again, and there's no point in you thinking otherwise. She and the children are going to stay up yer with me.' He gestured at the still-unconscious Steve. 'Can't see him stopping us, can you?'

Then something snapped inside Margaret Ann. Why should this boy, once her dearest, then her hated enemy, always an outsider, win in the end against all odds? What right had he? Her face twitching with the intensity of her rage, she jerked forward at him. 'It's this place . . . This accursed place!' A thin, cackling giggle dribbled from her lips. 'Don't think you'll escape it!' She turned with snake-like suddenness on Angela – 'Nor you, neither, you – you harlot! It do take good women, as well as bad.' She was giving off hatred now like some physical force, which drove Billie up the path towards the house ahead of her, backing away from her wrath.

'It will come for you in the winter, in the dark,' she hissed, 'just like it did for the Jobs, all them years ago, nudging, whispering . . . "anybody in there got somethin' for the poor Pwka'r? Anybody willing to keep him from the cold? Anybody been keeping his old room warm and snug for him?" And then he'll be in the house with you, whispering his bad words, turning you away from each other, driving you down the mountain to the brook . . . driving you, with the millstone tied round your ankle, mopping your cursed forehead with your big red spotted hankie till you'm in such a state you throw it down on the path . . . and in the end, like as not, it'll be one a them poor innocent children who finds you down there, Harry Job, dead in the sheep dip, and that Jenny back up yer, buried in the farmyard with the flesh all rotted around her poor wedding ring . . . '

Billie had stopped backing away now. He was gazing down at his mother with a mixture of pity and loathing. He put his arms around her shaking shoulders and tried to draw her into an embrace, but she stiffened and pushed him off. Hesitantly, Maureen Lawlor stepped in. 'Perhaps I'd better try to get her home, Billie,' she said, very quietly. 'I think she's worse than you'd believe at first sight.'

He glanced across at the doctor. 'Then she must be a bloody basket case,' he said. 'Only place I seen 'em like this before was on the Somme after a day's shelling.'

The doctor nodded. 'I think it might be something similar, though God knows how it happened. Let's get her in the car and then see about that great lump.' She jerked her head at the unconscious form of Steve Chandler.

Margaret Ann offered no resistance now. Nor did she show any sign of recognising them. They led her back along the path and eased her into the rear seat of the car, then went back for another look at Chandler.

For the first time since the awful incident started, Maureen Lawlor managed a smile. 'Really, Billie, I don't think I ever saw a dirtier fighter – and I was brought up in the back streets of Dublin!' she said.

He grinned back. 'In that case, I take it as a compliment, but havin' said that, what the 'ell do we do with 'im?'

'I'll take a look to see there's no permanent damage before we move him, then I think you and I can manoeuvre him into the car between us. If you could squeeze in the back with your mother and drive down with us, you and I could even get him on the last train to

Newport, I think. Willie Harris is probably on duty at the station and he owes me a couple of favours.'

'He'll have one hell of an 'eadache when he wakes up,' said Billie.

'I shouldn't think his kidneys will be doing him any favours, either, but any man as ready as this one to start a fight must have been in enough of them by now to be used to it. I'm far more concerned about whether he'll come back pestering you again.' She looked earnestly into Billie's eyes, marvelling as she did so that she had never before noticed their quicksilver colour.

He chuckled. 'I don't think he'll come back. I've run into big bullies before. They'm never as dangerous as the little 'uns. So used to winning all the time that they sort of lose heart if someone beats the shit out of them – 'specially when the someone is as small as me. It's the little skinny mean uns you gorra watch . . . and if he *do* lose his senses an' come back, I'll just give him more a the same. It ent the first time I've done it, you know.'

'No, I could see that.'

Somehow they shoe-horned the unconscious soldier into the front passenger seat, and Billie crowded over the back of the driving seat to get in with his mother. Margaret Ann was sitting gazing blankly through the window, muttering occasional unintelligible phrases, and dribbling slightly, but otherwise showing no signs of consciousness.

Billie waved goodbye to Angela and they shuddered off down the uneven track. 'I s'pose I should be more worried about Mam,' he said, 'but it do seem as if she've – I dunno – gone away, somehow. Can't see there's anything I can do to change it.'

The doctor shook her head. 'Nor I. I don't know whether I shall be certain, even after a thorough examination, but I'd guess this is something that's been building up for a very long time – something physical rather than mental – and the excitement up here this evening just completed whatever it took to trigger the attack. Try not to feel bad about it.'

He shrugged. 'Don't bother yourself on that account. I stopped feeling bad about Mam nearly forty years ago, when I was still not much more than a kid an' she blamed me for what went wrong with her marriage. Wasn't nothing to do with me, only I was too young to realise that and I spent years tearing myself apart trying to work out what I'd done wrong. In a way that's what got me in the Army in the end, and through that, to the War and the asylum.'

'Phew! That's quite a lot of fuel for resentment!'

'No point. There's a bitta Mam woulda liked to think I hated her. After a while I just made myself stop caring about it. Trouble is, when you do that, you stop caring altogether, so I don't give a damn what do happen now, or whether I'm to blame.'

She nodded, understanding. 'And do you still bear no malice for having ended up here, with such a solitary life all these years?'

He laughed. '*Duw*, no! Look around you. What place could be more beautiful? And if none a this had happened to me, I'd never have got my Angela, would I?'

'But Billie – almost a quarter of a century up here alone, just waiting for the woman of your dreams?'

'It woulda been worth a whole lifetime, not just half a one. You're looking at the happiest man alive, doctor. Now, let's concentrate on getting this piece a dead meat on that last train.'

They caught the train by a whisker, making sure the elderly guard punched Chandler's return ticket, and checking there was no possible way for him to return to Abercarn from Newport that night. Then they turned their attention to Margaret Ann.

'I was going to take her back to the Swan and examine her in my surgery,' said Dr Lawlor, 'but I don't like the look of her. I confess I thought she would have been coming out of it by now. If anything, though, she's worse.'

Margaret Ann had slumped back in her seat and her

eyes were half-closed. The thread of spittle at the side of her mouth had thickened to a rope-like trail, and the mouth itself was oddly distorted. 'Looks to me as if she's had a stroke,' said the doctor, when she looked more closely.

They got her inside the house and Billie went next door for Maisie, Haydn's wife. Lily had returned from her call with Charles Henderson and was with Maisie, having failed to find her mother at home when she called an hour earlier. By the time Billie returned, Maureen Lawlor had got Margaret Ann into her armchair by the fireplace and examined her.

She nodded briefly at Lily then turned back to Billie. 'As I suspected,' she said. 'It was a stroke. Seems to have got her right side. I don't think she's aware of very much at present. We'd better get her up to bed, or better still, get a bed down here. Lily, can either you or Maisie stay here tonight with her?'

'Of course. Charlie won't mind. He can lust after Sadie Ryder for the evening! Maisie, would you rather I did it?' Lily asked.

'Oh, would you, Lil? I'm up to the eyes at the moment, and someone will have to be with her tomorrow, won't they, doctor?'

Maureen Lawlor nodded.

'Well, I'll do all day tomorrow, Lil, so you can get back to the Swan, and p'raps we can set something up between us all from tomorrow evening on. How about that?'

'Thanks, Maisie. Go on, now, you get back in there and ask Haydn to come in yer and help Billie get a bed fixed up in the front room.'

While they worked, Lily sat on a low stool beside her mother's chair, and stroked her hand. It was limp and heavy, as though Margaret Ann were already dead.

CHAPTER TWENTY-SEVEN

Lily gazed down at the small, still figure in the bed and attempted to make sense of her feelings. Idiotically, her mind kept repeating: you're forty-six years old, not a child any more . . . not a child any more . . . not a child any more . . . For more years than she could remember, she had been treating Margaret Ann as if the old woman were her daughter, not her mother, with an indulgent kindness which owed nothing to their relative ages and everything to her own broader experience and her mother's small-town habits. The attitude had become so ingrained that it had never crossed her mind to consider her own needs. Now she saw the little, shrivelled form, scarcely kinking the bedclothes, and the child in her flinched at the thought of a world without her mother.

'Can I come in, kidda?' She glanced up. It was Haydn. 'Oh, aye, love. You won't disturb her. Either she's asleep or she don't know what's going on . . . I can't seem to take it in.'

Haydn barely glanced at his mother. He was looking searchingly at Lily. 'Come yer a minute,' he said. She turned to him and he put his arms around her, pressing her head down on his shoulder. 'Know your trouble, don' you? Too much thinking – too much thinking by arf. Some things don't change however much you try to think round them, and this is one, Lil. You can cry to me '

She did; endlessly, it seemed. After a while, ashamed, she raised her tear-stained face and said: 'Oh, Haydn, I'm an awful old cow, en I? She's your mother too, and you feel every bit as bad as me . . . '

The weeping swept over her again, and he interjected:

'Stop trying to put labels on everything.' They stood in silence for a while, comforting each other with their closeness, then he said: 'Some clever sod or other said no woman really feels grown up till her mother have died. I think p'raps he was right. Might even a been a she who said it, come to that. Stop thinking you shouldn't cry. There's nothing daft about what you're doing.'

Afterwards, she wondered if she would ever have stopped if Rose had not arrived. Rose was half-mad with grief and anxiety. 'It can't be a stroke! Can't be!' she was insisting to Maisie when Lily came out of the front parlour. 'She been tired lately. Just a bit of a black-out, that's all. Tell 'er, Lil, just a black-out, ennit?'

Lily brushed a hand across her eyes and said: 'No, love. Maisie's right. It's worse than that. A lot worse.'

'I gorra see 'er. She'll be all right when she do see me . . . have a little talk . . . maybe she'll feel up to a cuppa tea then . . . ' Rose's eyes were almost as unfocused as Margaret Ann's had been during the ghastly car journey from Trwyn Farm, but in her case shock was causing it.

Never one for the soft let-down, Lily said: 'No good trying that, Rose. She won't hear you or see you – and she can't move to sit up for a cup of anything. So why don't you sit down by there and try to calm yourself a bit? She've had a good innings, one way and another.'

Rose let out a wail worthy of a Greek tragic chorus. 'How can you be so hard? That's our Mam you'm talking about.'

'I *did* notice that, Rose. I helped get her into bed, remember? Rose, she's seventy-four years old. Apart from a few coughs and sneezes and when she was having babies, have you ever known her be ill?'

Rose shook her head dumbly.

'Well, then, stop having hysterics and thank this God of yours she've had such an easy time of it. If she hangs on a for a few months now, Mam won't feel it – we're the ones that'll suffer, coping with her. And if I know you and your delicate health, it won't affect you too much!'

'Now, Lil, don't be rough with her.' Haydn had just

emerged from the bedroom and had heard her last few words.

Lily made an angry little gesture. 'All this breast-beating won't help Mam, and wishing her still alive when she's in that state is plain hypocritical. I'm just trying to make Rose see a bitta sense, that's all.'

'Aye, well Mam is stirring a bit, so why don't you go an' have a look at her? . . . No, not you, Rose. I don't think you nor Mam would be up to that.'

Lily gave his arm a thankful little squeeze and pushed past him into the narrow passage.

In the dimly-lit makeshift bedroom, Margaret Ann was moving uneasily. Lily approached the bed and stood over her mother, showing herself as clearly as she could. Margaret Ann managed a series of anguished moans and with a huge effort, thrashed one arm about, gesturing downwards. Lily stood, bewildered, for a moment, then realised in horror what was the trouble. 'Oh, love, all right – don't worry! Just try an' hang on.' She raced upstairs and found a chamber-pot in the cupboard beside the double bed. Covering it with an old pillowcase, she took it back down to the parlour. Her mother's expression made it obvious that she had guessed correctly, but now it dawned on Lily that she had no easy means of helping a paralysed woman into a position where she could use the pot.

An instinctive understanding of her mother's ideas of propriety stopped her doing the logical thing and calling for Haydn to help. She balanced the chamber-pot on a low stool and then bent over her mother, picking her up from the bed as if she were a small child – indeed she weighed little more. Then, somehow, she managed to manoeuvre the helpless body into position and Margaret Ann used the pot, whimpering as she did so, Lily knew from shame that even her daughter should see her thus.

Afterwards she got her back into the bed and sat down, stroking her mother's forehead and murmuring nonsense words to comfort her. The wide blue eyes gazed up at her beseechingly, and Lily experienced new depths of distress as she understood Margaret Ann was fully aware of what was happening to her. Gradually, her mother's distress eased, as the weariness of the illness claimed her again and she sank into another doze, then into deep sleep. As soon as she seemed completely unconscious, Lily went back out to the kitchen.

'We gorra get a few things to help her – a commode for a start – an' a bedpan for when we can't shift her fast,' she said. 'And I think we're gonna need things like feeding cups an' all.'

Rose glared at Lily, and when she had caught her attention gave what she assumed was a subtly meaningful jerk of the head towards Haydn and their brother Lewis, who had come in while Lily was with Margaret Ann. Lily merely glared back, and said: 'If you're coming in an' out of yer the next few weeks, my lady, you'd better get used to hearing words like bedpan and commode in mixed company. There's gonna be an 'ell of a lot of wet sheets around if you don't.'

'Lily! I can't stand much more a this!' said Rose.

'Well you know what to do, then, don't you? Stay away and spend your time up the chapel praying for her. We can't use no shrinking violets yer at a time like this.'

Before a full-scale row could break out, there was a light knock on the back door and Charles Henderson came in. 'Maureen just told me what had happened and I came at once,' he said. 'Lily, I'm so sorry . . . Is there anything – anything at all – I can do?'

Lily smiled, deeply grateful for his mere presence, and shook her head. 'I'm glad you came straight up, but no. Maureen did as much as anybody could. I don't need either of you to tell me they don't take women of Mam's age into hospital in that condition. I'm sure you won't mind me sleeping up yer for a coupla nights until we sort out a routine – and you can probably give us all a bit of good advice about looking after her. Mais, be a love and wet the tea in that pot.'

While Maisie made the tea, Lily drove down to her own house, returning moments later with an unopened bottle of Bell's whisky. Charles gaped at her. 'Lily Henderson – I thought we'd seen the last of that a year ago. You must be the only woman in the village with one of those at this stage of the war!'

'Are you gonna report me or have some in your tea?' she asked, then proceeded to splash a hefty measure into every cup, including Rose's.

The spirits – and her desire to behave properly in her brother-in-law's company – steadied Rose's nerves and they sat around the kitchen-table for an hour, discussing the best way of helping Margaret Ann, drawing up an informal rota which enabled Lily to go on working and Maisie to run her household while Margaret Ann received round-the-clock attention.

'It won't be easy.' Henderson's tone was grim. 'Lily, you've helped nurse enough stroke cases around this village not to need my reminder that people can live for years in that condition. I know Sadie will take on more down at the Swan. But can any of the others be relied on for extra help up here?'

'You can forget about Kitty, for a start,' said Maisie. 'Don't like any reminders that we all gorra die one day, that one. She'll run a mile the minute she knows Mam's ill.'

'Forget about her. I wouldn't want her near our Mam anyway,' replied Lily. 'Sal will probably come down as often as she can, but Newbridge is a bit of a pull with the buses so bad these days. Jean will help, though, and she can probably manage a fair bit at weekends.' Jean was Eddie's wife, working as a nursing auxiliary at the local maternity hospital. 'We're better off than a lot I could mention. I've helped with some who couldn't find so much as a second cousin to move in and see to them. Mam had to get some benefit in the end from all them kids, didn't she?' she ended with a grim smile.

Rose blushed furiously. 'P-perhaps I – that is . . . as long as there wasn't no lifting, I could probably help out, Lil.'

Lily's expression was pure poison. 'Oh, no, Rose. We

couldn't risk your health an' all, could we?' Only
Haydn's mocking grin prevented her from delivering a
tongue-lashing when Rose responded with a smug little
smile and the words: 'Well, that's what I thought, an'
all.'

Finally, Henderson said: 'We've discussed everything
we can, and it won't help any of us to sit here brooding
about it. You'll all need to be on your toes for the foreseeable future, so I suggest you get as much sleep as
possible. Lily, are you going to move in here for the
present and just come to the surgery in working hours?'

'Yes. I don't think it's fair on Maisie, with Haydn and
the boys to see to. I haven't got anybody to fret over at
present, 'ave I, if Sadie will see to you?' Henderson
fought the impulse to scoop her into his arms when he
saw the desolate expression on her face. All this, and not
knowing if she'd ever see her only son again. But beyond
that moment, Lily herself seemed undismayed. 'You just
look in on her before you go, then I'll settle down in
there in a chair. Don't want to leave her in there alone
the first night.'

Henderson went into the parlour as Lily cleared the
cups from the table and Haydn went to empty the teapot.
Moments later, he was back. 'Lily, please come in with
me,' he said.

In the parlour, Margaret Ann lay utterly still, her eyes
wide open, gazing at the ceiling, the spotless cotton sheet
knotted convulsively in her hand. Henderson reached
down and gently pressed the veined eyelids closed, then
pulled Lily to him in an attempt to comfort her. 'No need
to organise yourselves now,' he said softly, 'she's gone
beyond it all.'

CHAPTER TWENTY-EIGHT

'D'you blame me for what happened to your mother, Billie?' Angela's pretty face was creased with worry.

'Good God, of course not! Mam had waited years to have a go at me like that. Apart from anything else, she was burning to tell me about the Jobs and Pwka'r. She tried twenty-odd years ago when I took the place, and I shut 'er up. You just gave her the final bit of impetus, that's all. Don't mean she wouldna done it anyway without you around.'

It was the day after Margaret Ann's funeral, and they were talking for the first time about the events that preceded his mother's death. Until then they had skirted it, carefully, like wary strangers, both of them excessively conscious of what each stood to lose if a wrong move were made now.

'It–it wasn't so much your mother, although I'll always feel guilty about it taking her like that. It was more, well, Steve and everything . . .'

'What *about* Steve and everything?'

'Well, what if he comes back? What if he won't leave us alone? What if . . . what if . . . ' Her lip trembled and she began to cry. 'Oh, Billie, what if he takes the kids away from me?'

He reached across and stroked her cheek. 'What will you do if he tries?'

'I've been thinking about it ever since the fight . . . and all I know is, I can't give you up, whatever happens.'

'I hoped you'd say that, 'cos I can't think of anything either side a the grave that'd make me give you up, either. Now let me tell you what I think. I think you've seen the last of your Steve.'

'Oh, no! We'd never be that lucky.'

'Don't be too sure. If he got his hands on you again, all he'd have would be the daily reminder of me getting the better of him. Do you think it would help him feel any happier about that if he separated us? I don't. And I think the same goes for Paul and Shirley.'

'How can you be sure?'

'Because I know the last thing he saw before I corpsed him. Paul and Shirley were just coming up over the top of the path as he took his big swing at me. They didn't just see me lay him out – they saw him make the first move. Every time he looked at them he'd think a them seeing him bested by – what did he call me? – a Welshman with one foot in the grave. I don't think he's made a the sorta stuff that could live with that day after day.'

'Oh, Billie, I hope you're right!'

'Course I'm right. And if I ent, we'll fight 'im every step a the way. I think you got pretty good grounds to contest anything he puts up, from what you've said about his behaviour on them home leaves.'

She blushed and nodded, unable to look at him. 'But it would be terrible to make the children give evidence.'

'Bloody sight better than losing them to that brutal bastard, if you ask me. You think it over – but honestly, love, I don't think you need worry. He'll leave us in peace now.'

'What about our baby?'

'What about it? I'm gonna be the proudest father as ever walked.'

'I know that – but he'll be – you know . . .'

'Illegitimate?'

'Yes. What do we do about that?'

'Give him so much love that when the time comes to tell him he won't care two hoots – oh, and we'll also change your name to mine by deed poll, and I'll legally adopt him when he's born.'

She was visibly happier, and wriggled more comfortably into her basket chair, smiling at him like a contented kitten. After a short silence, she said, 'While we're on the subject . . . '

'What particular subject would that be? My sainted mother, your loutish husband, your children or our child?'

'Stop teasing. None of them. The murder, and – and all that – weren't you ever curious, you know, when your mother had a go at you about it years ago?'

He laughed. 'What d'you think I am, inhuman? Of course I wanted to know. I was busting to know! Asked our Lily, but she didn't know no more than me. Mam had never said a word to anyone in the family. I didn't even know when it had happened. All I had to go on was Mam said she was friends with the wife in the early days after she was married.

'So I started from there. Turned out most of it was in the library down the workmen's institute. They had back numbers of the *Argus* right back to before the Prince of Wales pit explosion in the 1870s. When I had a bitta spare time, I used to sit down there in one a their little back store-rooms and comb through them papers, cover myself in dust . . . and in the end I found it. There was a coupla loose ends, and I followed them up and down the county library in Newport. Turned into quite a little hobby for me. Kept me happy for years, on and off.'

He told her what he had learned; first, from the old newspaper reports, about his mother finding Harry Job's drowned body in the sheep dip, weighed down with the millstone, then the police evidence about digging up Job's murdered wife beneath the millstone. He had traced Harry's mother's suicide, and the inquest report in a paper a generation earlier. And in both he had encountered inexplicable references to the mysterious Pwka'r which had figured in his mother's rantings. That had taken more investigation, but eventually he had found a couple of old books recounting county legends, both of which had referred to some family spirit which hung around the Job household.

As he finished, Angela gave a little shiver. 'Do this ghostly talk bother you?' he asked. 'I'll stop if it do.'

'No – I'll kill *you* off if you don't go to the end of the story now! This place has never worried me. You fill it with love, Billie.'

'Well, in that case, what are the chances of you regarding Pwka'r as being one a the family? I don't think he's wicked – I think the poor old sod is part a the place, and not unfriendly to them as welcomes him. Once I knew about him, I used to talk to him, over my shoulder, like, when I was milking, or out in the field. Better class a conversation when there's two of you, even if one's a spirit!'

'Just as well you're only telling *me* this, you old softy,' she said, laughing, 'or they'd lock you up again and say the shell shock had come back!' Then her voice lost its bantering tone. 'But funnily enough, I believe you. Why d'you think he's real?'

'If you feel like moving from this lovely patch a sunshine, I'll show you summat,' he said, standing up and extending his hand. She let him pull her to her feet and they walked into the house together. Inside, he led her up the back staircase and along the landing to the little room which the children used in winter for painting and reading, because it got the warmth from the big fireplace in the kitchen below.

'Over yer,' he said, going over to the small fire grate and pushing aside the rag rug which lay there. He squatted on the floor and slipped his hand into a notch in the broad old oak planks. Silently, a trap door opened.

'There's an old story in both the books I read,' he told her, 'about two household servants here in the days when the farm was fully manned. They was down in the kitchen, boasting about how nice the skin of their hands was. Story said one was a dairy maid and she was saying how the milk kept her skin white. All of a sudden, there was this little click, and a clear voice – they could never say if was a man or a woman – said, from somewhere up above them, "Pwka'r have got the fairest hands of all".'

He chuckled. 'Jesus! Can you imagine what it did to them? I bet they moved faster than they ever had before!

The worst bit was, they looked up where the voice was coming from, and there was this slim, soft, white hand, waving at them *through the ceiling!* Now looka that trap door. Don't you think that would be the perfect place where a real live Pwka'r could have sat and played his little trick?'

Angela was gazing at the door, entranced at the story. 'But didn't anybody try and explain it all?'

'Well, yes. But I like it as a fairy story. The one author do say it was some fugitive from the English king – either a Catholic running from Protestant royalty, or a Welsh nobleman hiding after he failed in some sorta rebellion. That's about as far as they go. It's certainly true that somebody once took a lorra trouble to hide someone in this room. There's the trap over here, and if you look outside, the door a this room is much newer than the others along the landing. Once upon a time, the trap was the only entrance. I think they walled him up for his own safety and passed him his food through the trap.

'I always liked the idea that the poor sod had hung around in the place where he'd been kept safe, sorta looking after it when his body was gone. Only unhappy people like that poor Job man and his mam just got the bad side, and they was already funny on their own account. If the old Pwka'r is still here, I think he's the guardian of the house.'

Angela had wandered away from him as he spoke, circling the room, taking in its atmosphere. 'If you're there,' she said, 'thank you, Pwka'r. Thank you for keeping him safe for when I came, and for keeping us safe now.'

Abruptly, the little trapdoor flopped shut with a hollow click. They both started violently and then laughed. 'You did that, you villain!' said Angela.

'Yeah, 'course I did,' said Billie, still chuckling. As he spoke, he thought: I could have sworn I'd fastened that back on its little catch.

Angela always swore it was the result of what she called

Billie's Adopt A Pwka'r Campaign, but whatever the reason, their luck seemed unbreakably good after that. Barely a month later, a small fat man in an incongruous pin-stripe suit toiled up the track to the farm in the summer heat, looking as if he were on the edge of an apoplectic seizure.

'You've never walked all the way up from the village?' said Billie in some admiration, wondering how the man had survived the trip.

The visitor took a couple of convulsive gulps of fresh air before he managed to gasp: 'Forester's lorry . . . brought me up to that clearing a coupla of miles back . . . Dear God, that was bad enough. You're safe from just about everything up here, aren't you?'

'I used to think so, but it don't look like it now, do it? You don't strike me as a man who've come up yer to see if we serve cream teas.'

'No . . . well, you're right. William Walters? Is that your full name?'

'Yes. What of it?'

'And is one – um – Angela May Chandler, née Harris, also resident here?'

Billie nodded, realising what was coming next. Angela, who had seen the stranger in the garden, came out on to the path. The man promptly turned away from Billie and approached her. 'Angela May Chandler, née Harris?'

Angela wiped her hands on her pinafore and said 'Yes. Who are you?'

'No matter,' he said, and reached forward to thrust a large sheaf of papers into her hand. Then, before she could respond, he was off, like a decidedly overweight whippet, down the track that eventually led back to Abercarn.

It was a divorce petition, accusing Angela of adultery with Billie. There was no application for custody of the children.

'Well,' said Billie, when he finished reading the document. 'That seems to be that. We've done it, love!'

'But the costs – they'll bankrupt you!'

He laughed. 'If that's the worst of our worries, we'll come through all right. A few weeks back we was wondering if he'd try to take Paul and Shirley, remember? I don't think they make people sell up to pay their divorce costs, so I expect they'll take the money bit by bit. My family been buying everything on the drip since the 1890s. I shouldn't think there's a lotta difference between getting a divorce on tick from getting a three-piece suite.'

'I love you, Billie.'

'And I love you, Mrs Chandler. Will you do me the honour of becoming my wife?'

Their miraculous good luck continued. The undefended divorce was rubber-stamped through the court by Christmas. 'Sorry I can't make an honest woman of you before our little friend puts in an appearance,' said Billie, 'but this bit about the King's Proctor and waiting six months will put paid to that. The minute it's over, all right?'

'More than all right.'

'I'll see a solicitor about it, anyway. I'm sure I've read about making arrangements in cases like this – the adoption thing, I expect. Will that be enough to be going on with?'

'More than enough, Billie. From today I have everything I want.'

He took her down to the Swan for the birth. 'You'll be crazy to try and get her in a nursing home, with them legal bills to pay,' Lily had said when he suggested a hospital. 'She didn't have any complications with the other two, did she?'

'None at all.' He uttered a little humourless laugh. 'She always says actually having the babies was the least painful bit of being married to that bugger.'

'Good. In that case, ask her if she can put up with our place and I'll see she gets the best. Me, Mrs Edwards the midwife, and Charlie. How about that?'

'Ennit a bit of a cheek to expect him to be around for it

just because you'm married to him? Home births is usually just the midwife, ent they?'

'Not when it's my brother's kid, it ent!' said Lily.

And that was how she arranged it. Angela duly gave birth to a big, healthy son after a shorter labour than Lily had believed possible. 'Popped out like a bloody pea out of a pod, kidda,' she told Billie, 'and his eyes is exactly the same colour as yours and mine and our Dad's.'

'Glad a that,' said Billie, ''cos I'd already decided to call him Evan.'

'What if it had been a girl? Couldn't see you calling it Margaret Ann.'

He had the good grace to blush. 'As a matter a fact, we was going to call it Lily, so stop your nagging, woman, and kiss the happy father.'

'Randy little sod!' she said, embracing him. 'You'm as bad as our Dad, an' all, producing in your fifties. But at least you had the self-control to wait until then and not make it a yearly habit like he did!'

They sat drinking some of Lily's black-market whisky later that night. 'I like it when it's quiet like this,' said Billie. 'It do always remind me of sitting with Dad after I'd come off afternoon shift, and I didn't wanna go to sleep, just enjoy the thought of not going down the bloody shaft again until the following afternoon.' He sighed and gazed into his cup. 'Lil, I been meaning to say thanks, and I haven't quite known how to put it . . . I don't arf appreciate you having Angela here and not kicking up no fuss – you know – about us not being married. Lotsa women wouldn't a done it.'

She gazed at him owlishly for a moment before throwing back her head and howling with laughter. 'Me? Me play holy Mary to anybody for misbehaving like that? Even if I wanted to, I'd never 'ave the nerve.'

'I don't understand.'

'Didn't you ever know about me and Peter? Peter Henderson?'

He shook his head.

'God almighty, the innocence of it! I fell in love with

Peter the first week he come to Abercarn, the year of the Strike. I fought it for ages, but he felt the same and in the end I gave in. Then we parted, because poor David was so ill and I felt guilty, but we loved each other so much we couldn't stay away from each other. It started again . . . '

'And when did it stop?'

'Haven't really stopped to this day. In practical terms, summer of 1936 when he took a bullet in the temple at Teruel.' She was dry-eyed but her face was ashen and a nerve twitched beside her mouth.

'How did you manage to come through, Lil – and not to let it show? I may be a bit of an innocent, but I swear nobody else knew, either.'

'Oh, yes. Charlie knew. Charlie knew the minute we looked at each other in 1926 and he suffered every minute from then till Peter died. He was never anything less than a wonderful friend to me through it all, though, and that's the one thing that kept me going sometimes.'

Billie was perplexed. 'He's quite a bloke on the quiet, ent he? I know it have ended all right for the two a you, but d'you sometimes wonder if you made a mistake when you broke off with him in the first place?'

'Oh, no. I loved the right brother. Peter an' me was made for each other. But you can't always have what you want . . . Funny, really, it seems – well, almost incestuous, but I've come to love Charlie again, as if I'd been getting to know him for the first time. If he'd been like this in 1920, p'raps I would have married him then. As it was, I had to learn about him properly – and he had to learn about me.'

'What about now?'

'Christ, kidda – you don' arf ask a lotta questions! I love the old bugger far more than most women of my age love their husbands. It have made us better lovers, that's all. Funny, ennit, after all these years? It looks as if he was the one I was waiting for after all. Now, drink your nice whisky and I'll top us up!'

PART FIVE

And I saw a new heaven
and a new earth: for the first heaven and
the first earth were passed away.

Revelation Ch. 21, v.1

CHAPTER TWENTY-NINE

London, Autumn, 1944

Bethan had been back on the wards again for some time –
for ever, she often felt. She did not exactly like the work,
but somehow it helped her to live without Max. Even
now, she found it hard to think about Max without a
lump of grief forming in her throat. All very well to say
they'd had seven happy years of marriage, and before
that awful business with James, their years as friends and
lovers. But she would always feel guilty at having let him
down; would never stop waking in the middle of the
night, agonisingly aware of the pain he must have
suffered when she deserted him.

It had been a long time before Bethan was able to look
the world in the eye again after she ran away from James
Norland on their wedding day. For a couple of months,
she had wondered whether she was losing her sanity. She
had no longer wanted the brittle world Norland offered,
but her spirit flinched at the prospect of a lifetime's
worthiness in the East End. Throughout it all, Max had
stuck by her, treating her like a precious piece of treasure,
never rebuking her for her appalling behaviour, allowing
her to indulge an increasingly waspish temperament as
the restrictions of her life impressed themselves upon her
afresh.

Finally it had been Joyce Gladstone, not he, who had
jerked Bethan out of her self-pity. As Bethan listlessly
drifted around the Hackney birth control clinic three
months after returning to work, pretending to organise
herself for the next day, Joyce snapped: 'Really, Bethan,

I'm beginning to wonder if I did the right thing in welcoming you back here with open arms.'

Bethan dropped her notebook and stared at the older woman. 'I don't understand you.'

'I wonder why not. I should have thought it was crystal clear. When Max scraped you up after your escapade with that dreadful Norland man, I was delighted at the prospect of getting you back. But really, what have you done since then to help either Max or us?'

With a faint stirring of satisfaction, she watched as Bethan's bewilderment began turning to anger. Perhaps this would knock a little sense into her.

'You were grateful enough at the time. I thought you said I was the best birth control adviser you had.'

Joyce forced herself to sound blasé. 'Yes, my dear, *had*. Everything changes, you know. It's a less ambiguous profession, nowadays – more well-trained women like ourselves are volunteering to come in. So you're less indispensable than you once might have been.'

'What a dreadful thing to say! I thought you were my friend.' Bethan's eyes were blazing, her face white with anger.

Joyce put a hand on her arm. 'I am,' she said softly. 'That's just why I'm speaking in this way now. You must stop throwing yourself away, Bethan, or the rest of us will follow your example.'

Bethan shook off the friendly touch. 'You're talking nonsense!'

'We both know I'm not. By now you should have settled back properly into what you do best, particularly with a man like Max backing you. But have you? Not a chance! Sometimes I wonder if you can only continue to function here as long as you think you're a little above it all. Well, you're not, and when our clients begin to notice it, I'm afraid I feel obliged to put their interests first.'

'Th-they've complained about me?'

'Not complained, exactly, Bethan. But before this unhappy business, they used to ask for you particularly, because you made them completely at ease and explained everything properly. Now they feel more often than not that you're doing them a favour by even talking to them. We both know that's not the right way to go about this job.'

As she spoke, she had watched Bethan stop her first burst of frenetic activity and sit on the edge of the desk, hands clasped, head down. Finally Bethan replied: 'You're right, Joyce. I'm no better with Max, and I owe him so much . . . Oh, I do dislike myself sometimes!'

'Are you sure of that?' said Joyce gently. 'It strikes me more that you feel sorry for yourself.'

Bethan's chin came up at that, and she seemed about to snap back, but then she shook her head. 'Perhaps you're right. I know I've made a frightful mess of things without any help from anybody else, and yet every now and then I still catch myself thinking: why should this happen to *me*? What have I done to deserve this? Of course I know the truth is I haven't done any more or less than anyone else. I've just let myself get used to being spoiled, and I'm a little too old for such childishness any more, aren't I?'

Joyce nodded, infinitely relieved that her friend had taken the advice instead of hurling it back in her face. Bethan sat silently for a few moments and then said: 'The trouble is, I have to struggle all the time to remember that. It's terribly easy for me to fall back on being a spoiled brat, Joyce. From now on, promise you'll rap my knuckles when I insist on doing it.'

Joyce laughed. 'Easier said than done, I'm afraid. I used the clinic as an excuse, but I think you'll mend your ways here without needing second reminders. It's the way you treat Max that worries me. I can't be your conscience there.'

She had refused to discuss the matter further, and secretly Bethan knew she was right. That was for her to make up to Max, not for a friend, however close, to arrange. After that she had made a sustained effort to please him, to give back even a little of what he had given her. It seemed to work, but from time to time she would catch him, in an unguarded moment, and see the pain on his face as he remembered her vast betrayal of him. Nothing could ever rub that out.

Then the War came and it began to look as if something could. Ironically, it was the Blitz which enabled her to start erasing his memories of her criminal selfishness.

They had been living with the bombardment of London for more than a month and, so far, apart from disturbed nights, it had not disrupted their lives. Then one afternoon, Bethan arrived home from the clinic to find Max showing a ramshackle quintet into the drawing room. As he saw Bethan, he closed the door on them, calling out, 'I'll get us all a nice cup of tea, Mrs Simms. You just sit down and get warm.' Then he turned to confront his wife.

Bethan could barely stifle her irritation. 'And who are they?' she asked, icily. 'Something tells me they're not patrons of the arts.' She flinched at his look, which was pitying above all else, and wished for the hundredth time that her natural impulse was not always towards the cutting remark.

'Perhaps if you'd seen them as I did, you'd feel a bit more compassionate,' he said. 'I was over in Paddington – working on those street lamp sketches I've been making – and I saw a splendid old gas fitting inside a little park. Just had to get it. I'd been drawing for a few minutes when I realised I was being watched. Looked up and there were two enormous pairs of eyes peering at me over the top of my sketch block. It was the two youngest Simms children.'

He told her the Simms's story, as Mrs Simms had told it to him. Billeted in a spacious Paddington house after their own Bermondsey home was flattened by a bomb, they had encountered nothing but hostility from the prosperous housewife who lived there. Mother and daughters were lodged in a double bed in one attic room, the boys in another. They were not allowed either to bring cooked food into the house, or to prepare their own in the kitchen, and it was made clear that they were expected to wash standing up at the handbasin rather than using the bath. They were not given a sitting room of their own, the landlady would not let them use hers, and expected them to vacate the attics during the daylight hours. In a chilly, damp autumn, their days were reduced to roaming through the parks of the neighbourhood, huddling together for warmth, eating cheap sandwiches to sustain them, and playing 'I-spy' games in a vain attempt to keep their spirits up.

As Max ended his tale of woe, he poured boiling water on to a mound of fresh tea leaves in their biggest, most seldom-used pot. 'I kept thinking,' he told her over his shoulder, 'of all the space we have here, of how many times I've thought of doing something about it and didn't get round to it. And in the end, I thought what the hell! Bethan won't mind if they move in with us.'

Now he turned to face her, his expression beseeching. Just as well he did, she reflected later, for she had been about to blast him with a scornful tirade. That look sealed her fate. As she sat there, momentarily frozen, watching him heft the huge black teapot, she suddenly realised that this might be a way to rehabilitate herself with Max. He was a kind, compassionate man, much more so than she could ever be, but he had little chance to demonstrate his better nature because Bethan was always there behind him, cutting down his altruistic schemes. Well then, if this was what he wanted, so be it.

'All right, Max – of course they can stay. Tell Mrs Simms not to bother with the rest of their belongings this evening. It's raw out there. We'll sort something out tomorrow.'

It was almost worth the inconvenience that lay ahead to see his face. He beamed, just remembered to put down the teapot, then lunged forward and embraced her with more enthusiasm than passion. 'You lovely girl! Promise you'll never stop surprising me!' he said, burying his face against her hair.

'Hmm, I find the charm of surprises has a habit of wearing thin after a while!' she responded, but he took no notice.

That was merely the first step. The second owed as much to Bethan's own sense of social justice as to her desire to please Max. The Simms family were a pleasant surprise to her – clean, quiet and friendly, never in the way, always anxious to help about the house to make some small repayment of the kindness they had been offered. Bethan softened sufficiently to realise that her skills might be at least as useful in more hard-pressed areas as in the birth control clinic.

The first tentative steps were being taken by local councils to appoint billeting officers who would sort out emergency accommodation for people like the Simmses. Within weeks of their moving in at the Hackney house, Bethan was at the town hall, volunteering her services as a billeting officer. Somewhat to her surprise, she was accepted with enthusiasm – as were Max's when he followed her example.

Elsie Simms studied Bethan carefully when she announced her new extra job. After a while, she said: 'I don' like to interfere, but I-I think I could help you, sorta get to grips wiv it quicker, if I took yer to see some a what people 'ave to put up wiv when they've been bombed out . . . ' Her voice trailed off, as though she feared Bethan's wrath at such a presumptuous suggestion.

But Bethan was already beginning to appreciate Elsie's unassuming intelligence, and she nodded eagerly. 'Where were you thinking of going, Elsie, and when? I think it's a marvellous idea. We could even make Max play nursemaid to the children while we're gone!'

Max managed an imitation of a ferocious scowl, but Bethan could sense his pleasure in finally having her whole-hearted backing for something he cared about. Elsie said: 'I was thinking of taking you dahn one a the tube stations they're using as shelters – not to spend the whole night, you'd like as not come back wiv lice and all sorter nasty fings – but just to see the filth they 'ave to put up wiv, night after night, wiv nowhere else to go, neither.'

What followed was a series of night-time and morning

adventures which would have been more acceptable in a Hieronymus Bosch painting than in one of the world's greatest cities half-way through the twentieth century. They had the effect of galvanising Bethan into the sort of radical her sister Lily had always been. After a week of it, she was saying to Max: 'We're doing it to our own, and we blame the Nazis for inhumanity! I could never hold up my head again if I let things like this go on happening.'

Max was somewhat bemused. Never a political extremist himself, he had always got by on a mixture of humanity, imagination and impulse, and had assumed that all other civilised people did the same. It had never entered his head that there were people like Bethan who dealt with the problems of society by refusing to acknowledge that such things existed.

Now, belatedly, Bethan had the bit between her teeth. What had started as a half-hearted personal campaign to prove her love to Max turned into a crusade, no less personal but enlarged, to improve the lot of the underprivileged. The real crunch came when Elsie took Bethan to Tilbury.

'You been reading about them new deep shelters they been building, haven't you?' Elsie said one morning over breakfast. 'Sound just what the doctor ordered, till you see one, that is. My sister May lives dahn Stepney. Tilbury deep shelter's her nearest port o' call in trouble. Won't touch it wiv a barge pole unless the bleedin' Luftwaffe's right overhead. I'm goin' dahn to see 'er today. They got some sorter deputation fixed up to try an' improve fings dahn there. D'you wanna come an' see what's what?'

Intrigued, Bethan agreed. Even the likes of her had heard rumours about Tilbury by now. It had been built to take twelve thousand people from the Stepney area, which was rapidly being reduced to rubble in the nightly raids. But although the authorities had dug deep, they had failed to dig efficiently. No one had thought it necessary to connect the shelter to a sewerage system. Every night twelve thousand people were packed in without any water supply or means of waste disposal. Nor was there any obvious way of disposing of accumulating waste, so heaps of excrement grew day by day and the stench hit anyone arriving at the entrance like the worst of underground gas leaks. There was no heating or ventilation, so the outside temperature dictated whether the shelterers froze or sweltered. Fortunately for Bethan's nostrils, London was going through a cold spell. Even in chilly conditions, the stink was virtually insupportable.

Elsie's sister, May, met them at the shelter and took them round it on a lightning tour. 'We've 'ad just about all we can take,' she said. 'We've done all we can for ourselves, but we can't dig our own latrines or nuffink. So we got a deputation, and we're going along to the ARP headquarters to tell 'em it's not nearly good enough. Wanna come along?'

'Nothing would stop us!' said Bethan. 'Come on, Elsie. If they want an interfering Welshwoman's expert opinion on public health risks, they can have it gratis.'

They tagged along with the forty-strong deputation which was straggling off from the shelter entrance towards the ARP headquarters. As they walked, May kept a little stream of the more active committee members chatting to Bethan, telling her what they planned. It all seemed very English and very moderate – decent sanitation; regular bulk allocations for people forced to use the shelters every night; ticket admission to prevent frightened people stampeding like animals.

They were a good-natured crowd, if angered by the authorities' apparent indifference to their plight, and they seemed reasonably optimistic about achieving what they had set out to ask for. Then the police arrived. As they approached the ARP headquarters, a mounted platoon abruptly charged out of the building's side entrance. Bethan was swept aside by the first swirl of hooves, and staggered against the wall, staring with disbelief at what was happening in front of her. A middle-aged man, head still bandaged from an air raid shrapnel wound, was seized by a foot constable and held while a mounted policeman beat him with a truncheon. Two younger men were chased by mounted police, who struck them repeatedly with their truncheons across shoulders and kidneys.

As yet another horseman swooped on a woman in her early twenties, Bethan leaped forward with a howl of protest and swung in front of her. 'Don't lay a finger on her or I'll have your badge!' she yelled.

It must have been the educated accent, which was a laugh in itself, she told herself bitterly later on. The man's raised arm faltered and fell, momentarily at least, to his side. 'Trouble with you middle class do-gooders is you don't know a Commie when you see one,' he muttered.

'What did you say?' She was capable of laying on such ringing tones when necessary, but this time her derision was quite genuine. 'For God's sake, man, *look* at her!'

He had the grace to blush and glance away, but repeated, parrot-fashion, 'Commies, I tell you, the lot of 'em!'

'Well, if your superiors are telling you that, and you're stupid enough to believe them, all I can say is there's no hope for any of us. Have you forgotten who we're fighting?'

'Don't need the likes of you to remind me, Lady Muck. Now, outa my way, or I may take a fancy to land one on you!' And he thrust his huge mount forward menacingly.

By now, a number of the deputation had been man-handled into the adjoining police station, and the little delegation was in tatters. May had not been taken in. Now she turned back to her two companions, defeat in every line on her face. 'Come on, girls,' she said. 'Forget it, eh? They'll never let the likes of us win, whoever's in charge. Sometimes I wonder if it makes any odds whether it's Churchill or Hitler.'

After that there was no stopping Bethan. She managed a part-time daily stint as billeting officer which was equal to what many regarded as full-time work. She continued at the birth control clinic, doing her normal job and also helping mastermind the change to a general medical advice centre concentrating on sexual diseases and other inevitable wartime social health problems. Between times she fitted in action groups and any sort of good cause which might galvanise London's local authorities into improving the lot of the working class Londoners who still bore the brunt of the Blitz.

After four months, Joyce Gladstone turned to her one afternoon, half admiring, half in exasperation, and said: 'One thing about you, Bethan, you never do anything by halves. Sometimes I wonder whether I was wise to have that word in your ear about standing by Max and helping him.'

Bethan gave her a wondering look. 'Good God, Joyce, I'd forgotten all about that. Yes, I suppose it was for Max at first. I was too stupid to see that some things are worth doing for their own sake. But that went long ago.' Before the other woman had time to protest, she added: 'Don't worry – Max is delighted at the change! What you set in motion had the desired effect. It's just that it turned out . . . well, differently to the way either of us might have thought, that's all.' She glanced down at her watch. 'Anyway, what are you doing over here at two-thirty on a clinic afternoon? You're usually far too conscientious for that sort of lead-swinging!'

She had meant the remark to be a slight tease, but Joyce blushed furiously. 'Actually, I'm feeling very guilty, if you must know . . . I've come to say goodbye.'

'Goodbye? What on earth are you talking about? The Gladstones and London as inseparable as bread and cheese.'

Joyce's smile was wistful. 'I wish that were still the case, but it isn't. Edwin's ill – very ill. May not last another year. It was a hard choice, Bethan, but my first loyalty is to him, always has been. You know Patricia moved to Cheshire last year when she got married? Well, she keeps asking us to go and live with her, and I've finally caved in. Virtually overnight, as it happens. I came to tell you first, but after that . . . well, we plan to leave in a week. I really don't know how long Edwin will last, you see, and I want him to have at least some peace and tranquillity before . . . ' She attempted to keep her smile in place, but it slipped and suddenly she was crying. 'Oh, God, Bethan, it's been such a terrible fight between loyalties! I'm still not at all sure I've done the right thing.'

Inwardly aghast at the prospect of losing this bulwark to her own strength, Bethan still managed a convincingly outraged snort. 'Of course you're doing the right thing! He's been your whole life. You don't give up something like that for a cause, even a cause like the war! I'm the one who says silly things like that, not Joyce Gladstone! You get off home and start packing. And come back to me the minute you need any extra help.'

After Joyce had gone it was another matter. Bethan sat huddled over her desk, reliving the times her friend had strengthened her, and wondering what would happen if she ever needed to call on such loving toughness again. It was not easily come by.

Inevitably, the crippling blow fell after Joyce had gone. Bethan had spent the day on her usual round of job, committee, meetings and voluntary work. Since Joyce's departure this had usually kept her out until late in the evening because, as one of the Birth Control Trust's most senior employees, she had considerable supervisory power over the federation of clinics which were strung across north and east London. Tonight was no exception. The air raid siren sounded as she was changing trains at Tottenham Court Road. She sighed with resignation. Would it be another overnight stay in a shelter, or would she manage to get back to Max tonight? No way of telling. Just have to sit it out. At least she was wearing a warm coat.

In fact the raid was not over-long, and after a couple of hours she was on her way again. She left the tube at the Angel and walked the last mile home. Oh, hell, she thought, exasperated, as her eyes caught the familiar dull glow of a burning building in the sky ahead. Some poor devil has copped it. Tomorrow would be taken up in haggling with some reluctant householder about allocating spare rooms to a homeless family . . . or perhaps not, the way that little lot was going up. It was quite a blaze . . . involuntarily, her pace quickened. It seemed to be in Pendlebury Road. Her road. Hers and Max's. And it looked to be about half-way down. Just where their cheery house with its absurd yellow front door stood. The door she would never let him paint another colour because the yellow paint had played a part in bringing them together . . .

Bethan was running now. She turned the corner into Pendlebury Road and her worst suspicions were confirmed. It was their house; theirs and next door. And Elsie Simms was rushing towards her, arms outstretched, like some half-blind animal groping along to help itself see better.

'Bethan – Bethan – they've gone, the two of 'em. My Jimmy and Max. It come dahn that side a the 'ouse, tore it right away . . . ' Elsie choked on tears for a moment. Jimmy was her twelve-year-old son. 'Took all a number eighty, and the top two rooms a your place . . . no 'ope, the fireman said . . . ' She stumbled to a halt, ' . . . not a bloody 'ope in 'ell . . . Oh, Christ. What we gonna do?'

And the two women clung together, silent in their grief, unable to offer one another anything but the warmth of an embrace to cushion the blow.

After the first burst of grief had stopped blurring her thoughts, Bethan knew what she must do, at least. Work was to be her only solution to pain. She knew Max had gone before she could prove herself a worthy companion for him. She chose to ignore the fact that he would have laughed to scorn the idea of her having to be a worthy companion, and that her deep sense of guilt would always have been there, had she lived to be a hundred. At least, thinking the way she did, Bethan could construct a reason for going on until the grief lessened to a manageable level. That was more than many bereaved, childless middle-aged women could manage.

Slowly, painfully, London was pulling itself together to help its suffering civilians. The repulsive tube station shelters Bethan had visited months earlier, where children were tied into narrow bunks to prevent them falling on to the sewage-flooded floors below, gradually became things of the past. Blitz victims were no longer means-tested before they received relief payments after losing everything. Slowly, steadily, the London County Council began establishing popular feeding centres. Laundry vans were despatched to blitzed areas so that people who had lost their water supply could at least clean their clothes. Emergency repairs were put into effect on bomb-damaged houses so that fewer people were crammed into inadequate rest centres. And someone, somewhere in the administration seemed to realise that the poor, too, needed to wash themselves and to eliminate body wastes, for they began attaching adequate washrooms and lavatories to the emergency shelters.

Through it all, Bethan worked like a demon, always striving to push aside her last memory of Max, laughing ruefully at one of her waspish remarks as she dashed off, late and without kissing him goodbye, to yet another committee meeting. Elsie Simms stoically re-assembled her own shattered life, took over at Pendlebury Road and showed remarkable resilience in bullying repair men and generally getting the house back in running order. When it was ready, Bethan knew exactly what she wanted to do with it. She volunteered all the spare rooms beyond the floor which she and Elsie's family now shared as billets for displaced bombed-out families. There was a time when she would have resented every midnight flushing of a lavatory or slamming of a door as an intrusion into her personal privacy. Now she welcomed it all. It held off the darkness.

With a shock, she realised it was two years since Max had been killed. The time had sped past, and the irony was that in the meantime she really had become the person she had only wanted to be in order to please him. Now he was dead, and Bethan Grant was a worthy, selfless woman who really cared about her fellow human beings. The first time she realised it, she shuddered with distaste. There was something appallingly provincial, respectable and middle-aged about the entire process. She had always wanted to escape her roots, but, dear God, not to this! She had wanted excitement, adventure, luxury . . .

Her wool-gathering stopped there. Well, what *had* she got? Compared with the life fate had marked her for, all of that. If she was honest with herself, Bethan was forced to admit she had started out as fodder for domestic service in a Cardiff mansion, or marriage to some Western Valley miner – God, that really *would* have been hardship, considering what the poor devils had put up with this past two decades! Instead, she had sailed through an easy school career, financed by an indulgent uncle, had qualified as a nurse, worked in London when most girls of her age never saw a town further than twenty miles from their home village, had been swept into the ridiculously artificial world of the Norland family, and out again into the entirely different riches of east London and the different bohemianisms of the Gladstones on one side and Max Grant on the other. She had experienced more variety, luxury and fun than any dozen other girls of her background, and still she was dissatisfied because she was not Lady Pamela Mountbatten or Mrs Charles Sweeney. Really, Bethan! she rebuked herself. You may think Max taught you a sense of reality, but you still haven't the intelligence to grasp the basics, have you?'

Abruptly, a memory flashed in her mind of a film she had seen with Max shortly before his death – *Now Voyager*, starring Max's favourite, Bette Davis. The movie had ended with her making one of her character-stistic chin-up-little-lady defiant gestures and saying: 'Why ask for the moon, when we have the stars?' Max had turned to her in the twilight of the cinema and said:

'You see? Everyone but you can see it, even Bette Davis.' And she had failed to understand him! No longer, though. She understood now. There was nothing wrong with her life. She had been given far more than many other women. It was about time she started giving some of it back – *really* giving it back, too, not simply dashing about acting the role of gallant wartime heroine. Time to do some serious work.

CHAPTER THIRTY

The first step was to return to work at St Thomas's. Times had changed beyond recall and Bethan was accepted with open arms as a senior ward sister. It was responsible, tiring work and at first she felt it offered her everything which had been missing from her life recently – everything, of course, except Max. But eventually she discovered that even this fulfilling job was not exactly what she thought.

She continued to live at Pendlebury Road with the Simmses and her tribe of transient lodgers, and to advise them about their rights as they awaited permanent re-housing or a return to their original, repaired, homes. And gradually that showed her what she wanted to do. The War would not always be raging across Europe. Come to that, there were times now when it appeared to be all over bar the shouting. The vast Allied army that had landed in France on D-Day was pushing the Germans steadily eastward. Paris had been liberated in the summer, and the ranks of lodgers at Pendlebury Road were thinning by the week. That was when she started asking herself what they were going back to. She could clearly remember the aftermath of the Great War, although she chose to think of it as little as possible. After that conflict, the miners thought they would be well-paid princes of their own industry. Women had believed they would never again be sentenced to domestic service. Home-coming servicemen had believed there really was a world fit for heroes awaiting them. And it had all been illusion. Within a couple of years, the old guard had been firmly in the saddle again, and the lower orders had been back where they belonged, at the bottom of the heap.

That time, Bethan had been too anxious to escape herself to identify with them. This time it was different. She had witnessed, and had participated in, the making of a better London for the people who were suffering in the Blitz. There could be no going back, now. It was time to make sure the world went on improving, and that needed participation, not polite applause from the sidelines. On her next rest day, Bethan went off and joined Hackney Labour Party. The least political of all Evan Walters's children had finally found her mission.

A couple of weeks later, she had arrived at St Thomas's and was just about to go on duty when the ward secretary asked her to take a personal telephone call. Bethan straightened her snowy cuff as she took the receiver, her vanity still giving her a small kick at the elegance of the white muslin against the midnight blue of the sister's uniform. A high-pitched voice, almost incoherent, jabbered at her: 'Bethan, the filthy bastards 'ave done it again. We've copped a V-2!'

She felt cold and the small office seemed to tilt on a crazy axis. 'Elsie? That *is* Elsie, isn't it? How bad?'

Elsie Simms was crying hysterically now. 'I can't find our Gillian. She was in the back attic, sorting out some toys for a coupla kids from down the street, an' it hit . . . Christ, Bethan, I can't lose anuvver one – not now, oh please don't let it . . . ' The storm of sobs wiped any further sense from her speech.

'Stay put. I'll be there the minute I can. I'm coming straight away Elsie. We'll find her.' Bethan slammed down the telephone and picked up her coat. 'Get Sister Wyllie over from Ward Three,' she snapped at the secretary. 'My house has been bombed. I'm needed immediately.'

As she hurried down into the hospital forecourt, a motorcycle despatch rider who had dropped off a package at casualty was wheeling his machine out. 'Are you finished for the day?' Bethan asked him. He nodded, surprised to be addressed by a hospital sister. 'Well you can do me one hell of a favour if you feel inclined,' she added. 'I've just been bombed out. What are the chances of you giving me a lift over to Hackney? I'll pay you for the petrol.'

He grinned. 'No need for that, love, no need at all. This 'ospital saved me dad's legs. 'Op on the back, then.' They careered out of the yard and he had her back in Hackney in well under half an hour.

The house was a hopeless wreck. Somewhere around where her sitting room had once been, a fire had started blazing over a severed gas pipe. Ranks of rubble and smashed furniture rose behind it to a tiny fragment of slate which was all that remained of the roof. Elsie Simms was across the road, clinging to the arm of one of the lodgers and still sobbing inconsolably. Bethan gritted her teeth and went to comfort her friend. It was obvious from the state of the building that Gillian could not have survived. Elsie saw her and reached out to her, the tears flowing afresh. Then her eyes lifted and she gazed past Bethan. 'There she is!' she gasped. 'Oh my God, there she is!'

Bethan turned and saw a scrap of bright scarlet – Gillian's last remaining good warm dress, she remembered. The top of a party wall had crumbled forward to reveal it. The little girl was still trapped – whether by clothing or by an injured limb it was impossible to tell – but it would clearly not remain thus for long. The wall went on cracking and falling as they watched. Gillian must already have been swept down through one full floor of the tall old house, but she was still a long way above ground and the battered remains of the fine cantilevered staircase petered out a dozen yards from where she was trapped.

Elsie was already struggling to get past a fireman, who was determined to prevent her going any further. 'Sorry, missis, I know it's awful for yer, but it'll add up to two a you instead of one . . . We're doin' our best . . . Don't even know if the kid's still breathin', yet.'

No, thought Bethan, and by the time you've made up your minds, she won't be. She dodged across the road, her nondescript grey uniform coat and the fading daylight making her less conspicuous than the weeping, lightly-clad Elsie had been. The team in front of the house had diverted their attention from the main door to concentrate on getting at the gaspipe fire and stopping it before it went out of control. By the time someone raised the alarm, Bethan was through the ruined front door and half-way up the staircase to the first floor. They might have built this place to last, but they weren't counting on high explosives, she thought, as she felt the previously rock-solid risers sway drunkenly beneath her.

On what had been the first-floor landing, half the balusters yawned into empty space. She looked away, suddenly conscious that she loathed exposed heights, and scuttled past the gap. There were shouts, now, from outside. 'Hey, you up there – don't be so bloody stupid! You'll kill yourself and bring everything down wiv you! Come on back . . . we'll . . . ' The voices faded as she ducked through the remains of Elsie's bedroom doorway.

On the other side she stopped with a sharp gasp of terror. There was no floor left. This had not been apparent from the street; it had looked as if there was merely a big hole along the front. But the whole thing had collapsed, leaving something which looked like a frail catwalk round the back wall. Bethan managed a shaky giggle. 'Oh well, dear,' she muttered, 'this is where you find out if you're *really* scared of heights or just putting it on!' She pressed herself flat against the wall that led back from the door, and squirmed along the impossibly narrow strip of wood and plaster. Somehow it no longer seemed important to establish whether Gillian were still alive before she made the attempt. Someone had to go to the girl. Otherwise Elsie would always feel her daughter had been left to die alone.

She was almost three-quarters of the way around the shell of the room before she dared look up towards Gillian. By now she was not even sure any longer if the child would still be there. There had been ominous shifts of rubble as her own small weight changed the precarious balance of the ruin. Now she risked a quick glance. Not only was Gillian still in position; she was conscious, and gazing in horror at Bethan as she crept along the ledge. As she drew closer, Bethan could see there was no obvious way to free Gillian. The child was pinned securely by an arm and a leg beneath a heavy mound of plaster and brickwork. Even at this distance, it was easy to see that shock alone was protecting her from the agony her injuries would normally have caused.

At that point, Gillian managed to speak. She whimpered: 'Don't leave me, Bethan, will you? Not all the way up here, on my own . . . ' As her voice died away, she extended a shaking hand towards her mother's friend. Gingerly, Bethan teetered a few steps further and managed to grasp it. Now she could see there was a slight widening of the rubble shelf beside Gillian. She managed a final lurch on to it and squatted beside her, pressing a comforting hand against her cheek. 'Oh, thank you, Bethan! I was so lonely . . . ' Tears fell from Gillian's eyes on to Bethan's hand as the girl turned to kiss it. Then there was a rumble that filled the universe, and with nightmarish slowness the entire chimney-breast swayed inwards, burying woman and child beyond hope of recovery in the basement, two floors below.

CHAPTER THIRTY-ONE

Abercarn, 1947

The figure that had clambered from an Air Force ambulance one bleak autumn day in 1945 had been unrecognisable as the big, rugby-playing, boisterous boy Lily had waved off to join the RAF before the War. Changi Jail, the Burma Road and the Japanese had seen to that.

When Tommy came marching home again, hurrah, hurrah! Lily had caught herself thinking, on the edge of hysterics, as she regarded her only son for the first time in nearly seven years. Would I have even recognised him as mine if I'd seen him in a crowd? she wondered, despairing. Then, pushing out all other thoughts, had come the terrible question: Dear God – how do I make it up to him?

As the months mounted to a year and more, it began to look as if she never would. Charles was every bit as considerate as she herself, but there seemed nothing either of them could do to staunch the awful spiritual wound he had suffered. He was not difficult in any way – quite the reverse. He thanked them punctiliously for the smallest courtesy; his behaviour was always beyond reproach; he was determined to continue his Forces career once the authorities declared him fit; and he was as remote as the Man in the Moon.

'If only he'd cry! If only something would crack, and he'd let it all out, just once!' Lily raged to Charles over a large drink one evening. 'I just can't cope with this polite silence all the time – it's killing me!'

Henderson patted her shoulder. 'Don't be tempted to

push him,' he warned. 'I think all he can *stand* is the polite silence. If he let that go, there would be nothing left, and how would we put Humpty together again then?'

'D'you really think he's broken?'

'I sincerely hope not. But I saw men who had gone through terrible experiences in Flanders, who coped brilliantly, but who were virtual recluses for years afterwards. For heaven's sake, you know a prime example yourself – your brother Billie.'

'Christ! Don't say he's gonna turn into another Billie!'

'I think Billie has done rather splendidly for himself. He's one of the happiest men either of us knows.'

'Now, yes. But it took him twenty-four years, mun! I don't want my boy serving a life sentence before he gets a chance of happiness.'

'I'm very much afraid it might come to that, darling. We've both read all we can get our hands on about what happened in the Far East. I sometimes wonder how any of them have come home with a shred of sanity left, but they seem to have done. Let's resign ourselves to looking out for his for as long as it takes. When he's declared fit to resume duty it may help him a lot.'

Tom's main physical problem was severe, recurring bouts of malaria. He himself sometimes thought of these as the least of his difficulties – his dreams were far worse than the fevers. But from the point of view of fitness to rejoin his unit, malaria was the drawback. He spent most of his time at Abercarn, staying with Lily and Charles, occupying the comfortable little flat over the surgery garage. Gradually he regained some of the weight he had lost over four years of starvation, but he remained remote, self-contained and uncommunicative. His only interest apart from getting fit and resuming his duties, seemed to be tinkering with anything mechanical.

In an effort to draw him out, Henderson played on this enthusiasm. Somehow, using his considerable wealth and contacts Lily had no idea he still possessed, he laid hands on a broken-down 1936 Morgan sports car, every boy's dream possession in the years leading up to the war. It was towed to the Swan one Saturday afternoon almost a year after Tom returned to Abercarn, and put into the rear section of the garage. For ever afterwards, Lily swore that was the first time she had seen Tommy smile since his release. From then on, every moment he did not spend harassing the RAF to declare him fit for duty, was passed in an intensive search for parts, or in work on the little car.

Henderson responded with a somewhat shamefaced grin when Lily asked him why he had thought a broken-down car would afford her son so much pleasure. 'I could have found the cash to get him a brand new one on the black market, as a matter of fact, but I guessed he needed something to take up every bit of his mind in every working moment. And what better for a trained, enthusiastic engineer than the wreck of the most covetable car of the thirties?'

'You never lose your touch, do you, Charlie? I just hope it do work, that's all.'

'If it doesn't, there's no other solution I can dream up, I'm afraid.'

Almost the sole good thing about the War, Lily often thought, was that it had reconciled her with her cousin Lexie.

They had never quarrelled over anything, parting the best of friends early in the 1920s. But Lily had always felt Lexie would want to run and hide from all who knew her unless she could demonstrate she had made a success of her life. Silence meant failure, and Lily had no wish to humiliate her cousin. In any case, there had been the problems of her mother's implacable refusal to acknowledge Lexie, and her own inability to afford the train fare to Cardiff on visits for most of the 1920s and 1930s.

She had received a long, sad letter when Rhys died, but since then there had been silence. As the War progressed, her thoughts had returned again and again to this closest companion of her childhood. She had never enjoyed a friendship quite as close as Lexie's – certainly never with her own sisters – and when Margaret Ann died she decided the time had come for a reunion.

It was an odd meeting. The War was almost over. External tensions were at a minimum. They were meeting after such a long parting that they had no true conception of the companions they had left behind. When they met again, neither woman saw what she had expected, and, strangely, they had drawn closer in taste and attitude.

Both were graceful, well-turned-out females of a certain age. Both fitted into the middle-class Queen Street tea room as though designed for it. They sat and exchanged polite nothings for five or ten minutes, then Lily said: 'I don't bloody believe this! You're the girl who took me to bet on the fan-tan, and told me what those Bute Street cafés really sold all them years ago – and here I am, sipping tea with you and talking about rationing! Come on, Lex! Uncle Rhys must be revolving in his grave!'

Lexie giggled. 'Ennit daft? But Christ, Lil, you didn't arf look dignified when you come through that door . . . They gorra new expression down the Bay – dead Cyncoed – and that's what I thought when I saw you.'

Lily gaped at her. 'I went up Cyncoed once – forget why, now – and I know what it means without you explaining. But Lex – *me*? Guess what I was doing in 1927?'

'Can't. Go on, tell me.'

'I was wearing a pinny made out of a hessian sack, an' I was picking coal off the South Celynen tip in the middle of the night. We'd get enough together to sell a coupla bags at full price next day, and the money would go in the fighting fund. But *me? Cyncoed?*'

'Tell you something our Dad said once – never trust the buggers from the way they do look. Well, maybe I shoulda known from you, Lil, but it wasn't easy. What have happened? You don't look like no miner's honourable widow to me. Not much suffering poverty in you, unless I'm mistaken.'

'Course there ent. I got out. I still live there, but I was

296

lucky. I haven't had to live on miner's pay for a hell of a long time, and I never will again. But I still remember. Thing is, you remember the poverty, you remember what went before, an' all, and I remember Uncle Rhys shelling out money for us to look smart. If you've 'ad that at the right time, it ent too difficult to pick it up again. I'm comfortable now, and I know what to do with it, so here I am, looking ever so Cyncoed, or whatever you called it. You don't exactly look like Black Bet on a bad night, either.'

'Don't say that! Bet was responsible for mosta this!' Lexie explained her father's last exploits, and Bet's involvement. From humble beginnings, she and Jean-Baptiste had built the only restaurant west of Bristol which commanded the homage of gourmets everywhere. Lily sipped her tea, ate her cake and wallowed in a success story which owed nothing to grand forces and everything to small people working in small ways.

'Nothing respectable about it, really, Lil. Always remember that. It's more like piracy on the high seas than anything else. Our kind do never get a decent chance playing fair. We always gorra cheat a bit. But bloody hell! If we do, the results ent arf spectacular!'

Lily grinned and gripped Lexie's arm. 'Lex, look at us. We survived. We survived all them buggers could throw at us, and we're gonna do even better. If we did it without the chances, think a what our kids can do with fair breaks. We'll rule the world within a generation – and not before time, neither!'

Lexie's expression clouded. 'Sure about that, are you? Wish I was.'

'What's the matter? Thought everything was perfect for you an' your Frenchman and your gorgeous daughter.'

'Yeah, well – it do just show the difference between the reality and the telling of it, don't it?' said Lexie.

She went on to describe Georgia's progress through Tiger Bay society. 'Wound up in Cathays High School. By then, Jean-Baptiste coulda financed her, but none a your soft touch. Our Georgie had to show the world.

Christ, Lil, she's bright! Frightens the living daylights outa me sometimes! Trouble is, it ent one thing. She can do just about anything, and it's about as feminine as blacksmithing!'

Apparently Georgia had just reached the age when university entrance applications were in order. She was the colour of a Fry's Five Boys bar, looked as beautiful as the Mona Lisa, and had every remotely feminist teacher at Cathays High School ready to march on Downing Street should her colour or sex deprive her of the medical school place which her academic qualifications and school reports indicated.

'Wonderful!' said Lily. 'So when does she start, and where?'

Lexie's expression was stormy. 'That's the soddin' trouble. She and Jean-Baptiste have had a row every other night the last fortnight, and in between it have been me and her.'

'What about, for God's sake?'

'Lil, she's saying there's enough time after the War for all that. She wants to get her medical school place, defer it until the War do end, and go in the WRAAF as a sodding mechanic until the whole shooting match ends.'

'What the hell for? No daughter of yours is a patriot, surely to God?'

'Nothing so easy . . . She reckons, the more women show they can do, the more people will *let* them do after. She says she understands theoretical mechanics like do-re-mi, and she wants to prove it in practice. Wharra my supposed to say?'

Lily opened her mouth to speak and then thought about what the girl was saying. It was true. The silence prolonged itself beyond politeness, then she said: 'Lex, I dunno how to say this, but she's right.'

Lexie glared at her. 'D'you realise what you're saying? With the exam results she's expecting, she can be safely inside medical school, place guaranteed, before all them male white heroes start coming home. If she do mess about now, by the time she settles down, there won't be room for nice little white girls, let alone a bar a chocolate like Georgie. What happens then?'

'If she's still thinking as straight as she appears to be now, she'll find a way around it, Lex. Let her have a try.'

'You're as bloody mad as she is!'

But it stuck. In due course, Georgia went for interviews at teaching hospitals in London, Birmingham and Cardiff. Eventually she was offered a place, and successfully deferred it while she donned khaki overalls and went off to help the RAF strip down jeep engines at St Athan. Lexie bit her elegant nails to the quick. Jean-Baptiste wondered who he was laying up a fortune for in the restaurant business. Lily went home to Abercarn and crowed to herself about a woman who would let nothing defeat her. Perhaps in the future they would all be like Georgia. She could only hope so.

All that seemed long ago now. Lily was watching her only son tear himself apart and fail to come to terms with a new world. Her priorities were Tommy and Charles, and she could see no help for the former. The hall telephone shrilled as she brooded on her problems over a cup of the watery coffee prescribed by post-war shortages. It was Lexie.

'Lil, I know this is just like my cheek, but can you gimme a bitta shelter for my ewe lamb? She's driving Jean-Baptiste daft, spouting nonsense all round the clock, and I can't stand much more of it. Look, I know she's about as inconspicuous as a barber's pole in your neck of the woods, but can you 'ave her up there for a few days? She've been demobbed now – her medical school term do start in six weeks – and there'll be blood on the moon if she's down yer much longer.'

Lily laughed. 'Always the understatement, eh, Lex? Course we'll have her. It'll be a pleasure. I don't know whether it's crossed your mind yet, but none of us has ever seen the kid, including me. I can't wait. D'you want one of us to fetch her?'

Lexie snorted. 'Christ, no! Thinks she's Lady Muck as it is! As long as there's someone to get her from the station, that'll be fine. Keep me posted, kidda. I'll send her tomorrow.'

Over the years, Charles Henderson's crippled leg had healed sufficiently for him to accomplish short car journeys on his own. Lily always undertook long drives, but for trips to the station or short medical calls he could manage. Now he was delighted to go off and meet his exotic young kinswoman unaccompanied. It held the hint of an adventure on a foreign shore and, because this archaic picture existed only inside his own head, he did not need to justify it to anyone.

When she dismounted from the train, he uttered a gasp of surprise. She was the most beautiful creature he had ever seen. Long before the War, he had been shown some Benin bronzes from an ancient Nigerian culture, and they had perfectly captured the woman he saw before him. Her skin was the colour of glossy, polished mahogany. The nose swooped in a perfect shape, almost a reverse echo of the plump curve of the cheeks. A porter helped her from the train and the sculpted lips parted to reveal teeth of spectacular even whiteness. The coarse, glossy black hair fell dead straight to shoulder level and was chopped off there, like the hair of a Pharaoh's wife. This was a woman whose like few men ever saw, and when they did, they must spend their life seeking to look at her again, he thought. God help Cardiff University Medical School!

She sat in the car with him and talked in an easy, soft voice which was the sound equivalent of that wonderful, flawless skin. He felt unmanned, a gauche youth trying to please the ultimate femme fatale. They drew up in front of the house.

'Really, my dear,' he sounded pompous, even to himself, 'I don't know what you'll find here to keep you from boredom.' He gestured helplessly around the yard outside the surgery and house. 'Perhaps you'd care to unpack and then join Lily and me for a drink.'

Her bright eyes were everywhere. She did not even look up when he mentioned the unpacking. Clearly an uninspired suggestion . . . Then her eyes lit on Tommy's Morgan. 'What's *that?*' she yelped, with a sharpness that almost made him leap out of the car.

'It-it's only my stepson's old Morgan . . . clapped out . . . bit of an idea I had . . . ' He stumbled to silence as he realised all her attention was concentrated on the car.

Georgia turned to him, every ounce of charm she possessed directed full on him. 'Would anyone mind if I just . . . changed into overalls, and . . . played . . . with it?'

Far away, he heard himself say: 'Of course not, my dear. As I said, it belongs to Tom, but he's hardly likely to mind . . . works on it all the time . . . just can't get it going . . . past it, I think . . . '

Afterwards, he felt deeply guilty. Tom was, in fact, willing to fight off anyone who tried to so much as open the Morgan's passenger door. Now, while he was off walking on his own somewhere, this beautiful hoyden had descended and appeared to be about to take spanner and feeler gauge to everything under the bonnet. Charles hurried indoors and took refuge behind a large whisky in the study.

Tom had gone through a thoroughly gruelling afternoon. He had felt faintly sociable early that day, and that invariably meant the same thing – Billie. Billie came closer to understanding Tom than anyone else in the family, so after breakfast, Tom had left the Swan and set out on foot for his uncle's remote farm.

They had walked on the hillside, and Tom had managed to dredge up a few of his night terrors in a form that was intelligible to someone else apart from himself. Billie listened, and talked long and calmly. The best thing about Billie was that he never tried to make his own experiences yours. He told you what had happened to him, then asked what had happened to you. Then he sat in silence and considered the two. Sometimes, after that,

301

he talked of himself. Sometimes – more often – he talked about you. But it always made sense. It always soothed. It always made you feel that however bad things were now, some day they might come right. He always made it possible for you to walk down the mountain again without wanting to lie face down in the brook until the life was washed out of you.

Tom strolled down into Abercarn High Street from the insignificant side turn which marked the start of the walk past the distillery pond towards Billie's farm track. He was almost home now. Home . . . funny, he could not remember when he had first regarded it as that. When he was lying half-starved in those pestilential huts in an Asian jungle clearing, home had seemed to be nowhere. Now, thanks to Billie, and Charles Henderson, and his mother, home was once more turning into this insignificant little village on the edge of the coalfield. Perhaps a gin and tonic would be nice before supper . . . Mentally he luxuriated in the taste of the tonic; one of those wonderful flavours that was truly wet, that quenched the thirst even in imagination. Yes, that would be good. And a bit of his mother's cooking. Maybe a little session on the Morgan's carburettor before the gin. For once his mind was fully and happily occupied as he strolled towards the Swan.

He was not concentrating fully as he started up the metalled drive towards the surgery entrance, or he would have realised immediately that something was amiss. Charles Henderson's roomy old Austin was outside the surgery. A couple of large open tool-boxes were scattered about in front of the garage. Inside all the lights were on, including a high-intensity inspection lamp which Tom seldom used. He stopped in his tracks . . . My God, some maniac visitor of Charles's or his mother's had lit into the Morgan . . . he'd kill them . . . He broke into a lopsided jog and burst into the garage, his weakened lungs already begging for air as he got there.

Sure enough, the Morgan's bonnet was up, and a brown boilersuited pair of legs disappeared inside.

'What the hell d'you think you're up to? Coming in here without a by-your-leave! I'll . . . '

The legs stiffened, the back straightened and the brown overalls popped upright as their occupant turned to face him. Tom took a deep breath which seemed to go on taking in oxygen for ever, then said: 'Oh!'

'What's your problem?'

The eyes swamped the face. The lips were as close to perfection as made no difference. A small, pointed tongue slicked across miraculously even teeth, its tip brilliant pink against their white enamelled brilliance and the brown of the skin. A voice like liquid gold said: 'Any man who screws up a carburettor like that should be put to sweeping up every morning.'

Instead of exploding, he burst out laughing. 'And who the hell are you?' he asked.

'Bloody better mechanic than you'll ever be, flower. Now, are you gonna get outa your party frock and come an' looka this carb with me, or do I have to do it all by myself?'

Two hours later they were still outside the garage. A slight chill eased its way into the evening air and Charles Henderson had given up preparing gin-and-tonics for their guest and his stepson when the first two had been left untouched.

He walked to the window and looked out at the two amateur mechanics. 'I hesitate to say this, Lily, but do I detect a certain . . . er . . . rapport, between them?'

Lily was grinning like a Cheshire cat. 'Oh, I think you could say that, Charlie.'

Caught on the hop, he turned and glowered at her for a moment. 'If I didn't know better, I'd think you'd engineered this.'

'Would that be so terrible?'

Charles sighed deeply, then moved over to the sideboard and refreshed his drink before returning to sit beside Lily on the sofa. 'I'm not at all sure how deeply you've considered this, Lily, but out there you have a young man, barely twenty-four, who's gone through worse experiences than many people ever understand. The girl you have thrown him in with is the wrong colour for her society and the wrong gender for what she wants to do with her life. You are sitting at the centre of events, chuckling secretly because you think you've created a possible solution to both his and her problems. I would be betraying you if I did not say here and now that I think you are laying up dreadful problems for both of them.'

To his discomfiture, she burst out laughing. 'If we're both alive in twenty years, come back and explain it then. I don't think you'll need to do it with them!'

'Lily, for a lifelong politician, you are a profoundly illogical woman.'

'Charlie, if you've lived to your age without realising this world haven't got any place for logic, you're a bloody sight more stupid than I ever thought.' She put down her drink, leaned across and kissed him full on the lips. 'But don't ever change. I won't know where I am if you do.'